THE EXILE

Spinrad stared away from Ellis into the artificial depths of the holo poster of the Pacific sunset tacked up on the kitchen wall.

"It's all still there," Ellis said softly. "The cities have changed, but the land . . . you know . . ."

"Yeah, I know," Spinrad said, refocusing his gaze on Ellis and smiling ruefully. "You tempt me, Mr. Ellis, you really do. It's a lost cause anyway, isn't it, the America I believed in is twenty years dead and more. I've got a right to some kind of personal peace in my declining years, don't I? To go home to the only stretch of land I've ever loved and see all my old friends from better days and live the life of a rich screenwriter in the bargain. And all I have to do is sign a couple of pieces of paper, write my screenplay and keep my big mouth shut. . . ."

"There *is* one final requirement," Ellis said. "You must fold the *Free Press de Paris* first."

"At last we reach the bottom line," Spinrad said knowingly. "You boys sure play hardball, don't you?"

Ellis grinned at him wolfishly. "It is, you will remember, the national pastime."

"Merde . . ." Spinrad said weakly. "Am I required to sign this contract in blood?"

OTHER WORKS BY NORMAN SPINRAD

Novels

The Solarians
The Men in the Jungle
Agent of Chaos
Bug Jack Barron
The Iron Dream
Riding the Torch
Passing Through the Flame
The Mind Game
A World Between
Songs From the Stars
The Void Captain's Tale
Child of Fortune
Little Heroes

Short Story Collections

The Last Hurrah of the Golden Horde
No Direction Home
The Star Spangled Future
Other Americas

Non-fiction

Fragments of America
Staying Alive: A Writers' Guide

Anthologies (editor)

The New Tomorrows
Modern Science Fiction

OTHER AMERICAS

Norman Spinrad

BANTAM BOOKS
TORONTO · NEW YORK · LONDON · SYDNEY · AUCKLAND

OTHER AMERICAS
A Bantam Spectra Book / October 1988

PRINTING HISTORY

STREET MEAT *published in* Isaac Asimov's Science
Fiction Magazine, *copyright © 1983 by Davis
Publications, Inc.*
WORLD WAR LAST *published in* Isaac Asimov's Science
Fiction Magazine, *copyright © 1985 by Davis Publications, Inc.*
THE LOST CONTINENT OF AMERICA *published
in* SCIENCE AGAINST MAN, *© 1970 by Avon Books.*

ISBN 0-553-27214-4

Published simultaneously in the United States and Canada

PRINTED IN THE UNITED STATES OF AMERICA

O   0 9 8 7 6 5 4 3 2 1

CONTENTS

STREET MEAT
1

THE LOST CONTINENT
45

WORLD WAR LAST
95

LA VIE CONTINUE
175

OTHER AMERICAS

An Introduction to the Volume

I HAVE ALWAYS BEEN fascinated—some might say obsessed—as a writer with the possible future destinies of America, and not just because I'm an American. Indeed much of the rest of the world shares this obsession, for America is not quite like other nations. Nor has it ever been regarded as such by the other peoples of the world.

Military might and economic dominance are obviously part of this worldwide fascination with America. The United States is still the most militarily powerful nation on Earth, with a network of fleets and bases that encompasses much of the globe. The American economy is so dominant even in its current travails that Arabs are constrained to price the oil they sell to the Europeans and Japanese in dollars and the world catches a financial cold when America sneezes.

But there's much more to it than that. The rest of the world has a complex and ambivalent *emotional* relationship with America that no other nation evokes, including its close military rival, the Soviet Union, and its close economic rival, Japan.

The United States is hated by the peoples of Latin America whom it thoroughly dominates, economically, politically, and militarily, and yet these same peoples gobble up its popular culture like cotton candy and dream of some other America of the heart's desire that will rescue them from poverty and domestic tyranny.

The French are forever complaining about "Anglophone cultural imperialism" and periodically attempt to purge their language of "Franglais," even as their best filmmakers seek to make Hollywood movies in English, their young people dance to American rock and roll, and their trendsetters emulate their own concept of American chic.

Our number-one economic competitor, Japan, plays baseball, is developing a weird fascination for American football, has its own Disneyland, and is becoming addicted to American-style junk food.

At the height of the Vietnam War, when America was the international villain throughout the Third World, a cargo-cult tribe in

New Guinea still attempted to purchase Lyndon Johnson to come and be their president.

Even our archenemies, the Russians, crave nothing so much as to be accepted as fraternal equals by the people of the United States.

Why should this be so?

The Soviet Union is almost our military equal. Japan is in some ways already our economic superior. Sweden, Switzerland, and Germany now have higher standards of living. From whence the magic of America?

In part, no doubt, the answer is the English language. As the dollar is the closest thing this planet has to a world currency, so is English the closest thing there is to a world language.

It is the first language of perhaps four hundred million people, and while more people may have grown up speaking the various dialects of Chinese, English is the *second* language of untold hundreds of millions more throughout the world. English is the language that binds together multilingual societies in India, in much of Africa, in the Philippines. It is spoken by more people than not in Scandinavia and the Netherlands. It is studied by every schoolchild in Japan and the Soviet Union.

English is the international language of aviation. A French pilot landing on a German airfield communicates with the tower in English. Indeed an Arab pilot landing on an Arab airfield will also communicate with the controllers in English. English is the language of international commerce. English has long since supplanted French or German as the language of international science.

But English can't be the whole answer, for Britain also speaks English, and it was the British, not the Americans, who spread English far and wide in Africa, who made it the, ah, *lingua franca* of India, and yet the peoples of the world do not really see English as the language of Great Britain. They relate to it emotionally as the language of America.

Show business probably has a lot to do with that.

English is also, of course, the international language of show business, the American market is by far the dominant English language market, and so American film, television, radio, and music have long since come to quite dominate international media.

And not only economically but in terms of iconography and imagery. There is no jungle so remote that American rock and roll cannot be picked up on a transistor radio. American film and TV stars are instantly recognizable almost anywhere on earth as are such purely American archetypes as the cowboy, the hardboiled private eye, the vigilante avenger and Superman. *Dallas, Miami Vice,* and even old *I Love Lucy* reruns inundate the airwaves in scores of countries, and, I kid you not, a famous book-length Marxist treatise in Spanish explores the imperialistic political significance of the mythic substructure of the adventures of Donald Duck.

But even the universality of American show business is not the whole answer. There is *still* something more. A something, that, in the end, is what I believe brought me to write the short novels in this book, as well as such novels as *Bug Jack Barron, The Mind Game, The Men in the Jungle, Songs from the Stars,* and *Little Heroes,* all of which are, in their diverse ways, American science fiction and America *as* science fiction.

For America—not as a geographic entity or conventional nation state but as a *concept*—has from its birth been a dream of the future, a kind of real world science fictional speculation, for the peoples of the Earth.

America was, after all, "discovered" in 1492 as if it were a virgin alien planet. And colonized by people from all over the world, much as people all over the world now dream of colonizing the Moon or Mars.

And became an independent nation as the embodiment of a radical utopian concept—namely that the populace could and should choose its own rulers as public servants rather than accept the divine right of kings.

Two hundred years later, it is difficult to realize just how radical, how speculative, how science-fictional a concept this really was at the time. Almost all of the world was ruled by hereditary monarchs, and had been, time out of mind. Greece had had democratic city-states of a kind, but they were really oligarchies, as was the Republic of Rome. Even Plato's science-fiction Republic was ruled by philosopher-kings.

That the right to govern might be something deriving from the consent of the generality of the governed and not from divine inherited right or even from a grant from some national elite, that there might be a human-given law superior to even the will of the chief executive, was something new under this sun, and quite arguably the most radical break with all of previous history ever to occur on Planet Earth. Out of it ultimately flowed the French Revolution and the Latin American republics and the revolutions of 1848 and the Russian Revolution and in a very real sense all the nonmonarchical governments that now form an overwhelming majority of the United Nations.

This, I believe, is in large part the genesis of the rest of the world's peculiar emotional relationship with America, a relationship not so much with a geographic entity as with a utopian vision made manifest in the real world, with America as a concept, with America as a kind of science fiction.

The American Revolution was a conceptual breakthrough that transformed the world, that altered forever the ideal concept of the relationship between government and governed, individual and body politic, legitimacy and the nature of the state. This is the true meaning of the so-called "American Dream"—the revolutionary concept that the people have a right to choose their own form of government and select their own governors by some form of democratic process, that legitimate rulers are those who are subordinate to the will of the people as expressed through law and electoral processes.

It is *this* American Dream that the peoples of the world have spent the last two hundred years trying to achieve and maintain for themselves. Absolute monarchy is now all but extinct and even constitutional monarchy is now a relatively uncommon form of government.

Alas, the Dream has been betrayed over and over again. The First French Republic became a Napoleonic Empire. Most of the revolutions of 1848 were eventually crushed. Latin American and African republics have degenerated into military dictatorships. The Russian Revolution degenerated into a bureaucratic tyranny. The Iranian Revolution gave birth to a grim theocracy.

But the Dream itself has never died. And, phoenixlike, its manifestations have risen again and again out of the ashes of defeat all over the world. For somewhere out there across the sea, there has always been an America of the spirit, the original democratic dream, a constitutional democracy that has somehow managed to keep the faith for two hundred unbroken years.

And a second homeland across the sea of time which the peoples of the world can rightly claim as in some sense their own, for America was settled by the sons and daughters of most of the nations of the Earth. No other nation on the face of the Earth has as many family connections to the rest of the world, no other nation was built by Englishmen and Scots, Frenchmen and Spaniards, Irish and Africans, Chinese and Germans, Poles and Italians, Russians and Jews, Japanese and Scandinavians, and certainly in no other nation of the Earth has such a diversity of former nationalities maintained their ethnic identities.

In the second half of the twentieth century, with its waves of refugees, its easy air travel, its European Common Market, its transnational corporations, its interlocked worldwide economy, this aspect of America has gained a new resonance.

For America, in a very real sense, is the model of the future transnational world. A world with porous international borders or no borders at all. A world in which ethnic groups from many origins intermingle in the same territory. A world that is halfway here already.

Can such multinational societies reach stability and flourish? Or will they degenerate into endless unresolvable ethnic strife of the sort we see in Northern Ireland and the lands that were Palestine and Lebanon and so many of the nations of Africa? Will the ethnic state be replaced by a higher transnational identity or will national states degenerate into the chaos of tiny tribalisms?

There is only one nation on this planet where an ethnic diversity exists that mirrors the interpenetrating ethnic diversity of such a future transnational world. The Soviet Union, India, and Nigeria may be thoroughly multinational states, but their nationalities are geographically distributed. Only America, all of whose territory was colonized by peoples from all over the world, is a truly mature transnational state, with an ethnic heterogeneity in all fifty states.

In this sense, too, America is the experimental laboratory, the living science-fiction story, of the transnational future world. And this is why the peoples of the world are fascinated by more than American foreign policy. This is why the peoples of the world pay such close attention to internal events in the United States.

If American democracy and culture survive and flourish, there is hope for a stable transnational future. If America destroys itself from within, that future will look grim indeed. On some level, the peoples of the world look at America, and for better or worse, they see their future selves.

Then too, the Industrial Revolution, which began in Britain, reached its full flowering in the United States, at least in terms of the accelerating pace of scientific breakthroughs and technological development. Consider just how many of the technologies that make the modern world what it is were invented or first developed in America.

The telegraph. The telephone. The Gatling gun, ancestor to the machine gun. Interchangeable parts for complex machinery. The assembly line The airplane. The transistor. The semiconductor. Computers. Nuclear fission. The atomic bomb. The hydrogen bomb. The broadcast satellite and worldwide live television. The electric guitar. Talking pictures. The synthesizer.

And of course the ultimate symbol of America as science fiction, Project Apollo.

It was 1969, the Vietnam War was at its height, and I was living in London when America landed the first men on the Moon.

It was a period in which anti-Americanism was quite strong in Europe. The United States, which had rescued Western European civilization from the Nazi darkness, which had rebuilt its shattered economy via the Marshall Plan, which had stood against Soviet expansionism in Greece and Berlin, which had long been seen as the champion of the democratic West, was now engaged in an ugly, evil, purposeless, and seemingly endless war against a small Third World country.

Like it or not, agree with it or not, that was the European perception of Amerika at a time when even many Americans were spelling it with a "k."

And then the Eagle landed.

And Western Europe partied through the night. People in London congratulated Americans on the street. There was more enthusiasm in Europe for the American Moon Landing than there was in the United States. For that one brief shining moment, a precious something that had seemed lost had come back to light up the world.

What was that something?

I was twelve in 1952, and I remember watching television coverage of the American army of occupation leaving Japan.

In 1945, before the atomic bomb was dropped on Hiroshima, it was generally assumed that the United States would be constrained to invade Japan, that millions would die, that the Japanese would fight the hated Americans to the death in defense of the Home Islands.

Then came Hiroshima. And the surrender on the *Battleship Missouri*. And the MacArthur Shogunate. And a democratic constitution imposed upon the defeated Japanese by the United States.

A mere seven years after Hiroshima, a peace treaty was signed with Japan, and the American army of occupation was withdrawn.

And when the occupying American army paraded through the Japanese cities on its way to the troop ships, something happened that had never happened before in the history of the world and that has not happened since.

A conquered people turned out to watch an occupying army leave their homeland. They did not jeer. They did not watch in stony silence. They tossed flowers. Thousands upon thousands of little paper American flags waved in their hands. Many people wept openly.

In 1945, an army of hated Americans had come to occupy a defeated enemy nation.

Seven years later, the people of Japan lined their streets to bid a fond farewell to their American friends.

I knew then as a boy as I know now as a man that no greater victory has ever been won in the history of the world.

That was what America once was. That was the America of the world's heart's desire. That was the America that reappeared for a brief moment out of the darkness when Neil Armstrong set foot on the Moon.

Alas, that moment was long ago, all too brief, and has long since passed.

The Vietnam War ground on for years afterward, and ended with an America defeated and dishonored.

The other America that its sons and daughters had been building, the other America that had forced an end to the war and given the nation a new kind of liberty, the other America that had released a new burst of creativity, that had fought for the rights of blacks and women and the maverick American spirit, was systematically crushed by the power structure in the name of American tradition itself, inflicting a spiritual, cultural, political, creative, and economic wound on the nation so profound that nearly twenty years later we are only beginning to understand the terrible cost.

An American president attempted a coup de main against the Constitution, failing only by the margin of a piece of tape across a door lock, and for the first time in history, the world watched an American president driven from office in disgrace.

And the world watched in numb disbelief as another American president allowed fifty-four American hostages to be held in Tehran for over a year in a pathetic demonstration of powerlessness, as the Ayatollah Khomeini broke the Carter presidency and elected Ronald Reagan, a former straight man to a chimpanzee, president of the United States.

And now the proud space program that put men on the Moon lies in utter ruins, destroyed not so much by the *Challenger* tragedy as by military co-option and a fatigue of the spirit.

America is engaging in nineteenth-century style interventionism in Central America even as it self-righteously condemns the Russians for doing the very same thing in Afghanistan.

The American economy groans under an enormous trade deficit and a crushing military budget and a national debt that has been tripled in less than eight years.

The American labor movement has been broken, the American standard of living is in decline, the broad middle class that was the backbone of American democracy is in the process of being proletarianized, the family farmer is an endangered species, and as a result the American spirit itself has become mean and crabbed.

The social fascist right is in the ascendancy and liberty is under siege to the point where small pressure groups are able to remove books from libraries and magazines from racks, a Supreme Court nominee must withdraw because he once smoked a few joints, and the best and the brightest of the American scientific and technological community are constrained to piss into bottles to prove their purity.

Not so coincidentally, American politicans of both major parties are generally perceived as intellectually bankrupt mountebanks, corporate executives as self-serving thieves, workers as goldbricking drunks and drug addicts, and American science, technology, and manufacturing are all losing their cutting edge.

America is now mistrusted, hated, feared, and psychoanalyzed all over the world, and, perhaps out of desperate longing, the peoples of Western Europe are looking eastward now, toward the Soviet Union of Mikhail Gorbachev, for a new light in a darkening world.

For America has lost its way and the world knows it, even if many Americans as yet do not. The American Dream is in eclipse, and the erstwhile light of the world now casts a baleful shadow in many corners of the globe.

And yet...

And yet America is still a nation of enormous diversity, still, for better or worse, the best model of the future that this world has, and still, for that reason, a kind of science-fiction story in real time, whose final outcome, the shape of whose future, is still, and perhaps always will be, in doubt.

For if science fiction itself teaches us anything at all, it is that there is no such thing as *the* future. *We* make our futures collectively, all of us, day by day, hour by hour, moment by moment, decision by decision, and those who do not ponder the possible futures will most certainly be condemned to inhabit the future they nevertheless cannot avoid making.

So here are four possible futures that we may or may not be making, as Americans, and as citizens of the Planet Earth. And if none of them are quite what our hearts might desire, if none of them are visions of other Americas we would wish to inhabit, they are not intended as such, but as cautionary tales.

In historical terms, they are would-be self-canceling prophecies pointing down roads to other Americas none of us would wish to see, in the hope that they will remain forever paths not taken. And in human terms, I believe, they are not, in the end, stories of terminal despair.

It is possible for life to go on even on the meanest streets of a decaying America. It is possible for the world to be saved by the very mountebanks and airheads who have put it in such mortal danger. It is possible for the American Dream to survive and inspire after the fall of America itself. It is even possible for an American to be true to that Dream as an exile on a foreign shore.

History passes. The human heart goes on. *La vie continue*.

Thus be it ever.

We never promised the world a rose garden.

Or did we?

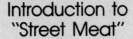

Introduction to "Street Meat"

How far away is the New York of "Street Meat"? Perhaps not as far as we would like to think.

There are already tens of thousands of homeless people living on the streets of Manhattan, there are already abandoned buildings a block or two away from luxury co-op towers, there is already a huge underclass of people who have grown up never knowing employment, and the economic gap between the streeties and the plushie tushies is currently just as extreme as anything in this story.

And while People Kibble has yet to be invented and rats have not yet quite surfaced as street food and private police have not yet come into vogue, give it the next recession, and a little inflation, and some more dollar devaluation, and an uptick in unemployment, and a decline in tax revenues, and "Street Meat" could stop being science fiction muy pronto, don't bet your sweet culo against it, muchacho . . .

STREET
MEAT

MAL SUERTE AND GOOD, so it goes in La Vida, no, and sometimes a streetie can't tell which is going to lead to which.

Bad luck for Gonzo that he lost his kibble kard when a city cop caught him trying to boost a roasted rat from a peddler who had the mother on the pad. Could you believe it, a rat peddler with the dinero to pad one of New York's finest?

Maybe a smarter streetie than Gonzo wouldn't have had so much trouble featuring that. Manhattan was full of rats, natch, but those ratones had more street smarts than, say, the likes of Gonzo, and half of them were rabid, so rat-catching was not for everyone. But a guy with the cojones and the talent could bag the buggers free, roast 'em over a garbage fire, and get five bucks a pop free and clear. A king ratter with a tight culo for dinero who held his luck for five years might even save up the bread to put a down payment on a room, or anyway a share in one. So slipping the local muni ten on the side every week was just playing the percentages, the closest a streetie could come to having his very own zonie.

But the street smarts to comprend all this Gonzo did not have, and so while the ratter was looking the other way, he hooked a fat sizzling one off the grill by its tail, not getting ten feet before he was collared with the evidence dangling still steaming from his hand. Good luck and bad.

First offense for street snatch was loss of kard, second was six months in the South Bronx digging holes on a cup of kibble a day, at the end of which, if you were one of the 60 percent who survived, you were issued a special blue kard, which marked you as a two-timer. And if a blue-karder got busted, it was lobe-job time, muchacho.

So the bad luck was the bust, and the good luck was that Gonzo *did* have enough street smarts to comprend the instant justice system. Most blue-karders had the smarts to throw the marker away, figuring a cup of kibble a day courtesy of the Welfare was not worth the inevitability of a lobe-job if you were busted with a blue ticket on your person. But Gonzo had the smarts to figure that the best course was to stay the hell out of the South Bronx in the first place. So after he lost his red kard the first time, he had spent a starving six days stalking streeties until he could bash a legit red-karder and steal a new one.

So even though this was really his *second* bust, he had a red kard in his possession to lose, and escaped with nothing worse than kard konfiscation. And of course, loss of the rat.

And muy pronto, one piece of good luck seemed to lead to another.

Street sex was not ordinarily Gonzo's bag—not because of excess scruples, but because, with his skeletal frame, stinking threads, and face full of pimples, he was not exactly equipped for a prime career as street meat. But what he needed more than anything else right now was another kosher kard and the best place to boost one was the meat rack at Fourteenth and Third.

These environs were about as low a meat rack as existed even in the Pig Apple, which was exactly the point. Any meat rack much more savory than this involved transactions between streeties and gainfully employed townies. Any market involving transactions between streeties and townies would be infested with muni cops, or even, if the market were patronized by pervos from a plush zone, by bad-ass zonies. Besides, townies, being employed, did not carry kibble kards.

Hard as it was for even Gonzo to comprend, Fourteen and Three was a meat rack in which the johns were *streeties*. Here *streetie* pervos could cop a come for a joint or a jug or a stringy old rat, and the cops there don't need you and man they expect the same.

The good luck was that Gonzo scored a geek almost at once, and a feeble old sack of shit at that. Leaning up against the wall of a burned-out building like barely able to stand, this white-haired old slimepot, wearing a drape stitched together out of the same potato sacking his street bag was made of, leered out of an alley at Gonzo dangling a half-eaten rat invitingly.

"Rat for a rack?" he croaked.

"Name your game, gaffer."

"Gum my goo, giggles."

Well any streetie willing to trade a rat for a rack was odds on to be carrying a kibble kard, who could ask for a better dig to do the dirt than this alley, and this gaf was in no shape to offer a tussle. As far as Gonzo was concerned, this was almost too good to be true.

The bad luck was that he was right.

Gonzo nodded his agreement and followed the gaf a few steps deeper into the alley. But as soon as the john began fumbling with his drape, Gonzo grabbed him around the throat with one paw and stifled his scream with the other. Frog-marching his victim even deeper into the alley, he demanded: "Koff your kard!"

The old geek's mouth muttered against his palm.

"Yawp you pervo, and I'll tear your tongue out," Gonzo said, removing the gagging hand

The pervo giggled quietly. "Yock's on you, younger," he said. "Ain't carrying no kard." His face suddenly went through some weird transformation, as did his voice. "In point of fact, you foul creature, you've just assaulted a townie. It's a lobe-job for you, sonny, if you're caught."

"*Townie?* Geek like you's a townie, I'm a plush zone slummer!"

"Vice verse, villain," the old man gabbled. "*I'm* the plushie tushie, primed for prole place plunder. Slumming for sleazo sex, son, see the scene?"

Dimly, dumbly, dubiously, Gonzo saw the scene. He'd heard the word from the bird on this kind of turd. Rich townie pervos from some plush zone palace day-tripping the streeties, copping their sick kicks in streetie drag. On the other hand, it could be a scam to let him lam.

But with both hands on this dirty mother, it didn't really matter. A red flash went off in Gonzo's brain, bolts of lightning seared down his arms, and, gibbering and screaming curses in some primal language of formless and innocent rage, he bashed the pervo's head against the wall with a dull sickening thunk and dropped the limp remains to the ground like the sack of shit he was.

Running on red-hot automatic now, Gonzo snatched up his victim's street bag and rat and fled up Third Avenue babbling and swearing, as if some cunning buried deep within his backbrain knew that no one on the sidewalks of good old New York was about to screw with a brain-burned screamer.

It was a *job*. She was a *townie*. That was all that Mary Smith knew and all that she needed to know, or so she continually told herself at times like these. She owned an entire room in what had once been a luxury building on Seventy-eighth and Riverside. There were twenty-five million people out of work in the US of A, and somewhere between five hundred thousand and two million streeties in New York who had neither jobs nor domiciles. Who thought themselves lucky when they got themselves a rat to supplement their kibble ration, assuming they even had kards. Who considered it the height of luxury if they stole a subway token and gained access to the Subterranio for the winter when the cold winds began to blow. She was a townie. She had a job. She owned a co-op room with thirty-seven years to go on a forty-year mortgage.

In point of fact, while this was all that Mary *needed* to know, when she let herself, she knew far more than that.

She knew that "Smith" was a "family name" she had given herself to celebrate the miracle of obtaining employment. She knew that she had grown up possessing only the name "Maria." She knew that until five years ago she had been a streetie, surviving by wits, hooking, and the considerable jungle judo she had been forced to pick up in the process. She knew that it had been only a fantastic piece of luck that had placed her in position to rescue a lousy plushie tushie from a mugger by practical application of these street-fighting skills and so secure this job as a zonie.

Of course she was *never* unaware that she was a zonie. She carried an old Uzi machine pistol, which required constant maintenance. Six days a week, she reported to work at the headquarters of the Upper East Side Security Zone Guard Force. Six days a week, she guarded the frontier or shepherded Upper East Side plushie tushies on their forays beyond the borders of the Security Zone.

She also knew, when she let herself, that she had killed and/or wounded any number of streeties in the line of duty. What she *never* let herself know was her body count. What she also never allowed herself to ponder, not even for an instant, was the moral ambiguity of being an ex-streetie protecting loathsome plushie tushies from the very reality from which she herself had escaped.

Indeed, she tried not to think of her charges as "plushie tushies" at all. They were Clients. They were People of Means. They were the Source of Employment. They had made her a Townie.

But at times like these, her doublethink wavered. It was plain impossible to think of Mrs. Gloria Van Gelder as anything but a plushie tushie. In fact it was impossible to think of this woman as anything but a brainless, arrogant, gold-plated bitch.

What else could you call a woman who required the services of a helicopter, a pilot, and a zonie to take her and her wretched cocker spaniel Dearie back and forth to the Ellis Island Recreation Zone in order to let the little monster frolic in the grass and pee against a real tree? The fuel bill alone was probably the equivalent of three months' salary for Mary. And while a million streeties subsisted on people kibble and the occasional rat, the wretched beast, sleek, fat, and yapping, devoured enough horsemeat daily to treat three streeties to a deluxe banquet.

And now, as the helicopter clattered over the gray canyons of Manhattan in the late afternoon twilight, the dog was squirming and yammering on the fat woman's lap as if its bladder was once again filled to bursting. Mary only hoped that the creature would piss right on Mrs. Gloria Van Gelder's pink satin jumpsuit. Or better yet, decide to take a dump.

Mrs. Van Gelder, however, now decided to forestall any such catastrophe. "We must land immediately," she told the pilot. "Dearie has to make a wee-wee."

"I'm afraid that's impossible, madam," the mournful-faced pilot said. "We're over an un-Zoned part of Manhattan. We'll be home in a few minutes, Dearie will just have to wait until then."

"Dearie is a *dog*, you imbecile!" Mrs. Van Gelder shrieked. "Do you think you can explain that to *him?* Do you think I intend to let him *make* all over me? You will land this machine at once! Right down there in that big burned-out crater! Down! *Now!*"

"He's right, Mrs. Van Gelder," Mary said. "That's not a safe area."

The plushie tushie stared at her with eyes of blue gimlet steel. "You're a zonie, aren't you?" she said thinly. "You've got a machine gun, don't you? What do *you people* think we pay you for? So that my little Dearie can piss on my pants?"

"I don't think—"

"You're not *paid* to think, you insolent creature!" Mrs. Gloria Van Gelder shouted. "You're paid to provide protection, and you, my man, are paid to fly this helicopter where I tell you to! Another word of argument out of either of you, and you can go back to eating kibble and dead rats! You will land at once!"

As if to agree with his mistress, Dearie began to make a horrible, whimpering, keening sound. It was almost enough to make Mary bash its stupid brains out with the butt of her Uzi and then turn the business end on the dog's mistress.

Almost enough. Instead, she gritted her teeth against the sound and her fury and double-checked her weapon as the helicopter descended towards the country of the streeties.

"Son-of-a-bitch-culo-cabron-bastard-plushie-tushie-chingada-mother..."

Screaming more or less the same limited vocabulary of rage over and over again, Gonzo walked more slowly up Third Avenue now, flinging old newspapers, crushed beer cans, wads of toilet tissue, and more amorphous high-class townie garbage from the pervo's street bag to the four winds.

For that was all that seemed to be in the bag—newspapers, empty aluminum cans, tampons, bits of cardboard, useless scraps of rag—a lot of townie crap without so much as an edible apple core or a gnawable rabbit bone, or any other potentially nutritive scrap of organic matter. As for the pervo's half-eaten rat, whoever had previously munched on it must have done his gobbling quite a while ago, seeing as how the morsel, on closer inspection, had proven to be liberally spotted with green velvet fungus, crawling with maggots, and dripping some kind of awful stinking brown mung. Even Gonzo was not ready to tear the thing apart for what edible bits might conceivably remain, at least not yet. Though he wasn't ready to throw the rat away either, seeing as how it might just be possible to slip it to a blind beggar with a bad head cold in exchange for a butt or a belt of meth.

"Stinking-culo-mother-plushie-pervo-cabron-bitch-bastard!"

If Gonzo hadn't been too pissed off to think, he might just have been able to realize what deep shit he was really in. A *real* streetie's *real* street bag would be filled with useful items—pieces of cloth big enough to stitch into something, fresh rat bones, bits of firewood, a brick that could be used as a weapon, maybe even a book of matches, a homemade shiv, or some real chunks of ratmeat if you hit the jackpot—not old paper and plushie tushie garbage that could have only come from a Zone. No real street bag, this. Meaning no real streetie, the stiff he had left in the alley. Meaning that if he were caught, it wouldn't be the South Bronx or even a lobe-job, but a one-way token to Tube City, where, so the word from the bird had it, his meat would be used to give kibble what little flavor it had.

"Goddamn-madre-jumping-son-of-a-cabron-bitch-puta— *aargh!*"

Verbally exhausted but still livid with rage, and still loping aimlessly northward, Gonzo upended the street bag, grabbed the bottom, and whirled it around his head, spraying the last bits of crap all over himself and another nearby screamer—a stooped, white-haired old woman dressed only in a ragged robe of crap-smeared brown paper and caught in an angry argument with an invisible Virgin Mary.

Nothing unusual about that. The street was full of babblers and screamers as always, gibbering to themselves or to invisible companions, and no streetie survived very long reacting to anything so trivial as being showered with old paper and garbage from someone else's shit-fit.

But what *was* unusual—so unusual that it caused Gonzo to react once more to his environment and start thinking again—was that the dirty old chocha suddenly belly-whopped to the filthy pavement, grimy paw out-thrust to cover something that had clattered from the bag.

Moving with street-smart instincts, Gonzo stomped on the hand with the full weight of his body, eliciting a liquid scream of pain, then kicked upward, catching the crone in the chops and flipping her over on her back, where she scrabbled and moaned like an overturned turtle drooling bloody froth.

And there on the cracked and filthy pavement was a metallic yellow coin. Prong a dong, a *subway token!*

A subway token! Five bucks in townie dinero! When the winter winds began to blow in a few months, could be worth a streetie's sweet life to get into the old Subterranio. Didn't snow down under the ground. Warm it wasn't, but you didn't freeze, either. Electric lights twelve hours a day, more or less. Tunnels full of rats! Fat City down under, or so the word from the bird had it! Good suerte again! Good luck too that only this old chocha had seen it.

All this passed through Gonzo's brain as he was scooping up his treasure and stuffing it safely into his jock. Only then did he pause to think that it had to be more than good luck that twenty other street-smart bonzos weren't even now kicking the crap out of him fighting for the prize. Only then did he dig that all the other streeties in the vecino were eyeing the sky and listening to the sound pound. And only after *that* did the clattering chattering penetrate his conscious attention.

Whop-whop, chop-chop, a goddamn *helicop* was descending through the jagged canyon of burnt-out factory loft buildings towards the big bomb crater on Third and Thirtieth. And this was no machine-gun chop from the muni cops, it was a *plushie tushie* helicop, and it must be in deep trouble to be dumb enough to come down here in a streetie zone like a fat juicy bone!

Snatching up the empty bag in case of swag, Gonzo joined the gleeful rush to greet this tasty meat dropping right down to the nonexistent mercy of the street.

A sinking feeling blossomed in Mary's stomach as the helicopter fluttered down past the burned-out buildings to land in a big rubble-strewn crater conveniently left as a landing pad by some thoughtful terrorist's bomb of days gone by. And not just from the drop. They were coming down right in the middle of a crowd of streeties, or rather, a crowd of streeties, maybe as many as three dozen of them, was forming up around the crater as they came down into it.

The pilot moaned as the skids touched down. Dearie whimpered and squirmed in the lap of Mrs. Van Gelder, who cuffed him across the muzzle. "If you pee on me, I'll *kill* you, Dearie!" she shrieked.

"Don't turn off the engine!" Mary told the pilot as she cocked the Uzi. "This could get rough."

The three of them sat there for a long moment as the circle of filthy, haggard, hungry-eyed streeties hesitantly began to converge, step by halting step, on the grounded helicopter, whose rotors turned slowly and throbbingly overhead as if to provide ominous background music.

But that stupid plushie tushie bitch had all the street smarts of her pissy little lapdog. "Well what are you waiting for, you idiot?" she said, jamming the leash into the hand of the ashen-faced pilot. "Go take Dearie for his walk before he makes all over."

Despairingly, imploringly, the pilot locked eyes with Mary for a long moment. She shrugged unhappily at him.

"Make it fast," she told him, brandishing her Uzi upwards like a spear. "Stay right by the helicopter and I'll cover you."

"Mama mia..." the pilot groaned. But he popped the canopy, and, as Mary stood up leveling the Uzi at the streeties as menacingly as she could manage, he snatched up the dog and stepped out onto the ground.

The circle of streeties seemed to ooze backwards a few steps as they caught sight of the machine pistol. But then, with an audible sigh of collective lust, they seemed to flow forward again as they saw the cocker spaniel already squatting and pissing as the pilot set it down.

Street-smart memories that she thought she had lost, that she had tried so hard to lose, flooded in on Mary. She knew all too well what was going through those perpetually starved brains out there. A dog! An actual dog! *Forty pounds of meat!* Twenty or thirty rats' worth, sleek and fat and well fed, enough for three months of luxury, maybe more if you didn't make a pig of yourself! She could all but feel the drool forming in her own mouth out of time-warped sympathy.

"Perro!" someone shouted. "Perro, perro, perro!"

"Dog!"

"MEAT!"

"MEAT! MEAT! MEAT!" more than one voice shouted.

Then they were all chanting it, inching towards the helicopter and working up their courage for a charge. "MEAT! MEAT! MEAT!"

Mary waved her Uzi in the air. "Get back!" she shouted. "Get back, you dirty—"

A chunk of stone came sailing up out of the anonymity of the mob, missing both her and the helicopter. Then a brick hit the canopy, shattering half of it into a webwork of cracks. All at once, bricks and stones and pieces of broken bottles were whistling overhead, raining down on the helicopter as the mob, with an animal growl, surged forward.

"Shoot!" Mrs. Van Gelder screamed. "Shoot! Shoot! Shoot! Kill the dirty sons of bitches!"

As dozens of wild-eyed howling streeties shambled like killer apes towards the helicopter, Mary didn't have to be told what to do. Her finger tightened on the trigger, sending a short loud burst of gunfire right into the mob. Streeties shrieked and fell. The mob abruptly turned tail and began to flee in all directions like the denizens of an anthill fleeing from the sudden shock of a boot-heel.

But Mary hardly noticed any of this. For the sudden screaming burst of machine-gun fire had passed not three feet from the pilot's head, scaring him out of his socks. He threw up his hands in panic, and in so doing, let go of the leash.

The panicked cocker spaniel, yelping and barking, went tear-assing across the crater right on the heels of the fleeing streeties.

Gonzo, stuck in the rear of the crowd of streeties by the press of bodies, was frozen for a moment by the sound of machine-gun fire and screams of agony, long enough to be knocked on his ass by some bonzo when the mob turned to flee.

Scrabbling to his feet in terror, he saw a black furry shape dashing right by his arm, barking and whining. The dog! What luck! Forty pounds of meat for the monster, muchacho!

Before his fuddled brain even had time to form these simple thoughts, his street-smart instincts had acted. With lightning speed and with every ounce of strength in his scrawny arm, he raised up his fist and brought it down on the head of the cocker spaniel.

Before the pole-axed dog could even hit the ground, he snatched it up by the tail, stuffed it headfirst into his street bag, shouldered the sack, and was up and running like a son of a bitch.

"My God, he's got Dearie!" Mrs. Van Gelder screamed. "Stop him! Stop him!"

But even as Mary fired, the plushie tushie bitch yanked at her arm, and the burst did nothing more than send chips of stone flying into the air not ten yards from the helicopter. "Don't shoot, you imbecile, you could hit Dearie!"

Then Gloria Van Gelder's pale powdered puss was inches from her own, as livid and drooling with rage as any Mary had seen in her previous incarnation as a streetie.

"You go out there, you incompetent cow, and you bring back my Dearie alive, or you don't bother to come back at all!" she snarled in a hysterical voice backed with cold steel. "I'll have you digging rocks in the South Bronx till you drop! I'll lobe you myself! I'll have you ground up into kibble! And don't you think I can't do it, you wretched scum."

Mary didn't. Not for a moment did she doubt that this

chocha could and would, with a wave of her fat-fingered hand, destroy everything she had become since she clawed her way off the street for a casual whim. But for one brief moment, she did toy with the delicious notion of jamming the muzzle of her Uzi right down this lousy plushie tushie's throat and emptying an entire magazine directly into her stinking guts. . . .

Then she was off and running.

High on the fly with swag in his bag, Gonzo's street smarts put brains in his feet. The mob was fleeing south on Third, the street was hot on the trot as the bird spread the word, and he knew he didn't have much chance of keeping forty pounds of dog in his bag on a streetie main drag. He needed to fade from this scene like a submarine, and so he turned east on the first side street.

His luck held. No one else had made this turn. There was nothing on this narrow street but burnt-out buildings mounded with ancient garbage. Somewhere in these ruins there must be something sharp enough to cut up the mutt into meat, and if he could score a match somewhere . . .

But as he paused for a moment to catch his breath and check out his chances, he heard the sound of running feet. Turning, he was brought right down to the ground, clown, by the sight of the zonie from the helicop halfway up the street behind him, running hard, closing fast, and waving that goddamn machine gun chop.

"Son-of-a-mother-jumping-puta-goddamn-zonie-bitch!" he screamed in outrage as he made his feet do their stuff. But with forty pounds of dog on his back, he wasn't going to outrun no zonie for long. And ditching the dogmeat to save his own was not even a thought that crossed his mind. She was starting to gain on him as he turned the corner and came out onto Lexington. Bad luck, boy, muy malo!

And then good.

He had come out onto the next main drag not a block from a subway stop! And for the first time in years, he had a token in his jock!

The shock of such an incredible roll of good fortune—a token, the dog, now a subway stop—was like a cold whack in the chops that brought Gonzo's street smarts rushing back.

Against all reasonable animal instincts, knowing that his pursuer would now be closing even faster, he forced himself to slow to a trot, and then to a mere brisky saunter as he entered the sphere of attention of the muni cop guarding the entrance against the more obvious chop-artists, screamers, psychoscum, and reamers. Be cool, don't be a fool, he told himself, flashing his token for the indifferent benefit of the bored muni as he descended the stairs to the subway station.

Mary turned the corner onto Lexington just in time to catch a glimpse of the top of a heavily laden street bag disappearing down the stairs of the subway entrance up the block right under the stupid eyes of some lobed-out muni. Or so she thought. At this distance, it was hard to tell one swag bag from another, and for a few moments she could still delude herself that maybe she wasn't going to have to chase the damn dog-snatcher through the subway, where her chances of catching him were slim and none.

But the mother was nowhere else in sight as she trotted up to the muni, waving her Uzi as a badge of zoniehood to cut any crap, and her brief interrogation of the cop put the seal on it.

"Skinny pimply geek with a dog in his bag?"

"Plenty of skin and bones with pimples, ain't seen no *dog* in three years, whaddaya think this is, Madison and Sixtieth?"

"What just went down the stairs. Pimples? Heavy bag?"

"Yeah, regular pimple-puss. Big bag of swag, now thatya mention it, musta had fifty pounds of crap in there. Flashing a token too."

Oh no! The odds against any streetie having a token were ten to one against. The odds against the one streetie that snatched the damn dog having one were forget it. Mary had hoped that if the bonzo *had* ducked into the subway entrance, he had simply panicked, wouldn't get past the barrier, she'd be able to corner him like a nice fat trapped rat. But if the mother got past the barrier and into the Subterranio itself—

"Mierda!" she snarled, and dashed down the stairs.

One bit of luck was that this was a small local station—this entrance only opened onto the uptown local platform. At the bottom of the stairs was the entrance barrier and a small one-man token fortress. The barrier was the usual floor-to-ceiling wall of rusting, bullet-pocked three-inch armor plate. The fortress was a seven-by-seven-by-seven cube of the same, with a rotating TV camera enclosed in bullet-proof glass on top, a single money-and-token slot at shoulder level and the muzzle of a fifty-caliber machine gun poking out just below it. One of the three revolving turnstile doors in the barrier was just turning shut behind someone. No one in sight, and no place here to hide.

Mary wasted no time interrogating the token clerk, seeing as how her eardrums and the soles of her feet were picking up the vibes of a train approaching distantly down the tunnel. She stuck a token in the turnstile slot and, with a belt from her shoulders, forced the rusty stile barrier to turn, valving her onto the subway platform.

The uptown platform was dim, gray-green, filthy, stinking, and pretty deserted. A muni armed with an M-16 lounged under one of the still-working lights close by the barrier. Four townies in subway masks stuck close by him staring across the tracks at the downtown platform. Up the platform towards the uptown end, a female streetie squatted, taking a grunty dump. Nothing out of the ordinary.

Mary could see the lights of a train approaching the platform from downtown. That end of the platform lay in darkness, all the lights there having long since ceased to function. Odds on, her quarry was down there somewhere. . . .

She turned to interrogate the muni. "Did you see where—"

—At that inopportune moment, with a roar, a squeal, and a gut-wrenching clatter, the train barreled into the station—

"—Wha—?"

"—Did you see—"

"—Huh—?"

—Hiss! Crunch! Squeal! Clang! The train came to a juddering halt and half the car doors slid open.

"I SAID DID YOU SEE A BONZO WITH A HEAVY STREET BAG?"

"Ya gotta scream in my face like that?" the muni snarled intelligibly in the momentary silence.

The masked townies (Mickey Mouse, Horseface, Clown, Frankenstein) dashed into the nearest car. The streetie daintily wiped her butt with the hem of her robe.

"I said did you—"

Way at the downtown end, a figure carrying a heavy bag and glancing in Mary's direction dashed out of the darkness into a subway car. The doors started to close—

"Crap!" Mary snarled, dashing for the nearest door, and

managing to wedge it just enough ajar with the butt of her Uzi to snake inside.

Clunk! Hiss! Whirr! Jolt! The train began to pull out of the station.

Safe for the moment, Gonzo had time to think, and once he began to think, he couldn't figure this crazy zonie. Why had she chased him this far? Natch, forty pounds of dogmeat would be a neat snatch even for a zonie, she must have the drool for the perro. But then why hadn't she chopped at him with her piece, she sure hadn't been slow with the blow back at the helicop. Loco in the coco, jamoco!

Gonzo dashed up the subway car to check out the doors at the uptown end. Days of yore, these had opened to connect the cars, but they had been long since welded shut for security isolation. Once he saw that the weld still held, that the zonie couldn't car-hop in here after him, he dropped down on one of the blue-green plastic benches that ran the length of the subway car to catch his breath and suss the scene.

There were only about a dozen people in this car, and they were all townies hiding behind their subway masks, staring into space trying to pretend that no one else existed in the hope that no one would notice *they* existed. No streeties to get any droolies for what might be in his bag. Good thing too, because now he could see that the bottom of the bag was oozing blood. Anyone with street smarts knew that fresh blood meant raw meat, skeet. Only these townies, lobed-out for the duration behind their dumb masks with goo jammed up their ears, too gutless to even let their faces hang out naked in the Subterranio, would make like they couldn't see he had mucho muncho in his poncho.

Hanging by one hand from a subway handle and dangling her chop from the other, Mary was given a wide zone all to herself by the masked townies, who sucked themselves even deeper into subway trance at the sight of this armed crazy, as she pondered the tactical situation. There were five cars between her and the bonzo and most if not all of the doors between would be welded shut. So you could say that she had him cornered in the extreme downtown sardine can. All she had to do was get to him.

Which, she realized, she could do at Thirty-fourth Street,

the next station. Timing and speed, that was her need. When
the train stopped and the doors opened, she would dash out,
run down the platform, and with luck get into the car where
he was holed up before they closed again. The trick was the
timing—she had to make sure that he didn't slip out as she
was slipping in. If he did, she'd be stuck in the train while he
stood on the platform waving bye-bye and then her only
chance would be to risk a head-shot on the fly-by and hope
she didn't hit Dearie in the bargain.

On the other hand, if she was willing to risk shooting at
all . . .

Not without a certain strain of the brain, Gonzo tried to
think like a zonie. What was *her* next move along this groove?

Hippity-hop, car-to-car at the next stop, that's what *he'd*
do if he were a zonie cop. And if he could hop out just as the
doors were closing and she was hopping in . . . It'd be fun,
son, she'd be off to the next station in the can, man, and he'd
be standing there waving adios to the heat still holding the
meat!

Mary leaned against the doors as the train clanked and
squealed into the next station, primed to move the moment
they opened. Grind! Squeal! Clank! Thud! Ziip!

The doors opened. Or rather one of them did, the other
jamming. Mary snaked through, elbowing aside a fat townie
in a devil mask who was trying to get in, made up one car,
slipped on some crap, stumbled into two more townies,
swept them out of the way snarling, made another car length,
saw the bonzo peering out of a door three cars ahead, made
another car length—

—The train doors started to close—

—She made for the nearest one, saw her prey starting to
dash out of the train onto the platform as she ducked inside—

And fired a long wild burst along the length of the
intervening cars, scattering screaming townies, pinning him
inside as the doors slid shut and the train left the station.

The townies caught in the car with this maniac and her
smoking gun sat motionless behind their silly subway masks,
cringing a bit as she glared at them while fitting in a fresh
clip, but otherwise earnestly ignoring everything that happened
in a punctilious display of standard straphanger manners,
though from the smell of things half of them had crapped in

their pants and the others were in the process. Only a couple of slimy streeties at the far end of the car were babbling and moaning.

"Snap your yaps, or I'll ice your dice, lice!" Mary screamed at them. "I'll drop that bop on the next goddamn stop!"

Gonzo knew he had to move now, like pow! or on the next pass, his ass was grass. The townies in the car were pissing and moaning, yet at the same time trying to pretend nothing had happened as they oozed as unobtrusively as possible towards the downtown end, away from the monster.

"Son-of-a-bitch-bastard-puta-mother!" he screamed at them as one switch in his brain clicked off, and another clicked on, and he grabbed a geek in a Mickey Mouse mask, who had been too slow in moving, by the throat.

"Snap your yap, jap!" he snarled as the townie gurgled and gargled. Street smarts took over, and, using the townie's head like a hammer, he began battering at the glass of the nearest window.

Clang! Screech! Thud! The train pulled into the next station. Mary squeezed through the half-opened doors, ran down the platform shoving townies out of the way with the muzzle of her Uzi, and made it into the extreme downtown car.

Two rows of townies huddled towards the end of the car, spaced and shaking behind their subway masks. Except for a geek in a Mickey Mouse mask who lay on the bench towards the middle of the car in a smear of blood, beneath a window whose glass had been battered out to form a jagged exit.

The doors slid shut. Gingerly, Mary stuck her head through the shard-guarded windowframe.

The train began to move.

Peering downtown as the train began to move uptown, she saw a figure carrying a heavy street bag on its shoulder tear-assing down the subway tunnel.

"Son-of-a-bitch-puta-mother-bastard!" she screamed, firing a wild burst after him without thinking. The bullets echoed and pinged harmlessly off the concrete walls, and then the sound was lost in the ear-killing noise of the subway train getting up to speed.

* * *

Now that he was home free all, Gonzo allowed himself the luxury of feeling his fatigue. Scattered blue lights bathed the subway tunnel in a dim pale glow. A line of pylons separated the uptown from the downtown tracks. Man-sized alcoves were incised into the tunnel wall at regular intervals for the benefit of track crews avoiding passing trains. Gonzo huddled in one of these. His feet were meat, his back was beat, and he really wanted a cool twenty-four on his seat.

But while he was pretty sure he had given the zonie the slip, he knew he wasn't quite finished with this run, son. Not until he had the dog butchered, dressed out, and cooked. For one thing, a forty-pound mutt was only maybe thirty for the gut, and after having his ass chased all over already, he didn't feature carrying the useless extra freight. For another, raw dogmeat would start to stink in a day or two, and then there would be maggots, and it would start to drip mung. . . .

With all the old metal junk down here, finding something to use as a knife wouldn't exactly be worth your life, but he couldn't cook his snatch without a match, and just sitting down in the open and barbecuing a whole dog would draw every streetie within range like birds to a turd.

Much as he disliked the notion, he had to admit that a few pounds of the dog could buy him everything he needed, if he could find a solo lobo with a secret hooch where he could poach the pooch. Some dumb suck too weak to try and push his luck.

Come to think of it, a *chick* would sure do the trick. . . .

Running on old street-smart reflexes without being dumb enough to take time to think, Mary got off the uptown train at Forty-second, fought her way through the rush crush in this town under the ground, slipped into a downtown just pulling out, rode it one stop, and got off again. Couldn't have taken more than five minutes.

Which meant that the bonzo who she had last seen running downtown through the tunnel had to be uptown from her now and heading her way down the uptown tunnel.

Fortunately for her, most of the lights at the uptown end of the downtown platform were long since gone, but there was still one burning at the uptown end of the platform across the tracks. Which meant that if she lay prone on the end of the platform, she would be invisible to anyone emerging from the tunnel, whereas *he* would become a nicely silhouetted target at point-blank range. Which meant that she should be able to drop him with a good tight head-shot without much risk of hitting the dog.

But once she took up this position, lying out of sight in the filth and shadows, she had nothing to do but listen and think and smell the stink.

Like most townies without plushie tushie bread, Mary was constrained to ride the subway back and forth between work and her room. Although she felt a certain contempt for herself for doing it, like most townies, she wore earplugs against the noise, and a subway mask between her private inner world and the collective bummer of the subway and her fellow straphangers. This was usually enough to space her into the traditional subway riding trance, which hypnotic state was usually enough to allow her to push full awareness of the olfactory component of her surroundings below the level of conscious awareness.

But now, unmasked, unplugged, lying right in the down and dirty, and forced by the pragmatics of the situation into full sensory alert, she really *smelled* the subway for the first time in either this or her previous life.

It stank. P.U. B.O. L.A.M.F. Like rank.

It stank of generations of piss and sweat and crap. It stank of the collective body odor of the tens of thousands of scum lower than streeties who actually *lived* down here. It stank of old broiled rat and garbage-fire smoke. It stank of the tension, suppressed fear, and sour despair of the millions of townies who found themselves processed through it twice a day. Once you let the smell penetrate your awareness, it permeated your whole being, it let you know that your *own* body odor was another part of the ghastly whole. It was a stink that made Mary think, and what she thought about was her own state of sweaty despair.

Dearie, the goddamn stupid mutt, might very well already be dead. She had seen the dog bashed on the head, hadn't she, and the sucker had really been brained. Come to think of it, she had never seen a struggling sign of life in the street bag, and had heard not a bark or whine of protest from the normally noisy creature throughout the whole chase.

And if the dog hadn't been dead when the bonzo had stuffed it in the bag, there was a good chance that he was killing it right now. Man, if *she* were the streetie with a dog in *her* bag, *she'd* sure as hell make sure the mother was dead as soon as possible. Even if he thought she had given up, he'd know that a bark or a yelp would attract attention, and any such attention you drew down *here* would mean nothing but trouble of the worst possible kind. . . .

Out of the corner of her eye, she clocked the comings and goings on the subway platform. The evening rush was in full swing. Train after train roared by scant feet from where she lay, rattling her brain. Masked townies zipped in and out through the crush trying hard not to see each other or anything else.

This not being one of the main station complexes, what they were really trying to avoid seeing was little in evidence— the permanent floating population of streeties, of things lower than streeties, that lived, or at any rate existed, down here full time, the Subway Scum that never saw the light of day.

Even in the worst times of her dimly remembered streetie days, Maria had never been dumb or desperate enough to spend the hours between nine P.M. and seven A.M. in the subway, not even when the streets above were filled with slimy slushed snow and the temperature at night hit ten below. When the subways shut down at nine, *all* the lights went out, and what hid in the tunnels and crannies during the subway "day" slithered out to claim a night blacker than a plushie tushie's heart. And the word from the bird was that anything that moved was meat.

You could get a hint of what that meant if you glimpsed out of the corner of your eye what lurked around the darker edges of the major stations like Times Square or Grand Central during the day. Babblers and screamers. Lumps of filthy flesh sleeping under mounds of newspapers. Bits and pieces of bone it didn't pay to look too closely at piled around last night's cookfires.

Even with plenty of ammo for the Uzi, Mary didn't have the dumb guts to risk being caught down here when the lights went out. She'd give up first, she'd take her chances with Mrs. Gloria Van Gelder, she'd go back to the streets, she'd . . .

Oh no!

Oh *yes*!

Mary snapped out of the hypnogogic reverie into which, in retrospect, she realized she had fallen. How long had she lain here? How many trains had gone by? She'd lost track. She'd lost count, or never taken it. But she'd certainly been lurking here more than long enough for the bonzo with the dog to come slinking up the tunnel.

If he was going to.

Crap, it figured! She'd been a zonie too long. She'd lost her street smarts, she'd forgotten how to think like truly desperate prey. If *she* were the streetie with a dog in her poke, if she had been chased and nearly nailed by a zonie with an Uzi, what would she do? She'd hole up in that tunnel between stations and stay out of sight until the lights went out, that's what she'd do! Figuring correctly that no townie, not even a heeled zonie, would want her ass bad enough to risk her own in the subway after nine. Then, and only then, would she sneak up the tunnel towards the nearest station, and, unless her luck was bad, escape to the street with the meat.

Face it Maria, that suck isn't going to come walking down these tracks while the lights are on. And even if you're crazy enough to wait here till they go out, which you are not, you won't even be able to see well enough to get a clean head-shot from five feet out.

You've been handing yourself a con, mon, she knew. Only two ways to go, mojo—into that tunnel after the suck before the lights go out, or hang it up and let the mother keep the pup, in which case your meat will be back on the street.

Mary got to her feet, pretending for a moment that she was making up her mind, that the possibility of true choice really existed. A train came roaring into the station not three feet from her nose. The rush was waning now, only about a dozen townies got on, and fewer got off. She had no more time to play games with her mind. It was now or never.

So when the train left the station, she slipped over the platform lip and onto the downtown tracks. Keeping close to the tunnel wall and away from the electrified third rail, she went trotting off uptown through the tunnel, following the dim line of blue bulbs ever deeper into the semidarkness, eyes alert for any movement up ahead, ears pricked to anticipate the rumble of trains approaching from the rear, nerves scraping rawer and rawer with the ever-building tension. . . .

Gonzo didn't feature this, he didn't like the look of it at all. He'd been slowly and ever so carefully making his way downtown through the tunnel, following the trail of blue bulbs, ducking into an inspection alcove every time an uptown train began to approach, long before he became visible in the oncoming lights. Starting and freezing every time he heard a rat scuttle or the unfathomable clank of distant machinery. Now he was approaching a totally dark section of the tunnel where all the lights were out, every last one of them, downtown and up, for as far ahead as his eyes could see.

As he squinted into the dark trying unsuccessfully to penetrate the ominous gloom, something seemed unnatural about the situation, you didn't expect things to be working down here very well, and there were always many dead bulbs, but...

Then he felt the pressure wave of an oncoming train moving uptown towards him from behind the blackness. He ducked into an alcove, and a minute or two later, the onrushing headlights of the train lit up the dark section of tunnel for a few moments as it came around a bend into visibility.

In those few moments, Gonzo saw that the dead bulbs up ahead hadn't merely been burned out and never replaced. Every last one of them on both the uptown and downtown sides of the tunnel had been smashed. And for a flash Gonzo saw, or thought he saw, or tried to convince himself he didn't see, a big, hairy, raggy-baggy shape shamble quickly across the tracks like a jungle ape. Clutching something that seemed to gleam like a well-cleaned blade...

Mary plastered herself to the tunnel wall as the train went by. When it had passed, she looked uptown with a sinking feeling in her guts.

The next whole section of the tunnel was dark. Dead black dark. So dark that she reflexively glanced behind her at the receding row of dim lights just to make sure that they were still on, that she hadn't lost track of time and been caught down here after nine. When she assured herself that the lights behind her were still feebly burning, a part of her, a big part of her, wanted to turn tail and follow them home rather than venture farther into the dark and deadly.

But she knew that if she followed those lights now, if she left this damn place without the goddamn dog, there wouldn't *be* any home to return to—no job, therefore no money, therefore no next month's payment on her room, therefore no room, therefore her ass would be back on the street.

Son of a chicken bitch! she told herself. You've got your chop, girl! Got your zonie moves, you mean jungle-mother! And if I was that gonzo sucker, I'd be right there in the dark lurking, figuring this poor little muchacha would chicken out and start twitching and jerking. Go get that suck, he's in there just waiting for mama with any luck!

Thus pumping herself up, Mary slowly began walking uptown again, into the darkened section of tunnel, up on the balls of her feet, her finger on the trigger, holding the Uzi before her like a spear.

Within twenty yards or so, the tunnel took a bend, and when she had rounded it, she was walking through total blackness. Her nerves started screaming in protest, but she couldn't let herself stop now. Even though every fall of her feet sounded to her like an elephant crunching along on broken glass. Even though she froze every few feet at little sounds, real or imagined.

The darkness seemed to go on forever in space and in time. Phantom shapes were flickering across the insides of her blinded eyes, glowing yellow eyes, gleaming mouths full of razor-sharp teeth, horribly flapping wings of night, and the squealing and scraping of rats and bats and things that—

—"Gargha! Eeegah!"

Something screaming, gibbering, puke-stinking foul, strong and heavy, suddenly smashed into her in the darkness, mewling and slavering and slamming her up against a tunnel pylon! Teeth sank into her shoulder sending a lightning bolt of pain down her arm, claws raked her face, the Uzi went flying into the darkness—

—Then there was a quick flash of blue light that engraved an awful afterimage on her retinas as it faded as fast as it had come—

—Muzzle first, the machine pistol had hit the third rail, fusing and sizzling in a shower of electric blue sparks that revealed—

—A huge hulking male thing, all muscles, rotten rags, crap-matted hair and beard, pinning her to the pylon with its body, lifting a face that was all hair and red eyes and brown jagged teeth dripping with her own blood, so close to her nose that she gagged on the fetid stench of its horrid breath as the afterimage faded to black.

"Puta-mother!" she screamed in the dark, and, bracing her back against the pylon, brought her knee up with desperate strength at where she calculated its crotch would be.

"Eeeeee!" A shrill burbling scream and something soft brushing against her kneecap. Claws at her eyes. Something hard hit her gut, knocking the wind out of her. Her knees started to fold and she began to fall. . . .

But not before she brought down the heel of her right hand where she hoped a neck would be and felt a satisfying resistance against it as she fell forward into a stunning jolt of head on head.

Something stabbed feebly at her chest. Then she was down on the dirt with a heavy weight atop her drooling and grunting and clawing at her face.

And the sound of a train clattering toward her from around the bend in the tunnel.

Somehow, she got her feet up, wedged in between her stomach and the creature. She could feel the pressure-wave of the approaching train now, see a light rushing towards her, eclipsed by the dark bulk pressing down on her body.

"Eee-YAH!" she shouted, putting all her remaining strength into a double-legged kick, flipping the thing up off her, back-first into the side of the train rushing past them at high speed.

The body bounced off the moving train like a basketball off a backboard and smashed into her as she tried to rise, knocking her over backwards—

—There was a sudden sharp pain at the back of her head and then her own lights went out.

Gonzo had no idea how long he had been frozen there, squeezing as deep into the alcove as possible, trying to become invisible.

He had seen a thing much too big for him to want to tussle with shamble across the tracks. He had heard screams and grunts and the sounds of bovver. Then an electric blue flash and two struggling figures as something hit the third rail. Then more screams and fight sounds. Then the lights of an approaching train outlining two nasty mothers rolling around on the tracks. Then nothing but darkness and silence up ahead for a long, long time.

No logician he, but this kind of calculation his street smarts could handle: he had seen something too big to mess with, that something had gotten into it with something else, therefore whichever one of them had come out on top, *he* did not feature facing it, in the dark or in the light.

No way he was going to go ahead towards whatever lurked in the dark. And unless the two of them had offed each other or the train had gotten them both, a percentage you had to be loco in the coco to play, *something* muy fuerte *was* up ahead of him in the dark, and might be silently creeping up the tunnel towards him right now.

So if he turned tail and fled uptown, he might be spotted by the whatever, little guy with a big bag outlined by the tunnel lights before him. Yeah, *he'd* be visible, and whatever was down there would be watching him out of the impenetrable dark.

So the scam, Sam, was to hold the line till the time was nine. When the whole subway went dark, the percentage would be his—he knew there was something down there, but *it* didn't know about him. He hoped. When neither of them could see, if he could move without tipping a sound, he could slink uptown home free.

Dashing down the snowy street five steps ahead of two dudes with open flies. She grabbed the rat by its tail and bashed its brains out against the wall. Grabbing up a brick from the pile of rubble, she smacked him across the chops with it. The dog ran yelping and screaming. Grunting and swearing, the john came. Gobbets of half-cooked ratmeat slid down her gullet. A throb of pain somewhere, and a deeper, duller thud of pain somewhere else.

Maria didn't really know when she had come to. Shoulder, right. Head, right. Fragments of dream images whirling behind her eyes at some point became fragments of fear images whirling in the dark. She had a head and shoulder somewhere, and they hurt like a son of a bitch. Body, right. There was a body laying on some hard rocks or something, didn't feel good. Her body. She had a body. It was lying in a twisted heap with a bonging header and a sharp pain in its right shoulder. *She* was laying on the ground with a pain in her shoulder and another in her head. She was waking up, or maybe she had been awake for a while without really knowing it. Open the eyes.

Nada. Big black nothing. Panic. What the—

Memories came flooding back. The dark section of tunnel. A fight. The train. A hit on the head. Then nothing. Until now.

She was Maria. No, she was a zonie named . . . Reflexively, she reached for the reassurance of her Uzi. It wasn't there. Then she remembered the gun hitting the third rail, and it all came back to her, and she knew where she was and what had happened.

Her Uzi was done for. She had kicked that filthy puta-mother right into a train, and then the body must have bounced into her, bashing her head against something which must have knocked her out. She didn't have any way of knowing how long she had been out cold in hours and minutes, but that didn't matter the way time was measured down here. Because what counted, *all* that counted, was that it was after nine in the subway, all the lights were out, and her chop would be useless even if she stumbled on it in the dark.

The panic returned, an informed, logical panic this time, and all the worse for its clarity. She couldn't see anything. She didn't know which way was uptown or downtown and there was no way to figure it out. She caught herself freaking before she realized that that didn't matter now. Because she was in deep enough shit without worrying about any god-damn dog anymore. And whichever way she went, she'd come to a station.

She took a deep breath, gathering her wits. Find the tunnel wall. Once she did that, she'd have the whole width of a set of subway tracks between her and the third rail. To be on the safe side, better crawl.

So instead of rising, she began crawling blindly through the muck and filth of the tunnel floor. She hadn't gone more than a few yards before her outstretched fingers recoiled from something warm and soft and sticky. Reflexively withdrawing, she reflexively stifled a reflexive scream. Nothing moved. The moment of panic passed as she realized this must be the corpse of her attacker. Whom she had bounced off a fast-moving train, and who therefore must be very, very dead.

She relaxed. She almost felt good. She had won. She had killed this great big crazy mother. And he had been armed with a knife.

A knife.

Efficiently, professionally, she ran her fingers all over the corpse until she found it, realizing, but not really caring, that the sticky wet stuff she was getting all over herself was blood. Then she touched something hard and metallic. Gingerly, she ran her fingertips along it until she touched rags. A rag-wrapped handle. She had it. She snatched it up. She had a knife. It might not be an Uzi, but at least it was a weapon.

It felt so much better to be heeled. Maria felt an almost sensual calm passing from the handle of the knife, down her arm, into her body, and thence to her brain, which slowly assumed a predator's icy calm. Having a weapon again made it possible to think clearly.

For one thing, it was stupid to be crawling around in the muck worrying about touching the third rail; it was after nine, *all* the electricity was off. She scrambled to her feet as soundlessly as possible, for silence was still golden down here in the dangerous dark. She reached down and took off her shoes, the better to simulate a predator padding through the jungle of the night.

Cunningly, methodically, she began to pad in ever-widening spiraling circles, until, inevitably, the outstretched fingers of her left hand touched the tunnel wall. Choosing an arbitrary direction, she pressed her body up against the concrete.

Feeling along the wall with her left hand, holding the knife cocked for action in her right, breathing in short, silent little sips, placing one foot softly and carefully in front of the other, she began creeping up the tunnel.

Gonzo had lost his nerve, and he was just on the verge of admitting it to himself. Fact was, as long as he stayed here frozen to the tunnel wall in the soundless dark, he was safe. Nothing could see him, and as long as he didn't move, nothing could hear him either. Whereas the moment he moved, anything that was waiting in the dark, anything that even now could be inches from his face could—

—a soft, warm, sweaty palm brushed against his cheek—

—He started, jumped, screamed, felt something whistle past his throat, wet his pants, and—

"I've got a knife, twitch and you croak, bloke!" Maria hissed in the dark, listening for something to slash at.

Silence. Darkness. The sound of ragged breathing over to the right, or her imagination? A standoff. She had the knife, but both of them were blind. A waiting game. The first one to make a sound would reveal their position, and then . . .

* * *

Slowly, ever so slowly in the silent dark, Gonzo's street smarts began to overcome his fear. A voice. He had heard a *chick's* voice. Did she really have a knife? Or was all that a scam, man? Or was she as scared shitless as he was? Or *more* afraid? *He* knew that what he was facing was only a muchacha with or without a blade, whereas *she* didn't know *what* he was. . . .

A chick . . . Hadn't he been planning to do a trick with a chick?

He made his voice as deep and menacing as he could, stepping back and aside as he spoke so she couldn't slash at the sound. "Deal, muchacha! Got a sweet deal for you."

Silence. Darkness. Nada.

"Come on, girl, give it a whirl," Gonzo said irritably now.

More silence. Then, over to the left, and maybe moving, a hesitant, harsh female voice. "What's the word, turd?"

Ah, got her talking now. If I can only. . .

"Got a match, snatch?"

"What if I do?"

"Take a peek, freak."

"What's your scam, Sam?"

"*Meat's* the treat, skeet!" Gonzo said seductively. "I got it, you cook it. Take a look, I won't bite."

Meat? *Dogmeat?* Maria could hear her heart pounding in the dark. Could it be? Could this be the bonzo who pinched the dog? Standing right there in front of her knife offering his life?

She had to. She had it made, she had the blade, and if she saw it *was* the suck, he was fresh out of luck.

Trembling, she fished around in a pocket with her left hand and extracted a book of paper matches. Still clutching the knife handle, she used both hands to get it open, tore off a match. Holding the matchbook in her left hand, the knife and the match in her right, she struck it and—

—the sudden light dazzled her—

—something leaped and battered at her hands—

—the match guttered back into darkness—

—the knife was gone—

Now that he had copped the blade, Gonzo had it made. He could leave her in the dark and make a run . . . or he could

really have some fun. And the snatch probably had another
match. . . .

"Hey, you got more fire, muchacha?" he said.

Nada. She was playing it cool, she was nobody's fool.

"Meat's the treat, skeet, like I say. I got a whole *dog* in
my bag! Come on, what do you say, a big piece of my meat
for a little piece of yours."

Ice-cold, red-hot, Maria did a slow burn in the dark,
cursing her own stupidity, but still praising her luck at finding
the suck. The puta-mother she was after! Her ticket back to
the Zone! But the mother had her knife, and after he had her
bod, it would probably be her life.

After he had her bod, she realized with slow delibera-
tion. Yeah, she'd be safe until he'd pronged her gong. And
she'd handled the big geek who'd had the knife in the first
place, hadn't she? And this was a scrawny little crud, she had
her zonie moves, and when he started to groove . . .

I know who *he* is, but he doesn't know what *I* am, she
realized. Better play it dumb and hook the scum.

"Dog . . . ?" she said in a little-girl voice. "You gotta *dog*?
I lube your tube, I eat the meat?"

"We got a deal, girl?"

"But . . . but how do I know you won't just feed me the
blade?"

"Dead gash ain't no stash."

Maria put all the dumb little chocha stupidity she could
into her voice. "Okay man, I take a chance. . . ."

"Gotta hooch where we can cook the pooch?"

Mother, the dumb geek thought she was Subway Scum!
Her confidence began to grow, that might be another angle
she could use. "Forty-second Street," she said, realizing
suddenly that if she had run into him, she must have been
heading uptown. Forty-second on the IRT East meant Grand
Central, a whole underground town, clown, where I can find
someplace safe to grass your ass.

"No quick moves," said a voice coming towards her.
"Don't freak." Then she felt an arm snake around her back
and a sharp little prick between her shoulder blades. "No
smart stuff, muff," he said beside her ear. And then they
started walking uptown through the dark tunnel together, just
like lovey-doves.

*   *   *

It had been a long, long time since Gonzo had spent a night in the Subterranio, and he'd *never* made the scene with anything in his bag worth a tussle to Subway Scum muscle, so his nerves began to twitch when he saw the smoky red glow of fires up ahead. Still, he figured he had an edge, or so he told himself. Primero, he had the knife, and for another, he had this chick as backup, and this snatch had managed to come out on top in a one-on-one with that big and bad back there. This was *Subway Scum* gash, muchacho, she knew how the land lay, she knew what games to play.

But he'd better not pop that he was really almost as cherry down here as some dumb muni cop. "Look, we stick together, right?" he said as they approached the flickering, smoldering, dull red light outlining the mouth of the tunnel. "We back each other up?"

"That's the scam, Sam. For tonight, you're my man."

"Okay, then no tricks, chick," he said, removing the point of the knife from the pit of her back, and letting it dangle from his hand in plain dangerous sight. "Just remember, I've still got the blade."

As they emerged from the cover of the tunnel and into the Forty-second Street station, Gonzo could see that there were dozens of fires burning in the station above. In the smoky smelly light, he got his first real look at his lady of the night. Subway Scum for sure, mon! She was wearing something that might once have been yellow but was now a raggy bag smeared with blood, and crap, and ashy grey mung. Her tough-looking face was more of the same—scratched, and bruised, and caked with crud and old blood.

She was one mean-looking mama, and that gave him cojones. They were a bad-looking combo, Mr. & Mrs. Kick-Your-Ass, with a bag and a knife, screw with us, and it's worth your life!

Maria had seen the Grand Central subway station often enough by day—it was the biggest there was, one of the main hubs of the whole system, an underground town with news-stands and veggie stalls, rag stores and smoke stands, rat peddlers and knife shops, porn racks and meat racks. Dozens of stalls and stands and stores and peddlers, hundreds of thousands of potential customers passing through, and the city taking its cut from all the action, meaning that there was always a small army of munis conspicuously in evidence to keep things cool.

But now, as they crawled up off the tracks onto the platform, it was a different world. All the floating peddlers were long since gone and all the stands and stalls and stores were sealed with armor-plate shutters that looked about three feet thick. Not a cop to be found, natch, and of course not a single electric light or townie in a subway mask.

But there sure was light and sound and plenty of raw meat around!

There were two platforms in this part of the station dividing four sets of tracks, and there were dozens of little fires burning on them where little solitary groups of shadowy figures hunched, rocking back and forth like spastics, mumbling and gabbling, and roasting rats and other morsels of meat. The flickering intermittent firelight turned the whole station into an ominous, endless, fluttering, guttering, formless human bat-cave, an illusive, ever-changing maze of shadow and dull red light, smogged with a thin, rancid, eye-watering smoke that stank of rat and grease and melting plastic and sizzling crap. Shadows, shapes, and human bat-things shambled and shuffled in the foul firelight, filled the air with chittering and mumbling and evil babble. It was truly the asshole of the universe, the nethermost pit of the Pig Apple.

"Come on, girl, let's get to your hooch!" her fellow traveler whispered nervously. She could hear the fear in his voice, smell his sour frightened sweat even through the gagging fog. Right, she remembered, this toilet bowl is supposed to be *my* turf!

"Stick close to me, mon, keep that blade ready, and we'll handle these geeks," she said with a certain contemptuous arrogance, pretending to herself that she was a zonie with a chop and he was her plushie tushie out for a streetside slummer. "Maybe you oughta give me the knife. I'm a bitch with a blade."

He just gave her a narrow sneer. "Move your ass, gash!" he snarled fearfully, waving the knife with one hand and shouldering his bag with the other.

"You're the man, Sam," Maria shrugged, snaking a protective arm around his waist and leading him off she knew not where.

*   *   *

At first, the bitch seemed to move like she really knew her stuff, weaving a wide twisting path across the platform, moving from shadow to shadow, keeping them lost in the gloom, giving what huddled around the fires plenty of room.

But as they wandered deeper and deeper into the station, the fires got farther and farther apart, the walls melted away into shadow, and she seemed to be leading him on a random path from light to light, from scene to ghastly scene, like a tour guide through hell.

Over there in the corner, just two filthy paws, each holding a fat rat by the tail over a stinking fire. Avoiding this, they practically stumbled over two raggy shapes humping and grunting in the dark. Starting away from these creatures in random flight, they blundered into two bags of ghostly white flesh ripping apart rats with their long, filthy nails and stuffing gobbets of raw flesh into their slavering yawps.

Pale eyes glowed at them speculatively, grinning mouths dribbling bloody bits of rat. The things started to move towards them, and instinctively, they ran off towards a dim red glow.

Only to plaster themselves into the shadows in terror at the scene outlined by the fire: two scrawny, naked, skeletal creatures carving up the corpse of an old woman with enormous rusty knives.

"Where the hell *is* it?" Gonzo hissed as they slunk off deeper into the darkness. "We can't—"

He was interrupted by a liquid gagging sound practically on top of him, and a mess of puke spattered horribly onto his feet. He kicked out and heard something moan in the black and then they were running blindly through the darkness.

Another dim firelight glow up ahead. Something slithered towards them out of the darkness on all fours, which she drove back with a kick in the chops.

"Where the hell is your hooch, bitch?" Gonzo snarled. "We can't last much longer out here!"

"Near here, man, don't freak now!" Maria said, not knowing what in hell she was talking about, but feeling a certain superior contempt through her terror, for him, and for the human slime that infested the deepest bowels of the city.

They emerged from the darkness into an area of the station lined with shuttered stalls and lit with four or five fires. There was no avoiding the light here, nor the attention of the denizens. Solitary Subway Scum and groups of two or three huddled around the fires cooking rats or bits and pieces of what might have been human flesh. Eyes turned greedily towards the big bulging bag as they threaded their way through this flotsam, mouths grunted empty threats. But a lot of knife-waving and snarling was enough to drive them back. Even though they could have rushed the two of them in a mob and feasted on a whole dog. The plushie tushies who owned the world somehow knew how to organize other people to serve them. The zonies knew how to coordinate themselves into a force. The townies could at least get it together to work and survive. Even streeties could come together to form a mob.

But down here these turds couldn't even do that. They were animals who didn't even have enough left to come together to rush a streetie with swag in his bag. One against all, even with their filthy asses to the wall.

Still, sooner or later, their luck would run out. Or sooner or later, he would realize she didn't know squat. Where could she find someplace to serve as "her hooch?" Jeez, she'd been down here during the day thousands of times, and this area was starting to seem familiar. . . .

She was leading him away from the fires now, down the line of shuttered stalls towards what showed signs of turning into a cul-de-sac, petering out into flickering shadows cast by the diminishing firelight behind them—

"Meat! Eat!"

A tall, fat, naked thing covered with scabs and old scars suddenly appeared from nowhere right in their path! A matted black beard framing a slack mouth full of snaggle teeth, a dripping nose, two bloodshot eyes. Swinging a huge piece of two-by-four caked with accretions of old dried blood.

The slimy-chicken gonzo shrieked, fell backwards, and waved his knife impotently. The club-wielding creature just giggled and drooled, not impressed one bit. But, mesmerized by the knife, it hunched forward like a killer ape, shambled forward swinging the big bloody board, and went after him.

Ignoring Maria, who stepped to the side as it went by and kicked it squarely in the groin. The creature screamed in pain and outrage, crumpled over, then began to turn towards her—

"Kill it! Kill it! Kill it with the knife, you lousy son of a bitch!" she screamed, as she ducked a clumsy swipe of the

club and delivered another karate kick to the creature's
crotch. The thing sank to its knees this time, and she
smashed it across the back of the neck with the heel of her
hand, kneeing it in the teeth in the same move.

Then, finally, her "man" worked up enough cojones to
stab it in the back again and again and again.

"Thanks a lot, hero!" she said when the creature finally
stopped moving. Jeez, what a—

"Come on, come on, come on," the bonzo babbled,
snatching up the bag again. "Everything down here must've
heard it! They're coming after us, bitch! Run! Run!"

Maria didn't hear a damned thing, and she didn't believe
the scum down here was about to go chasing after the sounds
of bovver either, but he was pushing and shoving at her in
panic, and so they went trotting off deeper into the
semidarkness.

And quite suddenly she realized where she was and
where she was heading and what should be only a few yards
ahead.

This corridor connected with the shuttle line. And there
was a toilet up here somewhere. All these big stations had
crappers. But no one had dared to use them in her memory.
They were so foul that no muni would take the patrol. And
without a resident cop, no one was dumb enough to go in to
take a flop. With one door in and the same door out, the
crappers were traps.

Or places to hide.

"Here we are, man," she said. "Be ready with that knife
this time. I'm gonna light a match."

Gonzo sure didn't need her to tell him to be ready for
trouble. She had led him back here into the deep dark,
where all he could make out by the dim distant firelight was a
rusted L-shaped barrier uselessly guarding a closed door from
nonexistent eyes. If she were going to try any crap, it would
be now, when she could feature that his eyes might be
blinded for a moment by the sudden light of the match,
hadn't he taught her that one himself—

She struck the match.

The tiny point of light blinded him for only a moment as
he squinted his eyes in anticipation of the shock. She made
no dumb move. "Good suerte," she said instead, picking up a

piece of brown cardboard lying in a pile of crap and lighting it to make a little torch. "Ready. . . ?"

"You first," he said, waving the knife. "I'll be right behind you."

She snorted at him, and then, with a real sharp move, she kicked the door open and dashed inside, with Gonzo right behind.

In the dim light of the torch, he saw a big room flaking peeling green paint. Along one wall was a line of urinals, their bowls heaped with paper, cracked bones, and old dried turds. Opposite, a row of crapper stalls with the doors torn off and more piles of mung and bones filling the ancient toilet bowls. Huge mounds of paper, bones, cardboard, and amorphous gray crud were heaped everywhere on the floor where there wasn't a puddle of piss. The stink was incredible.

"Jeez, do you—"

Suddenly one of the mounds of garbage exploded in a shower of paper, bones, and crap. Up out of it came a screaming filthy, white-maned pallid something brandishing a heavy length of pipe.

They moved like parts of the same deadly machine. Gonzo dropped his bag, sidestepped under a wild flail of the pipe, while she managed to hold onto her torch while she caught the creature in the guts with a well-placed kick, and he leapt forward, plunging the knife deep into its chest as a bone-thrilling jolt went up his arm. As the torch started to gutter out and the thing went down, they both kicked and stomped, howling like animals together in the dark.

He gave the motionless body one final kick as a match flared into brilliance and snatched up the pipe while she was lighting a fire in one of the garbage-filled urinals.

They stood there in the smoky toilet, facing each other hot-eyed and panting over their kill. With a little snarl, she kicked the corpse over onto its back with a flip of her bare foot.

Revealing a filthy old chocha with long stringy white hair, and thick red blood pooling between her naked withered dugs.

"Come on, man," she hissed, grabbing the body by the heels and starting to drag it towards the door.

"What you doing, girl?"

"Drag it outside. Give anyone coming by good reason to think twice about coming in *here*."

Gonzo tucked the pipe under his knife arm, and together they dragged and kicked the stiff out of the toilet, blocking the opening of the metal barrier with a barricade of dead meat.

"Gimme the pipe!" she demanded when they were back behind the closed toilet door.

Gonzo just sneered at her.

"Hey, you still got the knife," she said, fingering the doorknob. "Slip the damn pipe in behind here, like a lock, man!"

"Comprend," Gonzo said, wedging the length of pipe behind the doorknob so that the door was barred.

When this was done, he saw her staring at him with hot hungry eyes that made his groin throb. Oh yeah, this muchacha could really move, this was gonna be a groove. . . .

"*Now* . . ." she breathed huskily. "I want it *now!*"

"Sure baby," Gonzo moaned back, moving towards her. "Why not right now. . . ?"

She moved backwards as he came for her. "The *dog*, man!" she said. "Show me the dog *now!*"

Hunkered down in the light of the smoky garbage fire in the filthy stinking toilet deep down under the ground, sweaty, bloody, wounded, scabbed, tired, hungry, and aching, Maria was aware of none of these things. Her total attention was hot-wired to a narrow razor-sharp focus on the street bag as the bonzo reached in and dragged the dog out by the tail.

"Forty pounds of meat," he said proudly, leering at her in the flickering firelit cave like a mighty warrior home from the hunt.

Forty pounds of meat.

That was exactly what she saw.

Dearie's head was caked with sticky drying blood. The black fur of its body was matted with more of the same. The mouth lay agape, the swollen tongue lolling between its jaws.

Forty pounds of dogmeat.

Mrs. Gloria Van Gelder's cocker spaniel was dead.

Very, very dead.

As dead as the old woman outside the door. As dead as the creature with the two-by-four. As dead as the thing that had attacked her in the tunnel. As dead as her job as a zonie. As dead as Mary Smith, townie.

For now, Mary Smith *was* dead, Maria's escape from the

streets years ago was only yesterday's fantastic dream. Her whole goddamn life as anything but Maria the streetie was dead and gone into nothing. Mary Smith was dead. She had died back there at the helicop the moment this puta-mother's fist had brained Dearie. Mary Smith was as dead as forty pounds of dogmeat.

As dead as this son of a bitch was going to be before the subway lights went on again.

Oh man, did she look groovy! No woman had ever looked at Gonzo like that before. Her eyes glowed with animal lust in the orange firelight. Her mouth opened slightly to display pearly glistening teeth. She hunched forward like a cat just waiting to lap him up like a saucer of cream.

Since no woman had ever looked at Gonzo like this before, Gonzo had never felt anything like this before. They had killed together, they had run together, they had survived together. What a bitchin' chocha she was! Ah, he thought with a sweet sighing ache, we're two of a kind, girl! He felt himself going all soft inside, as soft inside as he was getting hard outside. All at once, he was proud of the forty pounds of dogmeat that he had laid before her, it became a token of offering rather than payment for a piece. You can eat all you want, girl, he thought. Maybe I won't ice you afterward... maybe we can run together... maybe... maybe...

If he could have comprehended the concept, Gonzo might have thought that he was in love.

"Wanna do it?" he said softly. "Wanna do it right now?"

"Yeah man," she said, slowly pulling off her rags. "Yeah, for sure I wanna do it."

She crouched there naked before him in the firelight, running a wet pink tongue over feral white teeth. "For sure I wanna do it right now."

Still reflexively holding on to the knife, Gonzo leaned forward across the dead dog and moved into her waiting arms. Then he felt the electric tingle of her hard little nipples against his chest, and they were rolling in each other's arms, biting and kissing, grabbing and ripping, moaning and grunting on the toilet floor.

Oblivious to his stink, oblivious to the ordure that was their bed, oblivious to everything but the knife in his right hand, Maria let him roll her over onto her back and hump away like the grunting, drooling beast that he was.

For nothing that was happening to her mattered, there was nothing in her world but that jagged piece of rusty steel and his hand pumping and squeezing it as he bucked and whined like a dog. Like a dead dog, like forty pounds of—

—he mewled in ecstasy as his body went rigid, then groaned in release as she bit down hard into the lobe of his ear—

Every muscle in his body relaxed as he came. Including the muscles of the fingers holding the knife.

Gonzo's bones were on fire from the tip of his toes to the end of his nose as he floated upwards to the sky so sweet he could die soaring above himself like a bird that knew the Word and the Word was—

"Die! Die! Die!"

An incredible torch of flame seared into his ecstasy, pleasure and pain merging into a sensation so total that he couldn't even tell them apart until it lanced into his back again! And again! And again! And again!

Through a fading red mist he saw a demon face, a nightmare thing out of hell with bulging, rolling red eyes, and the slavering mouth of a beast, screaming, and snarling, and twisting orgasmically as pain and pleasure met on the razor-edge of his soul why why why—

Rage and orgasmic ecstasy merged into a red-hot convulsive stabbing fire and then Maria lay spent and panting with a dead weight atop her, her hand still clutching the knife, the knife still planted in flesh.

Snarling and spitting, she rolled the stiff off of her and then dragged and kicked it into the nearest crapper stall. Only then was her body wracked by the dry heaves, gagging and choking, but producing nothing but thin bitter bile.

After this had finally passed, she crouched naked on the filthy toilet floor for a long time, for an interminably long time, thinking nothing at all.

Then, gradually, very slowly, a sense of being, the ghost of a feeling, began to creep back into her body, and, after another long while, began to register in her whited-out brain.

This feeling, this dim sensation, was all that existed in her world. Weak, and vague, and formless at first, it sharpened and focused, and expanded to fill the vacuum of her being with itself. It became a deep, hollow, cramped pain emanating from the region of her belly.

It spread until her every cell was screaming an outraged demand. She felt depleted, spent, lost, and drained. She crouched there for another long period clutching the bloody knife, becoming and then being this awful throbbing void.

Then a further small measure of self-awareness returned. And she knew what this feeling was.

She was hungry.

She was very, very hungry. She was hunger. That's all that she was.

Numbly and hesitantly at first, she inserted the point of the knife into the belly of the dead dog and ripped it open. Then, methodically, she began to rip out its innards. By the time she had the carcass cut up into manageable chunks, she was working with lustful abandon, her hands and arms covered with congealing blood, grinning like a happy beast in her firelit cave.

Maria awoke slowly, deliciously, lazily, with a heavy langorous contentment in a belly fuller than she had ever remembered it being.

But this did not prevent her from forcing down half a dozen big bites of succulent, crispy, well-charred haunch before stuffing the rest of her treasure into her street bag. Then she put her knife in the bag and pulled on a blood-and-crap-smeared remnant of what had once been her tunic. Shouldering the bag, she fumbled the pipe out from behind the doorknob and clutched it reassuringly as she opened the door and was blinded by the light.

It was the morning rush. Grand Central was jammed with hordes of empty faceless creatures hidden behind ludicrous masks, rushing in every direction. The station buzzed with the noise of their coming and going, with the babble of the stand owners and the rat peddlers, the hawkers and the talkers, the gabblers and the screamers. Trains roared and clattered in and out of the station with a gut-rumbling vibration.

Dazed and blinking, Maria hesitantly moved through the rush hour crush towards the subway exit, perplexed but pleased at the way the crowds seemed to part to grant her easy passage. Even the muni cop guarding the street en-

trance seemed to fade back with a curl of his nose and a look
of fear to let her by.

Then she was standing on the street in the bright
morning sunlight. Towering buildings reached for the hazy
sky. Armored taxis blared and clattered, carrying townies who
thought they mattered. Townie clownies rushed to and fro.
Streeties sidled by, giving her swag bag the eye, but one
good glance seemed enough to make them crap in their
pants.

She blinked like a mole emerging from her hole. With a
little sigh, she wondered why there were tears in her eyes.
Must be something in the air that made her cry. She had a
knife for her life and plenty of meat in her poke. Wasn't
everything else just a dumb plushie tushie joke? Screw all
this lousy townie jive!

Considering the alternative, wasn't little Maria lucky to
be alive?

Introduction to
"The Lost Continent"

It's not often that you can pinpoint the exact moment when the inspiration for a story struck you, but I know precisely when I got the idea for this one.

I was standing atop the hill of the Acropolis, one more tourist amid hundreds crawling over the magnificent ruins of classical Greece. I turned away from the Parthenon and looked out from on high over contemporary Athens spread out beneath me.

Shimmering beneath an appalling layer of hot summer smog, the view reminded me of nothing so much as lowland Los Angeles as seen from the top of Lookout Mountain in the Hollywood Hills, a rude reminder that this was in fact the Twentieth Century, and that the city below, with its dirty, noisy, crowded, tawdry streets, its economic dependence on tourists from far richer lands, had far more in common with Tijuana and the Third World than it did with its own past incarnation as the metropolis of what had then been the highest civilization in the world.

Somewhat depressed by this unwanted perception, I

descended the Acropolis through the Plaka, a hillside district of taverns, modest restaurants, and souvenir stalls, and swilled down half a liter of retsina, a resinous Greek wine best drunk as fast as possible.

The Plaka teemed with tourists, petty commerce, music, raucous street life, and the scene looked much brighter as I wandered about it with a retsina buzz on, for these latter-day Greeks were clearly a happy, life-loving people, living in their present with brio, leaving somber thoughts of a lost Golden Age to tourists from afar like myself.

But then I strolled out of the Plaka toward our hotel, deep in the traffic noise and tacky third-rate modernity of lowland Athens, and turned to look back, and the vision that I saw created the germ of this story in my mind's eye.

Atop the Acropolis, the Parthenon barely rose out of the choking smog, a ghostly specter of vanished glory floating over the tawdry present, over tacky lowland modern Athens, over the Plaka, where descendants of the civilization that had long ago built such magnificence, a poor Third World people now, eked out a precarious living off the ruins left by noble ancestors whose greatness had long since vanished from their land.

THE LOST
CONTINENT

I FELT A PECULIAR MIXTURE of excitement and depression as my Pan African jet from Accra came down through the interlocking fringes of the East Coast and Central American smog banks above Milford International Airport, made a slightly bumpy landing on the east-west runway, and taxied through the thin blue haze toward a low, tarnished-looking aluminum dome that appeared to be the main international arrivals terminal.

Although American history *is* my field, there was something about actually being in the United States for the first time that filled me with sadness, awe, and perhaps a little dread. Ironically, I believe that what saddened me about being in America was the same thing that makes that country so popular with tourists, like the people who filled most of the seats around me. There is nothing that tourists like better than truly servile natives, and there are no natives quite so servile as those living off the ruins of a civilization built by ancestors they can never hope to surpass.

For my part—perhaps because I am a professor of history and can appreciate the parallels and ironies—I not only feel personally diminished at the thought of lording it over the remnants of a once-great people, but it also reminds me of our own civilization's inevitable mortality. Was not Africa a continent of so-called "underdeveloped nations" not two centuries ago when Americans were striding to the moon like gods?

Have we in Africa *really* preserved the technical and scientific heritage of Space Age America intact, as we like to pretend? We may claim that we have not repeated the American feat of going to the moon because it was part of the overdevelopment that destroyed Space Age civilization, but few reputable scientists would seriously contend that we could go to the moon if we so chose. Even the jet in which I had crossed the Atlantic was not quite up to the airliners the Americans had flown two centuries ago.

Of course, the modern Americans are still less capable than we of recreating twentieth-century American technolo-

49

gy. As our plane reached the terminal, an atmosphere-sealed extension ramp reached out creakily from the building for its airlock. Milford International was the port of entry for the entire northeastern United States; yet, the best it had was recently obsolescent African equipment. Milford itself, one of the largest modern American towns, would be lost next to even a city like Brazzaville. Yes, African science and technology are certainly now the most advanced on the planet, and someday perhaps we will build a civilization that can truly claim to be the highest the world has yet seen, but we only delude ourselves when we imagine that we have such a civilization now. As of the middle of the twenty-second century, Space Age America still stands as the pinnacle of man's fight to master his environment. Twentieth-century American man had a level of scientific knowledge and technological sophistication that we may not fully attain for another century. What a pity he had so little understanding of his relationship to his environment or of himself.

The ramp linked up with the plane's airlock, and after a minimal amount of confusion we debarked directly into a customs control office, which consisted of a drab, dun-colored, medium-sized room divided by a line of twelvebooths across its width. The customs officers in the booths were very polite, hardly glanced at our passports, and managed to process nearly a hundred passengers in less than ten minutes. The American government was apparently justly famous for doing all it could to smooth the way for African tourists.

Beyond the customs control office was a small auditorium in which we were speedily seated by courteous uniformed customs agents. A pale, sallow, well-built young lady in a trim blue customs uniform entered the room after us and walked rapidly through the center aisle and up onto the little low stage. She was wearing face-fitting atmosphere goggles, even though the terminal had a full seal.

She began to recite a little speech; I believe its actual wording is written into the American tourist-control laws.

"Good afternoon, ladies and gentlemen, and welcome to the United States of America. We hope you'll enjoy your stay in our country, and we'd like to take just a few moments of your time to give you some reminders that will help make your visit a safe and pleasurable one."

She put her hand to her nose and extracted two small, transparent cylinders filled with gray gossamer. "These are government-approved atmosphere filters," she said, displaying them for us. "You will be given complimentary sets as you leave this room. You are advised to buy only filters with the official United States Government Seal of Approval. Change your filters regularly each morning, and your stay here should in no way impair your health. However, it is understood that all visitors to the United States travel at their own risk. You are advised not to remove your filters, except inside buildings or conveyances displaying a green circle containing the words FULL ATMOSPHERE SEAL."

She took off her goggles, revealing a light red mask of welted skin that their seal had made around her eyes. "These are self-sealing atmosphere goggles," she said. "If you have not yet purchased a pair, you may do so in the main lobby. You are advised to secure goggles before leaving this terminal and to wear them whenever you venture out into the open atmosphere. Purchase only goggles bearing the Government Seal of Approval, and always take care that the seal is airtight.

"If you use your filters and goggles properly, your stay in the United States should be a safe and pleasant one. The government and people of the United States wish you a good day, and we welcome you to our country."

We were then handed our filters and guided to the baggage area, where our luggage was already unloaded and waiting for us. A sealed bus from the Milford International Inn was already waiting for those of us who had booked rooms there, and porters loaded the luggage on the bus while a representative from the hotel handed out complimentary atmosphere goggles. The Americans were most efficient and most courteous; there was something almost unpleasant about the way we moved so smoothly from the plane to seats on a bus headed through the almost empty streets of Milford toward the faded white plastic block that was the Milford International Inn, by far the largest building in a town that seemed to be mostly small houses, much like an African residential village. Perhaps what disturbed me was the knowledge that Americans are so good at this sort of thing strictly out of necessity. Thirty percent of the total American gross national product comes from the tourist industry.

I keep telling my wife I gotta get out of this tourist business. In the good old days, our ancestors would've given these African brothers nothing but about eight feet of rope.

They'd've shot off a nuclear missile and blasted all those black brothers to atoms! If the damned brothers didn't have so much loose money, I'd be for riding every one of them back to Africa on a rail, just like the Space-Agers did with their black brothers before the Panic.

And I bet we could do it, too. I hear there's all kinds of Space Age weapons sitting around in the ruins out West. If we could only get ourselves together and dig them out, we'd show those Africans whose ancestors went to the moon while they were still eating each other.

But, instead, I found myself waiting with my copter bright and early at the International Inn for the next load of customers of Little Old New York Tours, as usual. And I've got to admit that I'm doing pretty well off of it. Ten years ago, I just barely had the dollars to make a down payment on a used ten-seat helicopter, and now the thing is all paid off, and I'm shoveling dollars into my stash on every day-tour. If the copter holds up another ten years—and this is a genuine Space Age American Air Force helicopter restored and converted to energy cells in Aspen, not a cheap piece of African junk—I'll be able to take my bundle and split to South America, just like a tycoon out of the good old days. They say they've got places in South America where there's nothing but wild country as far as you can see. Imagine that! And you can buy this land. You can buy jungle filled with animals and birds. You can buy rivers full of fish. You can buy air that doesn't choke your lungs and give you cancer and taste like fried turds even through a brand-new set of filters.

Yeah, that's why I suck up to Africans! That's worth spending four or five hours a day in that New York hole, even worth looking at subway dwellers. Every full day-tour I take in there is maybe twenty thousand dollars net toward South America. You can buy ten acres of prime Amazon swampland for only fifty-six million dollars. I'll still be young ten years from now. I'll only be forty. I take good care of myself, I change my filters every day just like they tell you to, and I don't use nothing but Key West Supremes, no matter how much the damned things cost. I'll have at least ten good years left; why, I could even live to be fifty-five! And I'm gonna spend at least ten of those fifty-five years someplace where I can walk around without filters shoved up my nose, where I don't need goggles to keep my eyes from rotting, where I can finally die from something better than lung cancer.

I picture South America every time I feel the urge to tell off those brothers and get out of this business. For ten years with Karen in that Amazon swampland, I can take their superior-civilization crap and eat it and smile back at 'em afterward.

With filters wadded up my nose and goggle seals bruising the tender skin under my eyes, I found myself walking through the blue haze of the open American atmosphere, away from the second-class twenty-second-century comforts of the International Inn, and toward the large and apparently ancient tour helicopter. As I walked along with the other tourists, I wondered just what it was that had drawn me here.

Of course, Space Age America is my specialty, and I had reached the point where my academic career virtually required a visit to America, but, aside from that, I felt a personal motivation that I could not quite grasp. No doubt, I know more about Space Age America than all but a handful of modern Americans, but the reality of Space Age civilization seems illusive to me. I am an enlightened modern African, five generations removed from the bush; yet I have seen films—the obscure ghost town of Las Vegas sitting in the middle of a terrible desert clogged with vast, mechanized temples to the God of Chance; Mount Rushmore, where the Americans carved an entire landscape into the likenesses of their national heroes; the Cape Canaveral National Shrine, where rockets of incredible size are preserved almost intact— which have made me feel like an ignorant primitive trying to understand the minds of gods. One cannot contemplate the Space Age without concluding that the Space-Agers possessed a kind of sophistication that we modern men have lost. Yet they destroyed themselves.

Yes, perhaps the resolution of this paradox was what I hoped to find here, aside from academic merit. Certainly, true understanding of the Space Age mind cannot be gained from study of artifacts and records—if it could, I would have it. A true scholar, it has always seemed to me, must seek to understand, not merely to accumulate, knowledge. No doubt, it was understanding that I sought here. . . .

Up close, the Little Old New York Tours helicopter was truly impressive—an antique ten-seater built during the Space Age for the military by the look of it, and lovingly restored. But the American atmosphere had still been breathable even in the cities when it was built, so I was certain that this copter had only a filter system of questionable quality, no doubt installed by the contemporary natives in modern times. I did not want anything as flimsy as all that between my eyes and lungs and the American atmosphere, so I ignored the FULL ATMOSPHERE SEAL sign and kept my filters in and my goggles on as I boarded. I noticed that the other tourists were doing the same.

Mike Ryan, the native guide and pilot, had been recommended to me by a colleague from the University of Nairobi. A professor's funds are quite limited, of course—especially one who has not attained significant academic stature as yet—and the air fares ate into my already meager budget to the point where all I could afford was three days in Milford, four in Aspen, three in Needles, five in Eureka, and a final three at Cape Canaveral on the way home. Aside from the Cape Canaveral National Shrine, none of these modern American towns actually contained Space Age ruins of significance. Since it is virtually impossible, and, at any rate, prohibitively dangerous, to visit major Space Age ruins without a helicopter and a native guide, and since a private copter and guide would be far beyond my means, my only alternative was to take a day-tour like everyone else.

My Kenyan friend had told me that Ryan was the best guide to Old New York that he had had in his three visits. Unlike most of the other guides, he actually took his tours into a subway station to see live subway dwellers. There are reportedly only a thousand or two subway dwellers left; they are nearing extinction. It seemed like an opportunity I should not miss. At any rate, Ryan's charge was only about five hundred dollars above the average guide's.

Ryan stood outside the helicopter in goggles, helping us aboard. His appearance gave me something of a surprise. My Kenyan informant had told me that Ryan had been in the tour business for ten years; most guides who had been around that long were in terrible shape. No filters could entirely protect a man from that kind of prolonged exposure to saturation smog; by the time they're thirty, most guides already have chronic emphysema, and their lung cancer rate at age thirty-five is over 50 percent. But Ryan, who could not be under thirty, had the general appearance of a forty-year-old Boer; physiologically, he should have looked a good deal older. Instead, he was short, squat, had only slightly graying black hair, and looked quite alert, even powerful. But, of course, he had the typical American grayish white pimply pallor.

There were eight other people taking the tour, a full copter. A prosperous-looking Kenyan who quickly introduced himself as Roger Koyinka, traveling with his wife; a rather strange-looking Ghanaian in very rich-looking old-fashioned robes and his similarly clad wife and young son; two rather willowly and modishly dressed young men who appeared to be Luthuliville dandies, and the only other person in the tour who was traveling alone, an intense young man whose great bush of hair, stylized dashiki, and gold earring proclaimed that he was an Amero-African.

I drew a seat next to the Amero-African, who identified himself as Michael Lumumba rather diffidently when I introduced myself. Ryan gave us a few moments to get acquainted—I learned that the Ghanaian was named Kulongo, that Koyinka was a department store executive from Nairobi, that the two young men were named Ojubu and Ruala—while he checked out the helicopter, and then seated himself in the pilot's seat, back toward us, goggles still in place, and addressed us, without looking back, through an internal public address system.

"Hello, ladies and gentlemen, and welcome to your Little Old New York Tour. I'm Mike Ryan, your guide to the wonders of Old New York, Space Age America's greatest city. Today you're going to see such sights as the Fuller Dome, the Empire State Building, Rockefeller Center, and, as a grand finale, a subway station still inhabited by the direct descendants of the Space Age inhabitants of the city. So don't just think of this as a guided tour, ladies and gentlemen. You are about to take part in the experience of a lifetime—an exploration of the ruins of the greatest city built by the greatest civilization ever to stand on the face of the earth."

"Stupid arrogant honkie!" the young man beside me snarled aloud. There was a terrible moment of shocked, shamed embarrassment in the cabin, as all of us squirmed in our seats. Of course, the Amero-Africans are famous for this sort of tastelessness, but to be actually confronted with this sort of blatant racism made one for a moment ashamed to be black.

Ryan swiveled very slowly in his seat. His face displayed the characteristic red flush of the angered Caucasian, but his voice was strangely cold, almost polite: "You're in the *United States* now, *Mr*. Lumumba, not in Africa. I'd watch what I said if I were you. If you don't like me or my country, you can have your lousy money back. There's a plane leaving for Conakry in the morning."

"You're not getting off that easy, honkie," Lumumba said. "I paid my money, and you're not getting me off this helicopter. You try, and I go straight to the tourist board, and there goes your license."

Ryan stared at Lumumba for a moment. Then the flush began to fade from his face, and he turned his back on us again, muttering, "Suit yourself, pal. I promise you an interesting ride."

A muscle twitched in Lumumba's temple; he seemed about to speak again. "Look here, Mr. Lumumba," I whispered to him sharply, "we're guests in this country, and you're making us look like boorish louts in front of the natives. If you have no respect for your own dignity, have some respect for ours."

"You stick to your pleasures, and I'll stick to mine," he told me, speaking more calmly, but obviously savoring his own bitterness. "I'm here for the pleasure of seeing the descendants of the stinking honkies who kicked my ancestors out grovel in the putrid mess they made for themselves. And I intend to get my money's worth."

I started to reply, but then restrained myself. I would have to remain on civil terms with this horrid young man for hours. I don't think I'll ever understand these Amero-Africans and their pointless blood-feud. I doubt if I want to.

I started the engines, lifted her off the pad, and headed east into the smog bank trying hard not to think of that black brother Lumumba. No wonder so many of his ancestors were lynched by the Space-Agers! Sometime during the next few hours, that crud was going to get his. . . .

Through my cabin monitor (this Air Force Iron was just loaded with real Space Age stuff) I watched the stupid looks on their flat faces as we headed for what looked like a solid wall of smoke at about one hundred miles per hour. From the fringes, a major smog bank looks like that—solid as a steel slab—but once you're inside, there's nothing but a blue haze that anyone with a halfway decent set of goggles can see right through.

"We are now entering the East Coast smog bank, ladies and gentlemen," I told them. "This smog bank extends roughly from Bangor, Maine, in the north to Jacksonville, Florida, in the south, and from the Atlantic coastline in the east to the slopes of the Alleghenies in the west. It is the third largest smog bank in the United States."

Getting used to the way things look inside the smog always holds 'em for a while. Inside a smog bank, the color of everything is kind of washed-out, grayed, and blued. The air is something you can see, a mist that doesn't move; it almost sparkles at you. For some reason, these Africans always seem to be knocked out by it. Imagine thinking stuff like that is beautiful, crap that would kill you horribly and slowly in a couple of days if you were stupid or unlucky enough to breathe it without filters.

Yeah, they sure were a bunch of brothers! Some executive from Nairobi who acted like just being in the same copter with an American might give him and his wife lung cancer. Two rich young fruits from Luthuliville who seemed to be traveling together so they could congratulate themselves on how smart they both were for picking such rich parents. Some professor named Balewa who had never been to the States before, but probably was sure he knew what it was all about. A backwoods jungle-bunny named Kulongo who had struck it rich off uranium or something, taking his wife and kid on the grand tour. And, of course, that creep, Lumumba. The usual load of African tourists. Man, in the good old days, these niggers wouldn't have been good enough to shine our shoes!

Now we were flying over the old state of New Jersey. The Space-Agers did things in New Jersey that not even the African professors have figured out. It was weird country we were crossing: endless patterns of box-houses, all of them the same, all bleached blue-gray by two centuries of smog; big old freeways jammed with the wreckage of cars from the Panic of the Century; a few twisted gray trees and a patch of dry grass here and there that somehow managed to survive in the smog.

And this was western Jersey; this was nothing. Further east, it was like an alien planet or something. The view from the Jersey Turnpike was a sure tourist-pleaser. It really told them just where they were. It let them know that the

Space-Agers could do things they couldn't hope to do. Or want to.

Yeah, the Jersey lowlands are spectacular, all right, but why in hell did our ancestors want to do a thing like that? It really makes you think. You look at the Jersey lowlands and you know that the Space-Agers could do about anything they wanted to. . . .

But why in hell did they want to do some of the things they did?

There was something about actually standing in the open American atmosphere that seemed to act directly on the consciousness, like kif. Perhaps it was the visual effect. Ryan had landed the helicopter on a shattered arch of six-lane freeway that soared like the frozen contrail of an ascending jet over a surreal metallic jungle of amorphous Space Age rubble on a giant's scale—all crumbling, rusted storage tanks, ruined factories, fantastic mazes of decayed valving and piping—filling the world from horizon to horizon. As we stepped out onto the cracked and pitted concrete, the spectrum of reality changed, as if we were suddenly on the surface of a planet circling a bluer and grayer sun. The entire grotesque panorama appeared as if through a blue-gray filter. But we were inside the filter; the filter was the open American smog and it shone in drab sparkles all around us. Strangest of all, the air seemed to remain completely transparent while possessing tangible, visible substance. Yes, the visual effects of the American atmosphere alone are enough to affect you like some hallucinogenic drug: distorting your consciousness by warping your visual perception of your environment.

Of course, the exact biochemical effects of breathing saturation smog through filters are still unknown. We know that the American atmosphere is loaded with hydrocarbons and nitrous oxides that would kill a man in a matter of days if he breathed them directly. We know that the atmosphere filters developed toward the end of the Space-Age enable people to breathe the American atmosphere for up to three months without permanent damage to their health and enable the modern Americans—who have to breathe variations of this filtered poison every moment of their lives—to often live to be fifty. We know how to duplicate the Space Age atmosphere filters, and we more or less know how their complex catalytic fibers work, but the reactions that the filters must put the American atmosphere through to make it breathable are so complex that the only thing we can say for sure of what comes out the other side is that it usually takes about four decades to kill you.

Perhaps that strange feeling that came over me was a combination of both effects. But, for whatever reasons, I saw that weird landscape as if in a dream or a state of intoxication: everything faded and misty and somehow unreal, vaguely supernatural.

Beside me, staring silently and with a strange dignity at the totally artificial vista of monstrous, rusted ruins, stood the Ghanaian, Kulongo. When he finally spoke, his wife and son seemed to hang on his words, as if he were one of the old chiefs dispensing tribal wisdom.

"I have never seen such a place as this," Kulongo said. "In this place, there once lived a race of demons or witch doctors or gods. There are those who would call me an ignorant savage for saying this thing, but only a fool doubts what he sees with his eyes or his heart. The men who made these things were not human beings like us. Their souls were not as our souls."

Although he was putting it in naive and primitive terms, there was the weight of essential truth in Kulongo's words. The broken arch of freeway on which we stood reared like the head of a snake whose body was a six-lane road clogged with the rusted corpses of what had been a regionwide traffic jam during the Panic of the Century. The freeway led south, off into the fuzzy horizon of the smog bank, through a ruined landscape in which nothing could be seen that was not the decayed work of man; that was not metal or concrete or asphalt or plastic or Space Age synthetic. It was like being perched above some vast, ruined machine the size of a city, a city never meant for man. The scale of the machinery and the way it encompassed the visual universe made it very clear to me that the reality of America was something that no one could put into a book or a film.

I was in America with a vengeance. I was overwhelmed by the totality with which the Space-Agers had transformed their environment, and by the essential incomprehensibility—despite our sophisticated sociological and psychohistorical explanations—of why they had done such a thing and of how they themselves had seen it. "Their souls were not as our souls" was as good a way to put it as any.

"Well, it's certainly spectacular enough," Ruala said to his friend, the rapt look on his face making a mockery of his sarcastic tone.

"So it is," Ojubu said softly. Then, more harshly: "It's probably the largest junk heap in the world."

The two of them made a halfhearted attempt at laughter, which withered almost immediately under the contemptuous look that the Kulongos gave them; the timeless look that the people of the bush have given the people of the towns for centuries, the look that said only cowardly fools attempt to hide their fears behind a false curtain of contempt, that only those who truly fear magic need openly mock it.

And again, in their naive way, the Kulongos were right. Ojubu and Ruala were just a shade too shrill, and, even while they played at diffidence, their eyes remained fixed on that totally surreal metal landscape. One would have to be a lot worse than a mere fool not to feel the essential strangeness of that place.

Even Lumumba, standing a few yards from the rest of us, could not tear his eyes away.

Just behind us, Ryan stood leaning against the helicopter. There was a strange power, perhaps a sarcasm as well, in his words as he delivered what surely must have been his routine guide's speech about this place.

"Ladies and gentlemen, we are now standing on the New Jersey Turnpike, one of the great highways that linked some of the mighty cities of Space Age America. Below you are the Jersey lowlands, which served as a great manufacturing, storage, power-producing, and petroleum-refining and distribution center for the greatest and largest of the Space Age cities, Old New York. As you look across these incredible ruins—larger than most modern African cities—think of this: All of this was nothing to the Space Age Americans but a minor industrial area to be driven through at a hundred miles an hour without even noticing. You're not looking at one of the famous wonders of Old New York, but merely at an unimportant fringe of the greatest city ever built by man. Ladies and gentlemen, you're looking at a very minor work of Space Age man!"

"Crazy damned honkies. . . ." Lumumba muttered. But there was little vehemence or real meaning in his voice, and, like the rest of us, he could not tear his eyes away. It was not hard to understand what was going through his mind. Here was a man raised in the Amero-African enclaves on an irrational mixture of hate for the fallen Space-Agers, contempt for their vanished culture, fear of their former power, and perhaps a kind of twisted blend of envy and identification that only an Amero-African could fully understand. He had come to revel in the sight of the ruins of the civilization that had banished his ancestors, and now he was confronted with the inescapable reality that the "honkies" whose memory he both hated and feared had indeed possessed power and knowledge not only beyond his comprehension, but applied to ends which his mind was not equipped to understand.

It must have been a humbling moment for Michael Lumumba. He had come to sneer and had been forced instead to gape.

I tore my gaze away from that awesome vista to look at Ryan; there was a grim smile on his pale, unhealthy face as he drank in our reactions. Clearly, he had meant this sight to humble us, and, just as clearly, it had.

Ryan stared back at me through his goggles as he noticed me watching him. I couldn't read the expression in his watery eyes through the distortion of the goggle lenses. All I understood was that somehow some subtle change had occurred in the pattern of the group's interrelationships. No longer was Ryan merely a native guide, a functionary, a man without dignity. He had proved that he could show us sights beyond the limits of the modern world. He had reminded us of just where we were, and who and what his ancestors had been. He had suddenly gained secondhand stature from the incredible ruins around him, because, in a very real way, they were *his* ruins. Certainly they were not ours.

"I've got to admit they were great engineers," Koyinka, the Kenyan executive, said.

"So were the ancient Egyptians," Lumumba said, recovering some of his bitterness. "And what did it get *them*? A fancy collection of old junk over their graves—exactly what it got these honkies."

"If you keep it up, pal," Ryan said coldly, "you may get a chance to see something that'll impress you a bit more than these ruins."

"Is that a threat or a promise, Ryan?"

"Depends on whether you're a man...or a *boy*, Mr. Lumumba."

Lumumba had nothing to say to that, whatever it all had

meant. Ryan appeared to have won a round in some contest between them.

And when we followed Ryan back into the helicopter, I think we were all aware that for the next few hours, this pale, unhealthy American would be something more than a mere convenient functionary. We were the tourists; he was the guide.

But as we looked over our shoulders at the vast and overwhelming heritage that had been created and then squandered by his ancestors, the relationship that those words described took on a new meaning. The ancestral ruins off which he lived were a greater thing in some absolute sense than the totality of our entire living civilization. He had convinced us of that, and he knew it.

That view across the Jersey lowlands always seems to shut them up for a while. Even that crud, Lumumba. God knows why. Sure it's spectacular, bigger than anything these Africans could ever have seen where they come from, but when you come right down to it, you gotta admit that Ojubu was right—the Jersey lowlands are nothing but a giant pile of junk. Crap. Space Age garbage. Sometimes looking at a place like that can piss me off. I mean, we had *some* ancestors. They built the greatest civilization the world ever saw, but what did they leave for us? The most spectacular junk piles in the world, air that does you in sooner or later even through filters, and a continent where seeing something alive that people didn't put there is a big deal. Our ancestors went to the moon, they were a great people, the greatest in history, but sometimes I get the feeling they were maybe just a little out of their minds. Like that crazy "Merge with the Cosmic All" thing I found that time in Grand Central—still working after two centuries or so; it must do *something* besides kill people, but *what*? I dunno, maybe our ancestors went a little over the edge, sometimes. . . .

Not that I'd ever admit a thing like that to any black brothers! The Space-Agers may have been a little bit nuts, but who are these Africans to say so, who are they to decide whether a civilization that had them beat up and down the line was sane or not? Sane according to whom? Them, or the Space-Agers? For that matter, who am I to think a thing like that? An ant or a rat living off their garbage. Who are nobodies like us and the Africans to judge people who could go to the moon?

Like I keep telling Karen, this damned tourist business is getting to me. I'm around these Africans too much. Sometimes, if I don't watch myself, I catch myself thinking like them. Maybe it's the lousy smog this far into the smog bank—but hell, that's another crazy African idea!

That's what being around these Africans does to me, and looking at subway dwellers five times a week sure doesn't help, either. Let's face it, stuff like the subways and the lowlands is really depressing. It tells a man he's a nothing. Worse, it tells him that people who were better than he is still managed to screw things up. It's just not good for your mind.

But as the copter crested the lip of the Palisades ridge and we looked out across that wide Hudson River at Manhattan, I was reminded again that this crummy job had its compensations. If you haven't seen Manhattan from a copter crossing the Hudson from the Jersey side, you haven't seen nothing, pal. That Fuller Dome socks you right in the eye. It's ten miles in diameter. It has facets that make it glitter like a giant blue diamond floating over the middle of the island. Yeah, that's right, it floats. It's made of some Space Age plastic that's been turned blue and hazy by a couple of centuries of smog, it's ten miles wide at the base, and the goddamned thing floats over the middle of Manhattan a few hundred feet off the ground at its rim like a cloud or a hover or something. No motors, no nothing. It's just a hemisphere made of plastic panels and alloy tubing and it floats over the middle of Manhattan like half a giant diamond all by itself. Now, *that's* what I call a real piece of Space Age hardware!

I could hear them suck in their breath behind me. Yeah, it really does it to you. I almost forgot to give them the spiel. I mean, who wants to? What can you really say to someone while he's looking at the Fuller Dome for the first time?

"Ladies and gentlemen, you are now looking at the world-famous Fuller Dome, the largest architectural structure ever built by the human race. It is ten miles in diameter. It encloses the center of Manhattan Island, the heart of Old New York. It has no motors, no power source, and no moving parts. But it floats in the air like a cloud. It is considered the First Wonder of the World."

What else is there to say?

*   *   *

We came in low across the river toward that incredible
floating blue diamond, the Fuller Dome, parallel to the ruins
of a great suspension bridge that had collapsed and now hung
in fantastic rusted tatters half in and half out of the water.
Aside from Ryan's short guidebook speech, no one said a
word as we crossed the water to Manhattan.

Like the moon landing, the Fuller Dome was one of the
peak achievements of the Space Age, a feat beyond the power
of modern African civilization. As I understood it, the Dome
held itself aloft by convection currents created by its own
greenhouse effect, though this has always seemed to me the
logical equivalent of a man lifting himself by his own shoulders. No one quite knows exactly how a dome this size was
built, but the records show that it required a fleet of two
hundred helicopters. It took six weeks to complete. It was
named after Buckminster Fuller, one of the architectural
geniuses of the early Space Age, but it was not built till after
his death, though it is considered his monument. But it was
more than that; it was staggeringly, overwhelmingly beautiful.

We crossed the river and headed toward the rim of the
Fuller Dome at about two hundred feet, over a shoreline of
crumbling docks and the half-sunken hulks of rusted-out
ships; then over a wide strip of elevated highway filled with
the usual wrecked cars; and finally we slipped under the rim
of the Dome itself, an incredibly thin metal hoop floating in
the air from which the Dome seemed to blossom like a soap
bubble from a child's bubble pipe.

And we were flying inside the Fuller Dome. It was an
incredible sensation—the world inside the Dome existed in
blue crystal. Our helicopter seemed like a buzzing fly that
had intruded into an enormous room. The room was a mile
high and ten miles wide. The facets of the Fuller Dome had
been designed to admit natural sunlight and thus preserve
the sense of being outdoors, but they had been weathered to
a bluish hue by the saturation smog. As a result, the interior
of the Dome was a room on a superhuman scale, a room filled
with a pale blue light—and a room containing a major portion
of a giant city.

Towering before us were the famous skyscrapers of Old
New York, a forest of rectangular monoliths hundreds of feet
high, in some cases well over a thousand feet tall. Some of
them stood almost intact, empty concrete boxes transformed

into giant, somber tombstones by the eerie blue light that
permeated everything. Others had been ripped apart by
explosions and were jagged piles of girders and concrete.
Some had had walls almost entirely of glass; most of these
were now airy mazes of framework and concrete platforms,
where the blue light here and there flashed off intact patches
of glass. And far above the tops of the tallest buildings was
the blue stained-glass faceted sky of the Fuller Dome.

Ryan took the helicopter up to the five-hundred-foot
level and headed for the giant necropolis, a city of monu-
ments built on a scale that would have caused the pharaohs to
whimper, packed casually together like family houses in an
African residential village. And all of it was bathed in a
sparkly blue-gray light that seemed to enclose a universe—
here in the very core of the East Coast smog bank, where
everything seemed to twinkle and shimmer.

We all gasped as Ryan headed at one hundred miles per
hour for a thin canyon that was the gap between two rows of
buildings facing each other across a not-very-wide street
hundreds of feet below.

For a moment, we seemed to be a stone dropping
toward a narrow shaft between two immense cliffs—then,
suddenly, the copter's engines screamed, and the copter seemed
to somehow skid and slide through the air to a dead hover no
more than a hundred feet from the sheer face of a huge gray
skyscraper.

Ryan's laugh sounded unreal, partially drowned out by
the descending whine of the copter's relaxing engines. "Don't
worry, folks," he said over the public address system, "I'm in
control of this aircraft at all times. I just thought I'd give you
a little thrill. Kind of wake up those of you who might be
sleeping, because you wouldn't want to miss what comes
next: a helicopter tour of what the Space-Agers called 'The
Sidewalks of New York.'"

And we inched forward at the pace of a running man; we
seemed to drift into a canyon between two parallel lines of
huge buildings that went on for miles.

Man, no matter how many times I come here, I still feel
weird inside the Fuller Dome. It's another world in there.
New York seems like it's built for people fifty feet tall; it
makes you feel so small, like you're inside a giant's room. But
when you look up at the inside of the Dome, the buildings

that seemed so big seem so small; you can't get a grasp on the scale of anything. And everything is all blue. And the smog is so heavy you think you could eat it with a fork.

And you know that the whole thing is completely dead. Nothing lives in New York between the Fuller Dome and the subways, where several thousand subway dwellers stew in their own muck. Nothing can. The air inside the Fuller Dome is some of the worst in the country, almost as bad as that stuff they say you can barely see through that fills the Los Angeles basin. The Space-Agers didn't put up the Dome to atmosphere-seal a piece of the city; they did it to make the city warmer and keep the snow off the ground. The smog was still breathable then. So the inside of the Dome is open to the naked atmosphere, and it actually seems to suck in the worst of the smog, maybe because it's about twenty degrees hotter inside the Dome than it is outside; something about convection currents, the Africans say, but I dunno.

It's creepy, that's what it is. Flying slowly between two lines of skyscrapers, I had the feeling I was tiptoeing very carefully around some giant graveyard in the middle of the night. Not any of that crap about ghosts that I'll bet some of these Africans still believe deep down; this whole city really *was* a graveyard. During the Space Age, millions of people lived in New York; now there was nothing alive here but a couple thousand stinking subway dwellers slowly strangling themselves in their stinking sealed subways.

So I kind of drifted the copter in among the skyscrapers for a while, at about a hundred feet, real slow, almost on hover, and just let the customers suck in the feel of the place, keeping my mouth shut.

After a while, we came to a really wide street, jammed to overflowing with wrecked and rusted cars that even filled the sidewalks, as if the Space-Agers had built one of their crazy car-pyramids right here in the middle of Manhattan, and it had just sort of run like hot wax. I hovered the copter over it for a while.

"Folks," I told the customers, "below you, you see some of the wreckage from the Panic of the Century which fills the sidewalks of New York. The Panic of the Century started right here in New York. Imagine, ladies and gentlemen, at the height of the Space Age, there were more than one hundred million cars, trucks, buses, and other motor vehicles operating on the freeways and streets of the United States. A car for every two adults! Look below you and try to imagine the magnificence of the sight of all of them on the road all at once!"

Yeah, that would've been something to see, all right! From a helicopter, that is. Man, those Space-Agers sure had guts, driving around down there jammed together on the freeways at copter speeds with only a few feet between them. They must've had fantastic reflexes to be able to handle it. Not for me, pal, I couldn't do it, and I wouldn't want to.

But, God, what this place must've been like, all lit up at night in bright colored lights, millions of people tearing around in their cars all at once! Hell, what's the population of the United States today, thirty, forty million, not a city with five hundred thousand people, and nothing in all the world on the scale of this. Damn it, those were the days for a man to have lived!

Now look at it! The power all gone except for whatever keeps the subway electricity going, so the only light above ground is that blue stuff that makes everything seem so still and quiet and weird, like the city's embalmed or something. The buildings are all empty crumbling wrecks, burned out, smashed up by explosions, and the cars are all rusted garbage, and the people are dead, dead, dead.

It's enough to make you cry—if you let it get to you.

We drifted among the ruins of Old New York like some secretive night insect. By now it was afternoon, and the canyons formed by the skyscrapers were filled with deep purple shadows and intermittent avenues of pale blue light. The world under the Fuller Dome was composed of relative darknesses of blue, much as the world under the canopy of a heavy rain forest is a world of varying greens.

We dipped low and drifted for a few moments over a large square where the top of a low building had been removed by an explosion to reveal a series of huge cuts and canyons extending deep into the bowels of the earth, perhaps some kind of underground train terminal, perhaps even a ruined part of the famous New York subways.

"This is a burial ground of magics," Kulongo said. "The air is very heavy here."

"They sure knew how to build," Koyinka said.

Beside me, Michael Lumumba seemed subdued, perhaps even nervous. "You know, I never knew it was all so big," he muttered to me. "So big, and so strange, and so . . . so . . ."

"*Space Age*, Mr. Lumumba?" Ryan suggested over the intercom.

Lumumba's jaw twitched. He was obviously furious at having Ryan supply the precise words he was looking for. "Inhuman, honkie, inhuman was what I was going to say," he lied transparently. "Wasn't there an ancient saying, 'New York is a nice place to visit, but I wouldn't want to live there?'"

"Never heard that one, pal," Ryan said. "But I can see how your ancestors might've felt that way. New York was always too much for anyone but a *real* Space-Ager."

There was considerable truth in what they both said, though of course neither was interested in true insight. Here in the blue crystal world under the Fuller Dome, in a helicopter buzzing about noisily in the graveyard silence, reduced by the scale of the buildings to the relative size of an insect, I felt the immensity of what had been Space Age America all around me. I felt as if I were trespassing in the mansions of my betters. I felt like a bug, an insect. I remembered from history, not from instinct, how totally America had dominated the world during the Space Age—not by armed conquest, but by the sheer overwhelming weight of its very existence. I had never before been quite able to grasp that concept.

I understood it perfectly now.

I gave them the standard helicopter tour of the sidewalks of New York. We floated up Broadway, the street that had been called The Great White Way, at about fifty feet, past crazy, rotten networks of light steel girders, crumbled signs, and wiring on a monstrous scale. At a thousand feet, we circled the Empire State Building, one of the oldest of the great skyscrapers, and now one of the best preserved, a thousand-foot slab of solid concrete, probably just the kind of tombstone the Space-Agers would've put up for themselves if they had thought about it.

Yeah, I gave them all the usual stuff. The ruins of Rockefeller Center. The U.N. Plaza Crater.

Of course, they were all sucking it up, even Lumumba, though of course the slime wouldn't admit it. After this, they'd be ripe for a nasty peek at the subway dwellers, and after they got through gaping at the animals, they'd be ready for dinner back in Milford, feeling they had got their money's worth.

Yeah, I can get the same money for a five-hour tour that most guides get for six, because I've got the stomach to take them into a subway station. As usual, it had just the right effect when I told them we were going to end the tour with a visit on foot to an inhabited subway station. Instead of bitching and moaning that the tour was too short, that they weren't getting their money's worth, they were all eager—and maybe a little scared—at actually walking among the *really* primitive natives. Once they'd had their fill of the subway dwellers, a ride home across the Hudson into the sunset would be enough to convince them they'd had a great day.

So we *were* going to see the subway dwellers! Most of the native guides avoided the subways, and the American government for some reason seemed to discourage research by foreigners. A subtle discouragement, perhaps, but discouragement nevertheless. In a paper he published a few years ago, Omgazi had theorized that the modern Americans in the vicinity of New York had a loathing of the subway dwellers that amounted to virtually a superstitious dread. According to him, the subway dwellers, because they were direct descendants of die-hard Space-Agers who had atmosphere-sealed the subways and set up a closed ecology inside rather than abandon New York, were identified with their ancestors in the minds of the modern Americans. Hence, the modern Americans shunned the subway dwellers because they considered them shamans on a deep, subconscious level.

It had always seemed to me that Omgazi was being rather ethnocentric. He was dealing, after all, with modern Americans, not nineteenth-century Africans. Now I would have a chance to observe some subway dwellers myself. The prospect was most exciting. For, although the subway dwellers were apparently degenerating toward extinction at a rapid rate, in one respect they were unique in all the world—they still lived in an artificial environment that had been constructed during the Space Age. True, it had been a hurried, makeshift environment in the first place, and it and its inhabitants had deteriorated tremendously in two centuries, but, whatever else they were or weren't, the subway dwellers were the only enclave of Space Age Americans left on the face of the earth.

If it were possible at all for a modern African to truly come to understand the reality of Space Age America, surely confrontation with the lineal descendants of the Space Age would provide the key.

Ryan set the helicopter down in what seemed to be some kind of large, open terrace behind a massive, low concrete building. The terrace was a patchwork of cracked concrete walkways and expanses of bare gray earth. Once, apparently, it had been a small park, before the smog had become lethal to vegetation. As a denuded ruin in the pale blue light, it seemed like some strange, cold corpse as the helicopter kicked up dry clouds of dust from the surface of the dead parkland.

As I stepped out with the others into the blue world of the Fuller Dome, I gasped: I had a momentary impression that I had stepped back to Africa, to Accra or Brazzaville. The air was rich and warm and humid on my skin. An instant later, the visual effect—everything a cool, pale blue—jarred me with its arctic-vista contrast. Then I noticed the air itself and I shuddered, and was suddenly hyperconscious of the filters up my nostrils and the goggles over my eyes, for here the air was so heavy with smog that it seemed to sparkle electrically in the crazy blue light. What incredible, beautiful, foul poison!

Except for Ryan, all of us were clearly overcome, each in his own way. Kulongo blinked and stared solemnly for a moment like a great bear; his wife and son seemed to lean into the security of his calm aura. Koyinka seemed to fear that he might strangle; his wife twittered about excitedly, tugging at his hand. The two young men from Luthuliville seemed to be self-consciously making an effort to avoid clutching at each other. Michael Lumumba mumbled something unintelligible under his breath.

"What was that you said, *Mr.* Lumumba?" Ryan said a shade gratingly as he led us out of the park down a crumbling set of stone-and-concrete stairs. Something seemed to snap inside Lumumba; he broke stride for a moment, frozen by some inner event while Ryan led the rest of us onto a walkway between a line of huge, silent buildings and a street choked with the rusted wreckage of ancient cars, timelessly locked in their death-agony in the sparkly blue light.

"What do you want from me, you damned honkie?" Lumumba shouted shrilly. "Haven't you done enough to us?"

Ryan broke stride for a moment, smiled back at Lumumba rather cruelly, and said, "I don't know what you're talking about, pal. I've got your money already. What the hell else could I want from *you*?"

He began to move off down the walkway again, threading his way past and over bits of wrecked cars, fallen masonry, and amorphous rubble. Over his shoulder, he noticed that Lumumba was following along haltingly, staring up at the buildings, nibbling at his lower lip.

"What's the matter, Lumumba?" Ryan shouted back at him. "Aren't these ruins good enough for you to gloat over? You wouldn't be just a little bit afraid, would you?"

"Afraid? Why should I be afraid?"

Ryan continued on for a few more meters; then he stopped and leaned up against the wall of one of the more badly damaged skyscrapers, near a jagged, cavelike opening that led into the dark interior. He looked directly at Lumumba. "Don't get me wrong, pal," he said, "I wouldn't blame you if you were a little scared of the subway dwellers. After all, they're the direct descendants of the people that kicked your ancestors out of this country. Maybe you got a right to be nervous."

"Don't be an idiot, Ryan. Why should a civilized African be afraid of a pack of degenerate savages?" Koyinka said as we all caught up to Ryan.

Ryan shrugged. "How should I know?" he said. "Maybe you ought to ask Mr. Lumumba."

And with that, he turned his back on us and stepped through the jagged opening into the ruined skyscraper. Somewhat uneasily, we followed him into what proved to be a large antechamber that seemed to lead back into some even larger cavernous space that could be sensed rather than seen looming in the darkness. But Ryan did not lead us toward this large, open space; instead, he stopped before he had gone more than a dozen steps and waited for us near a crumbling metal-pipe fence that guarded two edges of what looked like a deep pit. One long edge of the pit was flush with the right wall of the antechamber; at the far short edge, a flight of stone stairs began, which seemed to go all the way to the shadow-obscured bottom.

Ryan led us along the railing to the top of the stairs, and from this angle I could see that the pit had once been the entrance to the mouth of a large tunnel whose floor had been

the floor of the pit at the foot of the stairs. Now an immense
and ancient solid slab of steel blocked the tunnel mouth and
formed the fourth wall of the pit. But in the center of this
rusted steel slab was a relatively new airlock that seemed of
modern design.

"Ladies and gentlemen," Ryan said, "we're standing by a
sealed entrance to the subways of Old New York. During the
Space Age, the subways were the major transportation system of the city and there were hundreds of entrances like this
one. Below the ground was a giant network of stations and
tunnels through which the Space-Agers could go from any
point in the city to any other point. Many of the stations were
huge and contained shops and restaurants. Every station had
automatic vending machines, which sold food and drinks and
a lot of other things, too. Even during the Space Age, the
subways were a kind of little world."

He started down the stairs, still talking. "During the
Panic of the Century, some of the New Yorkers chose not to
leave the city. Instead, they retreated to the subways, sealed
all the entrances, installed space-station life-support machinery—
everything from a fusion reactor to hydroponics—and cut
themselves off from the outside world. Today, the subway
dwellers, direct descendants of those Space-Agers, still inhabit several of the subway stations. And most of the Space
Age life-support machinery is still running. There are probably Space Age artifacts down here that no modern man has
ever seen."

At the bottom of the pit, Ryan led us to the airlock and
opened the outer door. The airlock proved to be surprisingly
large. "This airlock was installed by the government about
fifty years ago, soon after the subway dwellers were discovered,"
he told us as he jammed us inside and began the cycle. "It
was part of a program to recivilize the subway dwellers. The
idea was to let scientists get inside without contaminating the
subway atmosphere with smog. Of course, the whole program was a flop. Nobody's ever going to get through to the
subway dwellers, and there are less of 'em every year. They
don't breed much, and in a generation or so they'll be extinct.
So you're all in for a really unique experience. Not everyone
will be able to tell their grandchildren that they actually saw
a live subway dweller!"

The inner airlock door opened into an ancient square-
cross-sectioned tunnel made of rotting gray concrete. The air,

even through filters, tasted horrible: very thin, somehow crisp without being at all bracing, with a chemical undertone, yet reeking with organic decay odors. Breathing was very difficult; it felt as if we were at the fifteen-thousand-foot level.

"I'm not telling you all this for my health," Ryan said as he moved us out of the airlock. "I'm telling it to you for *your* health: Don't mess with these people. Look and don't touch. Listen, but keep your mouths shut. They may seem harmless, they may be harmless, but no one can be sure. That's why not many guides will take people down here. I hope you *all* have that straight."

The last remark had obviously been meant for Lumumba, but he didn't seem to react to it; he seemed subdued, drawn up inside himself. Perhaps Ryan was right—perhaps in some unguessable way, Lumumba *was* afraid. It's impossible to really understand these Amero-Africans.

We moved off down the corridor. The overhead lights— at least in this area—were clearly modern, probably installed when the airlock had been installed, but it was possible that the power was actually provided by the fusion reactor that had been installed centuries ago by the Space-Agers themselves. The air we were breathing was produced by a Space Age atmosphere plant that had been designed for actual space stations! It was a frightening, and at the same time, a thrilling feeling: Our lives were dependent on actual functioning Space Age equipment. It was almost like stepping back in time.

The corridor made a right-angle turn and became a downward-sloping ramp. The ramp leveled off after a few dozen meters, passed some crumbling ruins inset into one of the walls—apparently a ruined shop of some strange sort with massive chairs bolted to the floor and pieces of mirror still clinging to patches of its walls—and suddenly opened out into a wide, low, cavelike space lit dimly and erratically by ancient Space Age perma-bulbs, which still functioned in many places along the grime-encrusted ceiling.

It was the strangest room—if you could call it that—that I had ever been in. The ceiling seemed horribly low, lower even than it actually was, because the room seemed to go on under it indefinitely, in all sorts of seemingly random directions. Its boundaries faded off into shadows and dim lights and gloom; I couldn't see any of the far walls. It was impossible to feel exactly claustrophobic in a place like that, but it gave me an analogous sensation without a name, as if the ceiling and the floor might somehow come together and squash me.

Strange figures shuffled around in the gloom, moving about slowly and aimlessly. Other figures sat singly or in small groups on the bare, filthy floor. Most of the subway dwellers were well under five feet tall. Their shoulders were deeply hunched, making them seem even shorter, and their bodies were thin, rickety, and emaciated under the tattered and filthy scraps of multicolored rags that they wore. I was deeply shocked. I don't really know what I had expected, but I certainly had not been prepared for the unmistakable aura of diminished humanity which these pitiful creatures exuded even at a distant first glance.

Immediately before us was a kind of concrete hut. It was pitted with what looked like bullet scars, and parts of it were burned black. It had tiny windows, one of which still held some rotten metal grillwork. Apparently it had been a kind of sentry box, perhaps during the Panic of the Century itself. A complex barrier cut off the section where we stood from the main area of the subway station. It consisted of a ceiling-to-floor metal grillwork fence on either side of a line of turnstiles. Beside the turnstiles, gates in the fence clearly marked EXIT in peeling white-and-black enamel had been crudely welded shut; by the look of the weld, perhaps more than a century ago.

On the other side of the barrier stood a male subway dweller wearing a kind of long shirt patched together out of every conceivable type and color of cloth and rotting away at the edges and in random patches. He stood staring at us, or at least with his deeply squinted, expressionless eyes turned in our direction, rocking back and forth slightly from the waist, but otherwise not moving. His face was unusually pallid even for an American, and every inch of his skin and clothing was caked with an incredible layer of filth.

Ignoring the subway dweller as thoroughly as that stooped figure was ignoring us, Ryan led us to the line of turnstiles and extracted a handful of small greenish-yellow coins from a pocket.

"These are subway tokens," he told us, dropping ten of the coins into a small slot atop one of the turnstiles. "Space Age money that was only used down here. It's good in all the vending machines, and in these turnstiles. The subway dwellers still use the tokens to get food and water from the machines. When I want more of these things, all I have to do is break open a vending machine, so don't worry, admission isn't costing us anything. Just push your way through the turnstiles like this. . . ."

He demonstrated by walking straight through the turnstile. The turnstile barrier rotated a notch to let him through when he applied his body against it.

One by one we passed through the turnstile. Michael Lumumba passed through immediately ahead of me, then paused at the other side to study the subway dweller, who had drifted up to the barrier. Lumumba looked down at the subway dweller's face for a long moment; then a sardonic smile grew slowly on his face, and he said, "Hello, honkie, how are things in the subway?"

The subway dweller turned his eyes in Lumumba's direction. He did nothing else.

"Hey, just what *are* you, some kind of cretin?" Lumumba said as Ryan, his face flushed red behind his pallor, turned in his tracks and started back toward Lumumba. The subway dweller's face did not change expression; in fact, it could hardly have been said to have had an expression in the first place. "I think you're a brain-damage case, honkie."

"I told you not to talk to the subway dwellers!" Ryan said, shoving his way between Lumumba and the subway dweller.

"So you did," Lumumba said coolly. "And I'm beginning to wonder why."

"They can be dangerous."

"*Dangerous?* These little moronic slugs? The only thing these brainless white worms can be dangerous to is your pride. Isn't that it, Ryan? Behold the remnants of the great Space Age honkies! See how they haven't the brains left to wipe the drool off their chins—"

"Be silent!" Kulongo suddenly bellowed with the authority of a chief in his voice. Lumumba was indeed silenced, and even Ryan backed off as Kulongo moved near them. But the self-satisfied look that Lumumba continued to give Ryan was a weapon that he was wielding, a weapon that the American obviously felt keenly.

Through it all, the subway dweller continued to rock back and forth, gently and silently, without a sign of human sentience.

* * *

Goddamn that black brother Lumumba and goddamn the stinking subway dwellers! Oh, how I hate taking these Africans down there. Sometimes I wonder why the hell I do it. Sometimes I feel there's something unclean about it all, something rotten. Not just the subway dwellers, though those horrible animals are rotten enough, but taking a bunch of stinking African tourists in there to look at them, and me making money off of it. It's a great selling point for the day-tour. Those black brothers eat it up, especially the cruds like Lumumba, but if I didn't need the money so bad, I wouldn't do it. Call it patriotism, maybe. I'm not patriotic enough not to take my tours to see the subway dwellers, but I'm patriotic enough not to feel too happy with myself about it.

Of course, I know what it is that gets to me. The subway dwellers are the last direct descendants of the Space-Agers, in a way the only piece of the Space Age still alive, and what they are is what Lumumba said they are: slugs, morons, and cretins. And physical wrecks on top of it. Lousy eyesight, rubbery bones, rotten teeth, and if you find one more than five feet tall, it's a giant. They're lucky to live to thirty. There's no smog in the recirculated chemical crap they breathe, but there's not enough oxygen in the long run, either, and after two centuries of sucking in its own gunk, God only knows exactly what's missing and what there's too much of in the air that the subway life-support system puts out. The subway dwellers have just about enough brains left to keep the air plant and the hydroponics and stuff going without really knowing what the hell they're doing. Every one of them is a born brain-damage case, and year by year the air keeps getting crummier and crummier and the crap they eat gets lousier and lousier, and there are fewer and fewer subway dwellers, and they're getting stupider and stupider. They say in another fifty years they'll be extinct. They're all that's left of the Space-Agers, and they're slowly strangling their brains in their own crap.

Like I keep telling Karen, the tourist business is a rotten way to earn a living. Every time I come down into this stinking hole in the ground, I have to keep reminding myself that I'm a day closer to owning a piece of that Amazon swampland. It helps settle my stomach.

I led my collection of Africans farther out into the upper

level of the station. It's hard to figure out just what this level was during the Space Age—there's nothing up here but a lot of old vending machines and ruined stalls and garbage. This level goes on and on in all directions; there are more old subway entrances leading into it than I've counted. I've been told that during the Space Age thousands of people crowded in here just on their way to the trains below, but that doesn't make sense. Why would they want to hang around in a hole in the ground any longer than they had to?

The subway dwellers, of course, just mostly hung around doing what subway dwellers do—stand and stare into space, or sit on their butts and chew their algae-cake, or maybe even stand and stare and chew at the same time, if they're real enterprising. Beats me why the Africans are so fascinated by them. . . .

Then, a few yards ahead of us, I saw a vending machine servicer approaching a water machine. Now, *there* was a piece of luck! I sure didn't get to show every tour what passed for a "Genuine Subway Dweller Ceremony." I decided to really play it up. I held the tourists off about ten feet from the water machine so they wouldn't mess things up, and I started to give them a fancy pitch.

"You're about to witness an authentic water machine servicing by a subway dweller vending machine servicer," I told them as a crummy subway dweller slowly inched up to a peeling red-and-white water machine dragging a small cart that held four metal kegs and a bunch of other old crap. "During the Space Age, this machine dispensed the traditional Space Age beverage, Coca-Cola—still enjoyed in some parts of the world—as you can see from some of the lettering still on the machine. Of course, the subway dwellers have no Coca-Cola to fill it with now."

The subway dweller took a ring of keys out of the cart, fitted one of them into a keyhole on the face of the machine after a few tries, and opened a plate on the front of the machine. Tokens came tumbling out onto the floor. The subway dweller got down on its hands and knees, picked up the tokens one by one, and dropped them into a moldly looking rubber sack from the cart.

"The servicer has now removed the tokens from the water machine. In order to get a drink of water, a subway dweller drops a token into the slot in the face of the machine, pulls the lever, and cups his hands inside the little opening."

The subway dweller opened the back of the water machine with another key, struggled with one of the metal kegs, then finally lifted it and poured some pretty green-looking water into the machine's tank.

"The servicers buy the water from the reclamation tenders with the tokens they get from the machines. They also service the food machines with algae-cake they get from the hydroponic tenders the same way."

The vending machine servicer replaced the back plate of the water machine and dragged its cart slowly off farther on into the shadows of the station toward the next water machine.

"How do they make the tokens?" Koyinka asked.

"Nobody *makes* tokens," I told him. "They're all left over from the Space Age."

"That doesn't make sense. How can they run an economy without a supply of new money? Profits always bring new money into circulation. Even a socialist economy has to print new money each year."

Huh? What the hell was he talking about? These damned Africans!

"I think I can explain," the college professor said. "According to Kusongeri, the subway dwellers do not have a real money economy. The same tokens get passed around continually. For instance, the servicers probably take exactly as many tokens out of a water machine as they have to give to the reclamation tenders for the water in the first place. No concept of profit exists here."

"But then why do they bother with tokens in the first place?"

The professor shrugged. "Ritual, perhaps, or—"

"Why does a bee build honeycombs?" Lumumba sneered. "Why does a magpie steal bright objects? Because they think about it—or because it's just the nature of the animal? Don't you see, Koyinka, these white slugs aren't people, they're *animals*! They don't *think*. They don't have *reasons* for doing anything. *Animals!* Stupid pale white animals! The last descendants of the Space Age honkies, and they're nothing but *animals*! That's what honkies end up like when they don't have black men to think for them, how—"

Red sparks went off in my head. "They were good enough to ride your crummy ancestors back to Africa on a rail, you black brother!"

"You watch your mouth when you're talking to your betters, honkie!"

"*Mr. Lumumba!*" the professor shouted. Koyinka looked ready to take a swing at me. Kulongo had moved toward Lumumba and looked disgusted. The Luthuliville fruits were wrinkling their dainty noses. Christ, we were all a hair away from a brawl. A thing like that could kill business for a month, or even cost me my license. I thought of that Amazon swampland, blue skies and green trees and brown earth as far as the eye could see. . . .

I kept thinking of the Amazon as I unballed my fists and swallowed my pride, and turned my back on Lumumba and led the whole lousy lot of them deeper into the upper level of the station.

Man, I just better give them about another twenty minutes down here and get the hell out before I tear that Lumumba to pieces. I had half a mind to take him back in there to that electric people-trap and jam one of those helmets on his head and leave him there. Then we'd see how much laughing he'd do at the Space-Agers!

The tension kept building between Ryan and Lumumba as we continued to move among the subway dwellers; it was so painfully obvious that it was only a matter of time before the next outburst that one might have almost expected the wretched creatures who inhabited the subways to notice it.

But it was also rather obvious that the subway dwellers had only a limited perception of their environment and an even more limited conceptualization of interpersonal relationships. It would be difficult to say whether or not they were capable of comprehending anything so complex as human emotion. It would be almost as difficult to say whether or not they were human.

The vending machine servicer had performed a complicated task, a task somewhat too complex for even an intelligent chimpanzee, though conceivably a dolphin might have the mental capacity to master it if it had the physical equipment. But no one has been able to say clearly whether or not a dolphin should be considered sapient; it seems to be a borderline situation.

Lumumba had obviously made up his mind that the subway dwellers were truly subhuman animals. As Ryan led us past a motley group of subway dwellers who squatted on the bare floor mechanically eating small slabs of some green substance, Lumumba kept up a loud babble, ostensibly to me, but actually for Ryan's benefit.

"Look at the dirty animals chewing their cud like cows! Look what's left of the great Space-Agers who went to the moon—a few thousand brainless white slugs rotting in a sealed coffin!"

"Even the greatest civilization falls sometime," I mumbled somewhat inanely, trying to soften the situation, for Ryan was clearly engaged in a fierce struggle for control of his temper. I could understand why Ryan and Lumumba hated each other, but why did Lumumba's remarks about the subway dwellers hurt Ryan so deeply?

As we walked farther on in among the rusting steel pillars and scattered groups of ruminating subway dwellers, I happened to pass close to a female subway dweller, perhaps four and a half feet tall, stooped and leathery with stringy gray hair, and dressed in the usual filthy rags. She was inserting a token into the slot of a vending machine. She dropped the coin and pulled a lever under one of the small broken windows that formed a row above the trough of the machine. A green slab dropped down into the trough. The female subway dweller picked it up and began chewing on it.

A sense of excitement came over me. I was determined to actually speak with a subway dweller. "What is your name?" I said slowly and distinctly.

The female subway dweller turned her pale, expressionless little eyes in my direction. A bit of green drool escaped from her lips. Other than that, she made no discernible response.

I tried again. "What is your name?"

The creature stared at me blankly. "Whu...ee...na..." she finally managed to stammer in a flat, dull monotone.

"I told you people not to talk to the damned subway dwellers!"

Ryan had apparently noticed what I was doing; he was rushing toward me past Michael Lumumba. Lumumba grabbed him by the elbow. "What the matter, Ryan?" he said. "Do the animals bite?"

"Get your slimy hand off me, you black brother!" Ryan roared, ripping his arm out of Lumumba's grasp.

"I'll bet you bite, too, honkie," Lumumba said. "After all, you're the same breed of animal they are."

Ryan lunged at Lumumba, but Kulongo was on him in three huge strides, and hugged him from behind with a powerful grip. "Please do not be as foolish as that man, Mr. Ryan," he said softly. "He dishonors us all. You have been a good guide. Do not let that man goad you into doing something that will allow him to disgrace your name with the authorities."

Kulongo held on to Ryan as the redness in his face slowly faded. The female subway dweller began to wander away. Lumumba backed off a few paces, then turned his back, walked a bit further away, and pretended to study a group of seated subway dwellers.

Finally, Kulongo released his grip on Ryan. "Yeah, you're right, pal," Ryan said. "That crud would like nothing better than to be able to report that I bashed his face in. I guess I should apologize to the rest of you folks. . . ."

"I think Mr. Lumumba should apologize as well," I said.

"I don't apologize to animals," Lumumba muttered. Really, the man was disgusting!

God, what I really wanted to do was to bury that Lumumba right there, knock him senseless and let him try to get back to Milford by himself, or, better yet, take him back to that crazy "Cosmic-All" thing, jam a helmet on his head, and find out how the thing kills in the pleasantest way possible.

But of course I couldn't kill him or maroon him in front of eight witnesses. So instead of giving that black brother what he deserved, I decided to just let them all walk around for about another ten minutes, gawking at the animals, and then call it a day. Seemed to me that all of them but Lumumba and maybe the professor had had their fill of the subway dwellers anyway. Mostly, the subway dwellers just sit around chewing algae-cake. Some of them just stare at nothing for hours. Let's face it, the subway dwellers *are* animals. They've degenerated all the way. I figured just about now the Africans would've had their nasty thrill. . . .

But I figured without that stinking Lumumba. Just when the whole bunch of them were standing around in a mob looking thoroughly bored and disgusted, he started another "conversation" with the professor, real loud. Real subtle, that black brother.

"You're a professor of American history, aren't you, Dr. Balewa?"

Got to give Balewa credit. He didn't seem to want any part of Lumumba's little game. "Uh... Space Age history is my major field," he muttered, and then tried to turn away.

But Lumumba would just as soon have run his mouth at a subway dweller; he didn't care if Balewa was really listening to him as long as I was.

"Well, then maybe you can tell me whether or not the honkies could really have built all that Space Age technology on their own. After all, look at these brainless animals, the direct descendants of the Space Age honkies. Sure, they've degenerated since the first of them locked themselves up down here, but degenerated from *what*? Didn't they have to be pretty stupid to seal themselves up in a tomb like this in the first place? And they did have twenty or thirty million black men to do their thinking for them before the Panic. Take a look around you, professor—did these slugs *really* have ancestors capable of creating the Space Age on their own?"

He stared dead at me, and I saw his slimy game. If I didn't cream him, I'd be a coward, and if I did, I'd lose my license. "Take a look at the modern example of the race, professor," he said. "Could a nation of *Ryans* have built anything more than a few junk heaps on their own? With captive blacks to do the thinking for them, they went to the moon, and then they choked themselves in their own waste. Hardly the mark of a great civilized race."

"Your kind quaked in their boots every time one of my ancestors walked by them, and you know it," I told the crud.

Lumumba would've gone white if he could have. In more ways than one, I'll bet. "You calling me a coward, honkie?"

"I'm calling you a yellow coward, *boy*."

"No honkie calls me a coward."

"This honkie does... *nigger*."

Ah, that got him! There're one or two words these Amero-Africans just can't take, brings up frightening memories. Lumumba went for me, the professor tried to grab him and missed, and then that big ape Kulongo had him in one of those bear hugs of his. And suddenly I had an idea how to fix Mr. Michael Lumumba real good, without laying a finger on him, without giving him anything he could complain to the government about.

"You ever hear about a machine that's supposed to 'merge you with the Cosmic All,' professor?" I said.

"Why . . . that would be the ECA—the Electronic Consciousness Augmenter. It was never clear whether more than a few prototypes were built or not. The device was developed shortly before the Panic. Some sort of scientific religion built the ECA—the Brotherhood of the Cosmic All, or some such group. The claim was that the machine produced a transcendental experience of some sort electronically. No one has ever proved whether or not there was any truth to it, since none of the devices have ever been found. . . ."

Kulongo relaxed his grip on Lumumba. I had them now. I had Mr. Michael Lumumba real good. "Well, I think I found one of them, right here in this station, a couple of years ago. It's still working. Maybe the subway dwellers keep it going—probably it was built to keep itself going; it looks like real late Space Age stuff. I could take you all to it."

I gave Lumumba a nice smile. "How about it, pal?" I said. "Let's see if you're a coward or not. Let's see you walk in there and put a working Space Age gizmo on your head and 'merge with the Cosmic All.'"

"Have you ever done it, Ryan?" Lumumba sneered.

"Sure, pal," I lied. "I do it all the time. It's fun."

"I think you're a liar."

"I *know* you're a coward."

Lumumba gave me a look like a snake. "All right, honkie," he said. "I'll try it if you try it with me."

Christ, what was I getting myself into? That thing killed people, all those bones. . . . Yeah, but I knew that and Lumumba didn't. When he saw the bones, he wouldn't dare put a helmet on his head. Yeah, I knew that he wouldn't, and he didn't, so that still put me one up on him.

"You're afraid, aren't you, Ryan? You've never really done it yourself. You're afraid to do it, and I'm not. Who does that make the coward?"

Oh, you crud, I got you right where I want you! "Okay, boy," I said, "you're on. You do it and I'll do it. We'll see who's the coward. The rest of you folks can come along for the ride. A free extra added attraction, courtesy of Little Old New York Tours."

* * *

Ryan led us deeper into a more shadowed part of the station, where the still-functioning bulbs in the ceiling were farther and farther apart, and where, perhaps because of the darkness, the subway dwellers were fewer and fewer. As we went farther and farther into the deepening darkness, the floor of the subway station was filled with small bits of rubble, then larger and larger pieces, till finally, dimly outlined by a single bulb a few yards ahead of us, we could see a place where the ceiling had fallen in. A huge dam of rubble that filled the station from floor to ceiling cut off a corner much like the one into which we had originally come from the rest of the station.

Ryan led us out of the pool of light and into the blackness. "In here," he called back. "Everyone touch the one ahead of you."

I touched Michael Lumumba's back with some distaste, but also with a kind of gratitude. Because of him, I was getting to see a working wonder of the Space Age, a device whose very existence was a matter of academic dispute. My reputation would be made!

I felt Kulongo's somehow reassuring hand on my shoulder as we groped our way through the darkness. Then I felt Lumumba stoop, and I was passing through a narrow opening in the pile of rubble, where two broken girders wedged against each other held up the crumbled fragments of ceiling.

Beyond, I could see by a strange flickering light just around a bend that we had emerged in a place very much like the subway entrance. The ceiling had fallen on a set of turnstiles and grillwork barriers, crushing them, but clearing a way for us. We picked our way past the ruined barriers and entered a side tunnel, which was filled with the strange, flickering light, a light which seemed to cut each moment off from the next, like a faulty piece of antique motion-picture film, such as the specimens of Chaplin I've seen in Nairobi. It made me feel as if I were moving inside such a film. Time seemed to be composed of separate discrete bursts of duration.

Ryan led us up the tunnel, both sides of which were composed of the ruins of recessed shops, like some underground market arcade. Then I saw that one shop in the arcade was not ruined. It stood out from the rubble, a gleaming anachronism. Even a layman would've recognized it as a specimen of very late Space Age technology. And it was a working specimen.

It had that classic late Space Age style. The entire front of the shop was made of some plastic substance that flickered luminescently, that was the source of the strange, pale light. There has been some literature on this material, but a specimen had never been examined, as far as I knew. The substance itself is woven of fibers called light guides—modern science has been able to produce such fibers, but to weave a kind of cloth of them by known methods would be hideously expensive. But Space Age light guide cloth, however it was made, enabled a single light source to cast its illumination evenly over a very wide area. So the flickering was probably produced simply by using a stroboscope as a light source for the wall. Very minor Space Age wizardry, but very effective: It made the entire shopfront a psychologically powerful attention-getting device, such as the Space-Agers commonly employed in their incredibly sophisticated science of advertising.

A small doorless portal big enough for one man at a time was all that marred the flickering luminescence of the wall of shopfront. Above the shop a smaller strobe panel—but this one composed of blue-and-red fibers that flashed independently—proclaimed MERGE WITH THE COSMIC ALL red on blue for half of every second, a powerful hypnotic that drew me toward the shop despite my abstract knowledge of its workings.

That the device was working at all in this area of the station where all other power seemed cut off was proof enough of its very late Space Age dating: Only in the decade before the Panic had the Space-Agers developed a miniaturized isotopic power source cheap enough to warrant installation of self-contained five-hundred-year generators in something like this.

The very fact that we were staring into the flickering light of a Space Age device whose self-contained power source had kept it going totally untended for centuries was enough to overwhelm us. I'm sure the rest of them felt what I felt; even Lumumba just stood there and gaped. On Ryan's face, even beneath the tight lines of his anger, was something akin to awe. Or was it some kind of superstitious dread?

"Well, here it is, Lumumba," Ryan said softly, the strobe-wall making the movements of his mouth appear to be mechanical. "Shall we step inside?"

"After you, Ryan. You're the ... *native guide*." Fear flickered in the strobe flashes off Lumumba's eyes, but, like all of us, he found it impossible to look away from the entrance for long. There seemed to be subtle and complex waves in the strobe flashes drawing us to the doorway; perhaps there were several stroboscopes activating the wall in a psychologically calculated sequence. In this area, the Space Age Americans had been capable of any subtlety a modern mind could imagine, and infinitely more.

"And you're the . . . *tourist*," Ryan said softly. "A tourist who thinks he knows what the Space-Agers were all about. Step inside, sucker!"

And with a grim, knowing grin, Ryan stepped through the doorway. Without hesitation, Lumumba followed after him. And without hesitation, drawn by the flickering light and so much more, I entered the chamber behind them.

The inside of the chamber was a cube of some incredible hyper-real desert night as seen through the eyes of a prophet or a madman. The walls and ceiling of the room were light: mosaics of millions of tiny deep-blue twinkling pinpoints of brilliance, here and there leavened with intermittent prickles of red and green and yellow, all flashing in seemingly random sequences of a tenth of a second or so each. Beneath this preternatural electronic sky, we stood transfixed. The dazzling universe of winking light filled our brains; before it we were as subway dwellers chewing their cud.

Behind me, I dimly heard Kulongo's deep voice saying, "There are demons in there that would drink a man's soul. We will not go in there." How foolish those faraway words sounded. . . .

"There's nothing to be afraid of. . . ." I heard my own voice saying. The sound of my own voice broke my light trance almost as I realized that I had been in a trance. Then I saw the bones.

The chamber was filled with six rows of strange chairs, six of them to a row. They were like giant red eggs standing on end, hollowed out, and fitted inside with reclining padded seats. Inside the red eggs, metal helmets designed to fit over the entire head dangled from cables at head-level. Most of the eggs contained human skeletons. The floor was littered with bones.

Ryan and Lumumba seemed to have been somewhat deeper in trance; it took them a few seconds longer to come out of it. Lumumba's eyes flashed sudden fear as he saw the bones. But Ryan grinned knowingly as he saw the fear on Lumumba's face.

"Scares you a bit, doesn't it, boy?" Ryan said. "Still game to put on one of those helmets?" The wall seemed to pick up the sparkle of his laugh.

"What killed them?" was all Lumumba said.

"How should I know?"

"But you said you'd tried it!"

"So, I'm a liar. And you're a coward."

I walked forward as they argued, and read a small metal plaque that was affixed to the outer shell of each red egg:

Two tokens—MERGE WITH THE COSMIC ALL—Two tokens. Drop tokens in slot. Place helmet over head. Pull lever and experience MERGER WITH THE COSMIC ALL. Automatic timer will limit all MERGERS to two-minute duration, in compliance with federal law.

"I'm no more a coward than you are, Ryan. You had no intention of putting on one of those things."

"I'd do it if you'd do it," Ryan insisted.

"No you wouldn't! You're not that crazy and neither am I. Why would you risk your life for something as stupid as that?"

"Because I'd be willing to bet my life any day that a black brother like you would never have the guts to put on a helmet."

"You stinking honkie!"

"Why don't we end this crap, Lumumba? You're not going to put on one of these helmets and neither am I. The big difference between us is that I won't have to because you *can't*."

Lumumba seemed like a carven idol of rage in that fantastic cube of light. "Just a minute, honkie," he said. "Professor, you have any idea why they died when they put the helmets on?"

It was starting to make sense to me. What if the claims made for the device were true? What if two tokens could buy a man total transcendental bliss? "I don't think they died when they put the helmets on," I said. "I think they starved to death days later. According to this plaque, whatever happens is supposed to last no longer than two minutes before an automatic circuit shuts it off. What if this device involves electronic stimulation of the pleasure center? No one has yet unearthed such a device, but the Space Age literature was full of it. Pleasure-center stimulation was supposed to be harmless in itself, but what if the timer circuit went out? A man could be paralyzed in total bliss while he starved to death. I think that's what happened here."

"Let me get this straight," Lumumba said, his rage seeming to collapse in upon itself, becoming a manic shrewdness. "The helmets themselves are harmless? Even if we couldn't take them off ourselves, one of the others could take them off. . . . We wouldn't be in any real danger?"

"I don't think so," I told him. "According to the inscription, one paid two tokens for the experience. I doubt that even the Space-Agers would've been willing to pay money for something that would harm them, certainly not *en masse*. And the Space-Agers were very conscious of profit."

"Would you be willing to stake your life on it, Dr. Balewa? Would you be willing to try it, too?"

Try it? Actually put on a helmet, give myself over to a piece of Space Age wizardry, an electronic device that was supposed to produce a mystical experience at the flick of a switch? A less stable man might say that if it really worked, there was a god inside the helmets, a god that the Space-Agers had created out of electronic components. If this were actually true, it surely must represent the very pinnacle of Space Age civilization—who but the Space-Agers would even contemplate the fabrication of an actual god?

Yes, of course I would try it! I *had* to try it; what kind of scholar would I be if I passed by an opportunity to understand the Space-Agers as no modern man has understood them before? Neither Ryan nor Lumumba had the background to make the most of such an experience. It was my duty to put on a helmet as well as my pleasure.

"Yes, Mr. Lumumba," I said. "I intend to try it, too."

"Then we'll all try it," Lumumba said. "Or will we, Mr. Ryan? I'm ready to put on a helmet and so is the professor; are you?"

They were both nuts, Lumumba and the professor! Those helmets had killed people. How the hell could Balewa know what had happened from reading some silly plaque? These goddamned Africans always think they can understand the Space-Agers from crap other Africans have put in books. What the hell do they know? What do they really know?

"Well, Ryan, what about it? Are you going to admit you don't have the guts to do it, so we can all forget it and go home?"

"All right, pal, you're on!" I heard myself telling him. Damn, what was I getting myself into? But I couldn't let that slime Lumumba call my bluff; no African's gonna bluff down an *American*! Besides, Balewa was probably right; what he said made sense. Sure, it had to make sense. That stinking black brother!

"Mr. Kulongo, would you come in here and take the helmets off our heads in two minutes?" I asked. I'd trust that Kulongo further than the rest of the creeps.

"I will not go in there," Kulongo said. "There is juju in there, powerful and evil. I am ashamed before you because I say these words, but my fear of what is in this place is greater than my shame."

"This is ridiculous!" Koyinka said, pushing past Kulongo. "Evil spirits! Come on, will you, this is the twenty-second century! I'll do it, if you want to go through with this nonsense."

"All right, pal, let's get on with it."

I handed out the tokens and the three of us went to the nearest three stalls. I cleared a skeleton out of mine, sent it clattering to the floor, and so what, what's to be scared of in a pile of old dead bones? But I noticed that Lumumba seemed a little green as he cleared the bones out for himself.

I pulled myself up into the hollowed-out egg and sat down on the padded couch inside. Some kind of plastic covering made the thing still clean and comfortable, not even dusty, after hundreds of years. Those Space-Agers were really something. I dropped the tokens into a little slot in the arm of the couch. Next to the slot was a lever. The room sparkled blue all around me; somehow that made me feel real good. The couch was comfortable. Koyinka was standing by. I was actually beginning to enjoy it. What was there to be afraid of? Jeez, the professor thought this gave you pure pleasure or something. If he was right, this was really going to be something. If I lived through it.

I put my right hand on the lever. I saw that the professor and Lumumba were already under their helmets. I fitted the helmet down over my head. Some kind of pad inside it fitted down on my skull all around my head, down to the eyebrows; it seemed almost alive, molding itself to my head like a second skin. It was very dark inside the helmet. Couldn't see a thing.

I took a deep breath and pulled the lever.

The tips of my fingers began to tingle, throbbing with pleasure, not pain. My feet started to tingle, too, and shapes that had no shape, that were more black inside the black, seemed to be floating around inside my head. The tingling moved up my fingers to my hands, up my feet to my knees. Now my arms were tingling. Oh, man, it felt so good! No woman ever felt this good! This felt better than kicking in Lumumba's face!

The whirling things in my head weren't really in my head, my head was in them, or they were my head, all whirling around some deep dark hole that wasn't a hole but was something to whirl off into, fall off into, sucking me in and up. My whole body was tingling now. Man, I *was* the tingling now, my body was nothing *but* the tingling now.

And it was getting stronger, getting better all the time; I wasn't a tingle, I was a glow, a warmth, a throbbing, a fire of pure pleasure, a roaring, burning, whirling fire, sucking, spinning up toward a deep black hole inside me blowing up in a blast of pure *feeling so good so good so good*—

Oh, forever whirling, whirling, a fire *so good so good so good*, and on *through* into the black hole fire I was *burning up in my own orgasm*. I was my own orgasm of body-mind-sex-taste-smell-touch-feel, I went on *forever forever forever forever* in pure blinding burning *so good so good so good* nothingness blackness dying orgasm *forever forever forever* spurting out of myself in sweet moment of total pain-pleasure *so good so good so good* moment of dying pain burning sex *forever forever forever so good so good forever so good forever so good forever*—

I pulled the lever and waited in my private darkness. The first thing I felt was a tingling of my fingertips, as if with some mild electric charge; not at all an unpleasant feeling. A similar pleasurable tingle began in my feet. Strange, vague patterns seemed to swirl around inside my eyes.

My hands began to feel the pleasant sensation now, and the lower portions of my legs. The feeling was getting stronger and stronger as it moved up my limbs. It felt physically pleasurable in a peculiarly abstract way, but there was something frightening about it, something vaguely unclean.

The swirling patterns seemed to be spinning around a bottomless vortex now; they weren't exactly inside my eyes or my head; my head was inside of them, or they *were* me. The experience was somehow visual-yet-nonvisual, my being spinning downward and inward in a vertiginous spiral toward a black, black hole that seemed inside my self. And my whole body felt that electric tingling now; I felt nothing *but* the strange, forcefully pleasurable sensation. It filled my entire sensorium, became *me*.

And it kept getting stronger and stronger, no longer a tingle, but a pulsing of cold, electric pleasure, stronger and stronger, wilder and wilder, the voltage increasing, the amperage increasing, whirling me down and around and down and around toward that terrible deep black hole inside me burning with hunger to swallow myself up, becoming a pure black fire vortex pain of pleasure down and down and around and around. . . .

Sucking myself up through the terrible black vortex of my own pure pleasure-pain, compressed against the interface of my own being, squeezed against the instant of my own *death*. Oh! Oh! *Death death death.* No No pleasure pain death sex orgasm everything that was me popping No! No! *On through!* becoming moment of death senses flashing pure pleasure pain terror black hole *forever forever* in this terrible universe was timeless moment of orgasm death total electric pleasure *no! no!* delicious horrible moment of pure *death pain orgasm black hole vortex no! no! no! no—*

Suddenly I was seated on a couch inside a red egg in a room filled with blue sparkles, and I was looking up at Koyinka's silly face.

"You all right?" he said. Now, *there* was a question!

"Yeah, yeah," I mumbled. Man, those Space-Agers! I wanted to puke. I wanted to jam that helmet back on my head. I wanted to get the hell out of there! I wanted to live forever in that fantastic perfect feeling until I rotted into the bone pile.

I was scared out of my head.

I mean, what happened inside that helmet was the best and the worst thing in the world. You could stay there with that thing on your head and die in pure pleasure thinking you were living forever. Man, you talk about *temptation*! Those Space-Agers had put a god or a devil in there, and who could tell which? Did they even know which? Man, that crazy jungle-bunny Kulongo was right, after all: there *were* demons in here that would drink your soul. But maybe the demons were *you*. Sucking up your own soul in pure pleasure till it choked you to death. But wasn't it maybe worth it?

As soon as he saw I was okay, Koyinka ran over to the professor, who was still sitting there with the helmet over his head. That crud Lumumba was out of it already. He was staring at me; he wasn't mad, he wasn't exactly afraid, he was just trying to look into my eyes. I guess because I felt what he felt, too.

I stared back into Lumumba's big eyes as Koyinka took the helmet off the professor's head. I couldn't help myself. I didn't like the black brother one bit more, but there was something between us now, God knows what. The professor looked real green. He didn't seem to notice us much. Lumumba and I just kept staring at each other, nodding a little bit. Yeah, we had both been someplace no living man should go. The Space-Agers had been gods or demons or maybe something that would drive both gods and demons screaming straight up the wall. When we call them human we don't mean the same thing we do when we call us human. When they died off, something we'll never understand went out of the world. I don't know whether to thank God or to cry.

It seemed to me that I could read exactly what was going on inside Lumumba's head; his thoughts were my thoughts.

"They were a great and terrible people," Lumumba finally said. "And they were out of their minds."

"Pal, they were something we can never be. Or want to."

"You know, honkie, I think for once you've got a point."

There was a strange feeling hovering in the air between Ryan and Lumumba as we made our way back through the subway station and up into the sparkly blue unreal world of the Fuller Dome. Not comradeship, not even grudging respect, but some subtle change I could not fathom. Their eyes keep meeting, almost furtively. I couldn't understand it. I couldn't understand it at all.

Had they experienced what I had? Coldly, I could now say that it had been nothing but electronic stimulation of some cerebral centers; but the horror of it, the horror of being forced to experience a moment of death and pain and total pleasure all bound up together and extended toward infinity, had been realer than real. It had indeed been a genuine mystical experience, created electronically.

But why would people do a thing like that to themselves? Why would they willingly plunge themselves into a moment of pure horror that went on and on and on?

Yet as we finally boarded the helicopter, I somehow sensed that what Lumumba and Ryan had shared was not what I felt at all.

As I flew the copter through the dead tombstone skyscrapers toward the outer edge of the Fuller Dome, I knew that I had to get out of this damned tourist business, and fast. Now I knew what was really buried here, under the crazy spooky blue light, under all the concrete, under the stinking saturation smog, under a hole inside a hole in the ground: the bones of a people that men like us had better let lie.

Our ancestors were gods or demons or both. If we get too close to the places where what they *really* were is buried, they'll drink our souls yet.

No more tours to the subways anyway; what good is the Amazon if I don't live to get there? If I had me an atom bomb, I'd drop it right smack on top of this place to make sure I never go back.

As we headed into a fantastic blazing orange-and-purple sunset, toward Milford and modern America—a pallid replica of African civilization huddling in the interstices of a continent of incredible ruins—I looked back across the wide river, a flaming sea below and behind us ignited by the setting sun. The Fuller Dome flashed in the sunlight, a giant diamond set in the tombstone of a race that had soared to the moon, that had turned the atmosphere to a beautiful and terrible poison, that had covered a continent with ruins that overawed the modern world, that had conjured up a demon out of electronic circuitry, that had torn themselves to pieces in the end.

A terrible pang of sadness went through me as the rest of my trip turned to ashes in my mouth, as my future career became a cadaver covered with dust. I could crawl over these ruins and exhaust the literature for the rest of my life, and I would never understand what the Space-Age Americans had been. Not a man alive ever would. Whatever they had been, such things lived on the face of the earth no more.

In his simple way, Kulongo had said all that could be said: "Their souls were not as ours."

Introduction to
"World War Last"

One night at a science fiction convention, I had a long bull session with Betsy Mitchell, editor at Baen Books, about nuclear weapons, terrorism, the Ayatollah Khomeini, Colonel Kaddafi, the mess in Lebanon, and related topics. It was really just for fun, and we ranged far and wide, and to tell the truth, I remembered little of it months later when she called me up to ask me to contribute a short novel to a book she was editing called After the Flames.

"It's a theme anthology," she told me, "three short novels about nuclear war or its aftermath."

I groaned. I virtually never write stories to order around a theme. My mind just doesn't work that way. I can't come up with a story idea on demand, let alone one that happens to fit someone else's thematic notion, and I told her so.

"But what about what we were talking about at that convention?" Betsy said.

And somehow I knew what she meant. It was a horrific and cold-blooded notion, but I was quite serious about it. Namely, that it might be a good thing if some unstable petty

Third World Dictator got hold of an A-bomb and used it. I had predicted that if such a thing happened once, it would never happen again, because the United States and the Soviet Union would be constrained to act together to teach any such small terrorist nation a lesson the world would never forget.

"Perfect for my book," Betsy told me.

I hesitated. Voicing such a notion in a private bull session was one thing, but detailing it in a short novel was something I didn't quite have the nerve to contemplate at the time.

"Yeah, sure," I drawled off the top of my head, trying to put her off, "but only if I can do it as a comedy."

"A nuclear war comedy?"

"Uh huh," I told her, figuring I had gotten myself off the hook.

"Just what I need. Do it."

"Anything I want?" I said, still searching for an escape route.

"Anything."

"Anything? No taboos?"

Jim Baen, her boss, had published Newt Gingrich's right-wing futurology book. He was a strong supporter of the Strategic Defense Initiative. Although he had also published my own short story collection, The Star Spangled Future, I knew that my politics were way to the left of his, and any nuclear war comedy I was about to write was sure to outrage him; indeed, it would have to if it was going to please me, or so at least at the time I thought.

"Anything," Betsy repeated, and she had me. I had always wanted to try my hand at an extended piece of comic writing anyway, she was giving me carte blanche, and so I threw restraint entirely to the wind and wrote "World War Last." When I was done, I figured I had a story with something to offend everyone.

I submitted the manuscript to Baen Books and waited for the screams of outrage and the rejection letter. They never came.

Betsy and Jim liked it.

A while later, while I was waiting for "World War Last" to be published in After the Flames, I was talking to Shawna McCarthy, editor of Isaac Asimov's Science Fiction Magazine.

"You have any unpublished fiction around?" she asked me. "I've got a big hole in my schedule that I've got to fill."

"Well . . . heh, heh, I've got this novella I wrote for Betsy Mitchell, Shawna, but no one is going to be able to publish a thing like this in a magazine. . . ."

"I published 'Street Meat,' didn't I?" she pointed out.

Well yeah, she had. She had rejected it, but called me back a few hours later and asked me to talk her into buying it after all, and I had. Shawna had more chutzpah than any other magazine editor I knew, but . . .

"But 'World War Last' is a lot grosser than 'Street Meat,'" I told her.

"Grosser than 'Street Meat'?" I could tell she found that rather hard to believe.

"Really, Shawna. You can't get away with printing it in Asimov's without bowdlerizing the hell out of it, and I don't want a cleaned-up version published."

"Try me," she insisted.

And I did.

And she bought it. And she published it with only three lines excised from the definitive version that appeared in After the Flames and that appear in this book.

Can you guess which three?

WORLD WAR LAST

SIX WEEKS BEFORE election day, Elmer Powell, the famous pollster, got a phone call from an anonymous someone at the Korami embassy who made him an offer he could hardly understand, let alone refuse.

Hassan al Korami wished a private consultation, for which he would pay the equivalent of one million dollars in a currency of Powell's own choosing.

There was only one catch: Hassan wanted to talk to him *right now*, meaning that Powell had to fly to Koramibad within the next four hours, take it or leave it.

Powell took it. Three hours later, a limo from the Korami embassy picked him up at his downtown Washington office, an hour and a half after that it had managed to fight its way through the traffic to Dulles International Airport, and fifteen minutes later he was aboard a Korami Airlines Concorde on his way to the tiny Arabian sheikdom.

He seemed to be the only passenger aboard, though it was hard to be sure, since the plane's interior was done up as a series of little private tents. He was served an excellent five-course French meal but no wine or other alcohol was available, though the hookah alongside his luxurious couch was provided with a chunk of hashish the size of a baseball.

After dinner, instead of a movie, a stunning and scantily clad young woman appeared, announced that she was his houri for the flight, and proceeded to transport him to an impressively realistic earthly version of Moslem paradise for as long as his body could take it.

So by the time the plane began its descent over the sere desert wastes towards Koramibad International Airport, Powell was stuffed to the gills, fried to the eyeballs, and screwed silly. He had read the stories on Hassan that appeared now and again in *People, High Times,* and *The National Enquirer,* but now he was beginning to believe them.

The Sheikdom of Koram was a desert principality about the size of Los Angeles County floating like a cork atop an immense pool of oil. The mild earthquakes that rocked the sheikdom from time to time were not, as the bedouins wandering the dunes in their Land Rovers and mobile homes believed, manifestations of the so-called Sacred Rage of Hassan al Korami, but manifestations of the fact that the entire state of Koram was slowly subsiding as the forest of wells that covered it sucked up the oil table below it into Swiss bank accounts.

Hassan the Assassin, Sheik of Koram, practiced and enforced his own stoned-out brand of Islam, which indeed made the Iranian ayatollahs and Shiite Mujadin seem like the effete liberals he often enough called them.

No alcohol. No movies. No TV. No newspapers. No jails. Even minor transgressions were punished by public beheading, unless Hassan was feeling particularly mellow that day, in which case a traffic offender might get off with a mutilation and a stiff warning.

Hashish, however, was legal to the point of being mandatory. Hassan al Korami, as the third son down and not figured to ever inherit the throne, had spent his early manhood playing a hippie Ali Khan in the more disreputable flesh and dope pots of the decadent West, until one day while supposedly reading William Burroughs on acid, he experienced the mystic revelation that made him a Born Again Moslem.

He suddenly began appearing on sleazy cable TV talk shows declaring himself to be the reincarnation of Hassan i Sabah, the legendary Master of the Hashishins. Soon thereafter, his elder brothers expired under rather suspicious circumstances, after which his father was conveniently trampled to death by a herd of camels.

Upon assuming the throne Hassan began preaching a stoned-out form of Islam in which he was the pope and hashish was the sacrament. All his government functionaries and troops were required to be stoned during duty hours in order to maintain the purity of their fanaticism. Random urine checks were done from time to time, and any soldier or official whose piss was found wanting in the residues of tetrahydrocanabinol was given a choice between castration and execution.

He also nominated himself all Islam's destined leader in a Jihad he declared against Israel and periodically proclaimed his intent to drive the Jews into the sea. Since the entire adult male population of Koram was less than fifty thousand, no one took this bellicosity very seriously, except, of course, for the international arms merchants, who supposedly took north of three billion dollars a year out of the bottomless Korami treasury.

Powell, like most westerners, discounted much of this as stoned hyperbole, but upon debarking from the Concorde onto the broiling tarmac, stoned as he was, he still had to admit that seeing was believing.

A soaring Bauhaus terminal highlighted with incongruous minarets and a great golden dome was the centerpiece of Koramibad International Airport. Surrounding this monstrosity and seeming to occupy every square foot of the huge airport save the main runway was a veritable junkyard of jet fighters of all nations, bleaching and rusting in the cruel desert sun.

American F-16s, F-15s, F-21s. Russian Mig 21s and 27s. French Mirage 3000s and Super Entendards. Swedish Saabs. British Super Harriers. Good lord, there were even Israeli Kfirs, as if Hassan just *had* to complete his collection.

It must have been the third largest air force in the world after the Russian and American, and surely the Israelis would be in deep shit indeed if Hassan ever found enough pilots to put half of it in the air before it rusted away to rubble. But fortunately, mercenaries avoided Koram like the clap despite the high wages, since they were required to live under the draconian laws of the self-styled Scourge of the Infidel and fly stoned as well, and the few Korami natives who tried their hands from time to time bought the farm after a month or two.

An air-conditioned Rolls waited at the foot of the ramp, presided over by two of al Korami's Hashishins, replete with kafiyahs, Kalashnikovs, and enormous spliffs, and Powell was ushered into the back seat, handed another of the gigantic joints, and treated to a wild ride to the palace.

Koramibad, such as it was, had been built from scratch in a few years at unthinkable expense in order to provide a sheikdom with a population of no more than one hundred thousand with Hassan al Korami's version of a world-class metropole and capital.

A huge lakebed had been excavated, lined with concrete, and then filled with water, which by now was as brackish as the Dead Sea. Koramibad itself was built on an artificial island in the middle of Lake Korami. The city could be reached only by air, since there were no bridges over the lake, and the island was encircled by a fifty-foot-high concrete wall studded at ten-meter intervals with machine-gun emplacements; Hassan al Korami had no intention of suffering the fate of Hassan or his own father.

An eight-lane freeway circled the city replete with electronic slogan boards and access control systems at the numerous on-ramps, though the only traffic on it were tanks and armored personnel carriers whenever Hassan's wacked-out troops managed to get some of them moving. Another freeway, somewhat more functional, connected the airport with the palace.

The rest of the city was one vast empty Potemkin Village. Broad radial avenues linked with huge parched-looking cedars kept barely alive with sprinkler systems at hideous expense converged on the central palace compound. Huge empty luxury apartment towers in perfect repair stood along most of these spotless and deserted streets. Other avenues sported ornate branches belonging to every major bank in the world. There was a Hilton, a Sheraton, a Meridien, a Ramada Inn, and a replica of the Waldorf Astoria, all subsidized and kept afloat by the Korami treasury. Similarly, the empty Macy's, Bloomingdale's, Harrod's, and GUM branches owed their survival to government subsidies, though Gucci, Tiffany, the Rolls Royce dealership, and Frederick's of Hollywood managed to survive on their own.

As the Rolls careened crazily toward the palace, Powell caught glimpses of what lay between the vast aisles of empty monoliths, to wit, enormous car parks choked with Hassan al Korami's impressive accumulation of tanks, armored personnel carriers, mobile artillery, Katushka rocket launchers, antiaircraft guns, jeeps, and assorted armored cars.

Powell found himself sucking nervously on his spliff and wishing for a few good, stiff drinks as the Rolls crossed the drawbridge over the moat that surrounded the palace, for the moat swarmed with huge, hungry Nile crocodiles and the spikes that studded the top of the palace compound wall were decorated with the rotting heads of minor criminals.

Inside, however, was a fair version of a desert-dweller's vision of paradise. The palace compound was built around a central garden done up as an Amazon rain forest. Scores, perhaps hundreds, of naked and splendid houris wandered about entertaining the troops. Parrots screeched, monkeys flitted through the treetops, and as Powell was ushered toward Korami's personal residence itself, he could hear a nasal version of Ravel's *Bolero* playing endlessly from hidden speakers.

Hassan al Korami's manse itself was a fifth-scale replica of the Taj Mahal replete wih reflecting pool, and the throne room was a large, round, high-ceilinged chamber dripping with gold filigree studded with rubies, sapphires, and emeralds.

On a black marble dais in the center of the chamber, a vibrating skeletal figure in a white silk burnoose heavily embroidered in gold reclined on a vast, cushioned, golden throne sucking avidly on the ivory mouthpiece of an enormous hookah. Flanking the throne were a brace of Kalashnikov-toting Hashishins gumming the standard-issue spliffs. A semicircle of huge plush cushions faced the throne, each provided with its own hookah. On one of these reclined an elegantly coifed silver-haired man in a tan Yves Saint Laurent suit chewing nervously on the mouthpiece of his hookah as the man on the throne ranted and raved at him.

"Nukes, Armand, *nukes!*" demanded Hassan al Korami. "Me want me *nukes!* It's not as if I were demanding Trident submarines, or Stealth Bombers, or SS-25s, or even MX missiles! A few dozen Tomahawk cruise missiles will suffice, a brace of Pershings, by the beard of the prophet, I would even settle for some of those ancient B-52s that the Americans are planning to sell for scrap anyway. I would even pay well for a few Vulcans, if worse came to worse, surely at least the bankrupt British cannot afford to turn me down!"

With his long wild black hair, great flowing black beard, and huge glowing brown bloodshot eyes, the Scourge of the Infidel reminded Powell of nothing so much as a speed-freak Rasputin.

"Were it up to me, mon ami," said the urbane, silver-haired man, "I would be pleased to provide your Sacred Cause with all the megatonnage and delivery systems you can afford. But alas, you have declared the Americans the Great Satan, the Russians godless atheistic devils, the British effete limey bastards, the Germans krautheaded sons of bitches, the Chinese opium-eating degenerates, and the French a nation of frog-eating faggots. This, unfortunately, does not quite entice any of them to be cooperative. . . ."

"What!" screamed al Korami. "You dare to blame my courageous declarations of Allah's own truth for your own failures, you effete krautheaded limey frog-eating degenerate devil running dog of the Great Satan!"

The guards cocked their Kalashnikovs eagerly. The silver-haired man coughed out a great lungful of smoke, trembling.

"Non, no, nein!" he exclaimed. "For who can deny the truth of your words, oh Lion of the Desert! Only spare this worthless servant, and I shall redouble my efforts in your behalf, for there may be a way.... Naturellement, it will be somewhat expensive...."

"Nukes!" roared Hassan al Korami. "Me want me *nukes*! Move your ass you perfidious infidel, and do not return without them!"

"I hear and obey, oh Scourge of the Infidel," the silver-haired man declared, rising to his feet and bobbing his head in an endless series of bows as he backed out of the throne room past Elmer Powell, who stood there transfixed, sweating in his socks.

He favored Powell with a little smile and a wink en passant. "You are in luck, mon ami," he whispered sotto voce. "He's in a good mood today."

"*Elmer Powell?*" demanded Hassan al Korami, glaring at him with his great, hash-reddened eyes.

"The same, your Majesty, your Magnificence, your ah...ah..." Powell stammered in no little terror.

"Be seated, Elmer Powell," Hassan commanded. "Toke up! Get your shit together with this primo Afghani!"

Powell collapsed onto the nearest cushion and sucked in a great lungful of smoke.

Hassan al Korami glowered at him. "One question you will answer, oh pundit of the infidels! Speak truly, and I will shower your Swiss bank account with tax-free hard currency, speak falsely, and I will add your head to the collection on my palace wall!"

"Trust me...." Powell muttered fearfully, wondering what was coming next. Some cryptic Sufic riddle? Some deadly zen koan? Some Koranic conundrum?

The Scourge of the Infidel puffed thoughtfully on his hookah. "Who," he finally demanded, "will be the next president of the United States?"

"*What?*"

"I have not yet torn out your tongue, have I? You are the same Elmer Powell who conducts the Powell Poll, are you not? Speak! Who is going to win the American presidential election?"

Elmer Powell let out a great sigh of smoke, befuddlement, and relief. "Samuel T. Carruthers," he said.

Hassan eyed him peculiarly. "You are certain?" he said. "That asshole? On this you stake your life . . . ?"

"Popular vote sixty percent to forty percent, plus or minus five points, minimum of three hundred electoral votes, unless he drops dead or turns into a raving maniac on the tube before election day, and even then it would probably be no worse than even money," Powell said confidently. "It's a lock. America loves Uncle Sam."

Hassan al Korami broke into raucous laughter. "America loves Uncle Sam!" he howled as if it were the punch line of his favorite joke, and then he broke up again, rolling his eyes, shaking with mirth, and spraying spittle, a wired Rasputin indeed.

Still fairly gibbering with laughter, he waved a negligent hand in Powell's general direction. One of the guards yanked Powell to his feet and began escorting him out of the throne room.

"That's it?" Powell exclaimed. "A million dollars? An eight-hour, round-trip plane ride? Just for—"

"Mysterious are the ways of Hassan the Assassin," said the guard, jamming another spliff into his mouth. "Be cool, and don't make waves."

Only three weeks to go until election day and Samuel T. Carruthers was riding high and wide if not exactly handsome toward the apotheosis of his American Dream, a success story such as was possible only in the Land of the Free and the Home of the Brave! Where else but under the Red, White, and Blue could the proprietor of a seedy used car lot in Santa Ana, California, rise in glory within a decade to become president of the United States?

After serving his country in the crummy jungles of Central America for three years as a supply sergeant, Carruthers had skimmed just enough capital to leverage the purchase of a tacky used car lot in Santa Ana and its unsavory inventory of ancient clunkers. Shortly thereafter, while cruising along the Santa Ana freeway in his five-year-old Buick, he had driven by a billboard near Knott's Berry Farm and been born again with the inspiration that was to change the course of history.

A cartoon Uncle Sam stood quite literally knee-deep in a sea of red ink glowering at the passing motorists and pointing an admonishing finger. Plowing through the waves around his kneecaps were a series of Chinese-type ships flying Japanese flags and piled to the gunwales with cars, VCRs, TV sets, and robots.

"Buy American!" shouted Uncle Sam in red, white, and blue letters, and lest anyone miss the point, the boats on the billboard also flew banners proclaiming, "Cheap Jap Junk."

"That's *it*, Margot!" Carruthers exclaimed, slapping his wife on the thigh with such distraction that he almost sideswiped the Toyota in the next lane.

"Up yours, you unpatriotic asshole!" he shouted at the Toyota driver when that worthy had the temerity to honk at his 100 percent red-blooded Detroit Iron. "Praise God, and our massive trade deficit, I've seen the light!"

And so, as it turned out, he had.

Carruthers sold off every foreign-made car on his lot at a dead loss, took out a third mortgage on his house, and restocked with the cheapest collection of crummy old American gas-guzzlers he could find. He renamed the establishment "Uncle Sam Carruthers's Red White and Blue One Hundred Percent American Used Car Lot." He bought himself a fraying Uncle Sam suit at a costume shop, had Margot let it out to more or less encompass his paunch, stuffed himself into it, bought commercial time on a local TV station, and, in the grand tradition of Southern Californian superstar used car salesmen, began starring in his own TV commericals, introducing the world to the spiel that, ten years and one bankruptcy later, was to make him president of the United States.

"Come on *down*, come on down to Uncle Sam Carruthers's Red White and Blue One Hundred Percent American Used Car Lot!" he would declare as he stood before his clunkers in his Uncle Sam suit. "Wouldn't you rather buy an *American* used car from your old Uncle Sam than some overpriced piece of unpatriotic crap from a traitor to the American Way of Life? If you can't trust your old Uncle Sam, then *who can you trust*? Come on down, come on *down*, lookee here, lookee here, my fellow Americans, why here we have a 1985 Dodge Van, AM-FM stereo, power everything, and only fifty-five thousand miles on the clock or fry me for a Rooshian, and the first five thousand takes it. Now I'm only willing to let this one go at such a loss because this cherry little darling was previously owned by a *genuine* American hero serving his country in Patagonia who was forced to put it on consignment due to war wounds, which necessitate trading it in on a hand-control model, and this brave lad can't get back on the road until I move this one off the lot and into the loving hands of one of you lucky patriots. . . .

"Come on down, come on *down*, and drive away with this 1980 Cadillac Seville, a mere seventy-five thousand on the clock, and every last mile put on driving to church by a Gold Star Mother forced to sell it off and go on *welfare* when her husband lost his job at the Ford plant to coolie labor in Korea. . . ."

Well what with the temporary oil glut of those years, and the rekindled sense of American patriotism, and the Buy American movement, and the unemployment, Uncle Sam Carruthers struck a chord in the public psyche. Not only was he able to move a lot of old moldy Detroit Iron at premium prices by wrapping his clunkers in the flag, he became as much a media hero as Ralph Williams or Cal Worthington ever had and then some, and was even invited from time to time to make the local LA talk-show circuit.

It was on one of these talk shows that he met the Reverend Allan Edward Wintergreen, and was born again as a franchiser.

Wintergreen was one of the most successful TV preachers in the country and certainly the richest, for he not only solicited contributions on his syndicated TV hour like all the others, he was the only one who sold *commercial time* between the sermons and the disco choir.

"God has brought us together to save the Nation and make mucho dinero in the process, my boy," he told Carruthers, and once the silver-tongued preacher and his accountant laid it out in dollars and cents, Carruthers Saw the Light again.

Why not *franchise* a nationwide chain of Uncle Sam Carruthers's Red White and Blue One Hundred Percent American Used Car Lots? For 10 percent of the gross, the franchisee got to use the name and reap the benefit of the commercials that Uncle Sam Carruthers did on the Reverend Allan Edward Wintergreen's nationally syndicated TV show.

And since Carruthers was already mortgaged up to the eyeballs, the Reverend Wintergreen, who was rolling in dough, easily enough persuaded himself to put up the necessary capital in return for a mere 49 percent of the action.

All went swimmingly until the Great Oil Famine, when the oil-producing countries wised up, suspended production entirely for three months, and then doubled the price.

All at once, Red White and Blue One Hundred Percent American gas-guzzling old Detroit Iron became virtually worthless and not all the patriotic appeals to national honor could move it off the lots, and franchisees went belly-up all across the country, soon to be followed by the home office itself, whose bankruptcy even threatened to drag down the Reverend Wintergreen's Church of Revealed Wisdom.

Broke, famous, without a pot to piss in or any prospects, what else could Uncle Sam Carruthers do but run for the United States Senate? It was an easy transition. He just continued to run more or less the same commercials on the Reverend Wintergreen's TV show peddling his own ass instead of used cars, and made his live appearances in the same Uncle Sam suit, railing against the A-rabs and the Nips and the Rooshians who had done his business and the national enterprise in.

When the long-retired Johnny Carson refused to run against him, his election as junior senator from California was assured, and he hit Washington already a national hero. His picture was on *Time* and *Newsweek* and *People* and he even made the cover of *Rolling Stone*. He refused to waste his time with boring committee assignments and instead concentrated on using the national TV coverage of the Senate floor to best advantage, rambling on for at least an hour a week for the next four years, so that by the time the presidential primary season approached, he had twice the face and name recognition of his closest rival in the polls.

So too did the election itself turn into a Red White and Blue Cakewalk, for Uncle Sam was the most seasoned TV performer presidential politics had seen since Ronald Reagan, and not even Reagan had had the chutzpah to do his act in costume.

To clinch it, Reverend Wintergreen had twisted enough arms in the party hierarchy to make them hold their noses and nominate his fellow TV preacher, Fast Eddie Braithewaite, for vice president.

Fast Eddie had first intruded upon the public consciousness as "The American Bob Marley," whose disco reggae records may never have climbed very high in the charts, but whose Reformed Rasta rap was good enough to launch him on a second career as a TV evangelist of a peculiar sort when his pipes began to give out in middle age.

"Lack of cash is the greatest evil in Babylon," he told his viewers. "All men are green in the eyes of Jah! No peckerwood's about to call you a nigger if you got a wallet full of credit cards, mon! Cast your bread upon the waters of Zion, and ye shall for sure be saved! It's *your* love donations that let me loan out money at two points under the prime! Together, we build our Zion in the Belly of the Beast, and together, we make the First TV Bank of Babylon a Fortune Five Hundred Company!"

It was a stroke of genius, for while most blacks viewed Uncle Sam Carruthers as a honkie asshole and while more blacks than not viewed Fast Eddie Braithewaite as a con artist, how many blacks, in the privacy of the voting booth, could refrain from voting for the first *black* con artist to make the national ticket?

Moreover, this was also a dream ticket that rednecks and bigots could vote for with pride; they could vote for Uncle Sam Carruthers's Red White and Blue jingoism and feel smug about displaying their nonexistent American sense of racial fair play in the bargain.

As for how either of these boobs could be expected to function as president, well, that was the sort of situation that the pros behind the scenes and the moneymen behind the pols knew could be professionally managed.

Three weeks from election day, riding high in the polls, Samuel T. Carruthers, accompanied by two Secret Service men, went into the men's room after gorging himself on rubber chicken at a fund-raising speech at the Century Plaza Hotel.

Five minutes passed, ten, a quarter of an hour, while the press secretary and the campaign manager fidgeted nervously, hoping Carruthers hadn't come down with the trots again, but somewhat fastidiously reluctant to interrupt the Great Man on the pot to inquire after the state of his bowel movements.

But after half an hour of this, there seemed nothing for it but to drag him off the crapper in time to make the plane to Minnesota.

The men's room was empty aside from two pairs of legs

visible in adjacent toilet stalls. These proved to be the two Secret Service men, bound and gagged with their pants down around their ankles. The last thing they remembered was entering the men's room and being assailed by a horrible stench. When they woke up, they were tied and gagged on the toilet seats, and the next president of the United States was gone.

Just as they were all about to dash out of the john to raise posse and pandemonium, the press secretary's pocket phone rang.

"This is the Mendocino Liberation Front, running dog of the Drug Enforcement Agency, and we've got Carruthers stuffed in a gunny sack on the way to our secret headquarters in the Sierras," said a shrill, nasal, female voice. "Now listen carefully, here's the deal. We just want to like *educate* the next president of the United States for twenty-four hours, if you do what you're told, you can have the asshole back after that and no one's the wiser. But if a word of this gets to the press or any police agency, we'll feed him feet first into a tree-chipper, and mail his head to the *Washington Post*. Power and profit to the Pot Farmers of America and our national trade balance! Boycott Colombian Imports! Buy American-grown Dope!"

The press secretary and the campaign manager did some fast, hard, professional management thinking. If these maniacs did kill Carruthers and mail his head to the press, they'd be left with *Fast Eddie Braithewaite* at the head of their ticket. If they lost, they'd all be out of jobs, and if they won, they'd be out on the streets anyway, because that crazy nigger hated their guts. If they did as they were told, there was at least some chance they would get their meal ticket back.

Bottomlinewise, the smart money said keep your mouth shut and manage the situation as best you can as long as you can, like the Russians had been doing with the corpse of Pyotr Ivanovich Bulgorny for at least five years. After all, they were sophisticated professionals, and Uncle Sam Carruthers had not yet even croaked. Surely if the Russians could pull it off for all these years, American know-how could manage such a situation for at least twenty-four hours.

Fast Eddie Braithewaite had smelled the unmistakable odor of bullshit since the closing couple of weeks of the campaign. For one thing, while he and Carruthers had never exactly partied together, now neither he, nor anyone he had talked to, had even been allowed in the same room with him by the campaign staff. They flooded the air with a blizzard of old taped commercials, they cut old footage into a phony live interview show, and Samuel T. Carruthers made only a dozen or so more live appearances, the news coverage of which made it seem that he was luded out and badly lip syncing a tape.

His victory speech had been broadcast late at night from his hotel room instead of in front of his loyal supporters and he had nodded off halfway through it and had to be elbowed in the ribs not quite off camera.

Between election night and the inauguration, they kept him closeted on some private estate in Palm Springs putting together his government, and sure enough the expected gang of the usual suspects was rounded up for the cabinet and the pros on the campaign staff segued into the White House.

Samuel T. Carruthers's Inaugural Day performance was more than Fast Eddie could finally pretend wasn't happening. He had taken the oath like a zombie on methedrine, babbling the whole thing out twice before the chief justice could more than open his mouth. During his speech, his mouth was hidden by a badly placed podium, and he stood there staring motionless into space as if his feet had been nailed to the floor.

The day after that, Fast Eddie had stormed into the White House staff meeting and demanded to see the president on threat of going to the press and telling them that he was taking over under the Twenty-third Amendment because the president had been captured in a palace coup.

"Don't say you didn't ask for this then," the White House chief of staff had told him with a peculiar expression, and he and the entire inner circle stuffed themselves into helicopters, which took them to Camp David.

The main lodge had been transformed. Half of it had been turned into an elaborate television studio and the other half of it was now some kind of medical facility.

"Where you got the fat boy stuffed?" Fast Eddie demanded.

"In a nice safe place."

They took him down a hall toward what had been the master bedroom. The wooden door had been replaced with a steel slab with a wire-barred window.

The press secretary whistled *Hail to the Chief*.

"Mr. Speaker, Members of Congress, Distinguished Guests, my fellow Americans," said the national security adviser, inviting Fast Eddie's attention to the window, "the President of the United States."

The entire bedroom had been turned into a huge and luxurious padded cell. Within, Samuel T. Carruthers sat naked on the pale-beige matting, babbling to himself and jerking off.

"Pussy, One Hundred Percent American Made Pussy in Red White and Blue cheerleader skirts put out for Uncle Sam as American as Apple Pie no cheap Jap junk..."

"As you can see," said the press secretary, "we are having temporary technical difficulties."

"But nothing that can't be managed in a professional manner," said the chief of staff, and before Fast Eddie could even get his gaping mouth to close, they had hustled him off into a nearby cabin to talk bottom line.

"Be special nice to me, turkies," Fast Eddie told them, "'cause I'm going to be the president of this Babylon in about the next two bars, mon! I mean, you got yourselves a crazy man in there, first time you need him live, they farm him to the bughouse and throw away the key."

The interchangeable faces of the White House staff had the same smug interchangeable smiles of bureaucratic patronization painted across them as the White House staff sat there in their interchangeable conservative business suits looking down their thin little noses at the nigger who unfortunately for them was about to become president of the United States.

Velveeta and Kool Whip on Wonder Bread, mon! Fast Eddie was going to enjoy kicking their tight white asses out onto the end of the long unemployment lines where they belonged!

"What happened to the man? How long have you guys been sitting on this?" he demanded. "Speak true, or when I take over and lift the lid off this garbage can, you'll all have free unpaid vacations in Allenwood!"

"The president has merely been the victim of a terrorist act, from which the doctors assure us he will soon recover, if they want to keep their jobs," said the chief of staff.

"Terrorist act?"

"Something called the Mendocino Liberation Front had him for twenty-four hours."

"We found him on one of those chicken ranches in

Nevada in a pretty heavy bondage scene," said the press secretary.

"To hear Uncle Sam tell it, they pumped him full of amphetamine, LSD, and L-dopa, and let him run wild in a roomful of jaded hookers for a day and a night. . . ."

"Disgust you to hear it. . . ."

"But nothing, Mr. Vice President, that we can't *manage*. . . ."

"Media techniques are much more sophisticated than you might suppose these days," the press secretary said. "We have enough audio and videotape we can computer-process to have Uncle Sam up and spouting brightly on the tube anything we want him to say. We have three actors undergoing plastic surgery to do live appearances. We can manage with a president who's crazy as a bedbug—"

"—After all, the Russians are still managing with Pyotr Ivanovich Bulgorny—"

"And everyone knows he's been dead for at least eight years."

"This may be Babylon, but it ain't Russia yet, my man," Fast Eddie said. "If the vice president of the United States goes on the tube claiming the president is nuts, you're gonna have to show the fat boy doing his thing live in public. I'll demand fingerprint tests, I'll have dentists do a hologram of his teeth with lasers, and when he gets thrown in the bin, I'll be president and your asses are grasses."

"I don't think you're going to want to do that," said the national security adviser. "I mean, that might compromise national security, if you get me, and you might have to be terminated with extreme cement overshoes."

"Mon, you think you can snuff the vice president of the United States before I get the people to listen to me?"

The press secretary laughed. "Credibilitywise, your Nielsen will be zero, kiddo," he said. "*No one* will believe that Uncle Sam is a drooling sex maniac because no one will *want* to. Because if Uncle Sam is a drooling sex maniac, then they've got themselves *you* for president. . . ."

"Besides," said the national security adviser, "there's always the Bulgorny option for the likes of you if you become too much of a problem."

"The Bulgorny option . . . ?" Fast Eddie said, suddenly quite sure that this dude meant some very extreme business.

"I mean, if the Russians can trot out Bulgorny to stand on Lenin's tomb twice a year and make a speech to the

Supreme Soviet just when people are getting to think he's gotten too moldy, you think we can't stuff and wire a vice president the same way to stand like a stiff at funerals?"

"And the first funeral you perform at if you open your mouth will be your own, Mr. Vice President," said the chief of staff. "We'll trot you out before the cameras and have you tell the Nation your ridiculous charges were the result of drinking too much cheap port wine and you won't feel a thing. You won't even be there."

"See, Mr. Vice President, it's all under control," said the national security adviser. "We've done a run on every possible scenario, we've covered all the angles. I'm sure that you'll now agree that we can manage just fine with a maniac in the White House and an audioanimatrated stiff for vice president if we have to."

"Well when you put it that way," owned the vice president nervously, "it's kind of hard to argue with your logic."

Purchasing hashish in Moscow, like everything else, required stable, secure connections, connections with a class self-interest in never selling you out to the authorities. Since no Soviet Citizen could reliably predict when or whether he might find himself in Lubianka negotiating his own survival, finding a hashish connection with a minimal risk was no mean feat.

And indeed, by very virtue of being free-market profiteers in the hashish trade, they were all both antiparty elements by definition and employees, if not agents, of the KGB.

The Red Army had not only lost considerable clout on the Politburo over the Afghanistan fiasco, they had so bungled the economic situation, that Sergei Polikov, the czar of the KGB, had come out of it with all-but-total control of the whole hashish trade.

Now all the caravans led straight across the border into Turkestan where 250,000 Soviet troops lurked conspicuously, ready to blitzkrieg their way back into Afghanistan, should the Mujadin violate their part of the bargain.

Under these conditions, the Red Army could more or less keep their troops free of hashish dependency as long as they were stationed far away from major cities, the Soviet Union secured desperately needed hard currency, and the KGB could control the supply, set the prices, and limit the amount of hash that filtered into the domestic market from the vast reexport trade.

No doubt having secured control of the total supply, the KGB could just as easily have entirely eliminated the vast population of hash smokers that had blossomed in the Soviet Union during the period when 200,000 soldiers rotating in and out of Afghanistan every year had gone into business for themselves as free-market profiteers.

But by the time they cut the deal to end the war, Sergei Polikov saw that there were political as well as economic advantages to allowing the domestic trade to continue. Every dealer had to get his supply from someone else who sooner or later had to get it from the KGB. So the KGB could access the identity of any one of the hundreds of thousands of petty economic parasites involved in the trade, which meant that any one of them could be induced to inform when required. And these dealers, in turn, knew the identity, collectively, of several million Soviet Citizens who were guilty of an infraction punishable by five years' internal exile.

Never before had the KGB succeeded in extending its fine tendrils this far into the tender flesh of the masses. Somewhere in that Great Interrogation Cell in the Sky, Joseph Stalin and Lavrenti Beria were no doubt turning green with envy.

Ivan Igorovich Gornikov, however, had found, or been found by, a source with the mystical power to render itself invisible to the KGB.

Mustapha Kamani was a cultural attache at the Korami embassy, and seeing as how Koram had no culture to speak of to export, Korami's true business in Moscow could be only one thing—purchasing agent for the government of Hassan al Korami, the largest single customer the KGB had.

No doubt the hash Kamani sold to a few favored Russian friends was skimmed from shipments going back to Koram, and therefore already signed, paid for, and disposed of on the KGB's books. Not even Sergei Polikov, indeed especially not Sergei Polikov, would ever arrest a golden goose with diplomatic immunity.

And indeed even if he did, Kamani knew what would happen to him if he stooled on his Russian contacts, for his Russian contacts, at least the ones that Ivan knew, were all, like himself, comrades in the Computer Underground. In fact, there wouldn't even *be* a Soviet Computer Underground were it not for the Korami involvement.

While Hassan al Korami was reputedly quite able to pay for the tons of hashish he bought each year from the KGB out of petty cash, Koram had contrived to force the KGB to accept a portion of the price in rubles, and these rubles were acquired by smuggling in computer equipment in return diplomatic pouches, and selling the stuff to hardware-starved Russians at obscene prices. An ancient MacIntosh could fetch fifteen thousand rubles, the latest IBM mini would set you back fifty thousand, and people had been known to shell out five thousand for a 16k Sinclair. As for dot-matrix printers, these were worth their weight in caviar, since one could distribute samizdat on discs and print out copies at two hundred cps.

There was only one thing that the KGB hated more than the Computer Underground, and that was the thought of losing the billions of hard dollars that Koram spent on hash in the Soviet Union each year.

But Ivan knew that if *he* were ever exposed as a member of the Computer Underground, if the KGB learned that *he* was being supplied with hash by the embassy of Koram, the whole game would be up for everyone.

For Ivan Igorovich Gornikov was the day-shift operator on the Bulgorny, one of the select few with access to the software that was the Chairman of the Central Committee of the Soviet Communist Party and President of the Union of Soviet Socialist Republics.

And Ivan had taken great care to inform Mustapha Kamani of the hacking he had done on the Bulgorny, the better to motivate him into hoping he was never exposed as the foreign agent who had known this and had continued to get him stoned.

Which was why there was no real tension in the apartment that Kamani maintained across town from the embassy, for everyone there knew each other, they were all desperate characters, and everyone had every reason not to betray anyone else.

There was Boris, the night-shift operator on the Bulgorny, and Tanya, who worked on the team that compiled the statistics at the Ministry of Agriculture, and Anatoly, who wrote programs that set production quotas for TV sets, cars, and toilet paper, and Grishka, who ran the computer that dealt with the waiting lists for apartments for all of Moscow. Among them, they had put enough bugs, practical jokes, and random noise into the software of state to send them all to Siberia for a million years if anyone found out, and they spent their stoned-out seances here in Mustapha Kamani's apartment vying with each other to do more.

"... so the half share in a one-room flat went to the professor of astrophysics, and the bubba who used to sweep the street outside got the luxury penthouse...."

"... which is why when next you crank him up to address the Supreme Soviet, Comrade Bulgorny will be able to boast that we lead the world in the production of toilet paper, though most of the people will still have to use *Pravda* since it has all been shipped to Novosibirsk...."

"If only we dared to really have him say that!" Boris exclaimed as Kamani wrapped up a take-home for him in toilet paper, as if to boast of his unlimited access to such luxury items.

"Why not?" said Ivan. "All we have to do is mail-merge some old speeches on toilet paper production quotas with the stock attack on distribution inefficiencies when they ask for something to have him boast about and something with which to belabor the petty bureaucrats who are responsible for everything that goes wrong."

"Low toilet humor, if you ask me," giggled Tanya. "Boys will be boys."

"Perhaps one of you would care to part with two thousand rubles in return for *this*?" Mustapha Kamini suddenly said theatrically, pulling a floppy out of a pocket.

"Two thousand rubles for a piece of *software*?" Grishka scoffed. "Come off it, Mustapha, we can all write our own, thank you."

"Perhaps you are right, I am far from versed in such matters, though those who are have told me that there has never been such an insidious little bedbug as *this*," Kamani said, toking on the communal hookah.

"Oh?"

"What does it do?"

"It is called the Joker, my young friends, all the rage in western circles, according to the bourgeois press. It is written around a random number generator that as you might say disappears into the system without a trace and overlays the interface of everything with everything. And once you've introduced it, there's no way of getting it out, short of wiping all the data and programs in the memory bank. . . ."

"Hashish for computers!" exclaimed Boris. "Why shouldn't they have some fun too?"

Ivan laughed. "Why shouldn't *Pyotr Ivanovich* have a chance to get stoned?" he said. "The poor bastard probably hasn't had any fun since he died."

"*The Bulgorny?*" exclaimed Boris. "You would randomize the programs and barble the memory banks of our beloved Party chairman? You would have the Bulgorny begin babbling like Khrushchev on vodka?"

"Even better than that," Ivan said. "Remember, if the forces on the Politburo hadn't been in such perfectly balanced deadlock all these years, they would long since have buried Bulgorny in Lenin's tomb where he belongs and agreed on a live successor. . . ."

"The decision-making program!" exclaimed Boris.

"That's right, this little bedbug would randomize that too!"

"I love it, Ivan, I love it!"

"What are you two *talking about*?" Tanya demanded crossly.

"The deepest, darkest secret of the Soviet state," Boris said, pulling on the hookah. "Shall we tell them, Ivan?"

"Are we not all comrades of the Computer Underground, Boris?" Ivan said, filling his lungs with smoke.

"The Politburo, as you can well imagine, is frequently deadlocked," he told them. "In the old days, when you had a live Party chairman and no one could muster a majority against him, that was that. Now they ask the Bulgorny to break deadlocks."

"*The Bulgorny!*" exclaimed Grishka. "But Pyotr Ivanovich has been dead for four years!"

"Eight."

"Six."

"Whatever. The chairman is just an embalmed corpse wired for motion and sound, how can such a thing decide anything?"

"Each member of the Politburo has a weighted vote calculated by the computer according to his current rating in the power struggle as determined by secret polling of his rivals. These are tabulated statistically via an Australian ballot system until a mathematical consensus emerges. This is interfaced with the memory banks via an index program, which selects and edits old Bulgorny speeches so that the chairman can announce his decisions in his own familiar, deadly prose."

"Bulgorny can write his own speeches?" Grishka said.

"Better than he did when he was alive," said Boris. "The computer that controls him remembers every boring word he ever uttered, and if he were alive to suffer that, it would surely kill him!"

"And if this Joker program inserts random interfaces between the statistical data and the tabulation..."

"And between the decision-making program and the memory banks, where the index program should be..."

"Then decisions of the Soviet state will be made by rolling the software bones...."

"And Pyotr Ivanovich Bulgorny will deliver them in gibberish...."

"Which no one will dare point out...."

"Which everyone must therefore pretend to understand...."

"And they won't be able to fix it without finally burying the chairman...."

"Which they'll never do until the corpse starts to rot!"

Mustapha Kamani had been lying back and sucking on his hookah during all of this, nursing a secret little smile. Now that smile became a supercilious grin. "Ah, you Russians are such a marvelous people!" he said. "In the effete West, this Joker program is used for mere sport, practical jokers insert it in each other's video games, and scramble the data of collection agencies, but here in Mother Russia, it becomes a weapon against the state."

"Come on, lighten up, Mustapha!" Tanya said. "We're not enemies of the state."

"We're hackers, not anti-Soviet elements."

"And hackers just want to have fun."

Armand Deutcher slurped down another oyster with a hefty swallow of Muscadet, then leaned back in his chair expansively, as if to wrap himself in the aura of La Coupole. Once, long ago, this noisy barn of a Montparnasse café had been a gathering place for somber Parisian existentialists, later a show business hangout, then a tourist trap, and now it was a huge house of assignations for the arms dealers, foreign agents, and American political exiles who were said to make up a quarter of Paris's current population. It was a place one went to for ambience, not haute cuisine or noble vintages, but there was little the chef could do to ruin raw oysters in season.

"Surely you would not wish to see this contract go to East Bloc sources, Zvi," Deutcher said. "You're my last hope, unless you agree to supply the warheads, Hassan will turn to the Soviets, and we'll lose the delivery system deal as well."

"Even from you, I can't believe this," Zvi Bar David said, spooning a gooey dark morsel of profitrole au chocolat into his mouth. "Even the Russians aren't crazy enough to sell nuclear missiles to a maniac like Hassan al Korami, and we both know it. *Israel* should sell him nukes? As if he'd buy them from us in the first place!"

"Ah but naturellement, he is never to know that his warheads are Israeli," Deutcher said. "You will deliver them to the South Africans, who will allow them to pass over to Zaire, who will sell them to the Angolans, who will assure the Koramis that they were made in Czechoslovakia and bartered to the Cubans through East Germany in return for mercenary troops to fight the Rastafarian resistance in South Jamaica."

"What can you possibly imagine would induce us to do such a thing?"

"What else?" Deutcher said good-naturedly. "Money!"

"Surely you cannot expect us to sell nuclear weapons to that anti-Semitic maniac at any price!"

"You sold him those Kfirs, didn't you?"

"We sold them to Singapore, who sold them to Taiwan, who moved them to the Chinese through Hong Kong, who bartered them to the Iranians for oil, and the Iranians told Koram that they had picked them up when the Brazilians overran Paraguay."

"Come, come, Zvi, be all that as it may, the Mossad certainly knew where they were going!"

Zvi Bar David shrugged. "Who could resist?" he admitted with a grin. "They were Yom Kippur War vintage junk. Not even the Haitians would buy them. If we had surplus Spitfires, we'd be happy to unload the mess on Hassan too! But we're certainly not going to sell Koram ordnance that they can really use against us, let alone nuclear warheads!"

"But of course, mon ami," Deutcher said slyly. "Au contraire, what I propose is that we together sell Koram twenty nuclear missiles for ten billion dollars that *you* can use against *him*."

Bar David eyed him narrowly now, wiping chocolate sauce from his chin. Armand Deutcher nodded.

"From Senegal via Algeria, I have acquired twenty truly moldy American F-111s that the Vietnamese appropriated way back when they overran Saigon," he told Bar David. "At ten percent over scrap prices, since their airframes and and engines have only a few thousand miles left in them and not even a kamikaze pilot would dare to try to fly them. . . ."

"They were dreadful dogs even when they were new, as I remember," Bar David observed critically.

Deutcher nodded. "A shining example of American overcomplication," he agreed. "But bon chance for us, for the Americans equipped these aircraft with low-level, terrain-hugging radar systems, the immediate forerunner of the cruise missile systems they developed later. . . ."

"I seem to remember some small problem with the swing-wings falling off. . . ."

"Ah, but that is not *our* problem, now is it, Zvi?" Deutcher said airily. "As fighter-bombers, they may be disasters, but imagine them as big, cheap, fast, highly unreliable cruise missiles!"

"I think I'm beginning to get your drift, Armand. . . ."

"But of course! Stick some kind of crude nuclear device in the bomb bay, wire it up with remote controls off your supersonic reconnaissance drones, and voila, twenty cut-rate supersonic medium-range cruise missiles that should cost us about half a million apiece at worst to sling together, and which we can then unload on Hassan al Korami for *five billion* dollars, and frankly, as you have already surmised, my ass is in a sling on the warheads, so I'll split the profits right down the middle, meaning Israel's balance of payment situation is improved by two billion dollars courtesy of the Scourge of the Infidel!"

Bar David scooped up a spoonful of his dessert and savored the heavy, dark chocolate sauce thoughtfully. "It certainly is tasty. . . ." he admitted. "But unthinkably dangerous! Three billion for us, one for you."

"Only to Hassan al Korami," Deutcher told him, knowing that this was the clincher. "For *you* will be supplying the remote guidance systems, n'est ce pas. Fifty-five, forty-five."

"So we will," Bar David said slowly. "So we will. . . . Sixty-five, thirty-five. . . ."

Armand Deutcher laughed. "Make it sixty, forty, and I'll also throw in a consignment of third-hand Japanese game-computers I bought in Shanghai complete with a cartridge called *Cruise Missile Commander*, which is close enough to the real thing to convince hashish-sodden maniacs who have never even seen a video game before that they're playing with real buttons."

"We could build a big fancy console around the video game computer for the controllers to play with, projection TVs, joysticks, maybe even stereo sound. . . ."

"And then jumble a great heap of junk with a lot of flashing lights and LCD readouts in the cockpit and hide the real control circuit on a chip somewhere in the works. . . ."

"So if they ever launch the things, we just take over. . . ."

"And drop them harmlessly into the sea!"

"Perhaps . . ." said Zvi Bar David.

Deutcher laughed. "You wouldn't be thinking of having the Scourge of the Infidel aim at Tel Aviv and hit, peut-etre, Mecca?"

"What a delicious notion, Armand!" Bar David exclaimed. "He would then be honor-bound to declare Holy War against himself!"

"Being first lady certainly hasn't been anything like what Sam promised so far," Margot Carruthers whined.

"Why are you bitching about it to me, moma?" Fast Eddie Braithewaite demanded. "You think I like this shit any more than you do?"

"No, Mr. Vice President, I don't," Mrs. Carruthers said coldly. "That's why I think you and I can make a deal."

For the first time since she had called him from a pay phone and insisted he meet her in the Watergate garage, Fast Eddie started to take the first lady seriously.

For sure, what with her old man confined in a padded cell by his staff and unable therefore to throw the White House parties and take her on the helicopter rides he had promised her, she had her reasons for being pissed off.

And as for himself, Fast Eddie was grinding his molars into stubs as he was constrained to attend funerals and keep his mouth shut, while all the while he should have long since moved into the Oval Office where he belonged.

"A deal?" he said. "What do you and me have to dicker over?"

Margo Carruthers slithered a little closer to him across the back seat of her rented Mercedes. "I thought *you'd* understand, Fast Eddie," she said breathily but hesitantly. "I mean, you people invented rock and roll, didn't you, you're in tune to the...ah...jelly roll vibrations...."

"*Say what?*"

She-yit, was Uncle Sam Carruthers's old lady *coming on to him?* He didn't know whether to laugh or puke.

"Sam and I hardly got it on together for years," she told him. "It got so I finally forgot what it felt like to be really turned on, so I hardly even missed it any more."

She sighed. She smiled blissfully. "But then, after Sam came back from whatever those terrorists did to him, before those White House staff creatures threw me out of our bedroom and turned it into a padded cell, Sam fucked my brains out. All night long. Over breakfast. On the toilet. I haven't had it so good in twenty years."

Fast Eddie goggled at her in amazement.

"Don't look at me like that!" she said. "I may not look like it now, but back when Sam was slogging around in Central America for three years, I had my little fling as a queen of the singles bars, I even turned a trick or two in my time for the hell of it. So when boring old Sam turned into a bright green pleasure machine, I had juicy enough memories to be reawakened, and now I'm so horny all the time I could scream."

Aghast, Fast Eddie sidled across the seat away from her until his back was pressed up against the door handle. "*Mrs. Carruthers,*" he said, "what *are* you trying to tell me?"

"Look at me," she told him, "not so bad for fifty-five if I do say so myself, but I'm not going to make out with the beautiful people at my age, and the First Lady of the United States would be a little conspicuous in a disco. Besides, it was like a second honeymoon, not that the first one was any great shakes in bed."

She gritted her teeth in determination. "I don't care if Sam is competent to be president of the United States or not, I want him in my bed, not in a padded cell, and I *don't* want him cured. I *prefer* my husband as a sex maniac."

"All right, mama, what did you have in mind?" Fast Eddie exclaimed. "I always was a sucker for true romance!"

"You get to fly around on Air Force One," Margot Carruthers said, creeping up on him again. "I get to visit Sam. I get him out of his cell and into a helicopter, and you have the plane ready and waiting at Dulles. We'll fly him to Los Angeles and put him on *America Tonite*."

"And they'll toss him right back in the bin!"

"But you'll be president, Fast Eddie. And if Ford could get away with pardoning Nixon as part of his deal, surely you can let us ride off somewhere into the sunset together. All I want out of this is my man."

"How you gonna get him out of the cell?"

"With a few twists and turns..." Margot Carruthers said, wriggling her thighs against him.

"And what about the captain of Air Force One...?" Fast Eddie said, leaning toward her.

"Oh he wasn't bad for someone who wasn't exactly my type," she said with a feral grin. "What about the next president of the United States? I mean, don't be insulted, but I always had this thing about the back seats of cars and black men."

"Funny you should say that, I always had this thing about married white women who had a thing about black men."

"Today is the day, now is the hour, now will the Scourge of the Infidel kick Zionist ass!" declared Hassan al Korami.

TV lights outshone the desert sun, befuddled reporters muttered idiot commentary into their mikes like color men in the fourth quarter of a very one-sided football game, and the palace guards surrounding the little reviewing stand upon which the Scourge of the Infidel stood stroked their Kalashnikovs nervously and hazed Hassan in a cloud of smoke from their spliffs, so that the cameramen cursed under their breath as they tried to keep sharp focus on the figure before the huge, makeshift tent.

Korami troops and officials and the foreign press corps alike eyed each other paranoiacally across the tarmac, the former scandalized at the unseemly sight of hundreds of running-dog mouthpieces of Satan polluting the purity of sacred Korami soil with their evil machineries, and the latter eying the drug-crazed, red-eyed, machine-gun-caressing troops with no little dread, and wondering why the Lion of the Desert had opened his borders to the foreign media for the first time in his reign for the purpose of staging this airport press conference.

Three days ago, the major European, American, Soviet, and Japanese news networks had been invited, indeed all but commanded, to produce their minions here in Koramibad International Airport for an announcement modesty promised to "change the course of world history."

One by one, their planes had landed and been surrounded by heavily armed and even more heavily loaded Korami troops. The reporters and crews were allowed to deplane with their equipment, and they were all hustled out here, where bulldozers had piled up rusty fighter planes in great heaps to clear an area in the great aerial junkpile large enough to erect the enormous tent, which apparently concealed Hassan's big surprise.

"Hear oh Israel!" the Scourge of the Infidel shrieked into his mike, sucking on the mouthpiece of a large hookah, and apparently beginning to work himself up into a proper rage. "Hear the words of Hassan al Korami, oh ye bloodsucking Zionist camel-fuckers and despair! Within four days and four nights, you shall remove your unclean presence from all of Holy Jerusalem and withdraw all your troops to the east bank of the Jordan River. Every Jew, every synagogue, every kosher delicatessen, must be cleansed from Jerusalem by the dawn of the fifth day, so commands Hassan al Korami, Sheik of Koram, Lion of the Desert, Scourge of the Infidel, Master of the Holy Hashishins!"

Mutters of astonishment, raucous laugher, and then an ugly growl of ire issued forth from the press. The crazy son of a bitch had finally OD'd on his own hash! He had been issuing asshole demands on the Israelis since he had assumed the throne, and now here he was standing in the midst of hundreds of junk fighter planes toking up and demanding their surrender!

That much was funny, but good enough to make the nightly half-hour news it was not, and that wasn't funny at all, because the crazy bastard had dragged them all out here into this miserable desert at great expense to themselves for a story that didn't exist. And there wasn't even any booze.

"You dragged our asses all the way out here for this!" the news director of NBC roared in outrage to a chorus of guttural agreement. "You can't treat the world press this way, you bedsheet-wearing little piss-ant! Believe me, you're going to pay heavily, imagewise, for this stupid little joke!"

The Scourge of the Infidel regarded him expressionlessly. He puffed on his hookah. He smiled thinly, and pointed at the Senior Network Figure with the little finger of his left hand.

Five palace guards forthwith trained their Kalashnikovs on him and blew him away.

"Do I have your attention now, mouthpieces of the Great Satan?" Hassan al Korami asked sweetly. "Here is what you came for," he said as the flaps of the great tent behind him began to fall away. "If one Israeli remains in Jerusalem or west of the Jordan River on the morning of the fifth day, I shall use *these*!"

But when the tent was down, the TV cameras found themselves recording the sight of nothing more earth-shaking than five more of Hassan's vast collection of moldering fighter-planes, notable only for the fact that they were even more ancient and decrepit than most of the rest of them.

"Jeez, those are F-111s!" someone exclaimed. "Thirty years old if they're a day!"

"You will observe their markings, infidels," said Hassan al Korami.

The five antique F-111s had been given new coats of Korami green, which was already starting to blister and flake off the rusting metal beneath. On the wings and rear fusilages, the Korami ensign—a marijuana leaf crossed by a machine gun—had been inlaid in gold leaf.

On the noses of the F-111s, a white circle bore words in Arabic, English, and Hebrew lettered in Israeli blue:

Tel Aviv.
Haifa.
Eilat.
Beersheba.
Galilee.

"Those are the targets we will destroy, Israel's population centers and its Jordan River irrigation system," declared Hassan al Korami. "We will turn the Zionist state into a radioactive desert cemetery where no one lives and nothing grows unless our commands are followed promptly and with perfection."

"*With those?*" a hidden voice called, and the press corps

had to choke back giggles for fear of arousing further admonitory gunplay.

But Korami ignored the lèse majesté this time. "You are now invited to come forward and examine the triumph of Korami military technology, the Sword of Hassan Supersonic Nuclear Cruise Missile," he said, his bloodshot eyes gleaming with the collector's true passion. "With a range of two thousand miles at a speed of a thousand miles an hour, with terrain-following radar that allows it to come in right down on the deck like an Exocet Three Thousand, the latest in computer control technology, and a quarter-megaton nuclear warhead."

For the better part of an hour, the reporters and technicians were allowed to pore over the aircraft. Whether half of these wrecks could fly from here to Israel before their wings fell off was problematical, but if they could go the distance, it would certainly seem that they could zip in under any radar, for the ancient, original, terrain-hugging guidance systems still seemed more or less functional, and that was what they had been designed to do.

They were handed geiger counters and allowed to probe the bomb bays with them amidst much clicking and moaning. The cockpits were crammed with enough electronic bric-a-brac to mix a record album, and there was a control van with enough monitors and keyboards and joysticks to impress the hell out of the reporters and air personalities and make wonderful high-tech footage.

But the camera and sound technicians were less than totally impressed, though they kept their amusement to themselves.

For the educated eye could detect that all this had been jumbled together out of crazily mismatched modules of this and that cannibalized from bits and pieces of Commodore game computers, Japanese TV sets, Build-a-Robot kits, and what looked like the imards of old Moog synthesizers. As to what it all did, one would have had to have been a member of the Russian Computer Underground to be crazy enough to try to trace the circuits out.

"Tell the world that Hassan al Korami speaks truly," the Scourge of the Infidel told the thoroughly shaken world press when these examinations were concluded. "If the Zionist oppressors do not obey my commands to the letter, in five days I shall nuke them into extinction!"

Then he nodded to his palace guard commander. "Remove these verminous mouthpieces of Satan from our Sacred Soil now," he said negligently.

And, with a disdain that would have made many a former American president rub his hands and chortle, the ladies and gentlemen of the world press were booted and prodded back to their planes at gunpoint, and sent on their way in a barrage of ink bottles and random automatic weapons fire.

"Come on Sam, get serious, just do what I tell you, and we'll get you out of here," Margot Carruthers said, as the president of the United States felt her up in his padded cell.

"Kiss my wienie and I'll follow you anywhere," he said, offering up the selfsame frankfurter of state for her inspection. "They haven't let me have any nookie for weeks! Old Oscar Meyer wants some sesame seed buns!"

"All right, all right, we'll play hide the banana," Margot told him, not at all displeased with the thought. "But when we do I'm going to scream and yell like you're forcing me to do it!"

"Oh boy, oh boy, oh boy!" said the president. "Can I tie you up with your nylons too if I promise to use slipknots?"

"No, Sam! Not *now!*" the first lady said. "Wait till we get to Burbank. When the guard comes in, leave everything to me, and do what I tell you. . . ."

"Rape! Rape! Ooo! Eee! Aaah! Aaah! Aaah! *Aaah!*"

Sergeant Carswell was under strict orders not to enter the Presidential Padded Cell, but when he heard the screams and grunts and sounds of struggle coming from within, gentlemanly instinct intervened, and he found himself dashing inside before he could think about it.

The president of the United States, naked, had the first lady's dress hiked up over her stomach, had her panties tied around her neck, and was humping away at her grunting *Hail to the Chief* as she scratched and bit at him.

The sight of this obscene state of the union shorted out a synapse in Sergeant Carswell's Christian and patriotic brain. Which is to say that Supreme Commander or no, no godfearing patriotic American could allow this shit to continue.

He dashed across the floor matting, and grabbed the president in a half-nelson, yanking him upward and backward off the first lady, then spun him around and flung him into a padded wall.

He felt something move up behind him, and turned around just in time to see Margot Carruthers's haymaker as it collided with his jaw.

"Remember, Sam, you're *the president,* don't let these flunkies push you around, show them who's boss," Margot Carruthers told the president when she had gotten him out into the corridor. "Don't take any lip."

Hand in hand with her stark-naked husband, the first lady walked down the corridor toward the first checkpoint, where two young Marine guards stood blocking their passage standing at ease.

"Aten-*shun!*" bellowed the ex–supply sergeant and used car salesman.

The two befuddled Marines popped to attention reflexively and then started fumbling with their holsters and staring at each other uncertainly at the sight of their naked commander in chief standing suddenly before them with an enormous erection.

"What are you fruits staring at?" the president demanded. "Haven't you ever seen such a Supreme Commander before?"

"Uh . . . ah . . . Mr. President, we have orders. . . ." stammered the white Marine.

"I give the orders around here!" bellowed the president. "I'm the president of the United States ain't I, and all those communists who didn't let me have any nookie are all fired as of now!"

"C-communists!" exclaimed the black Marine.

"That's right," said Margot Carruthers, "the White House staff has been taken over by Albanian agents and they've tricked you into believing my husband is crazy by taking away his clothes, feeding him Spanish fly, and forcing him to watch hour after hour of Russian soap operas."

"And they didn't let me have any nookie either, men," the president said petulantly.

"Help us to escape, and you'll both be heroes," said the first lady.

"Better than that, I hereby make both of you four-star generals as of now," said the commander in chief. "Now who do you say is crazy, boys?"

"Four-star generals?"

"Can he do that?"

"If he's still president."

"Shit man, *is* the dude still president?"

One Marine smiled at the other.

"He is as long as we say he is, now isn't he?"

"Where to, Mr. Prez...?"

"The nearest helicopter," said Margot Carruthers.

By the time the presidential party had reached the helipad, Camp David had been at least temporarily secured. The noncoms had been promoted to general, the privates had suddenly made sergeant, the officers had been busted and arrested for treason, the doctors and shrinks were assured of lucrative medicare payments, and all the TV personnel were promised presidential letters of introduction to big-time Hollywood producers.

The president, bundled into a blanket, and the first lady, doing most of the talking, boarded a helicopter, which speedily conveyed them to the airport, where it landed directly beside Air Force One, already warmed up on the runway and cleared for takeoff.

Once safely in the air, they were greeted in the plush presidential cabin by Vice President Fast Eddie Braithewaite and Captain Bo Bob Beauregard, the crew commander and pilot, a big, beaming, blond hunk, who winked at the first lady, saluted the president, and fixed his noble visage in his best heroic fly-boy expression.

"Don't worry, Mr. President, as of now you're safe in the hands of the United States Air Force," he said. "Margot here told me all about how those Cuban agents secretly replaced the White House staff with East German clones who kidnapped you and forced you to endure unspeakable perversions with Russian diesel dykes, makes my blood boil to think of it, but let me assure you that the Air Force of the United States is behind you one hundred percent! Why don't you have us take 'em all out with our Gorilla Killa mini cruise missiles? Shit, we can fly those sweet little sons of bitches right up their assholes!"

Fast Eddie looked as if he had fallen down a rabbit hole. The president stroked his erection reflectively as if considering it.

"Wait a minute Bo Bob... er, Captain Beauregard," the first lady said. "You just fly us to Burbank."

"Aw come on, Margot," the president whined, "let's have some fun."

"We'll have plenty of fun, Sam, when we get to Hollywood!"

The president's expression immediately brightened. "We're going to Hollywood?" he exclaimed. "Oh boy oh boy! I'm gonna get me some movie stars just like John F. Kennedy!"

"Better than that, Sam," Margot Carruthers told him, choking down her irritation. "You're going to go on *television*. You're going to address the Nation."

"I am?" said the president. "What am I supposed to say? Do I have to read a speech?"

"*Uncle Sam Carruthers* don't need no jive speech writer, now does he?" Fast Eddie told him, grinning. "You're the *president*, mon, you can say anything that comes into your honkie head, all you gotta do is let it all hang out."

"That's right Sam, you just go on as if you were still selling old Buicks and tell the American people whatever you think they ought to hear," Margot Carruthers said, giving him a little goose. "We'll see about movie stars later." And when they see what a horny old billy goat you've become, Sam Carruthers, she thought, I'll have you all to myself.

Somewhere over Colorado, Captain Bo Bob Beauregard reappeared in the presidential cabin, scratching his head. By now, Margot had gotten the president more or less into his Uncle Sam suit, though there was no way she could get him to keep his fly zipped up.

"Mr. President, there sure is some weird traffic on the air from down below," Captain Beauregard said. "Some crazy A-rab has got himself hold of some cruise missiles, and he's threatening to nuke the Hebes if they don't give up Jerusalem, and now the Israelis are sayin' screw you, Charlie, everybody knows we have no nukes, but if you lob one at us, we could acquire fifty Slings of David mobile ICBMs with one-megaton warheads faster'n hot baboon shit through a tin horn, and your entire ass is radioactive glass."

"Sure you're not listening to Radio Free Gonzo and doing spliffs up there?" Fast Eddie said. "Sounds like you've got some spaced-out DJ thinks he's Orson Welles."

Captain Beauregard frowned. "Hell boy, I've been on the horn to the button room, and they're freaking out, They sure as shit want to go on Red Alert, batten down, and get our SAC B-1s in the air just in case, but all they can get from

Washington is 'no comment' from the White House press secretary and 'it's not my job' from the secretary of defense."

"You tell them not to listen to anything those Commie spies tell them!" the commander in chief shouted. "Uncle Sam Carruthers is back in charge now! You tell my generals that I'm going on the air to address the Nation, and when I do, I want my Air Force to be ready to vaporize the Godless Atheistic Rooshians and the crazy Arabs and the smart-ass Jews and anyone else who gives us any crap when I tell them to!"

"Yessiree, Mr. President!" Captain Beauregard enthused, saluting. "That's just what the United States Air Force has been waiting to hear!"

"Wait a minute!" shouted Fast Eddie. "You can't do that!"

"Why not, boy?" demanded Bo Bob Beauregard.

"Because . . ." Because the fat boy is bugfuck bananas, Fast Eddie had been about to say, but one look at the granite set of this peckerwood's patriotic jaw disabused him of any such notion. "Because . . . because . . . because they won't believe you, mon!" he finally blurted. "The White House staff has got half a dozen actors who can fake the president's voice! They'll countermand the orders! They'll have the Secret Service grab us as soon as we get off this plane!"

"Can they do that, Captain?" the president said fearfully. "Can they lock me up again and take my nookie away?"

"You don't worry none about *that*, Mr. President," Captain Beauregard said triumphantly. "We're always prepared in the United States Air Force."

He went into a cabinet and came back with a bright red mobile phone. "This little sucker goes straight to a secure satellite in geosynchronous orbit, and then right down into the button room by tight laser beam. They got a voice-analyzer on the other end that will tell them it's you, and all I've got to do is verify it's a live broadcast. You just get on the horn and tell them to go to Condition Black. That means they put all strategic forces on full Red Alert, seal up the control center, and accept no orders that don't come right through that phone in the authenticated voice of the president of the United States."

Beaming, the president took the red phone.

"Sam, I don't think you should do this," Margot Carruthers

said nervously as he played with the phone with one hand and himself with the other.

"You're always telling me what not to do, Margot!" the president whined. "Don't you have another martini, Sam, Sam you're driving too fast, you keep your eyes off those cheerleaders, Sam! Well I'm the president of the United States now, and no one's going to tell me what I can't do, not my mother, not the Rooshians, and not you!"

"Give 'em hell, Mr. President!" Captain Beauregard said brightly, as he showed him how to get an operator.

"Hello, hello, this is the president . . . What do you mean I should hang up and dial directly myself?"

"This is Radio K-RAB, the Rockin' Voice of the A-rabs, beamin' a hundred thousand watts of Good Vibrations right at ya, all you crazy Shiite and Sunni mamas and papas you, from our Ship of Rock and Roll Fools out here in the Gulf, and here's the Big Number Twelve on Radio K-RAB today, *Jihad Jump* by Abou Abou and the Hashishins, right after this word from Kalashnikov, the state of the art in automatic rifles, and at a price you don't have to be an oil sheik to afford!"

Armand Deutcher turned off the air feed before the commercial could come on and returned his attention to the world news monitors he had had jury-rigged in the control room of the seaborn pirate radio station.

Even as Zvi Bar David had predicted, Hassan al Korami had not waited for the full shipment of Sword of Hassan cruise missiles to arrive before he did his dingo act. So far, so good.

Now NBC was reporting that the Israelis had issued their own ultimatum. Hassan had four days to surrender his nuclear cruise missiles to Israel or they would take them out with their mighty high-tech air force without the need to resort to nuclear preemption. Since Koram had threatened Israel with nuclear annihilation, they could hardly be blamed by world opinion if they launched an all-out air attack against the miscreant as long as they righteously kept their own nukes hidden under the rug.

And now Radio Msocow was reporting that Hassan al Korami was falling right into the trap. He had just declared that the moment an Israeli aircraft crossed his borders, he would annihilate Tel Aviv, Haifa, Beersheba, Eilat, and the Jordan River irrigation system.

They were goading Hassan into it. The Israelis would probably wait till the deadline just to keep him getting hotter. Then they would hit the Sheikdom of Koram with about a thousand or so drone fighter-bombers firing Pitchfork metal-seeking missiles, which would destroy Koram's forces utterly while the world stood on and cheered.

Deutcher only hoped that the Israelis wouldn't be *too* efficient. He had several billion francs riding on Hassan getting at least one of his cruise missiles off the ground before they were taken out by the Israeli luftblitz, and he would be a lot happier if the Israelis made sure he fired first.

After all, what difference did it make to them? Even if the Lion of the Desert managed to launch all five, the Israelis would just dump them all into the sea anyway, or so at least they should think.

Now there was danger of a major financial setback. Deutcher had counted on the Israelis wanting to let Hassan get at least one missile in the air so they could make him hit Mecca, indeed he had given Zvi Bar David the idea free of charge.

Then, with the mighty hundred-thousand-watt transmitter of K-RAB, the Rockin' Voice of the A-rabs, *he* could take control of the missile that the Israelis took away from Hassan's controllers and use it where it would do the most good.

It had cost him good money to rent this pirate radio ship too, let alone how deep he had dug to leverage his real-estate speculation, and now the Israelis threatened to throw a monkey wrench into the works!

Ivan Igorovich Gornikov had never seen the Politburo in such a state, and he had seen plenty as the day-shift operator of the Bulgorny all these years!

When Hassan al Korami had issued his first ultimatum to Israel, they had convened immediately, and when the Israelis had threatened to destroy his missiles by nonnuclear means, they had gone into permanent session, and when Hassan had declared he would launch his nukes on warning, they had panicked and repaired here, to the Dacha, to the emergency control center buried half a kilometer deep in the heart of the Urals.

And that had been the only consensus these Heroes of Socialist Labor had managed to reach. Marshall Borodin conceived the notion that this was somehow the ideal time to blockade Berlin. The Foreign Ministry advised a peace offensive, that they should side with whomever was attacked first. Sergei Polikov insisted they side with Hassan to protect his best hashish customer. The minister of finance agreed. The minister of propaganda believed that they should side with Israel, who would have world opinion on their side if they were nuked. And by now all of them were hoarse with exhaustion and repeating themselves endlessly.

And all the time, Pyotr Ivanovich Bulgorny, his skin varnished and polymerized to a high gloss and rouged to a ruddy glow, sat there at the head of the table, silent, motionless, and imperturbable. Admittedly, the chairman's failure to panic like the rest of them owed a certain debt to the fact that he was dead.

As for Ivan Igorovich Gornikov, his state of mind was anything but tranquil, for he knew the signs. The Politburo was quite thoroughly deadlocked, and by now most of them were drunk. The moment they found themselves faced with an unavoidable decision, they would ask the Bulgorny to speak.

And Ivan, alas, had already fed the Joker program into Pyotr Ivanovich's memory banks and decision-making software. He had no idea what kind of gibberish would issue forth from the speaker behind the corpse's teeth when they told him to put the question to the Chairman of the Central Committee of the Soviet Communist Party. For better or worse, the Soviet Union would soon be at the command of a randomized, collective, decision-making process.

"This was just received from our embassy in London," said a minor ministry functionary, handing a single piece of paper to the foreign minister. "It was called in from a pay phone by someone who claimed to represent the Mossad."

The foreign minister read it and went pale as a sheet.

"What is it, Nikolai?" demanded Polikov. "You look as if you have bitten into a turd."

"Apparently the Mossad is now afraid that their own government is about to go too far," the foreign minister said. "According to this, if any of Hassan's missiles should actually hit anything, they will use it as an excuse to destroy him using their own nuclear arsenal, announcing its existence thereby, and forcing the world to accept Israeli hegemony over the Middle East as a new nuclear superpower. The Mossad begs the Soviet Union to force Koram to capitulate to the Israeli ultimatum to prevent extreme Zionist elements from accomplishing this."

"They're right! We cannot allow the Israelis to rule the Middle East!"

"Preempt them!"

"Preempt *who*?"

"Israel!"

"Koram!"

"Berlin!"

They continued to scream and shout at each other, fortifying themselves with more vodka, but soon enough the unwholesome contumely began to run out of energy, and one by one, the members of the Politburo fell silent and turned their gaze to the tranquil and impassive leadership of Pyotr Ivanovich Bulgorny, who sat there like the corpse he was, loftily transcending this unseemly spectacle.

"Gornikov!" Marshall Borodin finally said. "It would seem we must consult Comrade Bulgorny on this matter. Boot him up, and load his decision-making program at once!"

Shaking, Ivan set to work at the control computer. "Be a good boy now, Pyotr Ivanovich," he whispered into the Bulgorny's ear. "For the sake of Mother Russia, and Ivan Igorovich's ass."

"It was *your* idea, Margot," the president complained. "*I* didn't want to make any speech, I just wanted to fly to Hollywood and boff me some movie stars!"

Air Force One had arrived at Burbank Airport without any Secret Service or FBI showing up, and it seemed they could have gotten Uncle Sam Carruthers to NBC's Burbank studios and on the air without being intercepted, as per the original plan.

But now neither the vice president nor the first lady could contemplate with any equanimity the notion of putting the president on the air with the command phone in his hand and the strategic forces gone to Condition Black. If Sam started raving about annihilating the Godless Rooshians or taking vengeance against the price-cutting Japs or even ridding Washington, D.C., of grafting pansy bureaucrats while the red phone was on, the Air Force would bloody well do it, and no one could get through to stop them.

And Samuel T. Carruthers kept stroking the damn thing and wouldn't let Margot take it away from him.

"It's too dangerous, Sam," she told him. "Once they know you've escaped and know where you are, they'll cut you off the air and send in the FBI and Secret Service."

"I got to admit the little lady's right, Mr. President," said Captain Bo Bob Beauregard. "You better stay right here on good old Air Force One where the Communists with the butterfly nets can't get at you." His eyes lit up. "In fact, just to be on the safe side, why don't I just get on the horn and get us some air cover? I reckon a couple dozen F-25s from Edwards would be enough to show the flag."

"I'm getting tired of sitting around on my ass in this airplane!" the president shouted angrily. "I want to go out and have some fun!"

"We could always nuke Washington," Bo Bob suggested helpfully. "The American people would understand. We had to destroy the city to save it from the Communist Conspiracy."

"It's full of nothing but pointy-headed bureaucrats, foreigners, and welfare chiselers who voted against me, isn't it . . . ?" the president said thoughtfully.

"You could say it's not a part of the real red-blooded US of A at all . . ." agreed Captain Beauregard. "I'd recommend four low-level airbursts with five-megaton Widowmaker airborne IRBMs coming in on the deck from B-7 Penetrator hypersonic bombers. That should take out the White House staff, wherever the slimy sons of bitches are hiding, six if you want to go for a little overkill. . . ."

"I'll show those ingrates what happens when they take away my nookie!" the president said, holding the red phone to his mouth.

"Wait, wait!" shrieked Fast Eddie. "I've got a better idea!"

"A better idea?" said Bo Bob. "Maybe you're right, boy! Now *New York City* is someplace a lot of people have always wanted to see sawed off from the rest of the country. . . ."

"No, no, no," said Fast Eddie off the top of his head. "Why don't you just call them up and make them surrender?"

"*Surrender?*"

"Give it a try before you start World War III over this jive, mon! Let them know you've busted out of the bin and tell them you'll go on the tube and whip up a lynch mob if they give you any more shit."

At which point, the White House staff would have no

choice but to finally turn over the presidency to *him* in return
for keeping their jobs, and he'd take considerable pleasure in
punching out this crazy old honkie and getting hold of the
phone to the button room himself.

"He's right, Sam, the sniveling cowards will give up
without a fight," Margot Carruthers said, fondling his privates. Or anyway they'll play along long enough for me to get
you into the sack and away from the red phone.

"Aw shit," said Captain Bo Bob Beauregard, "we're not
gonna get to take out Washington?"

"I guess I would enjoy telling the bastards what I think
of them first," the president decided.

"Don't look so sad, Bo Bob," said the first lady. "You can
still go play with your fighter-planes!"

"They say I am mad, but I am not mad," Hassan al
Korami cackled to himself. He took another great hit from his
hookah, and beamed happily across the throne room at his
assembled officers and ministers, sprawled on the cushions
before him, or standing at attention sucking on their spliffs.

Everything was falling into place exactly as his divine
inspiration had foretold. The American president was locked
in a padded cell masturbating, unbeknownst to the Israelis,
who believed the Americans would protect them from his
wrath. By now the Russian Computer Underground, which
he had created for just this purpose, had blown electronic
hashish into the computer that controlled the Russian corpse.

Now he was ready to kick over the anthill and watch the
Satanic vermin scramble and stagger to their doom.

"Vizier," he commanded, "order the evacuation of
Koramibad, for now will we return to the clean desert sands
from whence we came!"

"General, hitch up our Sword of Hassan cruise missiles
to the palace Rolls Royces!" he commanded.

"Scribe, release this pronouncement to the international
news media! We have evacuated Koramibad and disappeared
into the desert with our missiles where no Israeli aircraft can
find us before we launch. I, the Scourge of the Infidel now
therefore issue a new nonnegotiable ultimatum. The Zionist
oppressors now have three days to evacuate their population
to New York and Miami entirely, or we shall vaporize them all
where they stand!"

Even in the court of Hassan al Korami, this pronuncia-
mento was the cause for some concern, though of course no
one present dare declare anything less than perfect comprehension of the Wisdom of the Lion of the Desert for fear of
facing the Sacred Wrath of same. But no amount of hash
could convince any of them that the Israelis would ever
accede to such a demand.

Including Hassan al Korami.

It had all come to him in a vision last night.

Of course the Zionists would never give up without a
fight to the death! They might be Infidels, but they were no
wimpish cowards! Instead, they would do what he was forcing
them to do, openly brandish their own nuclear missiles, the
Slings of David, and threaten to use them first on Koram.

And then, ah then, the Russian bear would find itself
twitching and stumbling out of control onto the stage!

"The frigging Israelis have gone and done it!" the national security adviser said as he came back from the can to the
cabinet room still zipping up his pants.

"Oh no!"

"Done what?"

"Whipped it out!"

"Whipped out what, you don't mean—"

"Their frigging nuclear strike force, that's what! They're
displaying their Slings of David mobile ICBMs on television,
and they say they'll take out Hassan's missiles if he doesn't
surrender in twenty-four hours by the simple expedient of turning all of Koram into a two-kilometer-deep radioactive crater."

"That's nothing we can't manage, is it?" said the press
secretary. "I mean, imagewise, it's not our problem, is it?"

The cabinet meeting room, like the White House staff,
had certainly seen better days. Ever since Hassan al Korami
had trotted out his cruise missiles, they had been holed up in
here, holding themselves incommunicado from the press,
who wanted to ask them questions they couldn't answer, from
the Pentagon seeking orders they didn't know how to give,
and from the cabinet members and Congressional Bigwigs
demanding to see a president who on the one hand was crazy,
and who on the other would now seem to have escaped.

So there was nothing for it but to live on take-in junk food
and attempt to manage the situation, which, like the piles of
old pizza cartons, chicken bones, and half-eaten greaseburgers

that littered the big, long table, was beginning to get overripe.

"It isn't fair!" declared the chief of staff. "Isn't this what we hire ourselves a president for, to make the decisions that can only come out wrong, and then take the blame? We're here to take care of business, not run this mess ourselves!"

Ivan Igorovich Gornikov was sweating like a pig, and he would have given half a year's wages for a single hit of hash. He was getting the shakes, if not from withdrawal, then certainly from what these vodka-sotted assholes were putting him through.

Every time he thought he had finally gotten the last update entered, some other little apparatchnik would appear with another disaster report on the rapidly deteriorating situation, and he would have to sit around and listen to them discuss it drunkenly for an hour and then enter a new round of decision input yet again.

He was almost tempted to tell them that it didn't matter that Pyotr Ivanovich's software had been quite thoroughly randomized, so that additional data would only introduce additional noise into the system. But at least for the moment even the present situation was preferable to a log cabin in deepest Siberia or a bullet in the back of the head.

Which no doubt would come soon enough anyway, once the stuffed and wired mummy of Pyotr Ivanovich was ordered to speak.

"Broadcast my words to all the world!" declared Hassan al Korami. "Let the Zionist dogs piss unmanfully in their trousers!"

"You're not putting me on?" said the voice over his car radio. "This is really *the* Hassan al Korami, Lion of the Desert, Scourge of Infidel, and you're *really* listening to K-RAB, the Rockin' Voice of the A-rabs, well *too far out*, tell all our mamas and papas out there in the mystic sands, if you don't mind, Hassan, you wild and crazy guy, what's your fave rave of the month?"

"*Jihad Jump* by Abou Abou and the Hashishins," the Scourge of the Infidel found himself saying into his phone, which was only natural, since he owned the group that had made the charts with the heavy-metal version of the Korami National Anthem.

"But I did not call to do record promos!" the Lion of the Desert roared when he caught up on what had happened. "I have a proclamation that will shake the world and set the flag of Islam flying over Jerusalem! Hear, oh—"

"Hold on to your hookah, Hassan, we'll be right back to freak out on your Sacred Rage after this word from Harada, maker of fine samurai swords since before old Omar made his first tent, boys and girls!"

And the Scourge of the Infidel was constrained to wait through the commercial.

But for once, he found to his own surprise that he did not at all mind this pause between contemplation and act. For, for the first time in his life, he was actually feeling mellow.

The moment was perfect, and perfect too was the fact that he was passing through it out here in the endless desert sands, free under the sun and the sky, wandering the wastes once more, in the manner of his ancestors, though of course, as befitted the Lion of the Desert, he had much the best of it, riding in the capacious air-conditioned cabin of his outsized Rolls, rather than humping about and broiling on the back of some camel. And now—

"And now, Radio K-RAB, the Rockin' Voice of the A-rabs brings you a special treat, you spaced-out Shiites and Sunnis, you, live, direct from the ass-end of nowhere, that heavy rapper that's got 'em all rockin' and rollin' in the aisles in Moscow and Washington this week, a K-RAB exclusive preview, you heard it here first, boys and girls, the latest unconditional ultimatum from the Scourge of the Infidel, *Hassan al Korami!*"

"Hear the words of Hassan al Korami, Zionist vermin," Hassan began mildly. "For behold your futile threats to destroy our Sword of Hassan cruise missiles with your Satanic Slings of David are as the fartings of camels! My Hashishins and I have vanished into the desert with our nukes from whence we will annihilate you! Fire your missiles at Koram, villainous kikes, as you will, for I defy you!"

He paused, smiled to himself, and went on more calmly. "But before you do, know this, oh Israel know this, American running dogs of Zionist imperialism, I have just received iron-clad assurance from the Soviet Union," he lied, "that the moment a single nuclear explosion pollutes the sacred soil of

Koram, the Soviet Union will launch an all-out nuclear attack on the United States."

"Well *far out,* I'm sure we'll all be tuning in to see whether the world is going to hear the Big Bang before the weekend, and so while we're waiting, let's all get in the proper thermonuclear mood with *Brighter than a Thousand Suns,* that golden radioactive oldie from the Four Horsemen of the Apocalypse. . . ."

Hassan al Korami turned off the radio and sucked at his hookah, giggling to himself. Left to their own devices, the Americans would no doubt pressure the Israelis into at least surrendering Jerusalem and the West Bank now, while the Russians would be falling all over themselves to deny that they had ever promised Koram such a thing.

But of course Hassan had not left the twin limbs of Satan to their own devices! The American president had been turned into a raving maniac by the Mendocino Liberation Front, and the computer that controlled the Russian chairman had been confounded to Babel by the Russian Computer Underground.

Between them, an insane American president and a dead Russian chairman animated by a thoroughly barbled computer would surely contrive a way to blow each other and the Israelis to bits.

If the American did not preempt the Russians, the Russians would preempt the Americans' preemption, or the Israelis would preempt him, forcing the Russians and the Americans to simultaneously preempt each other.

It hardly mattered which Limb of Satan pressed the panic button first. Russian missiles would annihilate Israel and America, and American missiles would annihilate Russia, and then would the Lion of the Desert declare Jihad and victory at the same time and march into Jerusalem as the Imam of all Arabia and the Sultan of what was left of the world.

Admittedly, it was quite likely that in the process, Koram could expect to take some hits, but that was a price that the Scourge of the Infidel was quite willing to pay. For what was there in Koram to be destroyed but an empty city and some scattered tribes of bedouins? No amount of megatonnage could take out the true font of his power, the bottomless pool of oil upon which his sheikdom and his transcendent destiny stood. Indeed, with most of the world in radioactive ruins, he could up the price of petroleum to anything he chose!

Marshall Borodin read the latest communiqué that had been handed to him and fainted dead away. The foreign minister set to reviving him by pouring the remains of a bottle of vodka over his head and slapping his cheeks, while Sergei Polikov retrieved the communiqué, scanned it, went pale, and drank straight from the mouth of another bottle before summarizing it to those of the Politburo who were still conscious.

"Hassan al Korami has announced that the Soviet Union will react to any nuclear attack by the Israelis on his territory with an all-out preemptive attack on the United States. Furthermore, we have promised him we will do this even if he launches a nuclear attack on Israel first! Which he would seem to have every intention of doing!"

"Sergei, you imbecile, how could you promise him such a thing?" demanded the foreign minister.

"*Me?*" said the KGB director. "I never promised him any such thing. It must have been the Red Army."

Marshall Borodin, by now, had revived sufficiently to declare his indignation. "How dare you accuse the Red Army of such stupidity!" he roared. "*You* are the one who sells the maniac his hashish, Sergei Polikov!"

All eyes turned on the foreign minister.

"Don't be ridiculous," that worthy said. "Everyone knows I'm just a technician."

"What will we do?" wailed Marshall Borodin. "If we launch our missiles at the Americans, they will launch their missiles at us, and the truth of the matter is that we both have more than enough to annihilate each other."

"But even if we *don't* launch our missiles when Israel responds to Koram's first strike, the Americans will still think we might, and then *they'd* launch first," pointed out Polikov.

"We must announce that Hassan is lying," said the foreign minister. "We must inform the Americans publicly that we will not attack them no matter what Koram and Israel do to each other."

"Will they believe us?"

"Can we believe them if they say they believe us?"

"But if we let the Israelis get away with nuking Koram, it will turn all the Arabs against us, destroy our credibility in

Eastern Europe and cause a mass uprising, and leave the Middle East in the hands of a new nuclear power we have spent the past half century supporting terrorists against!"

"Perhaps we should strike preemptively at the Israelis?"

"Better to destroy that double-dealing parasite Hassan!"

"Someone must get on the hot line to the American president," said the foreign minister.

"Who?" sneered Marshall Borodin. "Certainly not you!"

"The Red Army certainly cannot expect to negotiate directly with a head of state!"

"Comrades," said Sergei Polikov," it is quite clear that both protocol and the fact that we will never agree on what to propose to the Americans ourselves requires that Pyotr Ivanovich, our beloved chairman and official chief of state, be the one to deal directly with his American counterpart on a summit level."

Ivan Igorovich Gornikov could all but smell the alcoholic sighs of relief as even now, at the ultimate hour of impending Armageddon, they gratefully reliquinished their responsibilities as the living representatives of the Soviet people to the animating software of a corpse.

"Activate Pyotr Ivanovich immediately, Gornikov," Marshall Borodin ordered.

"Da, tovarish," said Ivan, sending the first jolts of current to the steel exoskeleton concealed within the voluminous folds of the Bulgorny's traditional ill-fitting blue suit. Pyotr Ivanovich began to jerk and jiggle, his eyelids flapped open and closed asynchronously, his lips began to mutter to themselves, as the audioanimatronics warmed up.

Then the software took complete control, and Ivan brought the chairman to his feet, looming above the Politburo in all his ponderous bulk, staring out at them unwaveringly through his implacable glass eyes, dominating them utterly with his steadfast and tireless visage.

Even if his software *is* randomized, even if he *has* been dead for ten years, Ivan suddenly perceived, Pyotr Ivanovich Bulgorny certainly cut a better figure of a man than any of this besotted collection of generals, Chekist thugs, and time-serving Party hacks! Ironically enough, he thought, the antiparty elements, the Politburo, and myself now all find ourselves in perfect agreement.

The only good Party chairman is a dead one.

*   *   *

"This is the president of the United States, you effete eastern communist assholes, and I'm really pissed off!" roared the voice on the speaker-phone, and a great moan of woe went up in the untidy, smoke-filled cabinet room.

"It's Uncle Sam all right, we checked it out," said the national security adviser. "He's speaking from Air Force One, which for some reason is parked at the Burbank airport, and there's a squadron of F-25s overhead putting on a display of supersonic aerobatics that's shattering every window from Pasadena to Pacoima."

"You bastards had no right to lock me up without any nookie!" bellowed Samuel T. Carruthers. "I'm horny as a billy goat and mad as an ayatollah, and I'm *the president of the United States*, and from now on, I'm in charge here."

"Get the Secret Service out there! Get the FBI! Get a SWAT team from Los Angeles! Someone's got to get a net over the son of a bitch before the press gets wind of this!"

"Now you listen here, you miserable flunkies, I want your resignations right now, or I'm going on the air, and by the time I've finished telling the American people how you kidnapped their president, held him prisoner, and tortured him with a case of the blue balls, you'll all be breaking rocks in Leavenworth!"

"Oh my god . . ." moaned the press secretary, dropping a phone like a dead fish and holding his head in his hands. "The Russians have threatened to nuke us if the Israelis attack Koram!"

"What'll we do?"

"We'd better put our strategic forces on Red Alert," said the national security adviser. And he picked up the phone to the button room.

"And don't try to send your goons after me, either!" said the president. "My air cover will blow them away. And if you give me any crap, I'll let Bo Bob nuke Washington."

"Holy shit!" shouted the national security adviser, dropping his phone like a hot potato. "They've already gone to Condition Black!"

"Condition Black? What the hell is *Condition Black*?"

"The button room is sealed off and running on internal air and power. All I can get on the phone from here is a robot voice telling me the number is temporarily out of service. There's only one active line in now, and that's the red phone on Air Force One."

"That raving maniac has personal control of our nuclear forces?"

"You got it! The lunatic has taken over the asylum!"

Ivan Igorovich held the Party chairman at stiff attention while he keyed in the final update, exactly as he did on May Day and the Anniversary of the Revolution, when Pyotr Ivanovich stood heroically imperturbable for long hours in the dank breezes atop Lenin's tomb. At least the exoskeleton controls would seem not to have been affected by the Joker program.

But now it was time to run the thoroughly barbled decision-making software, and when he turned matters over to *that*, it would be terra incognita, for even stoned-out hacker's theory could not agree on what would happen when a randomized decision-making process interfaced with a scrambled data bank. Boris believed that feedback loops might be set up that would short the whole mess out. Tanya opined that the process of dialectical materialism itself might speak through this tossing of the electronic coins of a cybernated *I Ching*. Grishka likened it to feeding the entire Soviet Encyclopedia through a tree-chipper and publishing what came out as the next edition of *Pravda*.

Ivan Igorovich Gornikov had no such theories, but now he was the one who was about to find out, as he booted up the decision-making program.

Pyotr Ivanovich stood there silently and motionlessly for a while, and then the lips of the corpse began to tremble, and the glass eyes began to flick back and forth in their sockets, and then the chairman began to speak in a multitonal syntax cobbled together out of words and phrases from the recorded library of his old speeches.

"Fraternal greetings, peasants and workers of the Magnetogorsk refrigerator works, and welcome to the Five-Year Plan of Socialist Realism. . . ."

"What?"

"Gornikov! What's wrong with the chairman?" demanded Marshal Borodin.

Ivan shrugged innocently. "Aside from the fact that he's been dead for ten years, nothing."

"The correct Marxist-Leninist solution to the present crisis in hooliganism is to express fraternal solidarity with the

long-range class self-interest of the running dogs of agricultural production quotas. . . ."

"Then why is he babbling like that?" snapped Sergei
Polikov.

"Babbling?" said Ivan. "Don't tell me an educated Marxist-
Leninist intellectual like yourself has trouble following our
chairman's new Party line when it seems so crystal clear to an
ignorant but ideologically pure Soviet worker like me?"

"We must stamp out revanchist elements within the
Kirov Ballet and send the New Soviet Man to conquer the
stars on his way to Siberia. . . ."

"We can't put *that* on the hot line to the American
president!" said the foreign secretary.

"What else can we do?"

Marshall Borodin scanned another communiqué. "Spy
satellites indicate that the Americans have gone to Condition
Black!" he moaned. "Everything they have is now directly
controlled by this used car salesman, this bumbling *civilian*,
this Uncle Sam Carruthers!"

"They're preparing a first strike!" said Polikov. "We must
launch everything we have at once!"

"But maybe the president has instead seized control
from the militarist circles in order to *prevent* some crazy
general from acting on his own. Have you never seen *Dr.
Strangelove*?"

"He's right!" said the minister of production, arising
from his stupor. "It's an implied invitation to a summit."

On and on they went, as the clock ticked and the
Bulgorny babbled, and finally Ivan Igorovich Gornikov could
contain himself no longer. What did he have to lose by
speaking anyway, since if the world were not blown to
smithereens shortly, he would be shot for treason if the KGB
still existed afterward to find out what had happened.

"You'll pardon my saying so, comrades," he ventured,
"but why don't you ask *Pyotr Ivanovich* if he feels like talking
to the American president before we all blow ourselves to
bits? He may be dead, but at least he can always be counted
upon to be decisive."

"Well what about it, Pyotr Ivanovich?" Marshall Borodin
demanded directly of the stuffed and wired Party chairman.
"Do you wish to negotiate with the American president?"

". . . the Soviet Union is in favor of peaceful coexistence

with the complete disarmament of all neocolonialist tractor operators. . . ."

"*That* should give the American president pause. . . ." mused Polikov.

"Let no one mistake our determination to fulfill our sorghum production quotas or take a capitalist road toward the dictatorship of the party hacks, for we will never submit to American demands that we make a profit-motive revolution without breaking eggs. . . ."

"A powerful dialectical line would seem to be emerging, wouldn't you say?" said the minister of production.

"I find it impossible to fault its logic. . . ." agreed Sergei Polikov.

"It would appear you are our only hope, Pyotr Ivanovich," said Marshall Borodin. "Will you now speak with the American president?"

Ivan caused the corpse of the chairman to nod its assent, and managed to smear a rictus grin across its face. "We have nothing to fear but bourgeois tendencies in American ruling-class circles," said Pyotr Ivanovich confidently as the exoskeleton made his dead hand reach for the hot-line phone.

"Jesus," said the appointments secretary, "that's the Russian chairman himself on the hot line!"

"But he's *dead*!"

"He may be dead, but he's on the line demanding to talk with the president himself, and threatening to launch an all-out preemptive ideological dialectic against the class self-interest of malingerers and black-marketeers, whatever that means, if we refuse."

"What the hell can we do now?"

"Well, you assholes, I'm getting tired of waiting for your answer," the voice of Samuel T. Carruthers shrieked on the speaker-phone. "I'm horny, and I'm bored, and I want to go out and get some nookie!"

The White House Staff exchanged terrified speculative glances.

"We can't!"

"Got any better ideas?"

"Isn't this what we hired him for?"

"I'm gonna count to three, and then I'm gonna tell Bo Bob to have them drop fifty megatons on Washington. One . . . two . . ."

"He may be crazy. . . ."

"Two and a half. . ."

"But at least he won't take shit."

"I thought you were dead," President Carruthers said when they had patched Air Force One through on the hot line.

"The state will wither away only when all production quotas for sugar beets are exceeded by nonproliferation treaties between revanchist troglodytes and the vanguard of the working software," said the weird voice on the phone.

"My dong will wither away if I don't get me some nookie soon!" the president said crossly. "What do you want, you Rooshian stiff?"

"I want to take this opportunity to express my fraternal sympathies with decadent capitalist sensualism. . . ." replied Chairman Bulgorny. "Owing to temporary bad weather in the Ukraine, the nookie crap in Central Asia had been shipped to the Gulag by mistake. . . ."

"Oh," said the president much more sympathetically, "you're also having trouble getting laid."

"Socialist morality has advanced by leaps and bounds since Rasputin. . . ." Pyotr Ivanovich Bulgorny admitted. It figured. All those Rooshian women looked like science-fiction fans as far as Uncle Sam was concerned, and besides, it must not be so easy to make out in singles bars when you're a corpse.

"What you need, buddy, is some Red White and Blue One Hundred Percent American Used Nookie!" the president told him. "I hear tell that they got hookers in Las Vegas that'll make even a dead Russian chairman whistle the Star-Spangled Banner out his asshole!"

"Cultural exchange programs between our two great peoples should not be interrupted by linkage to ideological differences between trashy western popular literature and the Red Army Chorus. . . ."

"Tell you what, Mr. Chairman, why don't we have a meeting in the grand old American tradition?" the president suggested helpfully. "We'll go to Las Vegas and party with some hookers, and who knows, once we've gotten stewed, screwed, and tattooed, we might even get down to doing some business."

"Long live the solidarity between progressive elements

of social parasitism and to each according to his need," agreed the stuffed Soviet leader. "Let us conduct joint docking maneuvers together in the spirit of Apollo-Soyuz while continuing peaceful competition for the available natural resources."

"See you in Vegas," the president said happily. "For a Rooshian and a corpse, you sure sound like a real party animal!"

Blinking against the cruel glare, Ivan Igorovich Gornikov maneuvered the Party chairman down the ramp onto the broiling tarmac of McCarran Airport, following as inconspicuously as he could while of necessity lugging the portable control console.

"Two hours of this heat, and poor Pyotr Ivanovich will start to stink," Boris Vladimirov whispered unhappily in Ivan's ear as the full force of the noonday Las Vegas sun hit them in the face like a hot rocket exhaust.

Ivan groaned. No one had had time to think of that.

No one had really had time to think of anything. The hardware arrangements were as hastily improvised as the summit meeting that the chairman had somehow managed to arrange with the American president. Access to the main memory banks and mainframe software of Pyotr Ivanovich back in Moscow was a shaky affair involving a satellite link to the airplane, and a modem-mobile phone link to the control console that Ivan carried, cleverly disguised as what the decadent capitalists called a "ghetto blaster." It even had AM-FM cassette capability for the sake of realism.

But the KGB technicians, who admittedly had done heroic feats of socialist labor putting the electronic linkages together on such short notice, had entirely overlooked the limitations of even advanced socialist embalming technology. True, the corpse of the chairman had survived ten years of service without beginning to rot, but a few short appearances atop Lenin's tomb in brisk Moscow springs and falls were one thing, and the one-hundred-degree heat of the Great American desert quite another!

Ivan, Boris, and the chairman were met at the foot of the ramp by the vice president, the first lady, and a big, blond Air Force captain.

"Welcome to the monkey house, mon!" said the vice president.

"You look pale as a piss-ant parson, boy," said the Air

Force captain, regarding the chairman with an idiot grin. "Guess it's pretty hard to keep a tan back in Moscow!"

"I am pleased to convey the fraternal dialectic of the workers and peasants of the Lubianka collective gulag to the militaristic elements of progressive world youth," said Pyotr Ivanovich, grinning mechanically of its own accord, as it had taken to doing lately.

"Say what?"

"The chairman's English is somewhat less than perfect," Ivan said hastily. "Would you prefer we switch to Russian?"

"So you can do the talking?"

"Who *me?*" exclaimed Ivan. "I'm just the chairman's . . . how do you say it, *roadie,*" Ivan said. "And Boris here is my assistant."

"Where's the foreign minister and the defense minister and your KGB chief?" demanded the American vice president.

Cowering with the rest of the Politburo in the Dacha where they hope to save at least their own cowardly asses when the bombs start to fall! Ivan almost answered. Not one of them dared accompany the dead but gallant Party chairman on his eleventh-hour mission to save the world from nuclear destruction, the randomized decision-making software was not only in control, it was entirely on its own. Even Marshall Borodin, after a fatuous charade of reluctance, had readily enough in the end ceded direct computer-link control of the Soviet strategic forces to the decision-making software of Pyotr Ivanovich. Collective Leadership had been entirely surrendered to a new Cult of Personality.

"Our Glorious Chairman, Pyotr Ivanovich Bulgorny, Hero of Socialist Labor, inheritor of the mantle of Marx and Lenin, has the full unquestioned support of the KGB, the Red Army, and the Party Machinery which he embodies," Ivan was therefore able to declare quite truthfully. "But if there has been no militarist coup in American ruling circles, why is your president not here to greet him?"

The vice president and the first lady exchanged peculiar glances.

"Sam has . . . got his hands full at the Court of Caligula. . . ." the first lady finally muttered, grinding her teeth. *The Court of Caligula?*

"The hotel where the summit will be held," said the vice president.

"Don't worry boys," boomed the Air Force captain, "it's

got the wildest casino floor on the Strip, you're gonna love it!"

"Time to go down to meet the Rooshians, girls!" the president said, pulling up the pants of his Uncle Sam suit but forgetting to zip up the fly. If he had not yet gotten stewed or tattooed, he had certainly at last gotten quite properly screwed while Margot was occupied at the airport. He wondered if boffing four hookers in two hours might be one for the *Guinness Book of Records*.

"I hope your Rooshian friends don't think they can pay for pussy in rubles!" said the blond bimbo.

"Yeah, Mr. Prez," said the brunette, "I mean the world may be about to blow itself up, but business is business!"

"Don't worry girls, you just show old Pyotr Ivanovich a good time, and send the bill to the State Department," said the president. "Those Foggy Bottom fruits have been pimping for foreigners ever since FDR sent Eleanor to spread her legs for Stalin!"

The Air Force helicopter set down in the outdoor parking lot of the Caligula's Court Hotel and Casino, a huge, gleaming, glass phallus looming behind a half-scale replica of the Roman Coliseum domed like an all-weather stadium.

Ivan, Boris, Chairman Bulgorny, and the Americans were met at the collonaded entrance by a phalanx of body-builders done up as Praetorian guards, replete with spears, shields, and skin-tight rubber body-armor.

They were ushered down a short, wide corridor embellished with audioanimatrated Romans and animals cycling through entirely un-Disneylike couplings and through a great, vaulted archway overlooking the casino floor.

A long spiral ramp wound down around the circumference of the huge room where the grandstands in the real thing would have been, a continuous arcade of slot machines, where fat blue-haired women squeezed into pastel tights, small children, gum-chewing off-duty hookers, and bleary-eyed drunks stood pulling levers mechanically and staring into space.

Below, the roulette wheels, blackjack and poker games, and craps tables were interspersed with both live sex acts and audioanimatronic figures performing hideous tortures and perversions too beastly to contemplate. The cocktail waitresses wore black leather panty hose, chrome chains, and slave-collars. The dealers and coupiers were done up in rags as captive Christians, and the lurking bouncers were gladiators.

A big stage jutting out from the curving wall was presently dressed as the Emperor's Box, replete with two cushioned thrones, couches, fan-waving Nubians naked to the waist, groaning tables heaped with fruit and meats, and a plethora of nude serving girls.

The cocktail tables in front of the stage had been entirely taken over by reporters, cameramen, and TV technicians in the process of getting stony drunk, and the stage itself was garishly lit by bright shooting lights.

On one of the oversized thrones lolled Samuel T. Carruthers, the president of the United States. He was dressed in an Uncle Sam suit. Four hookers in red, white, and blue garter belts and pasties managed to drape themselves over various portions of his anatomy. He sat there stroking the red phone to the button room with his fly open and his staff at half-mast.

"Somehow, Ivan," Boris said as they made their way across the casino floor toward the presidential spectacle, "I don't think we're in Kansas."

"Sam Carruthers, how dare you!" Margot shouted before any more official greetings could be exchanged. "Get rid of these bimbos at once!"

"This is my new White House staff!" the president said. "Candy is the press secretary, Lurleen is national security adviser, Marla is chief of staff, and Sue Ellen is my new expert in domestic affairs."

"You can't appoint a bunch of whores to be the White House staff!" exclaimed the vice president.

"Why not?" said the president. "Why should I be any different from my illustrious predecessors?"

Fast Eddie shrugged. For once he had to admit that the old goat had a point.

"Well if that's the White House staff, then Bo Bob here is going to be my appointments secretary for the duration," the first lady declared. "Come on, Bo Bob, you sit down here with me and peel me a grape."

"Well come on and get your ass up here, Pete!" the president told Pyotr Ivanovich after the American delegation had sorted out its seating protocol, patting the cushion of the adjoining throne. "These lovely ladies are ready for some stiff negotiation."

Ivan hesitated, holding the Bulgorny motionless, for he wouldn't give Pyotr Ivanovich more than an hour or two under those hot lights.

But Pyotr Ivanovich, it would seem, had developed some more ideas of his own, or perhaps the linkage with Moscow was not quite as static free as promised with all these slot machines going off around the control console, for without any say-so on Ivan's part, the Bulgorny ascended to the stage and seated itself. Two of the prostitutes detached themselves from the president of the United States and turned their ministrations to the corpus of the chairman of the Soviet Communist Party.

"Greetings to the Plenary Session of the Supreme Soviet of the decadent West," said the chairman. "I wish to take this opportunity to propose a new five-year plan for drill press production."

Ivan and Boris collapsed behind a cocktail table and ordered a bottle of vodka, determined under these conditions to catch up to the American TV people, which, by the looks of them, would take some doing.

"Haw, haw! That's a good one!" the president exclaimed, slapping the chairman on the back. "Well you've come to the right town to do it!"

"Mr. Chairman!"

"Mr. President!"

The cameras started rolling and the reporters were up and shouting, and all at once a press conference had begun.

"Mr. Chairman! Is it true that you're dead?"

"The Cult of Personality has been tossed in the dustbin of history and the Party machinery now functions as the Collective Leadership of the Brezhnev Doctrine."

"Mr. President, if the Israelis ignore the Korami ultimatum, and Koram defies the Israeli counterultimatum, how will you respond to the Soviet threat to launch a nuclear attack on the United States after the Israelis reply to the Korami response to their rejection of the original demands?"

"Huh?" said Samuel T. Carruthers. What was the flannel-mouthed sucker talking about? He turned to his national security adviser. "Lurleen," he whispered, "what you got to say about that?"

"Tell 'em you'll think about it, hon."

"I'll just have to think about it. . . ."

"But Mr. President, within twenty-four hours, Hassan al Korami will launch his nuclear missiles at Israel if they don't capitulate, and if the Israelis retaliate, the Russians will nuke the United States! Isn't that what this summit meeting is all about?"

"They will? It is?" the president said perplexedly. He turned to face the chairman of the Central Committee, who sat beside him maintaining a perfect poker face despite this awful revelation. "I thought you just came here to get some nookie, Pete!" he complained.

"Mr. Chairman, do you deny that the Soviet Union has threatened to launch an all-out nuclear attack on the United States if the Israelis attack the Sheikdom of Koram?"

"The peace-loving Soviet people will never be the first to use nuclear weapons nor will we be the last. Long live the threat of long-range economic planning and mutual short-arm inspection between our two great nations!"

"Does that mean that Hassan al Korami was *lying* then? Are you now willing to promise the American people that Koram is *not* under the Soviet nuclear umbrella?"

"Owning to technical difficulties with the Proton supply rocket, the entire production of the Kiev umbrella factory was mislabled as fertilizer and shipped to Poland in place of the missing consignment of Marxist-Leninist dialectic. The Ministry of Production assumes no responsibility for the ideological reliability of misuse of the product."

"Just a minute now, let's get one thing straight, I'm the president here, this is *my* party!" said the president. This was getting out of hand. This smart-ass Rooshian was doin' all the talking.

"You tell 'em, Mr. Prez," said the presidential press secretary, nibbling at his ear.

"That's right!" said Uncle Sam. "Why don't you guys start asking *me* some questions?"

"Well then what will *you* do? Will you force the Israelis to capitulate to Koram? Will you preempt the Russians? Will you attack Koram before the deadline?"

Uncle Sam's patience was wearing quite thin. Koram,

Israel, and frigging Rooshians, they were all a bunch of foreign troublemakers, weren't they? "I'll nuke 'em till they glow blue!" he shouted, waving the red command phone.

"Russia?"

"Koram?"

"Israel?"

"Nuke who?"

"Nuke *you*, Charlie!" the president said crossly. "That's the part I haven't figured out yet!"

Slowly, the tumult began to subside, as the three major network anchormen rose to their feet in unison, and with the cameras rolling, went after the president before the world like a tag-team of wrestlers.

"Mr. President, within twenty-four hours, World War III is likely to break out between the Soviet Union and the United States unless you and the chairman can agree on steps to prevent it. . . ."

"The clock is ticking toward midnight. . . ."

"And there you sit before the American people with your fly open and the button in your hand telling us you'll think about it?"

"The American people have a right to know what you're going to do right now!"

"What am I going to do right now?" the president asked his chief of staff. She grabbed his crotch as she whispered in his ear.

The president grinned happily. "Right now," he said, "we're going to party!"

"Boy Mr. Prez, your friend is really weird," said the presidential press secretary, emerging from the adjourning bedroom on wobbly knees, and plunking herself down on the bed between the national security adviser and the chief of staff, who lay there torpidly dragging on cigarettes. "He's already worn three of us out, and we *still* can't make him come or quit!"

"And he talks so funny all the time while he's doing it, like some kind of speed freak phonograph record whose needle keeps slipping. . . ."

"He's a Rooshian, isn't he?" said Uncle Sam who, now quite thoroughly sated, was making an effort to pull up his pants and be presidential.

The domestic affairs adviser emerged from the other bedroom suddenly, ghostly pale and green around the gills. "Give me a lude quick!" she moaned "You're not going to believe this! It fell off!"

"You don't mean—"

"I am proud to award you all the order of Hero of Socialist Labor for your stakhanovite efforts in overfulfilling your production quotas by twenty-three percent!" declared Pyotr Ivanovich Bulgorny, clad only in his baggy blue boxer shorts and suit jacket.

As he regarded the Soviet chairman, standing there, grinning hideously, babbling communist propaganda, and with his pecker quite literally in his pocket, Sam Carruthers remembered what in his severe horniness he had forgotten, namely that Pyotr Ivanovich Bulgorny was in fact dead.

Now he finally noticed the green cast to the Soviet leader's skin, and once having observed that, he began to smell the faint putrid odor of deer that had been hung just a wee bit too high.

Well dead or not, thought Uncle Sam Carruthers, he can't complain I didn't show him a good time. And dead or not, he realized, Bulgorny was a man to be reckoned with, because dead or not, he had run the show over there in Russia for twenty years.

"Fair's fair, Pete," he said. "We've had our partying, and now, in the grand old American tradition, it's time to sit down to talk turkey. We can't let this little A-rab piss-ant pull this stuff on us! We gotta figure something out. Lurleen, give me my national security briefing."

"Say what, Mr. Prez?"

"Tell me what the hell is going on!"

"Well hon," said the national security adviser, as they all repaired to the couches in the suite's sitting room, "it's the same dumb game we girls get you johns to play with each other when we're feelin' mean. You know, some girl will get two big bruisers pissed off at each other and then stand back and laugh while they punch each other out. Well you and old Pete are the two nuclear heavyweight champs of the world, right, and this Hassan al Korami is the mean little bitch."

"That's right," said the domestic affairs adviser, "you jerks are letting him make monkeys out of you."

"Oh yeah?" said the president. "If you girls are so smart and Pete and I are so dumb, what would *you* do?"

The presidential press secretary eased herself down in between the president and the chairman and threw an arm around each of their shoulders.

"You guys don't *really* want to punch each other out, now do you?" she purred placatingly. "You're not really mad at *each other* now that you've partied together, now are you?"

"Right," said the national security adviser. "It's the creep that's been trying to get you to blow each other up so he can sit back and laugh who deserves to get his ticket punched, now isn't it?"

"What do you got to say to that, Pete?" the president asked the chairman. "Makes sense to me. Why don't we just get together and stomp the little piss-ant flat?"

"Marxist-Leninist doctrine clearly states that a fool and his missiles are soon parted," agreed Pyotr Ivanovich. "But on the other hand, the long-range interests of the Soviet consumer class cannot be decoupled from the national paranoia trip of Soviet prestige. *Pravda* by definition must always speak the truth."

"He means he'll look like a wimp if he backs down," explained the domestic affairs adviser.

"I guess I can see your point, Pete," the president was constrained to admit, seeing as how the poor bastard looked like a corpse with his pecker in his pocket already.

"Why don't you guys just go on *America Tonite* and yell at each other?" suggested the presidential press secretary. "Pete here, instead of threatening to punch you out if your pal Israel punches out Hassan, threatens to punch you out if *you* punch out Hassan."

"Right hon," said the chief of staff, "and you can jump up and down and threaten to punch out Pete if he punches out your pal Israel."

"You both get to look like big tough guys, and your troublemaking pals can't complain you let them down. . . ."

"But instead of blowing up the world, we all just get to sit back and laugh while the smart-ass that tried to start the whole thing gets the shit beat out of him."

"You girls sure beat all hell out of my previous appointments," the president said with satisfaction. "What do you say, Pete? It's almost show time. . . ."

"Long live dialectic solidarity between the collective leadership of working class software and the social parasites of decadent western oligarchs!" the Chairman of the Central Committee of the Soviet Communist Party declared, shaking hands with the President of the United States, and with that, the summit meeting was concluded, and the participants repaired arm in arm in arm to the casino floor.

America Tonite had been on the air for ten minutes, and Terry Tummler had already gone on and died with his opening monologue when the president of the United States, the chairman of the Soviet Communist Party, and four disheveled hookers finally shambled arm in arm onto the Emperor's Box state set and flopped themselves down under the hot shooting lights.

The primo front-row tables had been permanently commandeered by the by-now thoroughly sodden world press corps, and lousy tippers these freeloaders were too, to the dismay of the waitresses. Ivan and Boris managed to keep their front-row seats by offering hash joints and vodka to all and sundry, and the vice president, the first lady, and Captain Bo Bob Beauregard found themselves squeezed together at a small table next to the Russians.

The rest of the nightclub seats were jammed with a demographic cross section of ordinary Americans who had come to get drunk, lose their money, and tell the folks back home that they had seen *America Tonite* Live In Vegas, and instead found themselves sitting through dumb jokes waiting for the heads of state to emerge from their seclusion with the agreement that would save the world from nuclear holocaust.

And now, at last, with the deadline for doomsday only hours away, what they and the vast television audience beyond got was a former used car salesman in an unzipped Uncle Sam suit and a blotchy green corpse with its pecker in its pocket being interviewed by Terry Tummler bulging out of a comic Roman toga surrounded by fagged-out hookers.

"Well it's a pleasure to welcome two such extinguished world leaders to *America Tonite*," said the genial Terry Tummler, "and I'm sure we'd all like to know whether your writers have come up with any better material than mine have tonight. I mean, when *I* lay a bomb, only my agent dies, but if you bomb out the whole show gets canceled!"

"Don't get your balls in an uproar, Terry," the president said, waving the red phone. "Uncle Sam Carruthers takes no shit from Ivan the Terrible here!" He stuck his tongue out at Chairman Bulgorny and let fly a juicy Bronx cheer. "If you bomb Israel, Bluto," he told Pyotr Ivanovich with a wink, "old Popeye here will nuke Rooshia back into the stone age."

At this, even the unflappable Terry Tummler blanched, covering it as best he could with a sickly grin.

"Well . . . heh . . . heh . . . I guess these are the jokes, folks," he stammered.

"What have we *done*, Boris?" Ivan Igorovich Gornikov moaned drunkenly.

They had been unable to control the Bulgorny for hours, yet somehow Pyotr Ivanovich had managed to function autonomously. The randomized software had taken over entirely. There was nothing in any hacker's theory to account for it. If he were not a good atheist, Ivan would have crossed himself.

Come to think of it, he thought, making the motions, better safe than sorry.

"What about you, Chairman Bulgorny?" Terry Tummler burbled. "Got any hot new projects?"

Some sapient spirit seemed to peer out from behind the glass eyes of the corpse of Pyotr Ivanovich Bulgorny, which certainly was beginning to look a little worse for wear. When it spoke, Ivan wondered whether some chance conjuction between programming fragments and bits and pieces of randomized old speeches had not conjured the true spirit of the bureaucratic socialist state, the voice of pure dialectical determinism itself, the ghost in the Party machinery.

"The peace-loving malingerers and hooligans of the Red Army will not stand idly by while neocolonialist war criminals in high Pentagon circles vaporize reactionary Third World criminal elements," Pyotr Ivanovich Bulgorny declared forcefully.

"Oh yeah?" roared the president, mugging at the audience. "So's yer mother!"

"Now guys, come on, we've still got an hour of air time to fill, I mean, if we have World War III now, all that's left backstage to go on afterward is a chimp act and a gypsy violinist!"

"Well I'm ready to just sit back, open a six-pack, and watch the big fight on television if he is," said the president, leaning back, throwing one arm around a hooker, and elbowing the dead Soviet chairman in the ribs with the other.

"If our illustrious allies wish to beat the shit out of each other," agreed Pyotr Ivanovich, "then both the long-range interest of the international working class and the spirit of noninterference in the internal sporting events of friendly buffer states require that our two great peoples do nothing to interfere with their right to express their national identities outside in the alley."

"You tell 'em, Pyotr Ivanovich!" exclaimed Ivan. "Ah Boris, does not such sterling cybernetic leadership make you proud to be a member of the Russian Computer Underground?"

"Cowards! Camel-suckers! Perfidious Infidels!" roared Hassan al Korami when he heard the news bulletin on K-RAB. How dare the scorpions he had sealed together in a bottle refuse to fight each other to the death for his delectation?

"No more Sheik Nice Guy!" he screamed, storming into the control van where his missile controllers sat before their screens and joysticks ready to play *Cruise Missile Commander.*

"Launch all our missiles the moment an Israeli plane crosses our borders," said the Lion of the Desert. "But you will fire only *three* missiles at Israel. The ones we reserved for Beersheba and Eilat will instead be diverted to attack the American and Soviet fleets in the Mediterranean."

He rubbed his hands together, sucking on the nearest hookah. "Let's see the two arms of Satanic modernism talk their way out of *that* one!" he cackled maniacally, drooling smoke and spittle.

"Pyotr Ivanovich's nose has fallen off!" moaned Boris.

It was true. The chairman was visibly beginning to decompose under the shooting lights for all the world to see. His face had turned a sickly brownish green and gas bubbles pocked the surface of its varnish. Now the nose had melted like a piece of overripe cheese and fallen into his lap, exposing wet white bone.

*   *   *

Armand Deutcher sweated nervously before his news monitors in the control room of the Rockin' Voice of the A-rabs. An ABC camera satellite was trying to focus a clear picture of a flight of objects proceeding due south across Saudi territory from Israel, on their way to Koram. At the same time, Israeli TV was broadcasting *its* satellite coverage of the Korami cruise missiles waiting on the desert sands. Meanwhile, one of the other two American networks was running an old movie, while the third dominated the ratings with *America Tonite* as never before. Radio Moscow was playing patriotic music.

Now the NBC camera zoomed in tight on the formation of Israeli aircraft. Alors, they were neither Slings of David missiles nor fighter-bombers of the Israeli Air Force, but a few dozen cheap obsolescent light-weight drones powered by lawn-mower engines!

"Bedouin spotters report a vast armada of Israeli aircraft crossing our sacred borders, oh Lion of the Desert," declared Hassan al Korami's radio operator. "From horizon to horizon, the sky is black with F-21s, Super-Kfirs, and supersonic cruise missiles!"

"Launch all missiles!" shrieked Hassan the Assassin, biting through the stem of his hookah in his ecstasy and spewing splinters of bloody ivory.

Hurriedly, Armand Deutcher readied his own control console, and ordered K-RAB off the air so he could patch it into the Rockin' Voice of the A-rab's monster transmitter.

For the Israelis could have only one thing in mind by sending in this handful of old junk instead of a sophisticated all-out nonnuclear attack force.

Thanks to the crazy American president and the rapidly decomposing corpse of the Soviet chairman, his own plan was now back on course.

The Israelis obviously intended to provoke Hassan into firing his missiles first. Even now their own satellite cameras were showing the world five rusty F-111s wobbling shakily into the air then roaring off at supersonic speed right down on the deck in the general direction of Israel.

And, even as Armand had expected, the NBC satellite camera now showed the Israeli drones self-destructing just inside Korami territory.

Wonderful! Soon the Israeli controllers would take command of the Korami cruise missiles. They'd drop four of them harmlessly into the ocean off camera, and then use their satellite cameras to show the fifth one veering crazily off course and taking out Mecca.

Then they could nuke Koram out of existence while even their Arab enemies applauded, and when the dust cleared, they would sit astride the entire Middle East after having shot their way into the club as a nuclear superpower.

Or so they thought.

But Armand Deutcher had much better uses to put that cruise missile to than starting a nuclear potlatch, which, if it didn't escalate into World War III, would result in a Middle Eastern Pax Judaeaica which would severely suppress arms sales for decades to come.

His multibillion franc smart-money bet was on a far more profitable nuclear option. . . .

A battery of monitors had been dragged out onto the stage set of *America Tonite,* and Terry Tummler, the president, the chairman, and the hookers of the White House staff set there watching TV on camera, including, bizarrely enough, the live coverage of themselves watching it.

"Heh . . . heh . . ." burbled Terry Tummler. "Looks as if the boys in the bedsheets have launched their missiles. . . . Got anything funny to say about that, Mr. Prez?"

"I'll lay six to five against any of them hitting Israel," said Sam Carruthers.

"You're faded, Mr. Prez," said the national security adviser.

"I'll lay even money them Israelis clean old Hassan's clock in the next twenty minutes," declared the chief of staff. "Any takers?"

"The peace-loving revanchist vanguard of the Soviet people accepts your challenge to make a fast ruble," declared Pyotr Ivanovich Bulgorny, whose stainless-steel teeth and bony jaw were now clearly showing where more rotting flesh had fallen away from his face.

Israeli TV now made a great show of having its satellite cameras lose track of the wobbly F-111s as the five Korami cruise missiles peeled away from each other. On came the Israeli prime minister with a terse announcement.

"The Sheikdom of Koram has launched an unprovoked nuclear attack on the State of Israel. The Israeli Defense Forces will confine themselves to a nonnuclear counterstrike in the interests of world peace. Unless, of course, this maniac Hassan al Korami should actually manage to hit anything with his nuclear missiles, in which case we shall naturally be forced to nuke Koram out of existence in the interests of Biblical justice."

Armand Deutcher had the Korami missiles on his radar screen now. Three of them were zigging and zagging more or less in the direction of Israel, but the other two were making a beeline across the Mediterranean toward the Russian and American fleets! Good Lord, if the Israelis didn't dump those two missiles tout suite, all bets were off!

"What is happening?" demanded Hassan al Korami, chewing the soggy end of his huge spliff to bits, as his controllers twiddled furiously with their joysticks. On their monitor screens, fuzzy purple airplanes were bobbing and weaving over cartoon landscapes dotted with medieval castles, fire-breathing reptiles, and giant apes.

"We have racked up three million points already!" one of the controllers reassured him. "According to the control computers, we are approaching the arcade record!"

One by one, the blips dropped off Armand Deutcher's radar screen, as the Israeli controllers seized control of the Korami cruise missiles and ditched them into the sea. Now there was only one F-111 still on the screen, headed in the general direction of Tel Aviv. Suddenly it veered off, did a ragged one-eighty, and set off on a new tack to the south.

"Well that's four out of five into the drink, isn't it?" said Terry Tummler. "Maybe there won't be a fireworks act before the last commercial after all. . . ."

"It ain't over till the Fat Lady sings," said the president. "What do you say, Pete, will you give me three to one on at least one Big One going off before the show is over?"

But Pyotr Ivanovich Bulgorny sat there silently, his expression rendered all the more unreadable by the fact that most of his face had now fallen away, revealing a gleaming wet skull with two glass eyes set in its sockets, a hideous stainless-steel grin, and shards and tatters of shriveled skin and decomposing flesh clinging to the bone.

*   *   *

The Israeli satellite cameras had now managed to "find" the errant F-111.

"The last Korami cruise missile has now been spotted over Saudi Arabia and headed in the general direction of Mecca!" declared the Israeli TV announcer with a great show of outraged horror as the rusty old plane jerked into focus buzzing low over the head of a camel caravan.

"Whatever this maniac Hassan al Korami is up to, and whatever misunderstandings may have existed between our two great peoples in the past, the government of Israel wishes to assure our Arab friends that we will regard any Korami nuclear attack on their Holy City as an attack on our own and will retaliate accordingly with the full resources of our nuclear arsenal in the Spirit of Camp David."

Armand Deutcher keyed in the override command, which went out over the mighty Rockin' Voice of the A-rabs to the lamprey circuit he had planted on the control chips that the Israelis had secreted in the phony remote control machinery.

Reaching for his joystick, he bent the F-111's course slowly toward the west, fighting to turn the jury-rigged cruise missile around against the unexpectedly stiff resistance of the Israeli controllers.

On all the control screens, the same little purple airplane was weaving among giant black pterodactyls and laser-firing flying saucers toward a huge, dim black castle at the top of the screen. Robots and centipedes poured out of it and began firing frisbees and lightning bolts.

"A million bonus points for getting the Black Castle!" exclaimed one of the controllers.

Hassan al Korami squinted at the lettering on the screen. Where in Israel was "Mordor?"

"Merde!" grunted Armand Deutcher, stirring sweatily at his joystick.

All three American networks now showed the F-111 stunting crazily over Mecca as Deutcher fought the Israelis for control.

It buzzed low over the bazaar, sending goods and awnings flying with its supersonic shockwave, zigged and zagged among the sun-bleached buildings, suddenly shot straight up, then dropped down again and came within ten feet of taking out the Kaaba, before pulling out into another steep climb, and then—

—And then all at once Deutcher had it. He managed to bring the jury-rigged cruise missile back down on the deck and bend its course more or less to the north as its wings began to develop an all-too-familiar flutter. . . .

"Son of a bitch, look at that boy *fly!*" Bo Bob Beauregard exclaimed admiringly.

More monitors had been set out in Caligula's Court for the benefit of *America Tonite*'s live audience in order to hype the action, for by now even the tables and slot machines had been entirely abandoned as everyone in the casino watched the network satellite cameras track the Korami cruise missile upon whose eventual destination thousands of bets now hung.

"Wow," said the president, excitedly stroking both his red phone and his dong, "this is just like the fourth quarter of the Superbowl!"

The F-111 was putting on quite a show.

Jerking and bobbing about twenty feet above the Mediterranean like a drunken dragonfly, its wings shaking and juddering, the rusty old jet missed a supertanker by inches, buzzed a cruiseliner, decapitated a seagull, and then came in low over the crowded harbor of Saint Tropez, France.

It weaved crazily among the pleasure craft, scattering water skiers, starlets, beach bums, and Greek shipping tycoons, headed straight for the line of yachts lining the primo beachfront property, and then suddenly managed to veer off at the last moment, east along the Cote D'Azure in the general direction of Monaco.

It wobbled along the coastline until the prime beachfront real estate was replaced by rocky cliffs falling directly to the sea and then—

—the right wing of the F-111 sheered off and went sailing away like a kite as the plane went into a steep left turn—

—it skittered crazily across the sky and smashed directly into the sea cliff with a blinding flash—

And the satellite cameras pulled back to a medium shot of a mushroom-pillar cloud blossoming evilly on the southern coast of France.

*   *   *

A great groan of dismay rose up from the casino floor. No one had any money riding on *France*!

"All bets are off!"

"The hell they are! They didn't hit Israel, did they?"

"But they didn't hit Mecca either!"

"Fork over!"

"Pay up!"

"Screw you!"

"Tu madre tambien!"

Only Pyotr Ivanovich displayed admirable slavic stoicism during this unseemly tumult. There he sat, silent and imperturbable, as fistfights broke out among the gamblers, and the American president masturbated nervously with his red phone.

Indeed the chairman had not moved or spoken since the flesh had melted from his bones revealing the death's head grin within, as if he had become embarrassed by his poor appearance on television, or more likely, Ivan Igorovich Gornikov thought, as if his melting gush of body fluids had finally shorted the whole mess out.

But now a tremor went through the Bulgorny and the jaws of the skull clacked open and stuck, revealing the speaker grid within stuck like an overlarge morsel in its skeletal throat.

A horrible ear-killing shriek of static and feedback stopped everyone in their tracks and thin tendrils of smoke began steaming out of the rotting corpse's ears.

"... Brak! ... Scree! ... Wonk! ..." the Chairman of the Soviet Communist Party observed forcefully in a crackling, metallic robot voice. "The dialectical requirements of socialist realist esthetics require a beginning, a middle, and an end to all cautionary Russian folk wisdom in keeping with the Marxist-Leninist principle of from each according to his assholery, to each according to his greed."

"Are you saying what I think you're saying, Pete?" said the American president.

"You can't make a revolutionary omelet without breaking heads," Pyotr Ivanovich pointed out. "When confronted with homicidal reactionary maniacs and tin-pot nuclear pipsqueaks, all progressive peace-loving peoples must reach for their revolvers."

"Like the man says," agreed the national security adviser, as she soothed the president's throbbing dork, "nuke 'em till they glow blue!"

"Oh boy!" said Bo Bob Beauregard. "Do we get to take out the Rooshians now?"

"*The Rooshians?*" the president exclaimed. "Shit no, us and the Rooshians are going to bomb the bejesus out of that wormy little bugger Hassan al Korami! Why the hell should we be nuking each other with maniacs like that running around loose! Isn't that right, Pete?"

"As Chairman of the Central Committee software of the Party machinery, I hereby declare the extension of the Brezhnev Doctrine to encompass peaceful copreemption with the United States of all reactionary Third World autocrats who try to join the club."

Armand Deutcher, sipping cognac, puffing away at his huge Havana cigar, leaned back in his chair and watched the grotesque spectacle that all world news networks were now carrying with the wry amusement of a connoisseur of political buffoonery who no longer had any investments hanging on the outcome.

There for all the world to see was the president of the United States with a prostitute's head between his legs and the red telephone cradled against his cheek, and there sat the chairman of the Soviet Communist Party, a rapidly decomposing corpse out of some cheap Hollywood horror movie, with the last tatters of rotten flesh sliding off his skull and into his lap, and the smoke of burning electrical insulation pouring out of his ears.

Vraiment, thought Armand, as the anglophones have it, one picture is indeed worth a thousand words!

"This is the president of the United States. . . ."

"And the Personality Cult of the Party Machinery of the Union of Soviet Socialist Republics. . . ."

"My friend the chairman here may be a moldy corpse . . ."

"And Uncle Sam may embody the final pussy-obsessed imperialism of the stewed, screwed, and tattooed West on its way to the fertilizer production quota of history . . ."

"But even a corpse and a sex maniac know better than to let any little piss-ant who's even moldier and crazier than we are try to get his dirty little mitts on one of these red telephones again!"

"We will now bury an object lesson in the historical dialectic of socialist surrealism and peace-loving ass-kicking so that any revanchist reactionary oligarch with delusions of nuclear destiny will think twice before pissing us off again!"

"Go get 'em, Bo Bob!" the president ordered, and collapsed in sweet ecstasy.

"Overfulfill your nuclear production quotas where it will do the most historical good," said the chairman of the Central Committee as sparks shot out of his rictus grin, and he collapsed into a pile of old bones and burned-out circuitry.

The Black Castle was spewing forth bats and rockets and flying saucers and yellow munching circles in desperation now, for the little purple airplane had almost reached its target!

"Die, Zionist Dogs, die American Imperialists, die Russian Infidels, die Corrupt Modernism, die oh Great Satan!" shrieked Hassan al Korami as a huge, dark shadow-shape with a fiery grin arose out of the Black Castle. "Fire! Fire!"

The controllers pressed their joystick buttons.

The Great Satan laughed.

"YOU LOSE, SUCKER, DON'T TRY TO PLAY AGAIN," said the words that appeared on the screen just before a brilliant white light exploded.

Fast Eddie Braithewaite, president of the United States, gazed expansively out at Washington from the helicopter carrying him to his first weekend at Camp David.

When twenty ten-megaton American warheads and twenty ten-megaton Soviet warheads had slammed into the Sheikdom of Koram as an object lesson to nuclear upstarts in the name of newfound Soviet-American solidarity, Uncle Sam Carruthers had been a hero for a brief moment.

But two hundred megatons on an area the size of Los Angeles had been more than enough to shatter the collapsing rock-dome above the depleted oil table, and the entire sheikdom had plunged with a fiery splash into the oil pool beneath, setting it ablaze.

When the mushroom clouds cleared, there was nothing left but a huge cauldron of burning oil where the Sheikdom of Koram had been.

While this made for some spectacular footage on the evening news, when it became apparent that the fire was spreading like termites in balsa wood throughout the Middle Eastern oil fields, that was finally enough to convince the powers that be to give Samuel T. Carruthers the hook, and send him off to get his ashes hauled on an endless second honeymoon in Atlantic City.

Anyone who was *that* bad for business was, ipso facto, insane.

It was a good life being a member of the new Soviet elite in the dawn of the Moscow Spring, a life of luxury apartments, Dachas in the country, and Mercedes-Benzes, in a Russia freed from the dead hand of the moribund Party Machinery.

In the revision of Marxist-Leninist doctrine, which had been forced upon the Central Committee with the passage of the unifying figure of Pyotr Ivanovich Bulgorny from the scene, the Russian Computer Underground had emerged from the electronic catacombs as the only force capable of saving Mother Russia from total economic chaos.

The Communist Party and its functionaries had been retired honorably to the status of a collective royal family to preside at state funerals and make speeches atop Lenin's tomb on May Day and the Anniversary of the Revolution, and the practical matters of necessity had been put into the hands of the Computer Underground, who were the only people capable of keeping the newly decentralized and computerized Soviet economy going.

There were even those who called this the perfection of communism, since the state was indeed in the process of withering away.

But sometimes, late at night, Ivan Igorovich Gornikov experienced a perverse nostalgic twinge for the Bad Old Days of Pyotr Ivanovich Bulgorny, even as his parents had come to consider the memory of Stalin something of a sainted monster once he was safely dead and buried.

Say what you like, dead or not, the noble Pyotr Ivanovich was responsible for Ivan's present good fortune, and for the present Soviet-American detente! There was a man who, whatever his shortcomings, would live in history!

Besides, now that the KGB no longer had a customer like Hassan al Korami to soak, the filthy capitalist roaders had jacked the price of hash in Moscow 300 percent!

"Ce va, Zvi...?"
"Business, believe me, could be a lot better," Zvi Bar

David complained. "You were shrewd to get out and into real estate when you did, Armand. Ever since the Russians and Americans so forcefully discouraged Third World customers from seeking state of the art, all we can move are small arms and cheap old junk."

"Don't worry, Zvi," Armand Deutcher said expansively. "Someone will start a nice little war somewhere, they always do."

"Easy for you to say, Armand, look how you've made out!"

"I'm certainly not complaining!" Deutcher admitted.

There he sat on the terrace of his palatial mansion atop the highest point of the rimwall, looking down and out across the artificial bay carved out of the sea cliff when he had brought the F-111 down on this formerly empty piece of formerly worthless coast.

Land he had previously acquired for a relative song.

Ah, but now a gleaming beach of pulverized and certified nonradioactive glass ran around the noble curve of the bomb crater, crowded with sunbathers, and lined with brand-new luxury hotels, casinos, and marinas choked with yachts. Quaint age-old streets lined with souvenir shops, boutiques, and fancy restaurants had been laid out climbing up the crater wall to the heights, and what wasn't a deluxe emporium was a condo building or town house as the multibillion-franc development glittered and glitzed up the cliff like a Gucci amoeba.

And Armand Deutcher owned every square centimeter of the land it was built on, renting it out to his glitterati serfs for a third of the take.

"To tell the truth, Armand," said Zvi Bar David, "how well do you sleep at night? Almost we had World War III, and all for a petty real estate deal!"

"Come come, Zvi," Deutcher said good-naturedly. "*This* you call a *petty* real estate deal?"

"But what about your social conscience, Armand?"

"Pure as the driven snow!" Armand Deutcher declared. "Am I not the secret hero of the present era of easing international tensions? Thanks to me, no tin-pot little maniac will ever dare to acquire nuclear weapons again, the United States has accepted a black man as president, Israel and the Arabs have made peace, and the Russians have been forced to take care of business."

"True," admitted Bar David. "But on the other hand, an entire nation has been expunged from history, and the Middle Eastern oil fields are on fire."

"As for the first," said Armand Deutcher, "would you have preferred World War III to World War Last?"

"And as for the second?"

Deutcher shrugged philosophically. "As for the second," he said, "I'm already diversified into coal and horse-breeding, Zvi, and I strongly advise you to do the same."

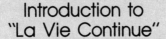

Introduction to
"La Vie Continue"

One of the trickiest problems a writer faces is the task of choosing the right form for a story concept, a commercial as well as an artistic consideration. La Vie Continue was originally conceived as a short story. Years ago, I wrote the first fifteen pages and then froze, realizing that what I had written was the beginning of a novel, not a short story.

A novel that no one was about to publish. There have certainly been novels published in which the author appears as a character—Jerzy Kosinski's The Painted Bird, J. G. Ballard's Empire of the Sun, Philip K. Dick's The Divine Invasion—but no one to my knowledge has ever published a novel in which his projected future self appears. The notion is just too outre, the concept involves too much hubris, yeah, sure, maybe, if you were Bellow, or Mailer, or Vidal . . .

So I put those fifteen pages aside. Until Bantam decided to publish this book and asked me to include a short novel written especially for it.

The novella has always been a liberating form, at least in the world of science-fiction publishing, where there have *always been and still are magazines and anthologies willing to publish stories of this particular length, unlike general publishing, where outlets for short stories this long (or novels this short) are few and far between.*

You can write a real novel in terms of formal structure, even if it is too short to publish as a book. Since a novella will only be part of a book or a magazine issue, you can deal with thematic material that no publisher will put out at novel length for fear of failing to get the book properly distributed, for instance something as politically controversial and stylistically extreme as "World War Last" or something as admittedly self-indulgent as fiction dealing with the author's own projected future self.

I have from time to time been in political hot water for ficton that I have published. My novel Bug Jack Barron, which deals with American presidential politics, among other things, was temporarily banned when it was serialized by New Worlds in Britain and got me denounced on the floor of Parliament. The Iron Dream, my alternate world novel about Adolf Hitler, was banned in Germany, a ban only recently over-ruled in the German equivalent of the Supreme Court after years of legal battle. The Men in the Jungle, my allegorical Vietnam novel, is still on the Index in Germany.

So my published work has already felt the weight of censorship in the real world, in Western democracies at that. And I have been told by American publishing executives that certain thematic material—a novel proposal about the Counterculture, another about America after twenty years of AIDS—cannot be dealt with noncircumspectly at novel length because book chains and distributors would refuse to handle it. And I wonder what would have happened if I had tried to publish "World War Last" at novel length.

Freedom of expression is presently under heavy attack in the United States. The religious right has been successful in removing many books from libraries and magazines from racks. The wife of a presidential candidate has led a crusade to censor rock-music lyrics. When Lorne Michaels, former producer of Saturday Night Live, was called back to inject life into the latter-day version, he was told he could not use certain sketches involving drugs that had proven successful back when his original version of the show was riding high in the ratings. A respected novelist of my acquaintance recently had a book effectively suppressed by the major book chains because of its homosexual content, at no little damage to his career.

It can *happen here. It* has *happened here. It* is *happening here.*

What if this process went just one step further? What if the powers that be, instead of merely coming down on the work of writers, began to come down on writers for what they had written? What would happen to American writers whose work challenged the bounds of the politically and culturally acceptable? What would happen to America?

What would happen to me?

Well Other Americas *was going to be a collection of my own short novels about Americas that might be, and if current trends continued, it was even possible that one or two of the novellas in this very book might in the future even land the author thereof squarely in the shoes of the Norman Spinrad of* La Vie Continue.

So it all came together. This was my collection. I was commissioned to write an original short novel for it. I was more or less free to write whatever I wanted to. I had a story to tell that I doubted could be published elsewhere.

And what more fitting way to conclude a collection of novellas about the possible futures of America than with the author himself standing outside both America and his present, looking back from the future on America from a foreign shore?

LA VIE
CONTINUE

Yours NOT TO REASON why, not that this assignment was do or die, but still, Eli Ellis found European anti-Americanism hard to swallow, the French particularly arrogant and obnoxious, Paris degenerate, and the thought of enriching a traitor like Spinrad, even in the national interest, even in the process of enriching himself, rather galling.

Not that he couldn't read the numbers well enough. Spinrad managed to publish only sporadically in the States and could never unblock a dime of the proceeds, but he had gotten together enough capital from all-too-nebulous European sources after the IRS came down to start the *Free Press de Paris*, and here in France the paper was beyond any American sanction save termination with extreme cement overshoes.

And while the *Free Press de Paris* reached the United States only as smuggled contraband, the wretched rag did its best to publish material that would embarrass the United States in Europe, and, given the political climate and the fact that it was the main medium of English-language publication for Paris's swarming hordes of American political refugees, not to mention an open conduit for every intelligence agency from the KGB to the Mossad, it always had plenty of muck available for the raking.

Washington, however, wanted no unneccesary hassle with the hostile French Socialist government, Spinrad was tight with the minister of justice, and besides, a live but caponized ex-exile living it up in Hollywood would be worth more propaganda-wise than yet another dead martyr.

So, in Washington as in Hollywood, a bottom-line calculation had been made. The silencing of the *Free Press de Paris* might not be worth the political complications of a forthright hit, but it *was* worth fifty mil in completion guarantees to a regime that spent more than that every day napalming mud huts in half a dozen shit-ass countries whose names the Administration could not quite correctly pronounce. Besides, *Riding the Torch* was an entirely nonpolitical piece of sci-fi and the stuff was golden again, so even on such an inflated budget, the film had a shot at breaking even and the Company might even recoup its investment.

Meaning that while failure to close down the *Free Press de Paris* would not be a one-way ticket to Central America or Central Africa or Central Ass-end of Nowhere to do his part for Old Glory in a more forthright fashion, failure to make the movie deal with Spinrad *would* kill a project that figured to make big bucks for BMA, and might very well be Ellis's ticket back to agenting third-rate TV writers, the moral equivalent of Colombia as far as he was concerned.

It was a vintage late September afternoon in Paris when his taxi, after a suspiciously expensive detour across the Seine from the Right Bank and through the heavy traffic around Saint Germaine and the Boul' Mich, doubled back onto the Ile Saint Louis from the Left Bank, and finally dropped him off on Quai de Bourbon, where the cabbie drove off cursing after Ellis stiffed the bastard on the tip.

For a moment Ellis would have almost been fond of Paris if only it weren't so full of Frenchmen. The streets of Saint Germaine had been full of color and life and promising-looking tail, and from this point in the prow, the Ile Saint Louis was like a big stone yacht plowing slowly along through the Seine.

Norman Spinrad had an apartment here on this perpetually trendy little island in the middle of the Seine just behind Notre Dame and just above Saint Germaine, hence on neither the Left nor the Right banks, though as far as Ellis was concerned, he was fooling no one.

From the dossier with which he had been supplied, Ellis knew that Spinrad had always lived in places like this—in New York it had been Greenwich Village; in San Francisco, Buena Vista Park on the fringes of Haight-Ashbury; in London, Bayswater not far from Notting Hill Gate, and in Los Angeles, never Beverly Hills, always Laurel Canyon.

What a waste! he thought as he was buzzed into the building and ascended a dim flight of rickety stairs to Spinrad's top-floor flat. Such a picturesque setting was wasted on the goddamn French, and on the other hand, America was pissing away half a trillion a year whipping a lot of essentially useless Third World banana republics into line, when the same investment in ordnance, treasure, and lives could have bought dominance over Western Europe, since everyone knew that

Battlestar America had long since reduced the Soviet Union to a nuclear paper tiger.

Spinrad's apartment was, well, weird. It was basically an attic space with the living room "ceiling" slanting down from a fifteen-foot apex nearly to the floor as a kind of enormous skylight-cum-window. One corner of the room was obviously a work space, with the traditional writer's desk, computer, printer, and clutter, and the rest of it was furnished with a set of vaguely art-deco black velvet sofas and rosewood tables. There was a kitchen area sectioned off by a very Californian-looking breakfast bar and stools, and through an open door leading into the bedroom, Ellis could see a corner of what appeared to be an actual fucking water bed.

But what made the place so unsettling and also somehow pathetic was the plants. The living room was a frigging jungle. Huge potted palms were everywhere, baskets of ivy, spider plants, and succulents hung from the high side of the skylight wall, and every table, shelf, and bookcase seemed to have at least three or four little cacti or venus flytraps or flowering something or other sitting on it. To complete the picture, there was a huge brass bird cage holding about a dozen vari-colored twittering little finches, like an avian tropical fish tank, and a big holo poster of a flaming Pacific sunset.

Spinrad himself wore a brightly patterned red dashiki over a crummy pair of blue jeans. The silver hair was longer and even more defiantly unkempt than in the usual photos. The gray eyes were large, keen, and somehow dangerous looking, but set deep in tired and blackly bagged sockets. The nostrils were red and sniffly; he seemed to have a cold.

There was something uncanny about the man. He didn't appear to be in his early sixties at all; instead he looked to be in his mid-forties, but with a severe hangover.

Somehow Ellis found the lion, such as he was, in his den, such as it was, encouraging, tactics-wise. Ellis was no horticulturalist, but he certainly had lived in Los Angeles long enough to recognize an attempt to transplant a Southern Californian ecosphere to a Paris garret when he saw it. Even without the dashiki, the jeans, the water bed, and the sunset poster to drive the point home.

Spinrad had not turned into some kind of synthetic Frenchman like so many of these American exiles; some part of him, and a big part by the look of it, was still California dreamin'. This could end up being a lot easier than he had supposed.

"Very nice..." he offered in his best Southern Californian accent.

"You mean *far out man*, don't you?" Spinrad drawled back. "Très Californien, n'est-ce pas?" Suddenly Ellis didn't like the amused look in his eyes at all.

Spinrad ushered him to one of the larger sectional sofas and then seated himself on a separate, smaller piece at a careful remove. "So, you said on the phone you were an agent...?"

"That's right."

"Certainement," Spinrad said, and all at once seemed to be looking right through him. "For sure. I'll bet you are. In every sense of the word."

"You don't believe me, you can call BMA in Hollywood collect right now and verify."

"Or some other acronym in Washington? I'm sure that would check out too."

Ellis flushed angrily. "Look here, Mr. Spinrad—"

"Peace, Mr. Ellis," Spinrad said, holding up two fingers. "Pax Americana, in fact. Pas problem. Paris is crawling with agents these days, so what's a few extra initials among friends, just testing your cool. Pretend you're in the Polo Lounge, and I'll come along for the ride. You, uh, said something about a movie deal?"

"That's right," Ellis said, relieved to assume familiar ground. "For *Riding the Torch*. We're packaging the deal for Universal. We've got commitments from a major director and very bankable male and female leads. Of course I can't tell you who they are until—"

"But you *can* tell me that all the principals are BMA clients, n'est-ce pas?" Spinrad said, suddenly flashing a Hollywood smile.

"You know the business, I see...." Ellis said, giving him a Hollywood smile back.

"Indeed I do. In fact Universal once *gave me* the business on *Riding the Torch*. They had it under option many moons ago...but naturellement, you know that, oui...?"

"Of course. But let me assure you that I didn't fly all the way to Paris to secure some cheap option. We're talking about a buy-out up front this time."

"Combien?"

"What?"

"How much?"

"How does six hundred thou sound?"

Spinrad's eyes widened. He hunched forward on his seat. Ellis could sense him sniffing the air. "Like beaucoup bullshit," he said. "No one pays that kind of money for a property anymore. If they ever really did."

"There is of course a catch," Ellis said slyly.

"Pas de merde?"

"But this one you're going to like. For six hundred thou, we get both the film rights to *Riding the Torch* and your screenplay. That's the deal."

"You hear this bullshit?" Spinrad said loudly, directing his voice and his gaze through the open bedroom door. To Ellis's shock and dismay, a woman emerged from within, carrying a magazine, a razor blade, a pack of Gitanes, and a walnut-sized lump of blackish brown hashish. She was slim, elfin, dark-haired, wore jeans and a black pullover, nodded silently as she sat down next to Spinrad, and was not in the dossier he had been given by his man in Langley.

Ellis had no way of knowing who in hell she was, or indeed whether she was American or French. And neither she nor Spinrad himself seemed about to give him any clue. He deigned not to introduce her, and she just sat there silently teasing tobacco out of a cigarette and onto a magazine with her long fingernails while the conversation went on as if she were not there.

"Que pasa, Ellis?" Spinrad said with an edge of anger in his voice. "What planet have you been on for the last ten years? You know damn well I can't get a dime out of the United States. You want to give me six hundred thou for the rights alone, bien, you want to give me a hundred thou for the rights, d'accord, you want to give me ten cents, that's okay too, because I'd like to see the film made, and I'll never be able to touch any of the money anyway. But I'm not about to do *new work* that I'll never be able to collect for."

"It's all or nothing," Ellis said. "No screenplay, no deal."

"Then it's nothing," Spinrad said harshly. "It's been charming, Ellis. You've really made my day."

The woman shaved hash onto the little pile of tobacco on her magazine and started stuffing it back into the flaccid tube of cigarette paper.

"You misunderstand," Ellis said evenly. "This is going to

be a major studio production. We want, we require, that you write the screenplay under direct supervision of the director. In Hollywood."

Surprisingly, Spinrad smiled ironically, and leaned back in the sofa. "Je comprend," he said softly. The woman lit the cigarette, took a big drag, then stuck the end of it in Spinrad's mouth. He sucked lightly on the joint and studied Ellis with hooded eyes. There was a long silence. "Well?" he finally said. "Aren't you going to finish your pitch? The bottom line, s'il vous plaît."

"I've just given you the bottom line," Ellis said.

"Je ne suis pas un naif, Ellis, and neither are you. We both know that the IRS has made it quite clear that one hundred percent of any dollar income I make for the rest of my life will go straight into napalm and nerve gas for wherever the current police action happens to be. If I go back to the States, they'll arrest me on umpteen counts of violating the National Defamation Act for all the stuff I've been printing in the *Free Press de Paris*, and they'll probably try to tag me for espionage too. And for that matter, once I'm out of France, my life insurance is no longer valid, compris?"

"You still don't understand," Ellis said. "We're . . . a very powerful agency. All that can be dealt with. This is your ticket home."

"Home is where the heart is," the woman said, speaking for the first time in an accent that could have been American or British or that of a Frenchwomam speaking perfect text-book English, and giving Spinrad a look that seemed to combine tenderness, possessiveness, and perhaps a wee bit of fear.

Spinrad laid a hand on her thigh but didn't look at her. Instead he stared straight at Ellis with eyes that began to betray a trace of weakness, a certain loss, a fatigue of the spirit.

"Do I understand you correctly, Ellis?" he said. "Am I talking to a representative of the American government?"

"I'm just an . . . agent, Mr. Spinrad," Ellis said with carefully deliberate fatuousness. "I represent only BMA and Universal. However . . ."

"*However . . .*"

"However, there are certain standard clauses in a screen-play contract . . . morals clauses . . . The screenwriter must warrant that he has committed no criminal acts, that he will not

o so in the future, that he will make no public statements
that might reflect adversely on the studio or the production,
or the government of the United States, that, in short, he is a
loyal patriot, and pure as the driven snow. . . ."

"That would seem to make the rest of this discussion
academic, n'est-ce pas . . . ?"

"Not at all, Mr. Spinrad," Ellis said smoothly. "In light of
our current difficulties with the IRS and certain other
charges that may be awaiting you in the United States, the
studio will in this case require public affidavits from the
United States government as to your status as a solid citizen
and a patriotic American. Affidavits we will guarantee to
secure before you set foot on American soil. All you have to
do is sign a screenplay contract containing a somewhat ampli-
fied morals clause."

"Saying what?"

"That you will in future publish no writings and make no
public statements casting aspersions or disrepute upon the
government of the United States, that you have voluntarily
signed the standard loyalty oath waiving your First Amendment rights required of all employees of the United States
government, and that you will refrain from making any public
statements on political matters without prior textual approval
by the appropriate official of the Justice Department."

"Merde . . ." Spinrad said weakly. "Am I required to sign
this contract in blood?"

"Then I take it you *are* interested . . . ?"

Spinrad sucked on his joint and stared away from Ellis
into the artificial depths of the holo poster of the Pacific
sunset tacked up on the kitchen wall.

"You know, I was born in New York, but I lived in
California on and off for twenty years. Been all up and down
the West Coast . . . Moro Bay, Big Sur, San Francisco, Ore-
gon, Seattle, Vancouver . . . There's no coastline like it in the
world, Ellis. The Midi is pretty, but . . . You know, I always
told myself that when I had the time I'd take a month or so
and drive slowly up the whole thing from LA to Vancouver or
even as far up as I could get into BC and Alaska before the
road ran out. . . . Never got around to doing it . . . and now . . . and
now . . ."

"It's all still there," Ellis said softly. "The cities have
changed, but the land . . . you know. . . ."

"Yeah, I know," Spinrad said, refocusing his gaze on Ellis

and smiling ruefully. "You tempt me, Mr. Ellis, you really do You make me feel lost and tired and old and so fucking far from home. No one can say I didn't try, right? It's a lost cause anyway, isn't it, the America I believed in is twenty years dead and more. I've got a right to some kind of personal peace in my declining years, don't I? To go home to the only stretch of land I've ever loved and see all my old friends from better days and live the life of a rich screenwriter in the bargain. And all I have to do is sign a couple of pieces of paper, write my screenplay, tend my garden, listen to the birds, and keep my big mouth shut...."

"There *is* one final requirement," Ellis said. "You must fold the *Free Press de Paris* first."

"At last we reach the bottom line," Spinrad said knowingly and seemingly without surprise. "You boys sure play hardball don't you?"

Ellis grinned at him wolfishly. "It is, you will remember the national pastime."

"The politics of America is business...."

"The politics of America is the bottom line," Ellis told him. "And the bottom line is that Washington calculates that the elimination of the *Free Press de Paris* is worth a film budget guarantee of fifty million dollars and your free ticket home."

"It's nice to know how much your soul is worth on the open market with such precision," Spinrad said dryly. "But what's *your* bottom line, Ellis?"

"My bottom line is that I think the film will make money and I get a point and a half...."

"But even if it doesn't, BMA still pockets ten percent of the budget courtesy of the Department of Media and you get to dip your beak in that for about half a mil, n'est-ce pas...."

Spinrad's accurate penetration to the essence of his deal took Ellis aback. This guy is supposed to be some kind of Bolshevik? He found it hard to fathom the fact that such an exile commie obviously had the down and dirty details of The Business down so cold.

"In other words, you have a heavy self-interest in having this deal go through," Spinrad said sharply. "I mean beside your patriotic dedication to duty, of course."

"So?" Ellis said cautiously, suddenly feeling that he had lost control of this meeting without quite knowing when.

"So just how much of this is negotiable?" Spinrad said tentatively.

"Just between you and me?"

"Yeah, sure Ellis, just between you and me."

"Well just between you and me, I think my principals might go another hundred thou. . . ."

"No, no, man, not the *money*. The terms."

"The morals clause and the loyalty oath are of the essence; surely you realize that."

"I just might be able to hold my nose and eat that," Spinrad said harshly. "But what about the *Free Press de Paris*?"

"As long as that rag is published on your money, there is no deal."

"You're quite sure there's no way we can—"

"Quite sure."

For only the second time, the silent woman spoke. "Norman, you're not, you wouldn't—"

Spinrad shot her a poisonous look. Their eyes locked for a long moment. Then she stormed out of the living room and into the bedroom, slamming the door behind her.

"Jeez, Ellis, I'm tired," Spinrad said weakly. "But if I'm really going to do this disgusting thing, I've got to salvage a little pride, compris? I've got to have a little victory to take the edge off. Before I sign any contract or any loyalty oath, I require a small gesture of good faith from your so-called principals. . . ."

"Such as?"

"Nothing that I'm not entitled to anyway," Spinrad said angrily. "I want my goddamn money! Fourteen fucking years worth of American royalties on all my old books! I want every last fucking dime that's been attached all these years plus the accrued and compounded interest at the average prime rate for the period. I want it in currency, I want it in Swiss francs, I want it coughed up to me here in Paris, and I want it before I sign anything."

"That's asking an awful lot. . . ."

"The fuck it is! Way I see it, the government of the United States has *stolen* about a half million dollars from me in the first place! I don't do business with people who have picked my pockets until they acknowledge the fact and pay me back with interest. Nonnegotiable, Ellis. I want my money. I really don't think that's asking too much."

"This is silly, Spinrad," Ellis said. "It makes no sense for you to endanger a seven hundred thousand dollar deal like this to get back a half million!"

"The seven hundred thou is *Universal* money, or so you say, Ellis. But the half million is *my* money."

Some Bolshevik *this* guy is! Ellis thought. "All right, all right," he sighed. "I suppose I can get *Universal* to give you half the difference as some kind of bullshit creative consultant, and you're right, I've got a heavy enough self-interest to pay you the rest out of my end."

"No way, José! It's a matter of principal. The IRS stole my money and the US government and no one else has to pay it back. In advance."

Ellis sighed. "Surely we both know I don't have anything remotely like the authority to negotiate anything like that," he said.

Spinrad smiled at him fatuously. "You're an agent, n'est-ce pas?" he drawled. "Well shit, I haven't had a Hollywood agent in years. The US government wants me to make this deal to fold le Freep, Universal and BMA want their federal completion guarantee, you want your piece of *Riding the Torch*, and I want the IRS to fork over. Seeing as how you're already representing America Incorporated, BMA, and Universal, why not complete the package and represent me too? Ten percent of my end of the *Riding the Torch* deal, and ten percent of what you recover from the IRS for me, and voila, you've got over a hundred thousand dollars' worth of incentive to get the deal done. That should cover the calls you're gonna have to make to Washington to do it. . . ."

"You're serious about this?"

"Precisely as serious as you are, Ellis. No more, no less. Get me half a million dollars in Swiss francs in a paper bag with a cover letter from the IRS, and you've got yourself a deal about a hundred thousand dollars sweeter than you thought it would be. Strike out as *my* agent, and what you get is bupkiss."

Spinrad lit up the joint and blew a thin stream of smoke in Ellis's general direction as Ellis tried to collect his scattered thoughts. "You mind . . . ?" Ellis asked, reaching for the joint.

"Not at all," Spinrad said with a laugh. "Ten percent of my dope is all yours."

Ellis sucked in a sip of smoke and thought fast. If Washington was willing to front fifty million dollars, they'd hardly be likely to balk at another five hundred thousand dollars, money-wise, would they? *He* wouldn't have to talk to the IRS himself, god forbid. He could two-track it. Tell BMA to get onto Universal about it, and let Universal put the pressure on through the Department of Media. Meantime, he could also go through Harris, his controller at the Company. Surely together they had enough clout to make the IRS cooperative. . . . At least it was worth a shot, considering the alternative.

"Okay, so you've got yourself an agent," he told Spinrad, handing back the joint. "No promises, though. And you realize this is going to take time. . . ."

Spinrad shrugged, stuck the joint back in his mouth. "Pas problem," he said. "Take all the time you want. Live it up in Paris on the old expense account till they pull the plug. Remember, I've been waiting to get my hands on this bread for so long that I'd just about given up. So I'm in no hurry now."

Alexander Sergeiovich Ulanov, as usual, took his petit dejeuner in his office high up in the Tour Montparnasse, though without his usual concentration on the quality of the patisserie. He bit off a piece of pain au chocolate, rolled it around in his mouth thoughtfully, staring out his big office window at the rooftops of Montparnasse far below, pondering how far he had risen and how far he had to fall, before washing it down with the remains of the day's first cup of powerful black coffee.

"What's he up to?" he said, more to himself than to Natasha Ivanova. "Why did he ask us to set up this charade in the first place?"

Natasha took it as a serious question from her boss. "Perhaps he wishes us to engage in a bidding war, Sasha?" she suggested. "It would be a severe setback to your career if Spinrad *did* fold the *Free Press de Paris*, would it not? Perhaps even a one-way, first-class Aeroflot ticket back to Moscow. . . or even . . . points east."

Sasha groaned as he pondered the horrid possibility. Norman is my *friend*, he told himself. He would never do such a thing to me! Would he . . . ?

On the other hand, according to Natasha, this deal, if it went through, would net Spinrad something like a million dollars.

Would Norman really turn down a million American out of friendship?"

Would *you*, Sasha?

You'd like to find out, now wouldn't you?

Alexander Sergeiovich Ulanov was a child of glasnost, of the Russian Spring, and a favored one at that. For him, the bad old days of Brezhnev were a dim childhood memory at best.

By the time he had graduated from Moscow University and gone to work as an entry-level copy editor for *Komosolya Pravda*, the "New Journalism" was already in full flower, the Old Dinosaurs were already well on their way to the boneyard of history, bright young novos like himself were being express-tracked, and his rise to his present position as head of Tass's Paris bureau had been charmed and swift, aided in no little measure by his peculiar relationship with the publisher and editor of the *Free Press de Paris*.

When Sasha was shifted from *Komosolya Pravda* to Tass and reassigned from London to Paris, Norman Spinrad was already in Paris, persona non grata in his own country, his American assets seized, and his American royalties frozen. Bitter, depressed, at loose ends, creatively blocked, he was living off the dwindling capital he had managed to bring out with him and the relatively meager proceeds from the western European rights to his old books.

While the old relationship between the KGB and the foreign bureaus of Tass had already been transformed from one of command to one of deal-cutting among equals, it was certainly true that favors, personnel, and assignments were still hopelessly entwined, and so it was that Sasha, still a rather junior reporter, had been assigned the task of turning Spinrad.

Norman Spinrad had never been more than a minor literary figure in America, but his books had long been much more popular in Europe, especially France, all the more so now that he had the cachet of the political exile. Such a figure could be of some value to the Soviet cause in Europe as a public turncoat, and all the more so if he was transformed into a European superstar by the media power of Tass.

Something which Tass now had the power to do. Glasnost and the New Journalism had given the Soviet Press Agency a heady and prominent new credibility in Western Europe, aided by its generous budget, rampant anti-Americanism, and the fact that the National Defamation Act had gelded its American competitors.

Tass had well-staffed bureaus in the major capitals and stringers everywhere as well. Tass had access to the formidable information-gathering apparatus of the KGB. Tass was now allowed to rake muck inside Mother Russia herself. Tass published its own free daily newspaper, *Europe Today,* in Paris, London, Munich, Barcelona, Amsterdam, and Milan, and its combined multilingual editions made it the best-selling paper in the world. Tass had its own dedicated satellite broadcasting twenty-four-hour TV news in competition with CNN. And unlike the Americans, it broadcast versions in English, French, German, Spanish, Dutch, and Italian.

And Tass, unlike any other press service or TV news network, supplied its wire stories and television programming to anyone who would carry them, free of charge. How could the decadent capitalists compete with *that*?

Norman Spinrad certainly had not been about to refuse a chance to plug into the media power of the Big Red Machine. Sasha had conducted that first interview in Tass's top conference room, a truly lavish parlor done up in a cunning simulacrum of nineteenth-century French rococo gilt and Louis the Something-or-Other furniture that belied its location high up in the sleek, glass precincts of the Tour Montparnasse, its only concession to modernity the truly daunting view from on high of the entire city from the Eiffel Tower and the Seine to the far-off white pinnacle of Sacre Coeur, all of Paris dwarfed like the ultimate model railroad city from the point of view of the media masters of Tass.

Spinrad was the sort of voluble interviewee who practically interviewed himself, the chemistry between them was good, he had plenty of juicy things to say about the American government, the IRS, the National Defamation Act, and the betrayal of the First Amendment, so the interview had been good copy in and of itself. So much for Tass.

Afterward, over vodka, cocaine, and caviar, Sasha had forthrightfully proceeded to KGB business.

"Believe me, we can do it," he told Spinrad. "This interview, we will place in *Le Monde,* and the *Guardian,* and the *Frankfurter Allgemeine Zeitung,* somewhere in Italy, Holland, and Spain, *Pravda,* and of course all editions of *Europe Today.* You watch—after this, the sales of your books will go up seventeen percent, that's what our marketing boys project. And we're not even talking television yet."

Spinrad had looked hungrily around the gaudy conference room, sipped at ice-cold pepper vodka, done up another line of Tass coke. "Okay, d'accord, so you're the Big Red Machine," he said. "So maybe you *can* make me the literary toast of Europe. Big deal. So what?"

"*So what?*" Sasha exclaimed perplexedly.

"So no big deal, Mr. Ulanov—"

"Please, Alexander Sergeiovich, better yet, *Sasha*," he said expansively. "But what on Earth do you mean by *no big deal*?"

"I mean the demographics suck, Comrade Sasha," Spinrad said dryly. "Let me give you a brief lesson in what the French call Anglophone cultural imperialism. I've always been more popular in Europe than in the States. My stuff has always done real well here in France, in Germany, Holland, from time to time even England, and my books have always sold mediocrely in the United States."

"So doesn't that mean—"

"No it doesn't!" Spinrad snapped irritably. "Even though I've long been a relative nobody in the States and a relative somebody here, the mediocre sales of my books in the US have *still* netted me four or five times the money they made in Europe and Japan. That's because the American rights area, which includes Canada and the Philippines and sometimes Australia, encompasses something like *four hundred million* English-speaking people. Why do you think top French directors go to California to make films in English? Why do you think even *Russian* rock groups record half their material in English? Political fortunes ebb and flow, but the English language reigns supreme. Which is why any writer in any country ain't gonna be able to live in the style to which he'd like to become accustomed without being able to sell American rights to his books. And get the fucking money out of the States!"

Sasha was not taken aback by the vehemence of Spinrad's tirade—indeed the anger and bitterness evident in every word of it seemed most promising—but he was thrown for a loss by its content.

For of course he knew full well that everything Spinrad had said was true, and indeed the situation was even worse from the point of view of the Ministry of Media. What with the naked American imperialism throughout the Third World, the National Defamation Act, the loathing of America in Western Europe, Battlestar America, and all the rest, the Soviet Union, aided by the fresh wind of the Russian Spring, should have been mopping the floor with the Americans, media-wise, should have long since shifted the cultural capital of the world from New York to Moscow or Leningrad. Soviet art and music and literature were creatively flowering, while their American counterparts were stagnant and dispirited schlock.

But the writers and artists and filmmakers of the world still looked to America. Because English was the closest thing there was to a world language and America was by far the largest English-speaking market. Even the most rabidly anti-American European writer still schemed and dreamed of a best-seller in the United States.

And Norman Spinrad knew this all too well. He could measure it quite accurately in the decline in his standard of living since he had been deprived of his American income. Even with the increase in European sales due to his exile status, he was still up against it in dollars and cents.

Then it was that Alexander Sergeiovich Ulanov took the first daring step toward his present exalted position. The junior Tass reporter took the big chance of speaking with authority he did not at all have and hoping that his superiors would not only back him, but would back him with sufficient clout back in Moscow, where such decisions still had to be made.

"Have you ever considered the money you could make in the Soviet Union?" he said.

"The Soviet Union?"

"Three hundred million people, most of them readers. Avid for novelty from the West. Editions not only in Russian, but in Ukrainian, Uzbek, Latvian, Estonian, and so forth. Big printings, immediately sold out. No returns. TV dramatization rights. Possible feature films. The lecture circuit, even if you don't speak Russian."

Spinrad scowled. "Right. Sure. You can make me a ruble millionaire. Big fucking deal. You know, a couple of my old books *have* been done in Russian. I've got the blocked rubles in a bank account in Moscow to prove it. It's play money, and you know it . . . *Sasha*. I can't take it out. The only place I can spend it is Russia."

"Would that be so bad...?" Sasha said slowly. "A lavish apartment in Leningrad or Moscow...a dacha in the Urals and a villa on the Black Sea...The restaurants are greatly improved. . . . The ballet is the best. . . . Good rock and roll...And of course as a hero of the Soviet Union there would be other perks as well. . . ."

"*That's* the game, isn't it?" Spinrad said sharply. "You guys will make me a ruble millionaire and a Soviet superstar if I defect?"

Sasha smiled. "Nothing as crude as...defection would be required," he said. "No heavy-handed endorsement of the Worker's Paradise. Just the occasional interview with Tass in which you will be free to speak your mind about the injustice done to you and other freethinking Americans by the government of the United States. You could come and go as you please. You could even keep your American citizenship and passport. . . ."

"My American passport has been lifted, remember!" Spinrad snapped angrily. "I'm pulling strings to get one from the Common Market."

"Well then, you could have a Soviet passport easily enough," Sasha offered expansively. "Or if that strikes you as too blatant, a Czech one, a Bulgarian one, even one from the DDR, which would mean Common Market credentials via the Greater German Confederation. . . ."

Spinrad made himself a caviar canapé from the fixings on the table, leaned back in his chair, chewed a bit of it slowly, savoring the taste of the best Beluga. "Under the circumstances, you do make it sound tempting," he finally admitted. "But..."

"But?"

"But there'd be no turning back, would there?" Spinrad said. "You'd have me by the short hairs. By the bank account. A rich man in Russia, but scrabbling to survive anywhere else."

"How would that be worse than your current situation, Norman? Indeed it *is* your current situation."

"It would be surrender!" Spinrad blurted.

"Surrender? To whom? To *us*?"

"To *them*, goddamnit!" Spinrad shouted. "To the motherfuckers who stole my money and lifted my passport! To the bastards behind the National Defamation Act! To the fascist

Reaganoid slime that have turned *my country* into the shithole it is today!"

He got up and began pacing the room, waving his arms and declaiming wildly. "I'm an *American*, damn it, despite it all I'm an *American*! And I've spent my whole fucking life fighting for *my* America in what small way I can! I love France, I've always been happy here, I speak the fucking language more or less, this country has nourished my spirit when it was starving, I have good friends here. But that doesn't mean I have any intention of becoming one of the pathetic American exile pseudo-Frenchmen that infest this city! Those bastards can kick me out, and steal my money, and drop me in Leavenworth, and throw away the key if they get their meat hooks into me, but I can't let them turn me into *that*! Still less a Soviet lapdog! I let that happen and I admit for all the world to see that the real America, the only America, is *them*!"

"You're telling me that after all that's been done to you, you're still an American patriot?" Sasha scoffed. "After all your public denunciations of the United States?"

"Fuckin' A!" Spinrad shouted. "I've *never* denounced the United States. The government, for sure! Conglomerate corporate capitalism, certainement! Star-spangled fascism, you better believe it! But not America! Not the America that once was! And someday must be again!"

"I don't understand. . . ."

"Don't you?" Spinrad said much more calmly, even insinuatingly. He sat down on the edge of the conference table and peered at Sasha knowingly with his deeply shadowed gray eyes.

"You're a Russian, aren't you?" he said. "A *modern* Russian, right? A child of glasnost. You're what, twenty-five years younger than me? But not *that* young. Not so young that you don't know what *your* country was like for the whole, dark, half century between Lenin and Gorbachev. What would *you* have done if you hadn't been so fortunate as to be born into the Russian Spring? Would you have become one of those faded White Russian exiles weeping in their vodka for the Czar in the Russian Tea Room? Would you have defected? Become a Russian expert for the CIA? Who are the real Russian heroes? The guys who turned their back on their country and split for the West? Or the poor bastards who stayed behind and fought as best they could? You know the

answer. Because without them, there could never have been
a Gorbachev, a glasnost, or a Russian Spring, and you wouldn't
be sitting here in this fancy joint in Paris laying out lines for
the likes of me!"

Spinrad picked up his glass of vodka, slugged it down,
subsided back into his chair. "Now do you understand why I
can't accept your gracious offer?" he said quietly. "Would you,
if you were in my shoes?"

"I think I do understand," Sasha had owned. But he had
left the second question hanging there. What *would* he do if
the wind changed again in Moscow and a new Stalin or even
Brezhnev arose and he were called back home onto the
carpet and told to toe a new hard Party line? And say
Reuters, or *Time*, or CNN offered him a fat salary for life in
the West in return for his defection?

The atmosphere in Moscow had been giddy and heady in
those days, and all the more so in Leningrad, but even then
Sasha had had free run of Europe long enough to know that
he had no interest in returning to the Soviet Union. Those
were good times to be young and a Russian, and these were
good times to be more mature and a Russian on a fat expense
account, and the wind from the East had not turned icy again
yet.

But then, as now, it was far better to be a Russian
serving the Motherland in the fleshpots of the West.

And now his old American friend was putting his life in
the West in jeopardy.

That first meeting had proven inconclusive at best, or so
Sasha had thought at the time, but about a week after the
interview was published, Norman Spinrad had invited him to
a rather unwholesome lunch in La Coupole, a huge noisy
Montparnasse brasserie, famous for intellectual and show-
business connections that went back to the Existentialists,
now frequented by American political exiles and everything
that swarmed around them, and somewhat notorious for
heavy-handed cuisine.

"I've been thinking over your proposal, Sasha," Spinrad
finally said over cognac and pastry. "I've got to admit that you
boys have delivered. . . ."

"And . . . ?" Sasha said, cocking his eyebrows in feigned
diffidence.

"And I've been talking to some people . . . people in the

know about the Soviet publishing scene. . . . Seems you haven't been exactly candid with me, Sasha. . . ."

"*Moi?*"

Spinrad swirled his snifter of cognac before his nose. "I've been talking to some western writers who sell rather well in the Soviet Union. . . ." he said. "People sympathetic to Soviet interests, if you know what I mean, people upon whom Party circles choose to smile. . . . *They* tell me that it *is* possible to get their rubles out. Rubles to east marks, east marks to west marks, and of course west marks to anything."

Sasha's ears pricked up. Suddenly this was becoming easier than he had ever dared to hope. "And you'd be interested in such an arrangement . . . ?"

"Mais oui!" Spinrad told him. "What's not to like? All my books in print in the Soviet Union in multiple editions and the proceeds here in Paris . . . No offense, but I much prefer the life here. . . ."

Sasha laughed. "No offense taken," he said. "I'm a loyal Soviet citizen, but so do I!" He took a sip of cognac, grew more serious, tried to phrase it as delicately as he could.

"You . . . ah . . . do realize that such arrangements can only be approved by . . . extraliterary agencies. . . ."

"Like the KGB?"

Sasha shrugged. "Let us not be crude," he said with a sardonic little smile. "Let us say that these . . . extraliterary agencies require . . . certain extraliterary services in return for such assistance with currency exchanges. . . ."

"Like a little espionage?"

"Please!" Sasha groaned. "We are no longer crude Chekist hooligans in the Soviet Union!" He laughed. "Besides, western writers openly sympathetic to the Soviet cause are not likely to have ready access to classified information, da. No, it's much more subtle than that. Attendance at certain events sponsored by the Soviet Union. Public support of the Party line. A little writing work for hire from time to time. From you according to your ability, to you according to your greed. . . ."

"And the flow of rubles to be contingent upon good behavior as defined by . . . those certain extraliterary agencies . . . ?"

"You have penetrated to the essence. . . ." Sasha said suavely.

"That's not the deal I had in mind," Spinrad said sharply.

"I'm not about to publicly salaam facing Moscow. But I am willing to offer you something better...."

"*Better?*"

"Something you've always wanted. Something you can't buy. Something none of those tame lapdogs can give you. A conduit for Soviet viewpoints into the West—"

"Tass already—"

"An *independent* conduit. A publication with unimpeachable credibility."

Sasha took a long, slow drink of cognac, sensing that Spinrad was about to venture out into terra incognita, that something that might very well be of interest to Moscow was about to be proposed. Something that might be of even more interest to his own career.

"Get my stuff published in the Soviet Union and get me the proceeds here and I'll use the money to start a weekly newspaper here in Paris, in English," Spinrad said. He looked around the noisy, crowded brasserie. "There are enough exiled American writers in this joint right now to staff it twice over."

"What interest do you imagine we would have in some pathetic English language emigre weekly with a circulation of ten thousand?" Sasha scoffed.

"None whatever," Spinrad said airily. "But I'm talking about something that will outsell the *International Herald Tribune*, which everyone knows has long since become an American government mouthpiece. I used to be involved in the old Underground Press a long time ago, a paper called the *Los Angeles Free Press*. Had a circulation over one hundred thousand in LA alone. What I'm proposing is to revive that concept on an international scale. We'll distribute it here, London, Amsterdam, maybe Rome, and, National Defamation Act or not, there are ways to get it distributed in the States."

"Why would anyone want to read such a thing? And why would *we* care if they did?"

"For the same reason, Sasha. I intend to revive the grand old concept of irresponsible yellow journalism. All the shit that fits, we'll print. All the juicy political dirt we can get our hands on. All the international scandals. All the crap that Washington would rather see swept under the rug."

Now it was Sasha's turned to sweep his gaze around the restaurant. "With a staff of American political exiles operating out of Paris, you're going to break all the news that the American press is afraid to touch?" he scoffed. "On a shoe-string? With no real resources?"

Spinrad grinned at him broadly. "What about with a little help from my friends?" he said.

"Oh . . ." Sasha said, his mind making the leap to what he in that moment thought was full comprehension. With the resources of Tass behind it, indeed with the full resources of the KGB channeling information to it through Tass, such a publication could indeed become a significant thorn in the American hide.

Indeed, it was rather ingenious. The KGB could discom-fort the Americans through such a paper with material that would have no credibility whatsoever if it was released overtly through Tass. The truth from the various war zones. Inside information from Washington through agents in place. Im-pending American military actions. American penetrations of Third World governments. And since the paper would be published in Europe, there'd be no way the Americans could shut it down. But . . .

"But such a paper would have no credibility for long," Sasha pointed out. "It would soon become obvious from what was published that it was merely a mouthpiece for us. . . ."

"Not if we kicked Russian ass too," Spinrad said.

"WHAT?"

"The *Free Press de Paris*, an equal opportunity ass-kicker! We'll be right up front about it. Any intelligence service in the world can leak anything they want about anyone they please through us. The British. The French. The Israelis. The Arabs. Hell, even the Americans if they want to, why not? And no one will dream of calling us a Soviet mouthpiece because our coverage of Mother Russia will be *really* juicy, seeing as how we'll have an inside pipeline through *you*."

"You're out of your mind!"

"Think of it as glasnost in action," Spinrad said dryly. "If I get the thing going, everyone else is going to be passing me Soviet dirt anyway, so why shouldn't you? Tass is releasing internal muckraking stuff these days anyway, so why shouldn't you pass the *Free Press* a little Russian scoop from time to time for credibility's sake? What do you say, Sasha, you walk this through for me, and you could be a big man at Tass. . . ."

"Da, I could end up a journalistic superstar in Siberia or worse still, Tirana!"

"Think about it. At least run it up the flagpole and see who sings the *Internationale*."

Carefully, not without misgivings, Sasha had. He had reported the conversation to the bureau chief. Who had stood to one side and referred him to the KGB resident. Who had listened without comment.

Who had apparently passed the proposal on without recommendation, for ten days later Sasha had been summoned to Moscow, sweaty and terrified, to present it to an undersecretary of media. Who had also listened without comment and sent him back to Paris.

Two weeks later, the KGB resident had summoned Sasha to his office and told him that Spinrad's proposal had been accepted. That Spinrad's books would be published in the Soviet Union and the proceeds channeled to Spinrad through him. That the *Free Press de Paris* would be Sasha's own little project. If all went well, his career would be significantly enhanced. If it did not, there were always plenty of jobs for agricultural reporters in Alma Ata or Novosibirsk.

Things did go well. They went very well indeed. The *Free Press de Paris* proved to be just the sort of scurrilous yellow rag Spinrad had promised. An American-backed coup in the making in Burma was thwarted by revelations in the *Free Press*. The Grossdeutschland Bund was unmasked as a CIA front. An American undersecretary of defense was sacked when the Freep published a story on his clandestine dealings with Lebanese arms merchants. CIA penetrations of Hollywood and American news organs were exposed as were White-House-ordered IRS audits of opposition politicians. There were many other, less dramatic, scoops.

The Americans were outraged regularly, the British, Israelis and Arabs occasionally, though Spinrad proved to have second thoughts about printing anything that might disturb the French. The KGB was happy for the most part, though it was a matter of gritting their teeth and bearing it when Sasha passed Spinrad a juicy morsel of essentially harmless Soviet scandal from time to time.

When Sasha moaned about some of these seances with the KGB station chief from time to time, Norman was always good for a prepublication bit of stuff on the Americans or

British or Israelis to keep his temper cooled, and the two of them became friends, or so at least it had seemed.

Promotion followed promotion, raise followed raise, expense account expansion followed expense account expansion, and finally, not long after the *Free Press* had printed an exposé of the offensive capabilities of Battlestar America—which came from disgruntled American rather than KGB sources—Kaminski retired, and Sasha was appointed chief of Tass's Paris bureau, a sinecure he would be happy to remain in for life.

He had a wonderful ninth-floor penthouse apartment close by the Luxembourg Gardens from the balcony of which he could view Notre Dame and the Bourbourg and the Opera and the magic roofscape of his beloved Paris rising wraithlike out of the early morning mists.

He had had a long succession of French girlfriends, culminating, perhaps, in Nadine, an artist's agent whom he had been seeing for close onto three years now, something of a record for him, a relationship that Sasha was beginning to contemplate making permanent.

He had a country cottage in the Maritime Alps, a Mercedes-Toyota, a well-stocked cellar, access to all the best parties, and a small circle of real friends.

Including Norman Spinrad, who was in good measure responsible for his pleasurable lifestyle, and vice versa. But now it appeared that his good life in the West was threatened, and by the very man who had helped him attain it in the first place.

For if Spinrad accepted this Ellis's devilish bargain and folded the *Free Press de Paris*, Sasha knew that at the very least he would be called back to Moscow to give an account of the fiasco, and of himself.

Just maybe be could talk his way back to Paris, but while the gulag was long gone, he knew full well that he would probably find himself "promoted" to the editorship of say, a local daily in Vladivostok.

He shuddered. Norman Spinrad had been his friend. Together they had collaborated to create the *Free Press de Paris* and both had profited thereby. Perhaps too well. Well enough for the American government to wish an end to their mutually advantageous arrangement badly enough to bribe an aging exile with a million dollars and a ticket home.

Would Norman turn down such a deal out of friendship

with a Russian? It was hard for Sasha to believe that he would, seeing as how, after all these years in the West, he knew damned well *he* would be tempted by a deal half so sweet.

And yet . . .

And yet Norman *had* come to him before his meeting with Eli Ellis. He *had* asked him to have Natasha Ivanova play the part of his outraged French girlfriend. But why?

As Norman had told him, just to tweak the noses of the American authorities by producing a mysterious live-in companion not in his dossier? Or to use the "outraged girlfriend" whom he would have to leave to jack the price?

Or was it something more subtle, something of which Norman himself might not be entirely consciously aware? Was there a part of his old friend that *wanted* Tass to have an agent in place in the middle of this thing? So that his old friend Sasha might be forewarned of his moves and act accordingly?

Sasha smiled ruefully to himself. He would like to believe that. But perhaps Natasha was right. Perhaps this was Norman Spinrad's way of telling Tass and the KGB and the money people behind them that he was placing himself on the auction block. Perhaps he *is* trying to get us into a bidding war with the Americans.

Certainly it made sense to assume that was the case and act accordingly.

"Should I return to his appartment?" Natasha asked. "Do I continue to play this little game?"

"What . . . ?" Sasha muttered distractedly.

"Do you want me to continue to play the part of Spinrad's mysterious girlfriend for this Ellis person, Sasha . . . ?"

"Yes, yes, of course. . . . As long as he wants you to. . . ."

"And you, Sasha, will you confront him now?"

Sasha thought about it. It was, of course, exactly what Spinrad would now expect him to do. Therefore he would not do it. He would do the unexpected instead, give *Norman* something to think about.

"No," he told Natasha Ivanova. "We'll simply act like good journalists and publish the story as an innocent bit of show-business gossip. *Free Press* publisher offered movie deal by Universal Pictures. A nice little scoop for the show-business section of *Europe Today*, don't you think?"

"But won't Spinrad know precisely where it came from?"

Sasha grinned. "Naturellement," he said.

"And Ellis will think Spinrad *himself* gave it to you!"

"Which will be true, in a way, will it not?"

"You hope this will blow the deal?"

Sasha shrugged. "Somehow I don't think it's going to be as easy as all that," he said. "So I think I'd better use a secret weapon. . . ."

"Secret weapon?"

"Katrina Charnov, the Red Metal Rose. I would imagine poor Mr. Ellis must be getting a bit lonely all by himself in the romantic City of Light."

"But she's a hooligan, she's totally unreliable," Natasha sniffed. "What does she have that I don't?"

Sasha laughed. "Only ten gold discs, a body that drives men wild, and a brother on the KGB shit-list."

"You really *are* a male chauvinist Rasputin!" Natasha said. "That's revolting!"

Sasha laughed. He chucked Natasha Ivanova under the chin. "Nyet," he said, "that's just show business, babes."

Alone in balmy Paris with plenty of time on his hands and a fat BMA expense account, Eli Ellis was still managing to have a lousy time.

They had booked him into the spanking-new Boulogne Hyatt up in the Port Maillot corner of the 16th, a large, ultramodern suite with a magnificent view of the Bois de Boulogne from the sitting-room balcony. The room service was top drawer, you could even get a real American breakfast, the restaurant was no-fault nouvelle Californian, the staff spoke perfect transatlantic English, and fancy hookers were available from the bell captain. It was almost the Beverly Hills, minus the pool and the Polo Lounge.

But Hollywood and Washington were giving him endless shit. He seemed to be spending thirty-seven hours a day on the phone, all to no avail, or worse.

Universal was slavering after that fifty-million-dollar government budget subsidy—even if *Riding the Torch* bit the Big One, they kept pointing out, this deal would be pure profit from the git-go, not to mention the ten mil or so they could skim from the budget.

BMA was on his ass to get the deal done so they could dip *their* 10-percent beak into the public trough, and outlining with increasingly vivid clarity the extent to which his ass would be grass if he didn't.

And the boys in Washington were being king-sized pricks about it. Numerous calls to Harris, his contact at the Company, and backstage machinations between Langley and the Justice Department that he didn't even want to think about, had finally gotten the IRS to agree to release Spinrad's blocked American royalties. More calls had even gotten them to swallow his demand for the accrued interest.

But *only* in dollars, and *only* in the States, and *only* after Spinrad had returned to Los Angeles, signed the contract, and waived his First Amendment rights by signing a loyalty oath under the terms of the National Defamation Act.

When he had called Spinrad to present this as a Grand Compromise achieved with much of his own blood, sweat, and tears, Spinrad had done a dingo act.

"You expect me to *trust* those fascist motherfuckers? What's to keep them from arresting me the moment I set foot on American soil?"

"They assure me—"

"*They assure you!* That and five francs will get you on the Metro! The only assurance that could be worth anything is *my money* here in Paris up front before I risk putting myself in their clutches, goddamnit! Earn your fucking ten percent, Ellis!"

And he had hung up.

Red-faced and pissed off as he was, Ellis had to admit that Spinrad had a point. But when he called Langley and made it, Harris read him the riot act too.

"*He* doesn't trust *us*? What's to prevent that subversive bastard from simply banking the money in Paris, telling us to get stuffed, and using it to keep putting out that filthy rag of his?"

"But then he'd lose the seven hundred thousand dollars for the rights and the screenplay—"

"While pocketing half a mil he never expected to see anyway without having to risk his ass or do a lick of work for it!"

"But—"

"But nothing, Ellis! This is the bottom line. Spinrad returns to the States and signs the necessary paper before we release a dime, or this deal is as dead as . . . as dead as your career in Hollywood afterward, I kid you not."

So much for business.

As for pleasure . . .

Ellis had nothing but time to kill, and Paris was supposed to be famous as a good-time city, but for an American who had never been there before, who had no local acquaintances except one man he had best avoid, who spoke no French, who didn't know the town at all, it was a matter of look but don't touch.

He rode to the top of the Eiffel Tower and plodded dutifully through the Louvre and the Pompidou and the Orsay. He took the sun in the Tuilleries and the Luxembourg Gardens. He puffed to the top of Montmarte. He took a tour boat down the Seine and gaped at Notre Dame. He walked the length of the Champs Elysées from the Place d'Etoile to Concorde. He wandered around the scurve of Pigale and took in a slimy sex show. He did Saint Germaine and les Halles and Montparnasse.

He ventured out of the hotel restaurant and had a magnificent and monstrously expensive dinner at the Tour d'Argent. He tried a quaint little bistro off the Boul' Mich and was served some horrible stew that nearly made him puke. He drank in the hotel bar, which was grim, at lively sidewalk cafés where everyone spoke nothing but French, at a dive called Le Drugstore which seemed like a pretentious Denny's.

Oh yes, the afternoons were bright, and the evenings fragrant and balmy, and the streets and cafés full of life and elegantly dressed pussy. People laughed, and jabbered, and cast looks of potential assignation at each other, and Ellis could see why they called the Frog Capital the City of Love.

But goddamn it, it was all going on in fucking *French*! It was like being stuck in some endless, tantalizing French film with no subtitles, let alone proper dubbing into English. The city teemed with life, and flash, and sex, and romance, but he could touch none of it. He was utterly alone. He was utterly frustrated. He felt like a boob, like a rube, like a horny hick from the English-speaking sticks.

Worse still, when he availed himself of one of the high-priced room-service hookers. She spoke good English, showed him a certificate of good health, gave a cold, professional performance, and informed him he could put it on his American Express card.

He even ventured to pick up a fancy streetwalker in a

leopard-skin coat from the meat rack on the Avenue Victor Hugo. She garnered him dirty looks from the hotel staff, spoke no English, gave him a terrific blow job, took her pay in francs, and departed.

When he pulled his pants on after a room-service breakfast the next morning, he discovered that she had cleaned out his wallet. While he was cursing the Frogs over this, the telephone rang.

It was his man in Langley.

"Have you read *Europe Today,* you cretin?" Harris said by way of greeting.

"*Europe Today*...? Of course not! That's a commie rag, isn't it?"

"It's *Tass,* you idiot! It's Spinrad's Bolshevik buddy, Ulanov! How the hell did *Tass* get this story?"

"Story...?"

"In the 'Show Biz Internationale' column. FREE PRESS PUBLISHER PONDERS JUICY IMPERALIST CO-OPTION. The Word from Our Hollywood Bird is that Norman Spinrad, editor and publisher of that troublesome tattling weekly, the *Free Press de Paris,* has been offered a fat deal from Universal Pictures for his moldy sci-fi oldie *Riding the Torch,* Spinrad to do the script back in Lotus Land, where one would think he would be facing heavy-duty agro from the US Justice Department. Hollywood golden boy Eli Ellis is ensconced at the Boulogne Hyatt in gay Paris putting the deal together now, BMA is the agency packaging the deal, or anyway the agency of record. Rubles to dollars, though, the ancillary rights are being handled by a certain other agency back in Washington whose initials start with C and also end with A. It would seem that the skids are being greased for Spinrad's bright, green return to Hollywood, wonder what else is slated to slide down them into the willy hole?"

"Oh shit..." Ellis moaned.

"Who have you been talking to, Ellis?"

"No one! Hell, everyone here speaks *French*!"

"If you're responsible for this, it might be a good idea for you to start learning French youself, get the message? People here are not happy with you, Eli."

"It wasn't me! It must've come from BMA...or Universal...."

"Right. Next thing you'll be telling me is that someone at

the Agency is working as a Hollywood gossip stringer for Tass!"

"Maybe Spinrad—"

"Sure. Spinrad planted this item in *Europe Today* to blow the deal and get himself in trouble with his own staff!"

"But—"

"Now you listen, Ellis, and you listen good! You are in deep, dark trouble. You close this deal, or you'll never work in Hollywood again, and your tax returns, such as they will be, will be audited to a fare-thee-well for the next ten thousand years!"

And with that, Langley hung up.

"Très drôle," Norman Spinrad said, flipping the Paris edition of *Europe Today* across Sasha's desk and into his lap. "With friends like you, who needs American agents?"

"Don't bullshit a bullshitter, Norman," Sasha told him with a little smile. "This is precisely what you wanted me to do, is it not? Otherwise, why have Natasha at your meeting with Ellis?"

Spinrad laughed, shrugged, pursed his lips, slouched into the chair before the desk. "C'est possible," he admitted. "But I really hate that line about a 'moldy sci-fi oldie....'"

"But why did you set such a thing up in the first place?" Sasha asked him. "For what would you do such a thing?"

Spinrad gave him his best, fake Gallic shrug. "Why else?" he said in a thick, stage French accent. "But of course, for money!"

"The film money? You think this will make the Americans, as they say, up the ante?" He studied Spinrad carefully. "Or perhaps you suppose such crude tactics will persuade Moscow to somehow produce a million rubles worth of unexpected royalties on your Soviet editions if you agree to turn down the American deal?"

Spinrad's eyes brightened. "Say, that's pretty good, I never thought about *that* angle," he drawled. "Tell you what, I'll give you the figures on the Universal offer, and you print them in—"

"Merde!" Sasha groaned, holding up his hands. "Please, I don't even want to hear—"

"Seven hundred thousand for the rights and the screenplay. Plus half a mil in blocked American royalties. Now you know my price."

"Mais oui," Sasha shot back. "Now the only question is what you are."

Spinrad laughed, then suddenly grew serious. "You really want to know what I am, Sasha?" he said rather somberly. "You want the truth?"

"It might have some novelty value. . . ."

"I'm confused, old buddy," Spinrad said. "I mean, I've got a chance to go home with more money than I've ever had in one piece in my life. To see my best short story turned into a movie. A good one too, with me doing the screenplay. I've always known that *Riding the Torch* could be one hell of a film. One that could finally make me the major-league reputation I've never really had. That might finally get me the recognition I deserve in my own country. That would let me live my declining years as a happy man. That might even get me writing fiction in English again. That would give the sad story of my life a happy ending."

"And all you have to do is fold the *Free Press de Paris,* betray everything you've ever believed in, sell out to your American tormentors, screw your colleagues at the *Free Press,* double-cross me, and send me on a one-way ride to Vladivostok. . . ."

"Well put, Sasha," Spinrad said tiredly. "I've truthed you, now you truth me, okay? Forget politics for a moment. Forget Mother Russia. Forget the US of A. Just two guys jackpotting. What would you do if you were me?"

Alexander Sergeiovich Ulanov pondered that a good long while before he spoke. He thought about being recalled to some boring daily in a grim, secondary city in Siberia. He thought about a young Tass reporter who had ridden to his present eminence on the coattails of the *Free Press de Paris.* He thought about what it would be like to have one million American dollars.

He thought about a fine American writer, a great one maybe, who had never received real recognition in his own native land, who had been forced to flee, who had been constrained to live for years in a country that spoke another language, to speak that language himself, to come to half think in it, to lose contact with the culture out of which his literary art arose, to slowly slide into a long, terminal writer's block, to become a mere journalist.

And for some reason, he thought of Aleksandr Solzhenitsyn,

who had never produced anything of real literary worth after defecting to the United States.

He thought of the politic answer and the answer of the heart. He sighed. He shrugged. Despite the cost to himself, he decided to tell the truth.

"If I were you, Norman," he said softly, "I do believe I'd take the money and run."

Norman Spinrad locked eyes with him for a long, quiet moment, deeply shadowed eyes, tired eyes, eyes that actually seemed to be moistening with tears.

"You are a cunning son of bitch, Alexander Sergeiovich," Spinrad finally said softly.

"And you are certainly another, Norman Richard," Sasha said.

"Takes one to know one, old buddy."

"So it does. . . . So what are you going to do, my friend?"

Spinrad laughed, fractured the long, poignant moment of bearish tenderness. "What I've been doing all along," he said. "Keep the pot boiling. Hope that if I toss in enough random factors, the God of Chaos will tell me what to do."

"You mean you *don't even know* where you want this all to lead?"

Norman Spinrad laughed again, got up, went to the door, opened it, gave Sasha a mock salute. "Old buddy," he said, "I haven't a clue."

The *Free Press de Paris* was located on the rue de Saintonge somewhere in the maze of narrow little streets between des Halles and the Place de la Republique. Even the cabbie seemed to have gotten genuinely lost for a while rather than just running up the meter, though Eli Ellis kept the tip to a mingy 10 percent just in case.

Ellis pressed a simple buzzer beside a plain little bronze plaque on a large, ancient, wooden door set in a filthy, brown, brick wall. He was buzzed inside without having to identify himself—so much for security—and crossed a grimy cobblestone courtyard to a crummy little two-story building of the same brick and vintage as the wall. It looked about two hundred years old, and as if it had seen long prior service as a warehouse, or a tannery, or an abattoir.

He entered directly into a big, open space partitioned into offices, work areas, and cubbyholes by cheap, unpainted fiberboard panels that went only halfway up to the high ceiling, which was hung with long, garish flourescent fixtures. Reception was a plain wooden desk cluttered with telephones, printouts, stacks of old newspapers, and unopened mail.

The girl behind it kept him waiting for a good five minutes, or so it seemed, while she jabbered in French to someone on the telephone. "Oui?" she finally said. "Qui voulez-vous, s'il vous plaît?"

"Uh... parlez-vous Anglish?"

The receptionist frowned. "Yeah, who do you wanna see?" she said in a faintly New York accent.

"Norman Spinrad..."

She picked up a phone, paused over the button console. "Who shall I say...?"

"Uh... Eli Ellis," Ellis said uneasily, for he had been dreading this inevitable moment of identification ever since he had decided to confront the lion in his own den. After the item in *Europe Today*, he knew damn well his name would be well-known to the staff here, and he could hardly expect it would be in good favor.

Nor was he disappointed. The receptionist gave him a look that would melt glass, hit an intercom button, and practically snarled into her phone. "Hey Spinrad, it's goddamn Ellis to see you, yeah *Eli* Ellis, who'd you think, ain't that sweet!"

She dropped the phone like a dead fish and busied herself opening mail.

"So...?" Ellis finally said.

"So he's coming to get you, asshole, what do you expect, a red carpet and a brass band?" she snapped without looking up.

Spinrad appeared a few minutes later, looking none too pleased to see him, nor did the receptionist seem exactly pleased at the sight of her boss. "Looks like he forgot his brown paper bag of blood money," she snapped. "Or maybe he just doesn't want to pass it to you in front of the hired help."

Spinrad scowled at her, said nothing, led Ellis down a long passageway through rows of open-doored offices, and into a big, open work space where half a dozen people were gluing strips of computer printout onto pasteup boards.

A big, red-bearded man in his mid-forties who had been

moving from board to board stopped in his tracks and glared at Spinrad.

"This is the big-time agent from Hollywood?" he demanded.

Spinrad nodded unhappily.

"The one who's going to make you a dollar millionaire?"

"That's the fantasy, Kurt."

"You got some nerve showing your face here, Ellis!" red-beard snarled, balling his hands into fists and taking a threatening step toward Ellis.

"Hey—"

The work around the pasteup boards stopped as the newspaper people dropped their knives and printouts and glue pots and became an audience for the confrontation and a nakedly hostile one at that.

"Kurt Gibbs, my managing editor," Spinrad said, quickly stepping between them. "Cool it, will you, Kurt!"

"*Cool it?* You're gonna sell the Freep down the Potomac to this slimy little spook, he has the chutzpah to walk in here, we're all gonna be pounding the pavements thanks to this fuckin' fascist Agency pig, and *you're* telling *me* to cool it, Spinrad?"

"Come on, man," Spinrad drawled rather unconvincingly. "You of all people should know better than to believe all the bullshit you read in the papers."

"You saying you're *not* gonna sell out to Hollywood now, Norman?" said a thin, mousey-haired woman.

"Hey Martha, if they're gonna give me seven hundred thousand dollars to make a movie I've always wanted to see made, I'm gonna take the money," Spinrad said. "Wouldn't you?"

"And write the screenplay in Hollywood?"

Spinrad shrugged. "Better me than some studio hack," he said.

"And what about the paper?" Gibbs demanded.

"You telling me you can't run the Freep for a few months by yourself, Kurt?"

"Cut the crap, Norman. You gonna fold the Freep or not?"

"Have I ever said word one about selling you guys out?" Spinrad demanded.

"You're saying you *won't* flush us down the tubes for

fame, fortune, and a ticket home?" demanded an ancient hippie with long, grimy gray hair.

"Jesus Christ, Eric," Spinrad said, bobbing his head nervously in the direction of Ellis, "I'm *negotiating!*"

"Negotiating *what?*"

"Come on guys, you forget who started the *Free Press* in the first place? You forget who put up the bread? You forget who's kept this operation afloat all these years?"

"Question is, have *you* forgotten who you are, Norman?" Gibbs said much more softly.

"Yeah," said the longhair. "The Norman Spinrad who started the Freep would tell this bastard to take his money and stick it right now!"

"Look, look, I promise you whatever happens, you guys will all be taken care of."

"Yeah, sure," Gibbs snapped, "like the IRS took care of me, right?"

"Yeah, like the porn maf took care of the original Freep!"

"Like Sherman took care of Georgia!"

"You're just going to have to trust me," Spinrad said.

"Yeah, sure, the check's in the mail."

"And you won't come in our mouths, either."

Ellis found himself backing away across the room. The atmosphere was so poisonous you could run a garbage truck on the fumes. Or so at least it seemed.

"My word isn't good enough for you, you can all leave right now!" Spinrad snapped, his voice suddenly hardening. "Go on strike! Stage a coup!"

He took Ellis by the arm, glared at his staff people. "Otherwise, get back to work," he said. "We've still got a paper to get out and only three hours to get this shit to the printer!"

But as the people in the makeup room did indeed go back to work as Spinrad dragged him into his office, Ellis began to wonder.

Was all this just an act Spinrad had put together for his benefit? If so, then *why?* If not, then why *were* all these commie exiles still working for him? Why *weren't* they on strike or trying to stage a coup or something? For all the anger, Norman Spinrad still seemed to be in charge here. Ellis had the feeling that maybe he had just been had.

Spinrad's office was just another fiberboard cubbyhole, with a desk, a computer, a phone, files, books, old newspa-

pers, folding chairs, and a musty old couch. At least it had a
door, though, which Spinrad slammed behind him as he sat
down behind the desk.

"*So?*" he demanded. "What the fuck are you doing here,
Ellis? You don't think I'm in deep enough shit with my own
people already?"

All during the cab ride down from the 16th, Ellis had
pondered what he was going to say to Spinrad, indeed what
he imagined he was supposed to accomplish by coming here
in the first place. He had finally decided that he was going to
see Spinrad at the *Free Press* because there was nothing else
to do. Now Spinrad's opening lines caused him to tell the
simple truth because he could think of nothing else to say.

"Not half as deep as I'm in with mine. They're blaming
me for that damn item in *Europe Today.*"

Spinrad laughed mirthlessly. "And *my* people are blaming *me* for it," he said. "Negotiating the price of the *Free
Press's* demise in public print. . . ."

"But *Europe Today* didn't say—"

"Are you for real?" Spinrad snapped. "These are *journalists*,
Ellis, shit, American political exile journalists! Gibbs was a
heavyweight on the *New York Times* before Washington came
down on him! Martha Mendez, who now finds herself dou-
bling as a pasteup girl, was a heavy-duty photojournalist
before she published those atrocity photos from Venezuela.
Eric Bradshaw was a White House reporter before he published
that leak that blew the Indonesian coup attempt. My people
have all had their careers pulled out from under them by just
the kind of creeps you represent, and they now spend most of
their time reading through elliptical leaks from intelligence
agencies. Reading between the lines is their line of evil.
We're talking about world-class paranoiacs who can add one
and one and come up with three every time."

"So what are you telling them?" Ellis asked nervously.

"You just *heard* what I'm telling them. Just what I advise
you to tell *your* people."

"Which is?"

"Go fuck yourselves!"

"Jeez," Ellis moaned, "get serious! I mean, I'm not just
talking about you'll never work in this town again, I'm talking
about . . . about . . ."

"Hardball players in trench coats, n'est-ce pas?"

Ellis nodded miserably. "They can fuck me up real bad . . . and they will. . . ."

"Tell me about it!"

"I'm trying to, goddamnit!" Ellis snapped. "My ass is gonna be grass with BMA and the Black Tower. They'll audit me for the rest of my life. . . . They'll . . ."

"Terminate you with extreme cement overshoes?"

Ellis broke into a cold sweat. "Come on," he said, "they wouldn't . . . they don't . . . *You're* still—"

Spinrad shrugged. "As long as I stay in France where the government protects me," he said. "But believe me, I'm not planning any trips to the Third World."

Ellis shuddered. This stuff was getting unreal. Or maybe *too* real. "But why in hell did you plant that item?" he demanded, determined to change the subject.

"*Moi?*" Spinrad said innocently.

"You're trying to tell me it *didn't* come from you?"

"Are you out of your mind? Where's my percentage in that? You think maybe I *like* having my own employees treating me like a traitor . . . ?"

"But if not you, who?"

"If not me, *you*, Ellis!" Spinrad said angrily. "Who else gains by it? You burn my bridges and force my hand, pretty fucking cute!"

"And blow the deal? And have Langley coming down on my head?"

"You're tell me it *wasn't* you?" Spinrad said.

"Are you kidding? With the hot water it's put me in?"

"Son of a bitch!" Spinrad exclaimed. "It's the only thing that makes sense. Sasha must've gotten it all by himself!"

"But how?"

"Are you kidding? We're talking *Tass*, Ellis, we're talking *KGB*! They're the Big Red Machine. Maybe they bugged your phone. Maybe they sewed a minimike in your boxer shorts. I'll bet you *do* wear boxer shorts, don't you?"

Ellis's head was reeling. Spinrad's logic was irrefutable. Yet some agent's instinct told him the man was lying in his teeth.

"Yeah, it's got to be the Russians. . . ." Spinrad was muttering. "*They're* the ones who lose if I fold the paper! Fucking goddamn Sasha! And I thought that Bolshevik bastard was my friend!"

"You can't trust a commie!" Ellis said, jumping on what seemed like a ray of hope.

"Maybe not, or so it suddenly seems. . . ." Spinrad mused. "But that doesn't mean you can trust the CIA either."

Sourly, Ellis had to admit that the man had a point. The CIA, the KGB, tapped telephones, who knew what else . . . ? Jesus, this was supposed to be a *film deal,* all he ever really wanted was his 10 percent of BMA's 10 percent of a nice sweetheart package. Now he was up to his chin in political horseshit and everyone in sight was trying to make waves.

"Look," he said rather pleadingly, "I don't like your politics and you don't like mine, but can't we put that aside and deal like . . . you know, Americans? Fuck the KGB! Fuck the CIA! Let's just do this deal so we can both go home in one piece!"

"What did you have in mind?" Spinrad said slowly.

"Oh man, I don't know. . . . Look, can't you just move a little, and I'll move a little, and we can meet somewhere in the middle . . . ?"

"Maybe . . . just maybe . . ." Spinrad sighed. "I've got to admit this is all getting a little ancient. What if . . . what if I sell the *Free Press* to a front of the CIA's choosing? For the half mil that the US government owes me. . . ."

"Huh?"

"Yeah, yeah," Spinrad enthused. "They deposit the money in a numbered Swiss account. I sign a predated contract of sale timed to the release date of *Riding the Torch*, contingent on receipt of the bank account number. . . ."

"Boy that sounds crazy!" Ellis exclaimed. But his agent's mind was working. This kind of deal-cutting was *his* line of evil. "You come back to the States, write the screenplay, they give you the number. . . ."

"And I take out a little insurance policy . . . another contract, with someone here in Paris, with my girlfriend, you know, you met her at the apartment. . . . If they arrest me in America, if I don't appear in Geneva on the release date of *Riding the Torch* to consummate the deal, the second contract goes into effect. Passing ownership of the *Free Press* to her for a token payment of one franc. . . ."

"So if they screw you in the States they screw themselves here in Paris," Ellis said, not without admiration and enthusiasm for the lunatic architecture of the deal.

"Do you think this will work?" Spinrad said. "Do you think you can sell this to your principals?"

Ellis shrugged. He thought about it. He managed a laugh. "To tell you the truth, I haven't the foggiest," he said. "Have you made me an offer they can't refuse?"

Norman Spinrad laughed back at him. "Quien sabe?" he said. "I think I've just made you an offer that *I* can't understand!"

Back at the Boulogne Hyatt, Ellis put in a call to Langley and outlined the deal, presenting it not as Spinrad's bright idea, which surely would not have gone down smooth, but as his own genius inspiration.

There was a long pause at the other end of the line after he had finished laying it out, which he took as a good sign.

"You thought this up all by yourself, Ellis?" Harris finally said.

"Well I let Spinrad fill in a few of the details himself, to let him convince himself it was really *his* idea, if you know what I mean," Ellis owned.

"*Hmmm....*"

"Well?"

"Well I can't decide something like this on my level, but I'll kick it upstairs.... At least you've got him talking, at least this gets things off the dime...."

By the time he was finished with Langley, Eli Ellis was feeling rather pleased with himself. He poured himself a Chivas from the minibar in the room, then pondered how he might celebrate today's success.

At which point, once again at a loss, he found his good mood beginning to sour. Put another lonely four-star dinner on the expense account? Order up another room-service hooker? Try for better luck on the Avenue Victor Hugo? Take in another porn show in Pigale? He poured himself a second, somewhat less celebratory, drink, sipped it out on the balcony, staring out at the Bois de Boulogne, feeling bored and horny, and beginning to feel sorry for himself again.

But before he could finish the second drink, before his spirits had a chance to sink much lower, the telephone rang, and there was a rather strange woman's voice on the other end.

"Hallo, this is Mr. Eli Ellis, da?" Sultry, weirdly accented, a bit spacey.

"Uh yes..."

"The Hollywood agent?"

"Uh that's right, what's this—"

"I wish to make the casting couch scene with you, babes. . . ."

"WHAT?"

"My English is not so bad, no? I want to fuck you for the purpose of you making me a big-time movie star in Hollywood. This is how such matters are accomplished in the decadent West, ain't it?"

Ellis chugalugged the rest of his Scotch in one searing bolt. "Ah . . . er . . . who the hell *is* this?"

"*You do not recognize my voice?*" whoever it was said in a tone of indignant incredulity.

"Lady, I don't think I even recognize your *planet!*"

In response, the woman's voice broke into a snatch of song, powerful, insinuating, sneery and learing, rocking and rolling.

"Feel the wind from the east
  Belly up to the beast
  For the bright red star is rising
  In my burning metal bed
  You'll be better red than dead
  Yes a bright red star is rising. . . ."

"*Katrina Charnov . . . ?*" Ellis stammered. "This isn't some kind of put-on?"

"Do you dare to presume that *someone else* could sing with the voice of the Red Metal Rose?"

"Uh . . . no . . . no . . ." Ellis muttered. Jesus Christ, *Katrina Charnov!* And she wants to fuck me? So that I'll help her defect?

Blood drained from Ellis's brain to his dick, but that did not prevent his agent's mind from going into overdrive. Katrina Charnov, the Red Metal Rose, was the only true Russian international rock and roll superstar. The girl every red-blooded American boy loved to hate and dreamed of screwing into submission, and her act played to it and had parlayed it into something like a dozen gold discs.

She stood about five feet tall, a perfect little miniature Amazon, vulnerability and danger in the same tantalizing package. Her hair was conked, dyed, lacquered, and metalized into a deco version of a giant rose. She performed in a variety of scanty and/or skintight costumes, all of which were bright red and featured the hammer and sickle. She usually wore jackboots and exaggerated epaulets and frequently wore the Soviet flag as a cloak. She was primo pussy and a rock-and-roll monster.

Ellis had never been into handling rock stars, but he knew damn well he could learn fast if he could get his hooks into a property like the Red Metal Rose. Ten percent of... no, screw that, a *personal manager* could get himself *25 percent*, now couldn't he? Properly exploited, discs, Vegas, a world tour, maybe even film, Katrina Charnov could pull in two, three, maybe five million a year... and with the defection PR angle...

"So, Mr. Ellis, you are overwhelmed, da, or surely it cannot be that you do not wish to discuss these matters...?"

"Uh no... I mean yes... I mean sure... I mean come right over to the hotel...."

"What kind of girl do you think I am? I detest the imperialistic plastic Hiltons...."

"It's a Hyatt."

"La meme chose, da? No, you will meet me for a drink, then you will take me to a lavish expense account dinner, then we will go back to my place, snort many lines of coke, and bang like bunnies, yes, is that not the way it is done in the decadent West?"

"Uh..."

"You will meet me in La Coupole in one hour, da? You of course know this place...."

"Uh no..." Ellis stammered, "but don't worry, I sure as shit can find it."

Ellis couldn't quite put his finger on what it was, but something about La Coupole made him nervous, and not just because Katrina Charnov was late, which he figured had to be SOP for female rock stars. It was a great, big, noisy barn of a place with a large dining room fronted by little café tables spilling out toward the sidewalk. It seemed kind of tacky and public for such an assignation, and all the more so, as his ears told him after he had sat down and ordered a martini, because the place was full of Americans. Ordinarily that would have put him more at his ease, but he *was* meeting a famous Russian, and these people seemed like the sort of political exiles whom he had seen at the *Free Press*—

Oh shit!

That was it!

He recognized Kurt Gibbs, and what was her name, Martha something or other, the photojournalist, sitting in a party of six about half a dozen tables over. And from the sidelong sneers and whispered conversation, it was apparent that *they* had seen *him*.

The waiter appeared with some kind of weird red wine over ice. "Hey, I ordered a *martini*..."

"*Oui, ce la!*"

"A martini, goddamn it, a *martini!*"

"*Qu'est-ce que c'est* la problem, Monsieur? *C'est* un Martini! Si vous voulez *blanc*, dites a moi *blanc*, crazy Americain!"

"What the fuck—"

"*Merde*—"

"Ah Mr. Eli Ellis, I see you est arrive!"

At this inopportune moment, the Red Metal Rose made her entrance. Katrina Charnov wore a rather ordinary sleeveless black minishift and golden velvet slippers, but the famous Red Metal Rose hairdo, the ice-blue eyes, the finely sculpted and vaguely Tartar face, were quite unmistakable, not only to Ellis, but to the waiter, nearby patrons, and the people at the *Free Press* table.

The waiter gave her the suave, gallic glad eye, heads turned, and Martha the photographer slipped a camera out of her purse.

"Oh shit," Ellis moaned, rising quickly to his feet, and managing to get his back turned just as the strobe went off.

"Come on," he said, grabbing Katrina Charnov by the elbow. "This place is a zoo, let's go right to dinner." The camera strobe went off again, Ellis fished a bill out of his wallet and slapped it down on the table without looking at it, and dragged her out of La Coupole, onto the street, and into a cab before she could even utter much of a protest.

"You certainly know how to sweep a girl off her feet," she said admiringly once he had stuffed her into the taxi. "Tres Hollywood!"

"Ou?" said the cabdriver.

"What?"

"He wants to know where we're going."

Ellis had given no thought to choice of restaurant, and indeed would have come up pretty dry even if he had. "Uh, how about the Tour D'Argent?" he said, coming up with the only name he could think of.

"Merde!" Katrina Charnov sniffed, turning up her nose. "This is how do you say, a clip joint for American and German tourists! Better we go to La Cuisine Humaine, yes?"

"Good choice, hear it's got a good reputation," Ellis lied suavely.

Katrina babbled to the cabbie in rapid-fire French and they whipped a short distance through the thick traffic to the Quai Voltaire, to just about the weirdest restaurant Ellis had ever seen.

A silvery building in the form of a recumbent 1930s art-deco spaceship floated on a barge in the Seine at quayside. A globe of the Earth revolved above the entrance. The doorman wore some kind of incredibly tacky old zoot suit and his face was so heavily made up that he looked like a department-store dummy version of himself.

Inside, black plastic toadstool tables and matching chairs seemed to grow out of a clear plexiglass floor through which the oily waters of the river were darkly visible. The walls and ceiling were muraled into an oddly cartoony composite landscape—greek columns rising out of desert sards, palm trees growing on an arctic glacier, Niagara Falls on a snowcapped mountain that looked like Fuji, a sky full of fleecy white clouds, whirling tornadoes, rainbows, aurora borealis.

The maitre d' and the waiters wore black tuxedo jackets, skintight blue jeans, loud Hawaiian silk shirts, Japanese sandals, and big white cowboy hats. And they all wore makeup that made them look like Disneyland versions of themselves.

"Jesus Christ . . ." Ellis muttered as the maitre d' showed them to their table.

"Très drôle, no?" Katrina Charnov said slyly.

"What the hell *is* this place?"

The Red Metal Rose laughed as the waiter handed them big menus that seemed to be made of flexible aluminum. "Just what it says, babes, La Cuisine Humaine, genuine human food, only as conceived by master chefs of the planet Mars," she told him. "Quite authentic, da? The robot waiters are even cunningly designed to look like real humans from Earth. But of course, this being a human restaurant on Mars, they have naturellement not quite gotten everything perfect."

Ellis opened the big menu folder. Ordinary menu French was bad enough, but this thing seemed to be gibbering in a

razy mélange of French, English, Russian, and German,
with Japanese kana and Chinese ideograms sprinkled through
it, just in case that got too comprehensible.

"Uh maybe you'd better order," he said. "To tell you the
truth, I've never been on Mars before."

Katrina laughed. "But of course," she said. "It is the *red
planet*, no? This is a chain, they have them also in Leningrad
and Moscow."

Katrina ordered Russian pepper vodka. This proved to
be ice-cold, clear, and about 150 proof, with big jalapeños and
maguey worms floating in it. It tasted like red-hot mescal and
seemed to explode with about five megatons in Ellis's brain.

"So now maybe you would like to tell me what this is
really all about?" he said, emboldened by the extraterrestrial
booze. "You want to defect to the United States, right?"

"*Defect?*" Katrina said. "How could the Red Metal Rose
defect? It would be like . . . like Superman would show up in
Leningrad and announce he is joining the Red Army. . . . My
act would then become ludicrous, da. . . ."

"Then what—"

The waiter appeared, jabbering in flat mechanical French
like a badly maintained robot. Katrina ordered Pizza de Fruit
de Mer, Cassoulet Soul Food for her, Hommard Stroganoff ala
Chinois for him, and a five-hundred-dollar bottle of Lafitte
Rothschild 1971.

"Okay, Eli babes, let us talk bottom line, yes?" she said
when the waiter had departed. "I have no wish to defect, why
should I? If I defect, my act goes to the toilet bowl, and I can
never go home again, where I am big star, Hero of the Soviet
Union, dacha, flat in Moscow *and* Leningrad, whole ball of
heavy-duty wax. Is Russian Spring, babes, I am number-one
blossom thereof, and I dig it!"

"But then—"

"I don't want to defect, I want to change agents!"

Ellis could hardly believe his ears. Was it really going to
be *this* easy?

The waiter arrived with the damndest "pizza" Ellis had
ever seen. A large, round piece of spongy Ethiopian bread
had been scored into many narrow wedges. Each wedge was
festooned with a different kind of sashimi—tuna, yellowjack,
salmon caviar, octopus, mackerel, sea eel, bass, red snapper—
and garnished with thinly sliced tomato.

Katrina rolled up a wedge into a neat little roll with her

fingers, gobbled it up, rolled another one, munching industri
ously as she spoke.

"Russian Spring or no, in Soviet Union, concert produc
ers, booking agents, film producers, everyone, are all sti
part of the same stupid Ministry of Culture bureaucracy. A
musicians have their deals made by Soviet Rock and Ro
Union, which is all part of same bureaucracy too. Eve
foreign deals are made by these same assholes. This suck
n'est-ce pas? Same bureaucracy sets performance fees an
royalty rates, books artists, produces discs, collects the mon
ey, and takes thirty-five percent for the state as payment fo
screwing artists. I am big rock star, but I make half what
should, and they do not get me film deal, which I deserve.'

Ellis rolled himself a wedge of tuna sashimi. Wasabi juic
was steamed into the Ethiopian bread. It was spicy and
delicious. And so was what he was hearing.

"Let me get this straight," he said. "You want to *fire th
Soviet Rock and Roll Union* and hire *me* to represent you?"

Katrina gave him a feral little smile. "Perhaps," she said
"Certainly I am fed up to the neck with *them*. Whether
wish to hire *you,* that is the purpose of tonight, Eli baby."

"This is legal under Soviet law?" Ellis said dubiously.

Katrina shrugged. "Who knows?" she said. "No one
thinks to do it yet. What can they do, send me to Siberia? I
game of bluff, babes. I let them think that maybe if they don'
let me have my own personal agent, *then* maybe the Red
Metal Rose defects and Mother Russia loses her number-one
rock star to the decadent West!"

They polished off the pizza while Ellis tried to digest
that one, and the waiter arrived with the wine and the
entrées.

His Hommard Stroganoff à la Chinois was chunks o
lobster stir-fried with fresh Shiitake mushrooms served in a
peppery sour cream and cognac sauce over scallion pancakes
and topped with a generous sprinkling of caviar. It was
wonderful.

Cassoulet Soul Food turned out to be a big earthenware
crock of black-eyed peas, individual baby back ribs, Texas hot
links, chunks of Virginia ham, and fresh baby corn on the
cob, baked in molasses and chili sauce, and topped with
stir-fried collard greens. It looked pretty disgusting, but the
Red Metal Rose wolfed it down with a will.

Over the entrées, Ellis laid out the numbers. Disc

sales. Vegas dates. World tours. His 25 percent. "I think I can make you three million a year for sure, maybe as high as five," he told her.

"Yes, yes, all that is very fine," Katrina said. "But I want to be a big movie star! You can make me the film deals too?"

Eli Ellis lay back in his chair sated and gave her his number-one deal-sealing shit-eating grin. "Katrina, babes, the movie business is my main line," he told her. "As a matter of fact, the deal I'm putting together now, *Riding the Torch*, has just the part for you. . . ."

"Da, da, Jiz Rumoku, I have read the story, why do you think I called you? I play this part, yes, and we make the movie a rock opera!"

"Uh . . . sure . . . why not? Terrific idea. . ." Ellis temporized. "Well, what do you say, do we have a deal? Should I have the papers drawn up?"

"Not so fast," said the Red Metal Rose. "Is one more thing my mother taught me."

"Your mother?"

Katrina leered at him, reached out under the table, and put her hand squarely on his crotch. "Never trust a man you haven't fucked," she said.

"Well I wouldn't want to piss off your mama. . . ." Ellis stammered.

The waiter appeared to bus the dishes. "Voulez-vous dessert, madam, monsieur?" he asked in his weird robot voice.

Katrina continued to squeeze Ellis's prick as she spoke to the waiter, who acted as if no such thing was happening. "Non, non, l'addition s'il vous plaît. Je ne mange pas dessert. Et pour le dessert, monsieur mange *moi*!"

Whatever all that French meant, it caused the waiter to flush under his heavy makeup, blow his robot cool, and shuffle off quickly in something of a daze.

"What in hell did you say to that guy?"

The Red Metal Rose laughed and gave Ellis's throbbing dick a good hard yank. "I ask for the check," she said. "I tell him no dessert here, I have something special for you chez moi."

"You're gonna make dessert for me at your place?"

"Le dessert, c'est plat de moi!" Katrina Charnov said. She broke herself up and absolutely refused to translate.

*   *   *

"C'est Paris, da?" Katrina said as she drew aside the curtains to reveal the truly spectacular view from the big parlor window of her apartment on the rue de Lillet, just behind and to the west of the Musee d'Orsay.

Ellis looked out across the empty plaza of the museum on a picture-postcard nightscape spread out before him. The dramatically lit Louvre shimmered across the Seine to the right, the dome of the Opera to the left, setting off the bosky darkness of the Tuileries gardens between them. Beyond, the jeweled lights and rooftops of the Right Bank, and the pinnacle of Montmarte outlined in the city glow against the dark sky in the far distance. From up here on the fourth floor, the brightly lit restaurant ships and tour boats plying the Seine looked like perfect child's toys, and the traffic on the Pont Royal, the quayside drive, the streets beyond, were rivers of red and white neon.

"Pretty spectacular, all right," Ellis agreed. And so was this apartment.

The ceiling had been removed between the fourth floor and the sloping atelier of an old building to form a large, loftlike space, and the huge picture window was two stories high. Opposite the window, a large sleeping balcony reached via spiral staircase ledged out over an ultramodern kitchen.

The living room itself was mostly empty space. A black wooden floor strewn with Persian rugs, and the whole skins of a polar bear, a lion, and a white Siberian tiger, complete with the heads. A wall of TVs, disc players, speakers, disc cabinets, arcane electronic instruments and keyboards. A big rainbow-painted rattan peacock chair. Zebraskin couches. A freestanding Swedish fireplace. Carved rosewood tables.

In the center of the room stood an enormous old antique wire bird cage in the form of a cathedral. In it, perhaps two dozen tiny finches of various spectacular colors chirped and hopped and flitted.

And one whole wall was just about covered with an enormous poster of the Red Metal Rose herself, rendered in the hoary, heroic, tractor-driver style of Socialist Realism. A huge Russian flag blew in a stiff breeze behind her over the Moscow skyline. Katrina herself stood before it with one hand on her hip, the other raising a fist, and her face rendered with starry-eyed patriotism. Except for red jackboots, red leather panties with the hammer and sickle on the crotch, and pasties in the form of red and gold onion domes, she was mother-naked. Something was lettered across the top in gold neon Cyrillic.

Ellis, who read not one word of Russian, knew what it said, for he recognized the poster as the cover art for *Red Star Rising*.

"Très drôle, no?" Katrina said, as she caught him oogling the poster. "Patriotic Soviet Heroine of Rock and Roll!"

Ellis nodded silently. He had been wondering whether the hair beneath the panties matched the hairdo of the Red Metal Rose. His dick throbbed expectantly, knowing it was about to find out.

"And now for dessert," Katrina said, dancing by him and into the kitchen. She took an ice-cold bottle of vodka out of the freezer, poured about a quarter of it into a blender, dropped in three whole limes, a shot of cassis, and a tray of ice. "The secret ingredient," she said, pulling a silver vial out of a drawer, and dumping in about an ounce of white powder. She hit a button and whipped the concoction up into a sherbet.

"I go upstairs, you wait here till I'm ready," she said, and ascended the staircase to the bedroom with the blender jar, leaving Ellis alone in the kitchen to contemplate the impending moment.

The whole thing seemed a bit unreal. A few hours ago, his best hope for a hot time in Gay Paris had been a fancy, solitary dinner and a room-service hooker. Now here he was in this fabulous pad with a crazy Russian rock star, and he had little doubt that the white powder was coke, or perhaps something even more exotic.

Eli, my boy, he told himself, the things a patriotic American is forced to endure in the service of his country!

"Hey, voilà!" Katrina called out from the bedroom, and he climbed up the staircase.

The bedroom of the Red Metal Rose appeared to be a corner of the original atelier, with a low, sloping, mirrored ceiling and open old-style French windows looking out over the rooftops of Saint Germaine. A red neon rose sizzled brightly beside a big water bed. A yellow neon hammer and sickle lamp stood on the other side.

The bed itself was covered with a huge Soviet flag, upon which lay Katrina Charnov, quite naked, slurping sherbet from the blender jar with one hand, and crooking the finger of the other at him.

Her body was tight and muscular, her breasts high and well mounded even in the recumbent position, and the erect nipples were rouged bloodred.

Entranced, Ellis drifted toward the bed, pulling off his jacket, unbuttoning his shirt, undoing his belt.... As he reached it, he could see that her pubic hair indeed matched her hairdo, but in a way that was entirely unexpected. It was shaved, and molded, and metalized into a perfect Red Metal Rose.

"No, no," she cried, "not yet. You must be a good boy, Eli. Before you are permitted to take off the clothes, you must eat your dessert."

She winked, she smiled, she slowly poured the drugged sherbert onto her pubic mound and leaned back luxuriantly with her arms outstretched. "Every last drop."

Ellis awoke at the magic hour of dawn to rose-red light tinging the sky over the rooftops and the sounds of the awakening city. Peculiarly enough, he knew exactly where he was, remembered every moment of the wildest night of his life, sighed, snuggled up against the sleeping Katrina, and found himself with an erection again as he ran it all back on the instant replay screen of his mind.

He had done as she commanded, burying his face in the icy sherbet between her thighs, slurping it up, not stopping till long after he was down to the native juices, his head clamped tightly in place by her muscular thighs, indeed not until she pulled him into a long kiss by his hair.

By then he was really flying high and had all but lost confidence in his ability to maintain by the time he had gotten his clothes off. But Katrina had filled her mouth with the remnants of the sherbert, and then taken him into it. It was ice-cold velvet, and it tingled, and by the time it had melted, there was no chance that he would, and they had made love for what seemed like hours before he finally came.

Afterward, strangely enough, or perhaps not so strangely considering the advice of Katrina's mother, they had talked business for a while before dropping off into thoroughly sated sleep.

"We will do this thing, yes, Eli?" Katrina said. "You will be my personal manager, I will give you twenty-five percent, and together we will make beautiful music and me a movie

star, da. . . . If you are half as good in the negotiations as you
are in bed . . ."

At that moment Ellis was ready to promise her the
world, and now, lying there beside this wondrous creature in
the rosy Parisian dawn, he realized that he just about had. Up
to and including the female lead in *Riding the Torch*, which
the two of them had decided together would be a rock opera.

What the hell have I gotten myself into? he wondered.
Could he convince Spinrad to allow them to turn his story
into a musical? And if he could, how the fuck was he going to
sell such a crazy notion to Universal? With *The Red Metal
Rose* as the female star in the bargain! And what would
Langley say to that?

It reminded him of a hoary Hollywood joke. A producer
dies and goes to heaven. But after a few hundred years of
playing harp and singing hosannas, he gets bored. He wants
to make a movie. He accosts Saint Peter.

"No problem," Pete says. "For the script, we got Shake-
speare, Goethe, Joyce, Tolstoi, none of them have worked
for centuries! Set design, Michelangelo, Dali, da Vinci, take
your pick. Renoir, Howard Hawks, von Sternberg, you name
it, they're all ready to direct. For male lead, you can cast
Garfield, Gable, Fred Astaire, Bogart."

"Great!" says the producer. "But what about a female
star?"

"Well . . ." Saint Peter mumbles furtively. "God's got this
chick. . . ."

The Red Metal Rose shifted in her sleep, snuggling up
tighter against him. He threw a possessive arm around her.
The sun was rising over a glorious morning. He was a
monster agent, wasn't he? This was his chance to make
millions, wasn't it? Fuck Norman Spinrad! Fuck BMA! Fuck
the KGB! Fuck Universal! Fuck Langley!

He might not be so young, but he was in Paris, he had a
golden opportunity, he had just passed through the most ma-
gical night of his life, and maybe he was in love. Fuck 'em
all, Eli baby, he told himself. Faint heart didn't just win fair
lady! Time to look out for Number One! Time to wheel and
deal! Time to rock and roll! Let's win this one for the Gipper!

"But why do you come to *me* with this, Norman?"
Alexander Sergeiovich Ulanov said ingenuously. "Why don't
you print it yourself?"

"Because I have the funny feeling that's exactly what you want me to do," Norman Spinrad said. "They find that their boy Ellis is screwing around with a KGB agent, they'll yank him out of here faster than hot baboon shit through a tin horn, and that'll kill the deal. That's why you sent him little miss Mata Hari in the first place, isn't it?"

"KGB agent? *Katrina Charnov*? Believe me, if you knew the lady, you'd know how ridiculous that idea is!"

"Go tell that to BMA! Go tell it to Universal! Go tell it to the paranoiacs in Langley!"

When Spinrad had asked to meet him clandestinely in this grimy little tabac on the Place Saint Placide, Sasha had been pretty certain what was on his mind.

As ordered, Katrina Charnov had enticed Ellis into a public meeting at La Coupole, a place known to be frequented by *Free Press* staff.

Unfortunately, the photos Norman had just shown him hadn't caught much more than the back of Eli Ellis's head in the company of the Red Metal Rose, but that little detail need not be a problem. Ellis and Katrina had been doing the town together for several days now, Sasha had recommended several dining venues in advance, and the Tass photographers he had planted had used the latest KGB minicameras with ultrafast film, no clunky Nikons with obtrusive flashes to alert the lovebirds that their trysts were being preserved for posterity. If and when the time came, he had plenty of good pictures to supply to Spinrad. Or, if Norman chose to sit on the story, to run in *Europe Today*.

"You're telling me you're *not* going to run this story?" Sasha asked, sipping at his cognac.

"Are *you*?" Spinrad shot back.

Sasha smiled. "It's your scoop, Norman," he said. "As your friend, my journalistic honor requires that I allow you to break it in the *Free Press*. Of course, if you don't run it in the next issue. . . ."

"Thanks a lot, old buddy," Spinrad said sourly. "Thanks for putting my ass in a sling. If I don't run this fucking thing, my staff will assume I'm going to sell out, and I'll have a revolution on my hands. If I do, I can kiss a million bucks good-bye. And if I let *you* break it, I get screwed both ways. Just when I thought I had worked the whole thing out with Ellis."

"Oh?" Sasha said.

Norman leered wolfishly at him. "So you don't know everything, eh?" he said. "Maybe the lady is holding out on you. Maybe Ellis doesn't talk in his sleep." He fell silent and took a long slow drink of kir, letting Sasha sweat.

"Are you going to tell me?" Sasha finally said.

"You have pictures, don't you Sasha?"

"What makes you say that?"

"Because I want them. The stuff I've got is shit."

"I thought you weren't going to run the story."

"I haven't decided yet. I think in all fairness, Mr. Ellis should get a peek first, don't you . . . ?"

"I could get you pictures . . ." Sasha said slowly. "We *do* have resources. . . ."

"I'll bet you do! What about it, Sasha, you give me the photos, I'll let you in on my deal with Ellis."

"You would trust me that far?" Sasha said, genuinely moved.

"About as far as I can throw you, old buddy. I don't *have* to trust you."

"Why?"

"Do the deal and find out."

Sasha shrugged. "It would appear I have nothing to lose," he said. "So tell me your little secret. . . ."

Spinrad did. When he was finished, Sasha laughed, shook his head in admiration. "A numbered Swiss bank account! How drôle! And if they *do* double-cross you back in the States, the *Free Press* continues to publish!"

He frowned. "Much as that would be in my interest, my friend, there is a possibility you should consider," he said more seriously. "Namely, that eliminating the *Free Press* may not be their primary goal. Maybe all this is just a ruse to get you back to the States where they can arrest you. Have you thought of *that* unpleasant possibility?"

Norman laughed. "You better believe it!" he said. "I haven't told you the cutest part. Guess who gets the *Free Press* for one franc if they double-cross me?"

"A member of the staff, I presume?"

"Wrong, old buddy!" Spinrad exclaimed. "*You* do!"

"WHAT?"

"I've told Ellis that the paper will go to my so-called French girlfriend if I don't show up in Geneva with the bank account number."

"*Natasha?*"

Spinrad nodded. "He swallowed it whole. If they try to fuck with me in the States, I'll tell them the truth. I'll tell them that *Tass* will end up controlling the *Free Press* through a proxy."

"But wouldn't they call your bluff?" Sasha moaned. "Make it all public? The *Free Press* would be entirely discredited if they broke the story that it had become a KGB front, it would almost be as good as killing the paper as far as the Americans are concerned."

Spinrad smiled. "Who would believe them? They've been calling the paper a commie rag since I started it. . . ."

Sasha slugged down the rest of his cognac. His head was reeling. If the Americans kept their part of the bargain, the *Free Press* would be folded. If they planned to arrest Norman in Los Angeles, they'd probably call his bluff, save the half million in Geneva, and play the KGB angle in public. Either way, Moscow would not be happy with the situation, nor would Alexander Sergeiovich Ulanov be likely to retain their favor.

"It would seem you're risking your freedom for a million dollars, my friend. . . ." he said.

Spinrad nodded. "And your ass, Sasha?" he said.

"The thought had crossed my mind. . . ." Sasha admitted.

Norman shrugged. "It's a gamble," he said, "but the odds are on my side."

"And if you win, I lose."

"Peut-être. But on the other hand, if I lose, you lose too."

"Surely there must be a safer alternative . . . ?" Sasha mused. But try as he might, he could not think of one.

"There just might be. . . ." Spinrad said quickly. "I'd have to write off seven hundred thousand dollars and the movie deal if it worked, but at least I'd be willing to consider it. . . ."

Sasha peered at him intently, dead certain that whatever this was, Norman had been leading up to it all along.

"If I could get my hands on the Swiss bank account number . . ."

"From Ellis!" Sasha exclaimed. "Of course! That's why the pictures . . . ?"

Norman nodded. A sad, faraway look came onto his face. "I'm caught between a rock and a hard place, Sasha," he said somberly. "God, I want this movie made! I want what I've never had, to be recognized as a major writer in my own country, to go home to California, to make my peace with it all before I die. But to have that, it seems I have no alternative but to sell out everything I've believed in, and people who have trusted me. Shit, this sucks! I wish Ellis had never showed up to tempt me! And I *am* tempted, old buddy. They've devised the perfect Satanic bargain. Fame, fortune, recognition . . . And all I have to do is sell out my principals, people who believe in me. . . ."

"And me," Sasha said softly, actual tears coming to his eyes.

"Yeah, old buddy. I know what will happen to you if all this fucks up. They'll yank you back to Mother Russia, won't they? You'll never see Paris again. And you love this place don't you?"

Sasha nodded silently.

"Yo tambien," Norman said. "Shit man, I don't want that on my conscience. So if I can get my half mil and save the *Free Press* too. . . ."

He shrugged sadly. "So I'll never see my work on the silver screen. So I'll die here in exile. So I'll never write anything of worth in English again. Fuck it, Sasha, I've had my run. Chip Delany said something to me once, and it's helped me sustain myself in this world of shit. If you've written great work, no one can ever take that away from you, Chip said. Whatever happens, you always have that. Even if you're the only one who knows. La vie continue, n'est-ce pas?"

"You'd do that for me?" Sasha said, reaching across the café table to touch his old friend's hand. "Give up the whole movie deal and all that it means?"

Norman's eyes were filled with bleary tears. "Fuck you, you commie bastard," he said softly. "I'd do it for myself."

"This may sound crazy," Sasha said, "but all at once, I don't really want to see that happen. . . ."

Norman grimaced. "Jeez, Sasha," he said. "You think maybe we've both been here too long? You think maybe we're starting to get soft in our old age? Shit, next thing we'll be kissing each other on the cheek like a couple of phony Frenchmen."

Life had certainly taken a sweet turn in the City of Light for Eli Ellis. Katrina spoke French, knew the city like a native, and with the Red Metal Rose as his tour guide, Paris opened up before him.

They ate lunch and dinner in two different restaurants every day. They toured the late night clubs. They took long walks along the Seine and took in the bird market. They lazed in the Luxembourg gardens and the Bois de Boulogne. They rented a little hover boat and flitted up and down the river.

And they snuck quickies in the most incredible places. Under the Pont Neuf. In the hover boat. In the Champ de Mars close by the Eiffel Tower. In an empty late-night Metro carriage. In dark Montmarte alleyways. Even in a streetside pay pissoir.

And of course these were only appetizers for the main courses that took place every night in her apartment. Ellis had certainly had his share of casting-couch starlets in Hollywood, but the Red Metal Rose was the hottest item he had ever known. The girl would do just about *anything*, and she had him doing it too. She had him snorting coke and smoking hash. She'd dress up in boots and whip and make him do her on his knees, and then she'd turn around and give him fantastic head. They gobbled all sorts of cuisine, haute and otherwise, off each other's bodies.

Am I in love? Ellis found himself asking himself. Did it matter? He was certainly in *lust* with the Red Metal Rose, and he never wanted it to end. He would have been perfectly content to spend the rest of his life in just this manner playing in Paris with Katrina Charnov.

But of course that wasn't going to happen. Things were either going to fall apart or get even better. Katrina kept bugging him about the movie deal. What was holding it up? When was she to make her break with the Soviet Rock and Roll Union?

Smitten as he was, Eli Ellis was not about to tell any Russian that the final approval for the deal was in the hands of the boys at Langley or even higher and mercifully nameless American political circles. *That* love crazed, he wasn't!

And while on one level he was impatient for the Word to come down from Langley, on another he found himself wishing they would *never* decide. Because whichever way it came down, his big mouth would have put him in deep shit.

If the Agency nixed Spinrad's deal, BMA would pull him back to Hollywood and demote him to agenting soap-opera stars, and there would be no *Riding the Torch* movie for Katrina to star in. She'd probably drop him as both lover and personal manager as the phony Hollywood bullshit artist he would have proven to be.

And if the deal *did* go through, he'd have to produce for her. He'd have to persuade Universal and the CIA to cast a Russian rock-and-roll singer who had never been in a film before and whom he was both managing and sleeping with as the female lead while the Russian Rock and Roll Union screamed bloody murder and insisted that she was still their client.

And then the Word came down from Langley. As luck would have it, it came on one of the few mornings that Katrina deigned to spend with him in the Hyatt hotel room, which she loathed. They were lying in bed together having a late room-service brunch when the phone rang.

"Congratulations, Ellis, it's a go. The Word just came down. Get on the horn to Universal and have the film contracts drawn up. We'll have our paper for Spinrad to sign in your hands in twenty-four hours."

"They went for it?" Ellis cried. "They really went for it?"

"I've got to hand it to you, Eli, you really put this one together. Your country owes you one. We'd put you in for a Medal of Freedom if this didn't all have to be on the QT. But just between you and me, I can guarantee you that the IRS will never ever audit you unless you do something *totally* outrageous on your returns."

"Uh thanks, that's great, I'll get right on it. . . ." Ellis muttered, and hung up the phone.

Katrina planted a brief wet kiss on his lips. "That was Hollywood, da?" she cried, hugging him. "The movie deal went through, yes?"

"Uh yeah . . . but . . ."

"Oh Eli, you filthy capitalist exploiter, you are *wonderful*!" Katrina shouted. She grabbed up the breakfast tray and flung it across the room with a grand gesture. "I am going to be a big Hollywood movie star!"

"Uh not so fast Katrin—"

She tore off the bedclothes. "The bright Red Star is rising over Hollywood!" she exclaimed. "And I owe it all to you! Oh Eli, Eli, you are magnificent!"

And for the moment all Eli Ellis's problems were blissfully forgotten as she gave him the most incredible, heartfelt blowjob.

Afterwards though, after Katrina left to do some studio work or something, it all came tumbling back onto Ellis like a ton of bricks. He put off calling Universal. What was he going to tell them? What magic words would convince them to turn *Riding the Torch* into a rock opera starring the Red Metal Rose? Procrastinating, he put in a call to Norman Spinrad at the *Free Press* to tell him the good news.

And while he was waiting for Spinrad to come on the line, the inspiration struck him. If *he* broached the notion of doing *Riding the Torch* as a musical vehicle for his new Russian client-cum-girlfriend, they would for sure laugh him out of town. But if it came from *Norman Spinrad*, if Spinrad insisted it be part of the deal, then maybe Langley would lean on Universal and—

"Hello . . . ?"

"Eli Ellis, Norman. Great news! They bought your deal!"

There was a long silence. "Far fucking out . . ." Spinrad said in a rather strange tone of voice.

This guy owes me plenty, doesn't he? Ellis told himself. I've just made him a million bucks, haven't I? He's never gonna be in a more receptive mood. . . .

"Uh look, Norman," he said tentatively, "could you come up to my hotel? Have some champagne and celebrate, and maybe talk a few details before I call Universal . . . ?"

Surprisingly, Spinrad readily agreed. "Certainement, for sure, Ellis. As a matter of fact, I've got a detail or two to discuss with you."

Maybe *too* readily. Ellis didn't like the sound of that. But then again, maybe he was just being paranoid, this certainly *was* a paranoid situation, wasn't it?

By the time Spinrad arrived at his hotel, Ellis had a bottle of Dom Perignon well iced, Beluga caviar with all the fixings laid out, and all his mental ducks in line, or so at least he thought. Fill the guy full of champagne, lay out some lines of Katrina's coke, play on his sense of gratitude. . . .

He popped the champagne bottle while Spinrad was coming up in the elevator, and met him at the door with glasses in hand. "We did it, man!" he said, handing Spinrad a glass. "Let's drink to *Riding the Torch*!" He clinked glasses, gulped his down, had another one poured before they had sat down on the couch before the imitation Italian-marble coffee table.

"I've got some great new ideas for this project, Norman," he enthused, pulling a vial of coke out of his pocket. "Do a few lines while we talk it over...?"

Spinrad raised his eyebrows. "Didn't think you had it in you, Ellis," he said as Ellis laid out half a dozen lines directly on the table.

"Hey my man," Ellis said, snorting up a line, "this is *Paris*, right? A long way from the DEA or pissing into corporate bottles!"

Spinrad honked a line with his left nostril. "I see your new girlfriend has loosened up your tight asshole," he said, and did up the right.

Ellis froze. "What?"

Spinrad eyed him narrowly. "We might as well start by laying all our cards out on the table," he said, reaching into a pocket, pulling out a sheaf of photos, fanning them out like a poker hand, and dropping them face up on the phony marble tabletop. "These are *mine*."

Ellis glanced at the pictures with a sinking stomach, knowing all too well what he would see. Nor was he disappointed. "Where did you get those?" he stammered, sounding inane even to himself.

Spinrad drank down his champagne, poured himself another glass, sipped at it, making Ellis sweat. He did up yet another line of coke before he spoke. "The two of you have not exactly been models of discretion. Not that you were supposed to be..."

Woodenly, Ellis snorted up another line of coke himself as Spinrad shook his head, exhaled a world-weary sigh. "Fucking Sasha set you up, Ellis," he said. "The lady is a Soviet agent."

"Impossible!"

"Do I have to draw you a diagram? He sends the Red Metal Rose to seduce you—who but a corpse could resist? —and at the opportune moment, he breaks the story in *Europe Today*. AMERICAN DOUBLE AGENT IN BED WITH LUSCIOUS SOVIET SPY. If I know Sasha, the story will *admit* that Katrina Charnov was working for the KGB, and he's sitting on his own pictures. The CIA will hit the ceiling, grow quite cross with you, and pull out of the deal, leaving the *Free*

Press as is, me out a cool million, and you quite high on the Agency shit-list."

"I don't believe it! You don't know—"

"Fortunately for both of us, my guys got *these* photos first. And Sasha doesn't yet know we're about to close the deal. So we've got time to think. . . ."

"To think of *what* . . . ?" Ellis stammered, pouring himself another glass of champagne and slugging half of it down.

"Good question," Spinrad said, shrugging. "I suppose I could sign the papers tout suite, scoop *Europe Today* in the *Free Press*, break it all myself, but with *our* topspin. You *knew* she was KGB, but you held your nose and screwed her for God and Country because . . . because . . . because you thought you could get a line into their Paris operation. . . ."

"Langley would never believe that. . . ."

"Of course not, but it would be in their interest to act as if they did . . . if . . . if I refused to go to Hollywood if they screwed with you. . . ."

"You'd do that for me?" Ellis exclaimed disbelievingly. His head was reeling, he was half drunk and more than a little stoned. And it seemed there was something he was forgetting. . . .

"I'd do it for certain considerations," Spinrad said.

"Considerations . . . ?"

"You get me the Swiss bank account number. I get the money out of Geneva before I go to Hollywood. That way my threat to back out if they come down on you will have credibility, and I'll have half a mil to console myself with if they call my bluff."

"How am I supposed to do that?" Ellis moaned.

Spinrad shrugged. "That's your problem," he said. "If you don't, I'll just let Sasha break this juicy story first his way, and then your problem will be a hell of a lot worse."

Something was hovering at the brink of Ellis's consciousness. He took another hit of coke to try to force it through.

"But even if I *do* get you the Swiss bank account number, and you get the money before you leave Paris, what's to prevent you from double-crossing *everyone* and pulling out of the deal?"

Spinrad smiled at him. "Only a seven hundred thousand dollar film deal," he pointed out.

But Eli Ellis wasn't really listening. The last hit of coke had burned away the fog and it suddenly came to him in a flash of white light. *He* had a hole card to play, and it was a good one.

"You're wrong about one thing, Spinrad," he said. "The KGB may have sent Katrina my way for *their* reasons, but take it from someone who's been there, the Red Metal Rose has ideas of her own!"

And he told Norman Spinrad a carefully edited version of the truth. Namely that Katrina Charnov was ready to defect in return for a career as a movie star in Hollywood.

"That's my hole card," he said, "the Red Queen of Rock and Roll. If I bring the Red Metal Rose over to the West, I'll be a *hero* with Langley for sleeping with her, not a bum!"

"She's really willing to do that, Ellis? You're *that* good in bed?"

"Uh not exactly," Ellis said. "She's got her price too. . . ."

"Oh no. . . ." Spinrad moaned.

"Oh yes," Ellis told him. "The part of Jiz Rumoku in *Riding the Torch*. And of course, the film will have to be a rock opera."

Spinrad goggled at him. "*My* movie starring your ditzy Russian girlfriend!" he cried. "A fucking *rock opera!*"

"You know any *other* way to save the deal?" Ellis said.

Spinrad took another hit of coke, studied him narrowly. "You set this up, didn't you Ellis?" he said. "You're gonna collect ten percent as her agent, aren't you?"

Ellis grinned at him. "Personal manager," he said. "Twenty-five percent!"

Spinrad burst out laughing. "Too fucking much!" he giggled. "Just too fucking Hollywood!"

"Well what do you say?"

"What do I say?" Spinrad said, choking back his laughter. "I say it's so fucking sleazy, so fucking crazy, I love it!"

He frowned. He took another sip of champagne. "But Universal will never buy it, man," he said. "She's got no acting experience. She doesn't even speak good English. And you've got such a conflict of interest they'd hang you by your nuts for even suggesting it!"

"Not if it comes from you," Ellis said.

"*Moi?*"

"You sign the papers, but you refuse to go to Hollywood to do the screenplay without Katrina as Jiz Rumoku. Langley doesn't care jack shit about what the movie turns out to be, right, all they want is the *Free Press* deal, and the propaganda coup when Katrina defects. They'll shove it down the Black Tower's throat."

"Christ," Spinrad moaned, "you expect me to put it all on the line so your fucking girlfriend can screw up *my* movie?"

"You expect *me* to weasel the Swiss bank account number out of Langley and pass it to you. . . ." Ellis pointed out.

Spinrad laughed. He shook his head. "Let me get this straight," he said. "I sign the Universal contract. The CIA puts the money in Geneva. You get the bank account number. When you pass it to me, I announce that I don't leave Paris for Hollywood without Katrina Charnov plays Jiz Rumoku. That's the deal?"

"That's the deal," Eli Ellis said.

"It's Hollywood sleaze."

"It's just show biz. . . ."

"You are a real motherfucker, Ellis."

"And you're another."

Norman Spinrad laughed, raised his glass. "I'll drink to that," he said, draining his goblet and tossing it against the wall.

Alexander Sergeiovich Ulanov was about to leave for lunch when Ivan Panov, the Paris KGB station chief, and a balding gray-haired man in a somber blue suit burst unannounced into his office.

Panov, a sprightly blond-haired fellow with a wry sense of humor, and an occasional carousing partner of Sasha's, seemed nothing like his usual good-natured self. The blue suit looked as if he were accustomed to biting the heads off small mammals for lunch and hadn't eaten since petit dejeuner.

"Uh, I'm afraid we are in a bit of trouble with Moscow, Sasha," Panov said nervously.

"I will do the talking, Panov," the blue suit said in a voice that seemed to blow out of the icy depths of Siberia.

"Uh . . . whom do I have the pleasure of addressing . . . ?" Sasha asked wanly.

"I am Igor Mikailovich Rostropov, Executive Assistant to the minister of media, I have had an unpleasant rushed flight from Moscow, I do not at all find this a pleasure, and neither will you."

"Would you like a drink?" Sasha offered inanely, pulling

open a desk drawer and extracting a bottle of excellent cognac.

Rostropov ignored this entirely and sat down on the edge of the only chair before Sasha's desk, sitting there ramrod straight, while Panov, wringing his hands, stood at the back of the office trying to fade into the woodwork.

"You are the one responsible for Katrina Charnov's relationship with Eli Ellis?" Rostropov demanded.

"Hardly a *relationship*, Comrade Rostropov," Sasha said. "We needed an agent, and she—"

"You were aware that Ellis represents BMA and Universal Pictures?"

"Of course. What's this—"

"I will interrogate, you will respond, Ulanov!" Rostropov snapped. "Were you also aware that Ellis was subject to CIA control?"

"Well, I assumed—"

"You *assumed*, you idiot! Do you realize what you've *done*?"

"Somehow, Comrade Rostropov, I doubt it. . . ." Sasha muttered miserably.

"The Red Metal Rose is threatening to defect, thanks to you, Ulanov!"

"WHAT?" Sasha exclaimed. He turned to Panov. "But Ivan, you assured me her brother—"

Panov shrugged, threw up his hands. "According to her dossier—"

"Shut up, Panov!" Rostropov roared. He turned his ice-blue eyes on Sasha. In them Sasha could see the cold, hard wastes of deepest Siberia beckoning. "The woman called the president of the Soviet Rock and Roll Union yesterday," Rostropov said. "She was most disrespectful and arrogant and appeared to be quite intoxicated. She tendered her resignation from the Soviet Rock and Roll Union and announced that henceforth she would be exclusively represented by Mr. Eli Ellis of Hollywood!"

"But . . . but she can't do that, can she?" Sasha stammered. "Under Soviet law, all artists must be represented by—"

"The president of the Soviet Rock and Roll Union is far better acquainted with these legal matters than you are, Ulanov. He pointed out the legal impossibility of such an action in considerable detail."

"Well then—"

"At which point, Charnov became quite abusive, outlining a long series of grievances against the Soviet Rock and Roll Union. She declared that her new representative, Ellis, had just closed a lucrative film deal for her in Hollywood, which was more than *we* had ever done for her, he had assured her she could be a big film star in the West, and therefore, unless the Soviet authorities acceded to her demand that we let him represent her, she would have no viable career choice but to defect to Hollywood, publicly and loudly."

"And what did the president of the Rock and Roll Union say to that?"

"Nothing!" Rostropov snapped. "She hung up and has refused to speak to Moscow since!"

"Merde..." Sasha moaned. "What are you going to do?"

"The question is, what are *you* going to do, Ulanov?" Rostropov said. "This matter is *your* responsibility. And unless you resolve it to the satisfaction of the Ministry of Media soon, you will find yourself reporting agricultural statistics in Kazakhstan!"

Shakily, Sasha poured himself a cognac and drank half of it down, using the time to rack his brains for a stratagem. "Well, couldn't we simply accede to her wishes...?" he finally suggested lamely. "From what you say, she *won't* defect if we let Ellis represent her, so—"

"And have every other damn Soviet artist signing with BMA or William Morris, you cretin? We cannot afford to set such a precedent."

"But why would they—"

"Because the Soviet Rock and Roll Union and the Soviet Actor's Union take thirty-five percent and the filthy capitalists take ten percent, Ulanov. Because American agents would be able to hold up Soviet film and disc producers for twice the fees and twice the royalties for *our own artists*."

"Oh," Sasha said glumly. "Any suggestion, Ivan?" he asked Panov forlornly.

"This is hardly the province of the KGB, Sasha...."

"Couldn't you abduct her and take her back home to...ah, listen to reason...?"

"This is the age of the Russian Spring, of the New Soviet Legality, we are not Chekist thugs in the KGB!" Panov shot back indignantly. "Besides, if the French let anyone get away with such direct action on their national territory, would not

the Americans have long since dealt more directly with your
friend Spinrad?"

Spinrad . . .

A ray of hope began to light up the icy Siberian wastes of
Sasha's gloom. *Riding the Torch* must be the film project in
which Ellis had secured a part for Katrina Charnov. Norman
was willing to forgo the film deal if he could somehow get his
American money and save the *Free Press* too. But his heart
yearned to see the movie made. Would he not be willing to
forgo the American money if he could have his film and the
Free Press too? Maybe, just maybe, there might be a way to
turn all this inside out and upside down. . . .

"If I may, Comrade Rostropov, just how much authority
do you have?" he inquired.

"I am the executive assistant to the minister of media
himself!" Rostropov said haughtily.

"Could you cut a film deal?"

"A film deal? We are not discussing a *film deal*, Ulanov!"

Sasha smiled. "Your pardon, Comrade Executive Assistant to the Minister of Media," he said, "but I'm beginning to
think we are. *Riding the Torch*."

"Is that not Spinrad's project at Universal?" Rostropov
said. "The deal that brought this capitalist swine Ellis to Paris
in the first place?"

Sasha nodded. "And rubles to zlotys, it's the film in
which Ellis has gotten a part for Katrina Charnov."

"Of course, that much is obvious," Rostropov said. "I
don't see . . ."

"What if we made it *our* deal, Comrade Rostropov?"
Sasha said. "Then the Red Metal Rose would be forced to
deal with *us*."

Did a thin, wintry smile actually crease Rostropov's thin
lips? "Take the project away from Universal?" he said slowly.

"Exactly," Sasha said. "Buy the rights from Norman
Spinrad before he makes the deal with Universal! Make the
film in the Soviet Union. We could pay Spinrad seven
hundred thousand rubles for the rights and the screenplay,
and still do it for half the American budget. The *Free Press*
would continue to function as before. Katrina Charnov would
be mollified, particularly since Ellis would be utterly discredited in Hollywood and would therefore no longer be
viable as her agent."

"Langley would be furious with Ellis!" Panov chimed in.

"They might even terminate him if he returned to the United States. . . ."

"You could persuade Spinrad to sell *Riding the Torch* to *us?*" Rostropov said skeptically. "But Panov has told me that part of his deal with the Americans is that he is to be paid the five hundred thousand dollars they owe him and be allowed to return to his country a free man. Surely—"

"He'll be eager to deal with us," Sasha assured him. "He's afraid of what may happen to him if he returns to the United States, and with good reason. And he doesn't want to give up his newspaper. From his point of view, a Russian film, seven hundred thousand rubles, the *Free Press,* and a safe life in Paris, is far better than an American film, a million dollars, the death of his newspaper, and an uncertain future in America."

Rostropov chewed this over slowly. For the first time, a genuine and unmistakable smile appeared on his stony face. "Save the *Free Press de Paris* as a credible independent conduit, deal with the Charnov situation, allow the CIA to give Ellis his richly earned comeuppance . . . the political logic, I must admit, is impeccable, Ulanov," he said.

He frowned. "But this film would have to gross fifty million rubles to break even," he said. "We would eat perhaps a fifteen million ruble loss. . . . The bottom line, as the Americans would say, does not compute. . . ."

Sasha shrugged. "So take a tip from the Americans," he said. "Could not the Ministry of Media account the loss to the *KGB's* operational budget?"

Now Rostropov really did smile, glancing at the miserable Panov. "Indeed," he said. "That *would* be true Soviet justice!"

"Oh fuck," Norman Spinrad moaned, dropping his chopsticks in the middle of his plate of Canard à la Pekinoise, and holding his head in his hands.

"What on Earth is the matter, Norman?" Sasha said. "It's wonderful news! Don't you understand? Haven't you heard what I've told you? We'll pay you seven hundred thousand in fully convertible *rubles* for the rights and the screenplay! You keep the *Free Press,* the film gets made, and you walk away a free man with about eight hundred thousand in dollar equivalents!"

Sasha had invited Spinrad to lunch at his favorite Chinese restaurant, Le Dragon Zephyr, to tell him the good news, and had even ordered the house specialty a day in advance with a truly magnificent white Bordeaux.

But now Norman looked like anything but a man celebrating his good fortune. In fact, he looked perfectly dreadful.

"What is so terrible?" Sasha said. "Don't you realize—"

"What's so terrible?" Spinrad groaned, looking up at him. "I signed the papers with Universal and the CIA yesterday!"

"You did *what*?" Now it was Sasha's turn to suffer a sudden disastrous loss of appetite.

"I signed the papers. Universal now owns *Riding the Torch*. The check is in the mail."

"The CIA deal too?"

Norman nodded. "The funds have already been transferred to Geneva," he said. "I'm waiting for Ellis to get me the bank account number."

"He hasn't gotten it yet?" Sasha said quickly.

"As you might imagine, he has some difficulty convincing Langley of his need to know. . . ."

Sasha's mood brightened. "Well then, all is not lost!" he said. "We'll publish the photos of Ellis and Katrina Charnov in *Europe Today* and they'll *never* trust him with anything again. The deal will be dead and—"

"Great!" Spinrad snarled. "Just fucking terrific! You're not listening. Universal has just paid me three hundred and fifty thousand dollars for the rights, they own *Riding the Torch* forever and ever. You run that story, Ellis gets shitcanned, I don't get the number or the money in Switzerland, the CIA pulls out of the deal, Universal doesn't make the movie, I'm out the screenplay bread too, and I *still* can't make a deal with you!"

Sasha sighed. "Well at least you keep the *Free Press* and three hundred and fifty thousand dollars," he said wanly. And if the story kills the American film deal and ruins Ellis in Hollywood, Katrina Charnov will probably stay with the Soviet Rock and Roll Union, he realized. Rostropov will be happy, the KGB will be happy, and I will have saved my tender ass from the frozen wastes of Siberia.

"You'd really do that to me, old buddy?" Norman snapped.

Sasha took a long sip of wine. At this moment, the noble vintage tasted quite sour. "I'd hate myself in the morning," he said. "But I have no choice. It's that or Siberia."

"Yeah, well maybe *I* have a choice," Spinrad said coldly.

"I can go to Hollywood, write the screenplay, and take my chances with the American government...."

"You'd really do that to me, old buddy?" Sasha snapped back. "You'd send me to Siberia... and maybe yourself to Leavenworth...?"

Norman sighed, took a long swallow of wine. "Unless Ellis gets me the bank account number, what choice do I have?"

"You wouldn't be bullshitting a bullshitter, would you, Norman?" Sasha said.

"Y tu tambien, Sasha? Why is it I get the feeling there's something you're not telling me?"

"Why is it I get the feeling there's something *you're* not telling *me*, Norman? Why do I get the feeling you don't really believe Universal will make this movie?"

"Ah fuck it!" Norman said. "I get the feeling we're both pointing derringers at each other's nuts under the table. Show me yours, and I'll show you mine...."

"D'accord...." Sasha said.

"Katrina Charnov," they both said simultaneously.

They both goggled at each other.

They both laughed.

"I get the Swiss bank account number from Ellis in return for which I have to insist she gets the female lead in *Riding the Torch* or I don't leave Paris."

"He's already told her she's got the part. She's leaving the Soviet Rock and Roll Union and making Ellis her agent."

"Universal will have a shit fit."

"The Ministry of Media will ship me to Kazakhstan."

"Ellis is counting on the CIA leaning on Universal."

"They'll never do it if *Europe Today* runs the story. And they certainly won't give Ellis the bank account number."

"Pas de merde, old buddy."

"Are you going to play along with Ellis?"

"Are you going to run the story?"

"What choice do I have?"

"What choice do *I* have?"

Norman Spinrad locked eyes with Sasha. Sasha stared back at his old friend. He thought about their first meeting. He thought about the day they had cut a deal to give the *Free Press de Paris* birth. He thought about his fancy office in the Tour Montparnasse, his penthouse apartment in the 6th, his cottage in the Maritime Alps, his whole life in Paris, about

Nadine, who would never accompany him back to Russia, about all he had to lose if he didn't run the photos of Ellis and Charnov in *Europe Today*. He thought about who had helped him to rise to his present treasured and precarious position. He thought about the grim Siberian winter.

And he thought about how Norman had been willing to give up seven hundred thousand dollars and his dream of fame, fortune, and recognition in his own land for friendship's sake. It was a lot of water under the Pont Neuf.

He threw up his hands. "Are we going to let these bastards make us do these things to each other, Norman?"

"Are we, Sasha?"

"Not if I can help it, one phony Frenchman to another."

"So what do we do, old buddy?"

"I run the story," Sasha said. "You give *Europe Today* a big scoop. NORMAN SPINRAD SIGNS UNIVERSAL FILM DEAL FOR RIDING THE TORCH STARRING THE RED METAL ROSE. With all the juicy details of Ellis's affair with Charnov."

"Universal will have an embolism!"

"So will the Ministry of Media!"

"And the CIA!"

"And Eli fucking Ellis!"

"In the service of *what*, Sasha?" Norman said.

"In the service of Chaos!" Sasha said. "I have read all your books, that one, too."

Norman laughed. "Is that all there is to it, Sasha?" he said. "Two phony Frenchmen giving the finger to everyone?"

Sasha smiled. "Mais non, mon ami!" he said. "The publication date will be most carefully timed."

"To what?"

"To your party! All Paris knows Norman Spinrad's crazy parties! And this will be the craziest of all!"

"What party?"

"The one you are going to throw to announce this deal. Next Friday evening. The very hour *Europe Today* hits the kiosks with the story, n'est-ce pas?"

"And where am I going to throw this party?"

"You will rent a bateau-mouche, the kind they redo to order, and our Ship of Fools will wheel and deal down the Seine. Très Hollywood, oui?"

"That's gonna run me a lot of bread."

"You've just made a big movie deal. You can afford it."

"So can Tass."

"Bien sûr."

"Your nickel, Sasha."

"D'accord. Let it not be said that the New Soviet Man doesn't know how to boogie."

"I'll drink to that!" Norman Spinrad said, downing a full glass of wine. "Right now, I'll drink to anything."

He smeared hoisan sauce on a pancake, stacked it with skin and duck meat, rolled it, popped it into his mouth.

"Did I ever tell you about the first time I ever had Peking Duck?" he said. "It was in Los Angeles. A wonderful birthday present from a very special lady."

"I still do not think I should be going to this soiree, Eli," Katrina Charnov said as their cab pulled up at the Port de la Conference on the Right Bank just east of the Pont de L'Alma. "Neither Ulanov nor Panov has tried to speak to me since I fired the Soviet Rock and Roll Union. . . ."

"So?" Eli Ellis said.

"So the vibes I do not like," she told him. "They will surely be at this party, and they must be furious. . . ."

"So what?" Ellis said, pecking her on the cheek as they climbed out of the cab. "*I* was furious with you a few days ago, and *we've* kissed and made up, haven't we?"

He had indeed been royally pissed at her after Spinrad unmasked her as a KGB agent. He had stormed into her apartment that night and thrown a shit fit.

"You've made a fool of me all along!" he screamed at her. "You're working for the KGB! You don't love me! It's all been a con!"

But instead of trying to deny it, Katrina told him a heartfelt sob story about her brother Dimitri, a big-mouthed dissident whom the KGB had threatened to send to Siberia or worse if she didn't play ball.

"Da, I was sent to seduce you in order that Tass might obtain compromising photographs," she admittedly blithely. "But then, the chemistry between us, Eli, this I did not expect! Nor that you would *really* be able to make me the big star in Hollywood! Ulanov certainly had no interest in my continuing to see you after he got his photos, da. Nor can he be pleased that I have left the Soviet Rock and Roll Union for you!"

She threw her arms around his stiff neck and kissed him, long and deep. "All this I did for *us*, Eli," she said. "Even as you got the part for me, my capitalist Hollywood agent darling!"

"So you say. . . ." Ellis said, still dubious.

"Ah, but I prove it!" she cried. "Tonight I have called Moscow and fired the Soviet Rock and Roll Union! They are furious, the exploitative swine! *This* was the act of a KGB spy, mon cher?"

"*You did what?*"

"I fired the cheapshit bastards! I told them that from now on you were my manager, I was going to make a movie in Hollywood thanks to you, and if they gave me any of the hassle, I would defect to America before I would break my deal with you!"

"Without consulting with me? Before your part in the film was nailed down? Before the damn deal was even nailed down?" Ellis didn't know whether to be angry or touched.

Katrina decided for him. "You are pleased, no? When a Russian is in love, when the hot Slavic blood begins the boiling, one must be brave, one must *do it*, and think later, if at all. Is not la même chose with Americans, Eli?"

And she had flung herself into his arms, grabbed him by the cock, tumbled him over backward onto the polar bear skin rug, pulled down his pants, and that had ended their first lovers' spat in forthright fashion.

"One does not kiss and make up with the KGB and the Ministry of Media as one does with *you*. . . ." Katrina said nervously as they walked across the pier to the restaurant boat waiting at dockside. "It is a different kind of screwing, and they are accustomed to top position, Eli. Panov, at least, should be screaming and threatening. This silence . . . is ominous, I do not like. . . ."

"Come on Katrina, what are they gonna do, try to snatch you in front of all these people?" Ellis said. "Lighten up! Spinrad's throwing this party to celebrate the *Riding the Torch* deal. It's going to be full of reporters. And he's promised me that tonight's the night he's gonna announce that he doesn't go to Hollywood without you. You *had* to come! You're gonna be the star of this party, Katrina!"

"You wait and see, Eli, Alexander Sergeiovich Ulanov, he will throw, how you say, a curveball!"

The bateau-mouche that Norman Spinrad had rented was one of the restaurant tour boats that had plied the Seine for decades. With a single big deck enclosed by an angularly faceted, but somehow sleek, greenhouse affair, it was a prime piece of moldy French futurism that reminded Ellis of the Parc de la Villette or the Pompidou or for that matter, the escalators at the Beverly Center.

Through the big glass facets, Ellis could see that the party was well underway—he had successfully timed it so that Katrina could make her grand entrance—and there was a short line at the gangway, where one beautiful blond in a stylized black tuxedo was checking the guests against the list and another was handing them some kind of newspaper as they boarded.

"Eli Ellis and Katrina Charnov," Ellis said.

The first girl checked them off her list. The second one handed them newspapers.

Ellis glanced at his as they boarded, did a take, and cursed. "Motherfucker!"

"Merde!" Katrina shouted at roughly the same time.

The paper was *Europe Today*. It had been neatly folded open to page 12. The headline on the lead story ran RED METAL ROSE TO STAR IN RIDING THE TORCH. The slugline read "Soviet Rock Star Scores Big on Hollywood Casting Couch." There was a nicely framed photo of Ellis and Katrina making goo-goo eyes at each other across a café table.

"*Free Press de Paris* publisher Norman Spinrad has signed a fat deal with Universal Pictures to do a screenplay for a fifty-million-dollar picture based on his novel *Riding the Torch*," Ellis read. "*Europe Today* has learned that he is tailoring the scenario as a starring vehicle for Katrina Charnov, the Soviet Union's own Red Metal Rose—"

"—curiously enough, the very same Eli Ellis who has been romantically linked to Russia's top rock star—" Katrina read aloud.

"—the deal was put together by top BMA agent Eli Ellis—"

"—seen painting Paris red together—"

"—'perfect for the part of Jiz Rumoku,' Spinrad declared—"

"—could be a step toward reviving cultural détente—"

"—always thought it would make a great rock opera—"

"—wouldn't dream of making the film without her—"

"—according to sources, Ellis has already signed up the Red Metal Rose to a lucrative seven-figure contract, though the Soviet Rock and Roll Union refuses to comment—"

"This is good, Eli, I think?" Katrina said perplexedly.

Tass announces whole deal for Spinrad's party, means they give me no shit about leaving Soviet Rock and Roll Union and becoming Hollywood star, yes?" She squinted at the paper. "But then why this cheap gossip column crap about how I suck you for the part like sleazy capitalist starlet? And why does *Tass* hint I am maybe KGB agent?"

Slavic or not, Ellis's blood came to a quick, rolling boil. To kill the deal!" he snapped. Good god, they must be chewing the rug at the Black Tower! Even at six thousand miles' remove, he could feel the ax whistling toward the back of his neck, hear a mighty chorus of voices screaming, "You'll never work in this town again, Eli Ellis!"

And *Langley*! he realized. Oh shit, of course! The commie bastards must've done this to put me and the deal on the agency shit-list! Langley must be burning the wires to the Black Tower right now!

"I do not understand," Katrina said. "Deal is already signed, sealed, delivered, no?"

"No!" Ellis snapped.

"*No?* But you tell me—"

"You tell *yourself*, Katrina!"

"What shit is this, Eli?"

"Deep shit, that's what, damn it!"

"You tell me, Eli Ellis, or I—"

"Not *here*, fer chrissakes!" Ellis hissed, grabbing her by the elbow.

They had boarded the boat reading the newspaper story to each other, and they had wandered inward as they started shouting at each other, and now they were right in the middle of things, drawing no little attention to themselves.

The old bateau-mouche had been completely redone for the party. The standard tables had been removed and a long buffet table ran down the centerline of the deck, laden with sushi, Chinese food, French fare, taco fixings, chili, salads, fruit, cheese, pastries, huge mounds of caviar with all the trimmings. Tuxedoed waiters dispensed assorted booze from full bars at both ends, though there were three bowls of poisonous-looking amber punch on the main table.

Small café tables were set out around the periphery of the deck close by the glass enclosure. On each was an onyx ashtray holding what looked to be half a dozen actual joints and matching black slabs with soda straws and lines of coke already laid out.

A black curtain cordoned off the prow section, guarded by what looked to be two bouncers in tuxedos. An afro-electro band, replete with dashikis, talking drums, congas, and key boards played quirky background music at the stern.

Ellis and Katrina had entered via the amidships gangway and now they stood in the middle of the boat, in the middle of the crush, close by the buffet table. Heads were turned, eyes were upon them, a red-haired woman in a long, red sheath dress accosted them, balancing a huge plate of caviar on one hand, holding a champagne glass in the other.

"Cynthia Goodman, *Time*, Miss Charnov, would you say—"

"Piss off!" Ellis snarled.

"Hey, Mr. Ellis, Derek Spencer, *Rolling Stone*, is it true—"

"No comment!"

"Pierre Laconte, *Paris Match*, c'est vrai que—"

Reporters were swarming around them. Someone pulled out a camera and flashed it in Ellis's face, momentarily blinding him.

"Leave us alone, will you!" he snarled.

"Mais un moment—"

"Our readers—"

"Tokyo Shimbun—"

"FUCK OFF!" Ellis shouted, brandishing his fist. "Get lost, you assholes!" .

Throughout all this, Katrina had been striking poses, smiling into lenses, playing the big-time rock star. "Merci, please, bitte, kudasai, we will do the press conference later, first you must let me get righteously loaded yes. . . ."

It only served to exacerbate the feeding frenzy.

"Hey guys, come on, be cool, let 'em *breathe*, willya, pas de bullshit, there'll be a press conference later, d'accord!"

Norman Spinrad, resplendent in a garish red tuxedo and ruffled paisley shirt, had appeared from somewhere. "Hey, this is a party!" he shouted into the melee. "And you're all guests! Cut this shit out, or get off my boat! I mean it, I really mean it!"

Grumbling, muttering, balancing overflowing plates of food and brimming glasses, the press crush reluctantly retreated.

Spinrad smiled at Ellis. "Sorry about that," he said, taking him by the elbow and leading him and Katrina to a café table up by the prow.

"What the fuck is going on here, Spinrad?" Ellis snapped
: him. "You *knew* your commie amigo Ulanov was going to
reak that goddamn story when you planned this party, didn't
ou? You got copies of the damn thing to hand out! I thought
e had a deal!"

Spinrad eyed him peculiarly. "We do," he said. "I've told
e world your girlfriend has to star in the movie, haven't I?
Vhen Sasha told me he was gonna break this thing, I gave
im exactly the statement you wanted me to, didn't I?"

"No! Yes! I mean—"

"Quit your bitching!" Spinrad told him. "*You're* the one
ho's welching on our deal. Or do you finally have that Swiss
ank account number for me?"

"No . . ." Ellis moaned. "And now Langley will never . . . oh
od, listen man, we gotta talk!"

"Oh we will, we will, Ellis, we'll wheel and deal like you
ouldn't believe," Spinrad said with a shit-eating grin. "But
ter, much later, when we're all good and loaded!"

And he waltzed away from the table and disappeared
ehind the black curtain into what was obviously the VIP
ection.

Ellis trailed after him. One of the tuxedoed bouncers
tepped into his path.

"Pas d'entrée," he said, folding his burly arms across his
hest. "Seulement par invitation."

"What?"

"Invitation only. No crashers, comprais? Or I break votre
neecaps, monsieur, get the message, motherfucker?"

"What's the matter, Ellis," said a familiar voice behind
im, "don't you like it out here with the peons?"

Ellis turned to confront Kurt Gibbs, the managing editor
f the *Free Press de Paris*. The big, red-bearded man was
cowling, but somehow Ellis got the feeling that his ire was
ot really directed at him.

"What's *your* problem, Gibbs?" he snapped irritably.
"You should be enjoying this!"

"I should?" Gibbs said perplexedly.

"It's what you wanted, isn't it?"

"It is?" Gibbs snapped. "Spinrad's sold out the Freep
nd you—"

"He's killed the whole fucking deal, that's what he's
one!" Ellis blurted.

"He *has*?" Gibbs said, knotting his brows in confusion.

"If you think that Langley's gonna swallow—" Ell
caught himself short. *Oh god, why am I blabbing to th
asshole?*

But it was too late. Gibbs's eyes lit up in sudde
comprehension. "So you *admit* it's all been a Company dea
do you Ellis?" he said. "And someone's thrown a monke
wrench into the works... Tass, no doubt. But then wh
would Norman...?"

The big man frowned. "Doesn't add up," he said slowl
He eyed Ellis much more sympathetically. "Look man, th
only sure thing is that you're in deep shit with some very ba
people...."

"What are you talking about?" Ellis stammered.

"Come on, Ellis, even you can't be that much of a nai
The Company doesn't like its operatives crawling in bed wit
KGB agents, and you've been asshole enough to get caugh
doing it in public...."

"It's not... she's not...."

"How about it, Ellis, you give me an exclusive on you
inside story, I can sell it to *Spiegel, Paris Match,* mayb
Scoop, and I'll help walk you through a political asylum de
with the French, I know the ropes, I had to do it myself—

"Piss off, Gibbs, I'm a loyal American, I'm not about t
defect to the Frogs or anyone else!"

"Ah yes," Gibbs purred at him. "My very own words o
many moons ago. Ask not what *you* can do to your country
Ellis, think about what your country can do to *you.* Think
over, Ellis, I'll be around after the party's over if you chang
your mind."

"Fuck you," Ellis muttered, throwing up his hands
turning his back on Gibbs, and retreating toward their table
where Katrina was snorting up a line of coke.

"Now you will finally tell me what is going on, da, Eli?

"First things first," Ellis said shakily, sniffing up a lin
sloppily himself. "This is gonna take quite a bit of explaining....

Alexander Sergeiovich Ulanov cocked an inquisitve eye
brow as Norman Spinrad came back into the VIP sectio
shaking his head, an ironic smirk plastered across his face.

"The commotion, I take it, was Charnov and Ellis mak
ing their grand entrance?" Sasha said.

"Yeah," Norman said, "reporters all over them like flie
on horseshit."

Igor Mikailovich Rostropov scowled, or anyway his normally somber expression deepened a degree or two. "You *left* them out there to be interrogated by reporters?" he snapped. "That was most stupid. Why did you not bring them in here?"

In here was a curtained-off section at the bow of the boat done up for all the world like some Hollywood mogul's opulant private conference room, which in a sense, Sasha realized, it was for tonight, or anyway a movie set for same.

Norman had had a large crescent-shaped mahogany table placed in the bow of the bateau-mouche, with the horns of the crescent pointing toward the stern. A big, black, leather recliner sat in the focus of the hollow like a captain's chair, looking forward through the glass enclosure over the prow down the Seine toward the brilliantly illuminated Eiffel Tower looming in the distance over the Left Bank like a logo.

Half a dozen similar chairs, all slightly smaller, were placed around the outside of the crescent, backs to the dramatic forward view. Each of these seats had two telephones before it, while the captain's chair had three, plus a speaker-phone, and an elaborate switching console. There were two ice buckets of champagne, another of vodka, a bottle of cognac, a bowl of hashish joints, and a Japanese teacup half-filled with cocaine on the table. In the corners of the enclosure stood two large potted palms, blatantly emblematic of Hollywood.

"Let them stew in it a while, n'est-ce pas," Spinrad said, plopping himself down in the captain's chair, which he had clearly appropriated for himself. "Let them get good and loaded. Let them sweat. Let them scream at each other for a while. Old Hollywood technique."

He picked up a phone, punched a button on his intercom. "Tout ici . . . ? Bien! Avanti, mon capitain!"

The boat's engines began to thrum. A moment later it warped away from the dock, glided out into the middle of the river, and headed westward down the Seine.

Spinrad leaned back in his chair, lit up a joint, poured himself a cognac, smiled at Rostropov. "Our Ship of Fools is underway," he said. "Relax, have some dope, have some coke, have some booze! This is a *party*, remember?"

Rostropov grimaced, began tapping a nervous forefinger against the tabletop. Sasha glanced at the cocaine, glanced at the joint. Under the circumstances, he was sorely tempted.

But one glance at Igor Mikailovich Rostropov convinced him to settle for a large glass of ideologically correct vodka.

"You have been handing me the Hollywood bullshit all along, Eli Ellis?" Katrina said indignantly. "You have never even *spoken* to Universal about me?"

"I told you, I told you, I *told* you," Ellis said for what seemed like the fifteenth time. "It had to come from *Spinrad* first! Otherwise, I'm going in there saying you guys gotta put my girlfriend and my client in this movie I put together, which is like this awful old joke, they'd tell me to get stuffed!"

Katrina snorted yet another line of coke and washed it down with a belt of pepper vodka. "Then what is problem?" Katrina demanded. "Spinrad has done this thing, now you call Hollywood and negotiate my movie-star contract, yes?"

"No," Ellis moaned. "Don't you see? I can't do that now!"

"No I do not see," Katrina said belligerently. Her eyes were red, her skin was flushed, she was already rather loaded, and seemed determined to go higher. This was not making it any easier for her to understand the situation.

Ellis had had a few lines and several glasses of the poisonous bourbon punch himself, and that wasn't making it any easier for him to comprehend it either, let alone explain it to the Red Metal Rose.

The boat was now gliding between the Eiffel Tower and Trocadero, and they had been sitting here arguing like this ever since it left the dock, while the party swirled around them. Press creeps kept drifting past their table trying to overhear snatches of their conversation, but none dared approach Ellis's angry snarls. A couple of them had pulled out cameras, but Spinrad's bouncers had taken care of that. Still, Ellis had the feeling he was buck naked in a forest of eyes.

"Is telephones on this tub, no?" Katrina insisted. "You call Hollywood, make deal right now!"

"I told you I can't do that!"

"*Why?*"

"Because the CIA won't buy it now!" Ellis blurted.

"*The CIA?*"

Oh Lord, Ellis realized, now it's come out! He shrugged. He snorted two more lines of coke and drank more insidious bourbon punch. And more or less laid it all out for her.

"The CIA is subsidizing this movie. They want to kill the *Free Press de Paris*, it's worth fifty million dollars to them, so they made a deal with Universal to front the budget if Spinrad returned to Hollywood to do the screenplay and folded the paper. I figured that if Spinrad threatened to pull out of the deal if you weren't in the movie, the CIA would make Universal swallow it because—"

"The CIA forces Hollywood to make the Red Metal Rose a movie star?" Katrina shouted. "You are really loaded, Eli!"

People froze in their tracks. Heads turned. Reporters inched closer, craning their ears.

"Cool it, will you?" Ellis hissed, pulling her face closer to him by the chin.

"Makes no sense," Katrina said a tad more quietly. "CIA makes *me* a movie star? Why would they do that?"

"They won't now, that's what I've been trying to tell you," Ellis said. "Not after Tass has hinted that you're working for the KGB! Looks like *you've* subverted me instead of—"

"You tell the CIA that you get the Red Metal Rose to *defect!*" Katrina shouted. She reeled to her feet, waving her arms, and addressing the goggling audience of reporters and rubberneckers. "I make the statement! Never will the Red Metal Rose defect to America! Katrina Charnov is no traitor to Mother Russia! I want to be big Hollywood movie star, but I am loyal citizen of the Russian Spring! Fuck all politics! Fuck the CIA! Fuck the KGB! Fuck the show-business running dogs of the Soviet Rock and Roll Union and the CIA!"

"Katrina! Fer chrissakes!" Ellis grabbed at her arm.

She pulled away. "Fuck you, Eli Ellis!" she screamed. "You make love to me for the CIA!"

"Look who's talking!" Ellis shouted back, finally quite losing it. "You screwed me for the KGB!"

"I make the casting couch scene to become movie star, is all!"

"Ms. Charnov—"

"Mr. Ellis—"

"Is it true—"

"Do you deny—"

Norman Spinrad was higher than a kite, Sasha had gone through a quarter bottle of vodka, Igor Mikailovich Rostropov was pacing around the VIP area stone-cold sober and muttering imprecations under his breath, and the boat had made a 180 opposite the Eiffel Tower and was heading back up the Seine when all hell seemed to break loose in the main salon beyond the curtain.

"—true that you are an agent of—"

"—have you ever considered defecting to—"

"—is the deal—"

"—did you know that she was—"

Dozens of loud voices were drowning each other out in fragmentary questions like a hostile press conference in sudden full swing. But above the journalistic tumult, Sasha could hear the voices of Katrina Charnov and Eli Ellis loud and clear.

"You tricked me, Eli Ellis—"

"Shut the fuck up, Katrina!"

"CIA spy!"

"KGB whore!"

"Uh Norman, don't you think you'd better—"

But Rostropov cut Sasha off. "Get them out of there right now, Spinrad, or I'm leaving!" he roared, and headed for the curtain.

Spinrad was out of his chair faster than Sasha would have believed possible, considering his state of inebriation, and blocked Rostropov's path. "Just what I have in mind," he said with a foolish grin. "The secret of wheeling and dealing is all in the timing." And he waltzed into the main salon.

Sasha could hear him shouting into the whirlwind. "I told you the press conference is *later*! And I promise you the story is gonna be a lot juicer than you think now, incredible as that may seem! *Come on*, damn you, come *on*!"

And Katrina Charnov and Eli Ellis came staggering through the curtain, with Norman propelling them with nudges and shoves.

"What the hell is this?" Eli Ellis demanded. The conference table. The leather chairs. The man in the elegant tan suit lounging in one of them. The older, ominous type in dark blue. All the telephones. The fucking potted palms.

Were it not for the unmistakable nightscape of Paris drifting by beyond the glasswork and its shimmering reflections on the rolling Seine, he would have sworn that he had just been propelled into some corner office high up in the Black Tower.

"Sasha Ulanov, you running dog son of a bitch!" Katrina shouted at the man in the tan suit.

"Charmed to see you too, Katrina," the tan suit drawled.

"*Ulanov?*" Ellis cried. "What are you doing here?"

Norman Spinrad stepped in front of him, executed an ironic little bow. "Eli Ellis, Sasha Ulanov, Sasha Ulanov, Eli Ellis," he said silkily. "I thought it was about time you guys met."

"And who is *this?*" Ellis demanded, nodding at the blue suit.

Ulanov slithered up from his chair and mimicked Spinrad's little flourish. "Igor Mikailovich Rostropov, executive assistant to the minister of media of the Union of Soviet Socialist Republics," he said.

"Is bullshit!" Katrina muttered, dropping down into a chair unbidden and folding her arms across her chest belligerently. "Is KGB."

"Nyet," Rostropov said harshly. "But perhaps, maybe later. . ."

"Well now that we're all acquainted, let's start this meeting, okay," Spinrad said blithely, for all the world like some studio executive, seating himself in the presiding catbird seat. Ulanov subsided back in his chair. Rostropov hesitated, finally took a seat at the far end of the table, one chair removed from his compatriot, as if making some unfathomable Hollywood brownie point.

"What's this all about, Spinrad?" Ellis demanded.

Norman Spinrad beamed at him. "Show business," he said. "Pretend you're in the Black Tower, Ellis. It's time to get to the bottom line."

Woodenly, Ellis took a chair beside Katrina, who poured herself a glass of vodka from the fixings on the table, and leaned closer to him, her fury apparently at least temporarily forgotten. "You will play the hardball for me, yes, Eli?" she whispered in his ear. "Now you will make for me the deal, da?"

Ellis poured himself a vodka. Loaded as he was, he still knew he was in deep, dark shit. But loaded as he was, a strange energetic calm came over him. Somehow, insane as it was, he felt he had suddenly been warped onto his own well-worn turf.

"Okay, Spinrad," he said, "let's cut the crap and talk turkey."

"Do you have the Swiss bank account number for me, Ellis?" Norman said.

Sasha watched Eli Ellis squirm, glancing at Rostropov, who sat there as stony and unreadable as the legendary Andre Gromyko.

"It's all right, Mr. Ellis," Sasha said to break the ice. "We all know about the money in Geneva."

"I'll bet you do, you commie bastard!" Ellis snarled.

"Do you have it?" Norman persisted.

"No . . ." Ellis muttered unhappily.

Norman nodded toward the phones in front of him. "Then call Langley right now and get it," he said. "I'm tired of waiting, I want it now, or the whole deal is off."

"Don't be ridiculous!" Ellis said shrilly. "They won't even give me the time of day now, thanks to Ulanov!"

Norman nodded unconcernedly, sipped at a snifter of cognac. "Bien," he said. "The old deal has evaporated, and Universal is now left holding a three hundred fifty thousand dollar rights bag. Mr. Rostropov . . . ?"

"The Ministry of Media is prepared to buy out *Riding the Torch* from Universal," Rostropov said. "Provided of course that we are not held up for something outrageous."

Ellis's eyes fairly bugged out. "You're talking *turnaround*?" he exclaimed.

"Just so," Rostropov said. "We wish to make the film in the Soviet Union." He leered a wintry smile at Ellis. "You are no doubt in considerable foul odor with your clients at Universal now," he said. "Would not your situation be improved if you could aid them in unloading the property on us? But we will not be exploited by Hollywood profiteers. You must secure us the rights for no more than four hundred thousand rubles. I am not authorized to go further."

I can't be *this* loaded! Eli Ellis thought vertiginously. "You . . . you want me to act as your *agent*?" he stammered.

"I offer you the chance to redeem yourself with your capitalist masters," Rostropov said coldly. "Do not expect a commission! You have too many fingers in this pie as it is!"

Ellis's brain shifted into agent overdrive. I can get my

commission from Universal, he thought. Or anyway ten percent of the turnaround profit if worse comes to worse. . . .

He reached for the telephone.

Katrina batted his hand away. "Wait a minute!" she said. "What about me, Eli?"

"Hey come on, Katrina, this is my ass—"

"It is *my* ass you have been having, Eli Ellis! You are my manager, are you not? You must look out for my interest! And your twenty-five percent of the same, da?"

Ellis thought about it. He thought about the money. He gazed out at the Parisian night drifting by like a wonderful and illusive dream from this fake Hollywood perspective, and he thought about golden days and red-hot nights that were. And might be again. He thought about how the CIA had used him. About how the Russians had used Katrina. About how *he* had been willing to use her, come right down to it. He looked around this ersatz mogul's office and pondered that sometimes questionable virtue known as agent's honor.

It suddenly seemed quite real now. As did the City of Light. The Black Tower, BMA, Hollywood, even Langley and all that it implied, seemed long ago and far away.

He glared at Rostropov. He lit up a joint and blew smoke in his direction.

"The lady has a point," he finally said. "Her starring role has already been announced." He glanced at Ulanov. "By your own boys at Tass," he said. "Besides, she's the biggest box-office star you have. With the Red Metal Rose, you might even be able to get some American distribution."

Rostropov looked squarely at Katrina. "All this is true," he said. "But Katrina Charnov must be represented by the Soviet Rock and Roll Union, not you. We give you the part, Charnov, but only if you stay with the union."

"You will at last make me a movie star in Mother Russia?" Katrina said, locking eyes with him.

Rostropov nodded.

"And all I must do is fire Eli?"

Rostropov nodded again. "What do you say, Charnov?"

Katrina drained her glass of vodka, folded her arms across her chest. "I say fuck you!" she said. "The Red Metal Rose does not betray her lover and her honor! Fuck you! Fuck the Ministry of Media! Fuck the Soviet Rock and Roll Union! Eli Ellis is my personal manager till death do us part!"

She grabbed Ellis's arm with both hands and hugged it

to her breast. "You and me, yes Eli?" she said softly, kissing him on the cheek.

A wonderful warmth spread up Ellis's arm. His eyes began to water. "You heard the lady," he said.

"This is totally unacceptable!"

"Oh is it?" Ellis purred. Never in his life had he felt so brave and clean and strong. "You listen to me, you Russkie bastard, and you listen good. You need me to make your deal with Universal. All you political bastards have been jerking me around, and I'm fucking tired of it! Like the lady says, fuck you, fuck the CIA, fuck you all. Well we're talking movie business now, and that's *my* turf. And I don't pick up this telephone without you deal with *me* for the services of *my* client. And that's the name of the game, my man."

"Right on!" Katrina cried.

"Jeez Ellis, I didn't think you had it in you," said Norman Spinrad.

Igor Mikailovich Rostropov was turning fairly purple. Sasha could all but feel the cold, Siberian blast of the explosion to come. Norman was leaning back in his chair, amused by all this, and sucking on a joint. Katrina Charnov glowered at Rostropov. Ellis clung to her side, the determination of his expression set in stone.

Why me? Sasha asked himself.

Because there is no one else, Alexander Sergeiovich.

He slithered across to the chair next to the executive assistant to the minister of media. "If I may, Comrade Rostropov. . . ?" he whispered in his ear.

Rostropov deigned to cock an inquisitive eyebrow, nothing more.

"A compromise would seem to be in order," Sasha said into Rostropov's ear. "Let Ellis deal with Universal. If he succeeds, if he succeeds . . . make him the American representative of the Soviet Union in this matter! He gets ten percent of the profits to Sovfilm from the American distribution. He gets nothing from the Russian distribution."

"But that is worth almost nothing," Rostropov hissed.

"Exactly," Sasha said.

Rostropov nodded, turned away from Ulanov. "Very well, Mr. Ellis, I offer you the following proposition," he said. "You will negotiate the turnaround with Universal. Katrina Charnov will star in our film, but her interests will be represented by the Soviet Rock and Roll Union. In return for which, you will receive ten percent of the net proceeds to us of the American distribution."

"Say what?" Ellis said. "That's not worth jack—"

And suddenly it came to him. A brilliant inspiration. The opportunity of a lifetime. Millions and millions of dollars sitting right out there in front of his face.

These guys are *amateurs*, he realized. They don't know what they're doing! Turnaround? Fuck turnaround! Put yourself together a coproduction deal, and you're set for life, my man!

But go slow, Eli, go slow, gotta suck them into it. . . .

"I just might be willing to go along with that. . . ." Ellis said slowly.

"You would betray me, Eli!" Katrina Charnov cried.

Ellis held up a hand for silence. "Provided we can get together on Katrina's representation problems," he said.

Rostropov scowled. Sasha moaned to himself, knowing that this was the essence of the whole deal as far as the Ministry of Media was concerned.

"I am Katrina Charnov's *personal manager*, not her agent, technically speaking," Ellis said. "I might be willing to let the Soviet Rock and Roll Union continue to be her agent of record when it comes to anything inside Russia, about which I do not know diddly-squat, provided *I* represent her in all dealings with western promoters and producers, about which *they* do not seem to know beans. I split my commissions fifty-fifty with the Soviet Rock and Roll Union and they split theirs fifty-fifty with me."

"Sounds reasonable, does it not?" Sasha told Rostropov.

Rostropov gave him a poisonous look en passant and locked eyes with Ellis. "And what *is* your commission on western deals, Ellis?" he demanded.

"Twenty-five percent."

Rostroprov snorted contemptuously. "The Soviet Rock and Roll Union gets *thirty-five* percent," he said. "Half of twenty-five percent in return for half of thirty-five percent does not seem to be what you Americans would call a kosher deal. . . ."

Norman Spinrad, who had been sipping cognac, smoking his joint, and listening to all this with wry amusement, finally spoke up. "Listen you guys, I'm tired of all this penny-ante shit! Get your acts together fast, or I just might decide to do my dealing with Langley after all!"

"He means it," Sasha whispered in Rostropov's ear. "And he's right. If you accept this deal, the *Free Press* survives as an independent conduit and Charnov stays wih the Soviet Rock and Roll Union, more or less. This is what you came from Moscow to accomplish, da? If it is learned there that you threw all that away over the difference between twelve-and-a-half and seventeen-and-a-half percent, we will *both* find ourselves in far Kazakhstan!"

"I will not be blackmailed by this capitalist swine!" Rostropov hissed back.

Lord what an asshole! Sasha thought. But he held himself in check and continued to whisper sweet reason in Rostropov's ear. . . .

On the Right Bank, the darkened trees of the Tuilleries gardens tossed in a gentle breeze as the bateau-mouche moved up the Seine toward the prow of the Ile de la Cité, and on the Left, the Musée d'Orsay drifted by the boat; behind it, not quite visible from this perspective, out of sight but far from out of mind, the rue de Lillet and Katrina Charnov's apartment, where Eli Ellis had spent what he now knew were the best moments of his life.

He nodded in the direction of the darkened bulk of the museum and what lay just beyond and squeezed Katrina's hand while the two Russians continued to whisper to each other as they had for what seemed like a thousand years. Katrina squeezed back and rubbed her thigh against his under the table.

Ah, to be in love, in Paris, gliding up the Seine in the catbird seat on a perfect September night!

Finally, Rostropov's scowl lightened, he nodded agreement to something, and Ulanov spoke.

"You keep your whole commission on any American revenues, the Soviet Rock and Roll Union keeps the whole commission on all Comecon revenues, they handle the rest of the world, give you twelve-and-a-half percent, and keep twenty-two-and-a-half themselves, that's our bottom line deal."

With manful effort, Ellis managed to keep a straight face, managed to feign grudging acceptance. "You commie bastards drive a hard bargain," he managed to tell them without laughing, "but you got yourself a deal."

And he picked up a phone and put in a call to Elliot Friedman, head of production of Universal Pictures.

Surprisingly enough, the switchboard put him right through to Friedman without the usual telephone status games, as if Friedman had been waiting for this call all along.

Which, as it turned out, he had.

"Elliot . . . ? Eli Ellis—"

"Ellis, you imbecile, where are you, we've been calling your hotel all day! What the hell have you been *doing* over there in Frogland? Have you seen *Europe Today*? Have you spoken to BMA?"

"Uh no, Elliot—"

"Well don't bother! You've been fired! You better believe that was the first call I made after I told those CIA bastards where to stick it!"

"*You* told off *Langley*?" Ellis exclaimed.

"You better believe it! This whole idiot project was *their* idea, remember? We buy this stupid sci-fi property, and they back the deal with fifty million dollars. Now, thanks to you, Ellis, we've already paid that commie bastard Spinrad *our* money, and *they're* welching on their fifty mil. Now we've paid three hundred fifty thousand dollars in rights money for a property that would cost forty million dollars to film, meaning we'd need to gross a hundred mil to break even, which we cannot do, meaning the project is dead, and we are fucked. And so are you! And so is the CIA!"

"The CIA . . . ?"

"Those bastards have gotten far too big for their britches out here," Friedman declared indignantly. "They've stuck their greasy little fingers in film and TV production for the last time. Subsidizing propaganda films, backing TV shows, using foreign location crews as Agency cover, okay, okay, for that kind of crap who needs to make waves with Washington. But by God, Langley is going to learn that when you screw the *Black Tower* to the tune of fifty million dollars, you'll never work in this town again!"

Ellis could not help laughing.

"What are *you* laughing about, Ellis?" Friedman snapped. "You're as dead in Hollywood as they are."

"I think not, Elliot," Ellis drawled.

"You think not!" Friedman screamed.

"You heard me, Elliot. I'm gonna save your ass."

"*You're* gonna save *my* ass?"

"How would you like to have the American rights to a completed master of *Riding the Torch* with forty million dollars' worth of production values for a cost to Universal of ten million dollars?" Ellis asked.

"How would I like to have a magic wand that makes gelt from dreck!" Friedman roared. "You're drunk, Ellis, you're stoned, that's it, isn't it?"

The bateau-mouche was passing south of the Ile de la Cité now and the gothic towers of Notre Dame rose ghostly in the distance in a klieg-light aura. And here I sit with a bunch of Russians and an American exile, Eli Ellis thought, dribbling the most powerful man in Hollywood like a basketball.

He laughed. He sipped slowly on an ice-cold pepper vodka, savoring the moment as the fire suffused from his stomach into his brain. "Drunk as a skunk and high as the Eiffel Tower," he admitted. "But I'm also sitting here with Igor Rostropov of the Soviet Ministry of Media and the sweetest little coproduction deal you ever heard of. . . ."

Eli Ellis glanced at Norman Spinrad, who did something with his console, and a madly incongruous disembodied voice from Hollywood came through the speaker-phone as Sasha watched the illumined spires of Notre Dame loom larger and larger as the boat moved under the Pont Michel just north of the Left Bank's legendary heart, the intersection of Saint Germaine and the Boul' Mich, electronically linked in this crazy transcontinental moment with the mythic corner of Hollywood and Vine.

"This is Elliot Friedman at Universal, are you there, Mr. Rostropov?"

"Da," Rostropov said into thin air. "We are prepared to pay—"

Ellis made frantic slashing movements across his throat with his finger. Sasha watched in perplexity as Norman nodded, hit another button. Oh no, he thought, what now?

"I know this guy, Rostropov, so let me do the talking," Ellis said. "And I can cut you something much better than a rights buy-out. A coproduction deal with Universal."

"Coproduction . . . ?" Rostropov said slowly.

Ellis nodded frantically. "You can shoot this thing in Russia for twenty million dollars, right? You put up ten,

Universal puts up ten. You distribute the film in the East Bloc, they distribute it in America, we work something out for the rest of the world, and the net proceeds worldwide get split down the middle...."

Rostropov frowned in confusion. "But you said—"

"Forget what I said, we gotta wheel and deal right now, I can't keep *Elliot Friedman* on the line forever, yes or no?"

"Too complicated... I don't know...."

"*Do it*, Comrade Executive Assistant to the Minister of Media," Sasha broke in. "It's a work of genius!"

"*It is?*"

"Da, da," Sasha babbled. "Our American distribution has always been horrible, no Soviet film has ever been a hit in the States..."

"Yes, yes, we are restricted to art houses, cheap cable channels, and a few rental outlets by the capitalist—"

"Well don't you see?" Sasha exclaimed. "*Universal Pictures* will distribute *Riding the Torch* in the States, it'll gross at least seventy million dollars in America alone...."

Rostropov's eyes lit up in rubles. "And with *Soviet* star, another seventy million rubles in Russia...."

"And think of the political ramifications," Sasha cooed at him. "The Red Metal Rose in a big American hit without a defection! Maybe a general distribution deal with Universal will come out of it too! The conquest of Hollywood! When Gorodin retires, who do you suppose will be the next minister of media...?"

Igor Mikailovich Rostropov actually broke into an unequivocal grin. "Brilliant, Mr. Ellis," he said. "I'm glad I thought of it."

"Sorry about the bad connection, Elliot, we're on a *boat*, if you can believe that," Eli Ellis said as the bateau-mouche sailed very slowly now along the brilliantly lit gargoyled bulk and gingerbread buttresses of Notre Dame, as if the captain too wished to savor and prolong the sweetness of this moment.

"Here's the deal. You put up ten million, the Russians put up ten, we shoot the thing in Russia, where there are no union problems and production costs are dirt cheap, and bring it in for twenty million dollars. They distribute in the East, you distribute in the States, let the lawyers haggle about the rest of the world, and the proceeds get split down the middle. Can you read the numbers, Elliot?"

"Don't treat me like an asshole!" Friedman's voice rasped over the speaker-phone. "Minimum gross of fifty mil to Universal on a budget outlay of ten mil. It's a sweetheart of a deal, all right, and it'll teach those fuckers in Langley a lesson they'll not soon forget! Can you hear me, Mr. Rostropov?"

"Da."

"Are you empowered to close this deal for your principals?"

"Da."

"Is it acceptable as outlined by Mr. Ellis?"

"Da..." Rostropov said. "With certain understandings...."

"Go," said the voice of Elliot Friedman.

"Katrina Charnov must be the female star, big box office in the Soviet Union...."

Friedman's voice groaned. "Big risk here...." he said.

"You may choose an American for the male lead."

"Done. What else?"

"Russian supporting cast."

"For sure! But at Russian wages."

"What else?" Rostropov agreed. "We certainly cannot afford American scale."

"Fuckin' A! The idea is to keep the budget down and dirty."

"So the film must be released in Russian with English subtitles."

"No way, José! The American star acts in English, you dub him into Russian on your release print, and we dub everything else into English on ours, except Charnov's vocals on our version. She *can* sing in English?"

"Like Yankee nightingale, you better believe it!" Katrina chimed in.

"And I write the screenplay," Spinrad said.

"Done."

"In Paris, not Hollywood."

"You can write the thing in Outer Fucking Mongolia, for all I care," Friedman's voice said. "Anything more?"

Rostropov scratched his head. "I think we have nailed it down, da?" he said.

"A pleasure doing business with you, Mr. Rostropov," Friedman said. "Too bad our asshole politicians are too stupid to reach the bottom line like this."

"I *am* a representative of my government, Mr. Friedman," Rostropov pointed out.

Friedman's voice laughed. "Me, I'm just in show business," he said.

"C'est la politique d'Amérique," said Norman Spinrad.

After the press conference, Eli Ellis snatched up a bottle of cognac off the buffet table and repaired with Katrina to a café table on the starboard side of the main salon. This time, the reporters left them alone; the press had more than had its feeding frenzy satisfied by *this* story, and they all huddled around the buffet table waiting impatiently for the boat to dock so they could file it, and passing the time fitfully by scarfing up the remains of the free food and booze.

Ellis poured them both big snifterfuls, clinked glasses. "Here's lookin' at you, kid!" he said in a boozy Bogart voice.

"Here's to Hollywood, even if I do not go there yet, yes?" the Red Metal Rose said, and they both took big sips.

"Here's to good old Mother Russia, da?" Eli Ellis said, waxing expansive.

"Here's to the famous Black Tower!" Katrina toasted back. "Here's to America, da?"

Ellis frowned. "Right now I don't know whether I'm ready to drink to that," he said, suddenly somber. "I don't know what will happen to me if and when I go back home. . . ."

"But you will be big man in Hollywood, no?"

"No doubt. . . ." Ellis muttered. "But I'm on the CIA shitlist for sure, Katrina! And the IRS will audit me for life . . ."

"Pah!" Katrina spat. "You put your money in Switzerland! I have account in Geneva, but you must not tell Rostropov, yes."

"Things are not so hot in America these days, Katrina, everything is politics, and the politics suck," Ellis found himself admitting for the first time. "If it is Spring in Russia, it is Autumn in the States, and the Agency and the IRS have their meat hooks into everything. . . . I could be in deep, dark shit when I go home. . . ."

"But the Black Tower, it will protect you, yes?"

"Could be . . ." Ellis mused. Elliot Friedman *had* read Langley the riot act. Still . . .

Katrina Charnov leaned over the table and touched a hand to his cheek. "Do not be sad, Eli," she said softly. "You Americans, you think too short. In Russia, we have centuries of winter from Terrible Old Ivan to glasnost, where it seems cold wind will never change. But one day Spring comes to Mother Russia, and you will see, it comes back to America too."

She smiled. She kissed him. She spoke more gaily.

"And until it does, we have each other," she said. "We have lots and lots of money, da, we have big movie deal, we go to Russia, and I show you Leningrad, and Moscow, and Siberia in the summer, is very beautiful, I kid you not . . ."

The bateau-mouche had sailed past the southern bank of the Ile Saint Louis during the press conference, rounded the island, and now it was moving through the narrow channel separating it from the Ile de la Cité. Dramatically lit by spotlights, Notre Dame towered to the right, and the lights of the Ile Saint Louis cast a silver sheen on the waters of the Seine.

"Et maintenant, we are young, and rich, and in love, and in Paris," said the Red Metal Rose. "Is hardly fate worse than death, da? Home is where the heart is, yes, not in some far country. La vie continue, n'est-ce pas?"

A momentary shadow moved over them as the bateau-mouche passed under the Pont Louis, but then the flash and glitter and joie de vivre of Saint Germaine appeared like a very bright light at the end of a very short tunnel on the Left Bank before them, a Parisian brigadoon rising from the mists, and all the more sweet because this fantasy of the heart was quite real.

Eli Ellis sighed a little lost American sigh, laughed a little American laugh, and shrugged what he knew was quite a gallic little shrug.

"I'll drink to that," he said raising his glass to Katrina, to himself, to the two of them, to the City of Light.

"Fuckin' A!" exclaimed the Red Metal Rose. "Is never a winter so cold that somewhere is not Spring."

After the press conference was over, Eli Ellis and Katrina Charnov repaired to a private table in the main salon to make moony eyes at each other, Rostropov began belatedly filling his belly from what remained on the buffet table, and a dozen *Free Press* staff members filed into the VIP section to make their peace with Norman Spinrad and vice versa, leaving Alexander Sergeiovich Ulanov to wander aimlessly around the detumescing party sipping vodka out of a big champagne glass.

People began filing out of the VIP section as the bateau-mouche rounded the Ile Saint Louis and headed west along the Quai d'Anjou, looking satisfied but somehow pensive. Last to leave was the managing editor, Kurt Gibbs, who came up to Sasha shaking his head rather ruefully.

"Maybe you oughta go in there and talk to him, Ulanov," Gibbs said. "He's taking all this kind of peculiar. I mean, he's gotten what he wanted, or so he says, but . . . you know. . . ."

"Yes, I think I do," Sasha said, and he topped off his champagne glass with more vodka and then went forward.

The VIP section, its phones quiet, its big conference table strewn with dirty glasses, its air thick with stale smoke, already seemed like the morning after, no longer the electric arena of wheeling and dealing it had so recently been.

Norman Spinrad sat alone on the edge of the table, gazing out at the Ile Saint Louis as the boat rounded the Quai de Bourbon and headed toward the point of the island.

Sasha sat down beside him, handed him the glass, and they both sat there silently, sharing the vodka, and looking out on Paris, their mutual city of exile, for a long, long while.

"So Norman . . . ?" Sasha finally said.

"So, old buddy . . . ?"

"It is beautiful, is not?"

"Paris?"

"Da . . . How fortunate it is that we do not have to leave this place, yes?"

Norman continued to track the passing bank of the Ile Saint Louis with his eyes. "Fortunate for *you*, old buddy," he said quite somberly. "You're here by choice, I *can't* go home. . . ."

"But you could have," Sasha pointed out.

"Yeah, sure, I could have been a big-time screenwriter in Hollywood, maybe. Had forty years' worth of work recognized for what it was in my own country while I was still alive."

"But it has been, Norman."

"Say what?"

"Recognized for what it really was," Sasha said. "That's why you're stuck here in exile, isn't it, mon ami?"

Spinrad laughed bitterly. "Touché," he said.

"And that too was a choice," Sasha pointed out.

Now Norman turned to look at him. His eyes were quite bloodshot and deeply hollowed, but a small smile lit up his face. "You got a point, old buddy," he said. "Like the old song says, no retreat baby, no surrender."

He shrugged. He sighed. "You know, I think I could be happy here, one phony Frenchman to another," he said. "If only I could see my work published in my own country again. Or even just find the energy to write something worthwhile again after all these years. . . ."

"There is the screenplay, Norman. . . ."

"Screenplay!" Norman Spinrad said contemptuously. "Creative typing! I'm talking about a *novel*, Sasha, a novel in English. . . ."

"Why have you never—"

"Because I'm an *American*, damn it, whether I like it or not," Norman snapped with sudden passion. "All my best stuff was always about America. It was my theme and my energy source, compris? Here . . . shit, I'm cut off from all that, from America, from the rhythm of the language, from the spirit of . . . Ah!" He threw up his hands in frustration.

"That in itself is an American story, is it not?" Sasha said.

Norman's eyes snapped into sharp focus. "*What?*" he said.

"Often I have heard you complain that it was not you who left America but your America that left you abandoned on these shores. Paris is full of Americans like you these days, n'est-ce pas? You have staffed a newspaper with them. Is *that* not an American tale worth your telling?"

"You commie son of a bitch!" Norman cried. He grinned. "Why not?" he exclaimed. "It has everything—a rock star, the movie deals, the CIA, the KGB—"

"Oh no! I did not mean—"

"—sex, foreign intrigue, double- and triple-dealing—"

"Norman, Norman," Sasha moaned, "I never meant that you should tell the story of *this* hideous mess, which we have escaped by the skin of our teeth! Moscow would . . . Washington would . . ."

But Norman Spinrad was looking out at the passing lights of the Ile Saint Louis again, indeed at his own home in exile on the Quai de Bourbon.

"Don't say it, Sasha," he said brightly. "Because it isn't true, old buddy. They can rant and rave and tie up my royalties, but you just reminded me of the one thing they can't take away from me. . . ."

"Which is . . . ?"

Norman laughed uproariously. He took the glass from Sasha's hands, raised it in a toast to Paris, and slugged the rest of it down.

"No one but myself can keep me from working in *this* town again!" he declared. "La vie continue, mon ami, la vie continue!"

Alexander Sergeiovich Ulanov shook his head, wishing very much in that moment that Norman had left something in the glass for *him*. "One phony Frenchman to another, mon ami," he said, "I do hope you are right!"

ABOUT THE AUTHOR

Norman Spinrad was born in 1940, graduated from the City College of New York in 1961, published his first story in 1963, his first novel in 1965, and has not held a job since. In addition to somewhere between twelve and fourteen novels (depending on the counting method used), three books of short stories, two non-fiction books, and two anthologies, he has published literary criticism, film criticism, political commentary, and essays on various scientific subjects.

Spinrad has been a literary agent, has had a radio phone show, and is past president and vice-president of the Science Fiction Writers of America. He has written a couple of song lyrics and has cut a single, vocalist record in Britain and France, which never came close to making the charts.

His novel *Bug Jack Barron* was banned briefly in Britain, and two of his novels, *The Iron Dream* and *The Men in the Jungle* are currently on the Index in Germany, where they are nevertheless selling quite well under the table. His latest novel is *Little Heroes* and he is currently at work on his next novel.